THE HERO RULE

THE HERO RULE

BRANDON HUGHES

TENSION
BOOKS

TENSION
BOOKS

TensionBooks.com

Library of Congress Control Number: 2023905650

Trade Paperback ISBN: 979-8-9879233-1-3
eBook ISBN: 979-8-9879233-0-6

Cover design by Glen M. Edelstein
Book design by Glen M. Edelstein

Printed by IngramSpark in the United States of America.

First printing edition 2023

For my wife Karen

"*In any moment of decision, the best thing you can do is the right thing, the next best thing is the wrong thing, and the worst thing you can do is nothing.*"

—THEODORE ROOSEVELT

"*History will decide if I'm a villain or a hero.*"

—HARLAN ELLISON

JUSTICE (JUHS-TIS) *NOUN:*

- The quality of being just; righteousness, equitableness, or moral rightness;
- Justness of ground or reason;
- The administering of deserved punishment or reward.

THE HERO RULE

CHAPTER 1

THERE WAS NOTHING PARTICULARLY unique about courtroom four in the Towne County courthouse— dark mahogany walls, worn carpet, the judge's dais, witness stand, jury box, and the Alabama state seal on the wall behind the bench. If you've seen one courtroom, you've pretty much seen them all. What was different about this particular courtroom, though, was the presence of the lawyer sitting at the counsel table. The lawyer's presence wasn't unusual in and of itself, of course; after all, it was a courtroom. However, it was after midnight on Friday morning and precisely one hour since the jury handed down its verdict.

Duncan Pheiffer was the lawyer at the table, and it was his client who had been convicted of capital murder. As he sat there in a chalk stripe charcoal suit, looking just as put together as when he had arrived at the courthouse some seventeen hours ago, there was only one thing on his mind: absent a minor miracle, he knew that be it at the hands of the executioner, a fellow inmate, or God Himself, his client would never again see the sun rise in the east as a free man.

As Duncan sat, he turned reflective and looked back on how he had arrived at this point. He was more than nine years removed from the bar exam and just over two years removed from the Towne County District Attorney's office, where he had spent the first seven-plus years of his legal career as an assistant district attorney. When Duncan began his career at the DA's office, he had six-figure student loan debt courtesy of law school, and seven years of fighting the good fight was showing up quite negatively in his bank account. Being a public servant did not pay well, especially compared to most of his law school pals who went straight into civil practice.

He was closing in on four years of marriage to his wife Molly when they had begun seriously considering starting a family. As is the case with many prosecutors, money became an issue. Neither he nor Molly had grown up with much, so they did not aspire to be wealthy, but they did not want to scrape by for the next fifty years either. Moreover, the skill level of the lawyers he was opposing was so incongruous with the fees they claimed to be collecting that he began to wonder what a former prosecutor with his trial experience and skill set would be worth on the open market. This had been weighing on his mind when the most venerated and senior member of the Towne County bar approached him about joining his one-man firm, which he did. The old lawyer later retired, leaving Duncan his practice.

The decision to leave the DA's office was not easy, and the most challenging part was telling the district attorney, Maggie Gamble. She hired him fresh out of law school, giving him an opportunity when no one else would. She made it clear that though she was unhappy about losing him, she had been doing this long enough to understand.

Duncan's cell phone buzzed in his coat pocket, bringing him back to the here and now, and all thoughts went to the man whom he had just let down in the worst way possible: Charlie Calvin Clements was the client whose case he had just lost.

❀　❀　❀　❀　❀

Duncan was not an idealist, far from it. He was not opposed to the death penalty and had a healthy respect for law enforcement. He was well aware of what people were capable of and, as with most experienced prosecutors, had developed a keen bullshit detector. By his estimation, he figured that about eighty-five percent of his clients were absolutely guilty of the crime they were charged with, and about ten percent were probably guilty; the police did not get it wrong very often. However, roughly five percent of his clients were utterly innocent of the crime charged. Five percent was probably being generous, but the number just sounded better than two or four. He knew they weren't all saints, nor were they all free of some wrongdoing on some level at some point in their lives, but they weren't guilty of the offense he was representing them on at that moment. It wasn't the evil he had seen in his nine-plus years as a prosecutor and defense attorney that kept him up at night—it was the five-percenters.

Duncan remained sitting at the counsel table, the same table at which he and Charlie had sat, side by side, for the last ten days. He could not will himself to leave the courtroom as if remaining in the dugout after the game ended would somehow change the score in his team's favor.

It wasn't merely that he lost—he had lost cases as a prosecutor and a defense lawyer—it was believing that justice had not been served by the jury's verdict. Justice was a term recklessly bandied about, and attempting to define it was near impossible. However, he knew it when he saw it, and this verdict was the antithesis of everything he believed justice to be.

The quiet was interrupted by the door opening behind the judge's bench. A short, middle-aged black woman with close-cropped hair wearing a brown deputy's uniform appeared: "We're about to take your guy on to the jail so we can lock the courtroom up for the night." Looking down at her watch, she corrected herself, "For the morning, rather. You need to see him?" It was Deputy Carla Maples of the Towne County Sheriff's Department. She acted as security in this courtroom, a job she had held for the past fifteen years.

"Oh, hey, Carla. Yes, I do. I'll try and be quick."

"Ah, don't worry about it. I will be here for another couple of hours, regardless. Paperwork." She shook her head wearily.

Duncan followed her to the holding cell to meet with his client; he hated this part. When a defendant takes a case to trial, no matter the evidence against them, they almost always convince themselves they would be found not guilty. If they weren't convinced of it, their families certainly were, and they were often the ones paying his fee. Many times, for the guilty, as the trial wore on, they knew. For some, though, no matter what they did or the evidence against them, it never sounded that daunting—until the state's closing argument. That's when all the facts and all the evidence were laid out before the jury. Then, at least for some, it began to set in. For those that it did not set in for and for those who indeed were innocent of the offense charged, particularly those who were taken into custody on the spot, the brief post-trial meeting rarely went well. Duncan was dreading this post-trial meeting more so than any he had ever had.

"I'm sorry," was all Duncan could come up with in the dank, musty, institutional-green cell as he and his client sat across from each other on stainless steel benches affixed to the cinderblock walls. The two men looked as lawyer and client as they conceivably could at that moment. Duncan in his Hart Schaffner and Marx suit with Brooks Brothers shirt and rep tie and his client wearing faded black slacks with a well-worn white button-down shirt—both at least a size too big—and a shiny pair of silver bracelets linked together by a short silver chain all courtesy of the county jail. He'd have to return the slacks and shirt to the jail as they had come from the closet that maintained clothes for inmates going to trial with nothing better to wear. The handcuffs would be returned as well—eventually.

"Sorry, huh," Charlie Calvin Clements said with a quick humorless laugh. "You're sorry." It was a statement, not a question. "Motherfucker, I'm the one gonna die in here," he said with a rising voice, chains rattling as he pointed toward the ground with both hands out in front of his body.

BOOM, BOOM, BOOM came three raps on the metal cell door. "Keep it down in there," yelled the deep male voice of a guard.

Duncan, getting refocused, said, "We aren't finished yet; there's still more work to do. We have the penalty phase next, and my focus now is keeping you out of the death chamber. After that, we can start the appeal process." Duncan paused, gauging Charlie's demeanor before continuing. "Outside all of that, I may have something else that could help you." As Duncan said the last part, he hoped Charlie heard more confidence in his voice than he felt.

Duncan knew that appeals of murder convictions, particularly those in death penalty cases, were rarely successful. Appellate judges were elected, and they were loath to set a convicted killer free. Especially in the law and order deep south.

"More work to do? This isn't the same type of work you did that got me convicted, is it?" said Charlie.

Running a hand through his dark brown, slightly mussed hair, Duncan leaned back against the peeling paint of the chipped and scuffed cell wall and said quietly, "For your sake, I hope not." This response saw a very slight smile escape his client's lips, and Duncan felt the tension beginning to melt away, if only slightly. "Is there anything you want me to tell your momma or your sister? Anything you want me to get them to bring you?"

"Naw, man," his client said, staring down at the floor. He lifted his head, gazed directly into Duncan's eyes, and held the stare. After a beat, in a much softer tone, he said, "Just get me out of here, man. Just get me out. I don't belong in no prison."

"I know you don't, Charlie. I know you don't." Duncan stood, put a hand on his client's shoulder, and squeezed. "I will be by to see you tomorrow."

Duncan knocked on the door letting the guard know he was ready to leave. The door opened, and Duncan exited the cramped confines. As the guard was closing the thick steel door, Duncan stole one last glance into the cell.

"Hey, Pheiffer," said Charlie rising from his seat. Duncan grabbed the edge of the door and looked expectantly at the condemned man. "I trust you."

The guard tapped Duncan on the back, and Duncan released the door allowing it to close. Hearing those last words spoken by his client, Duncan realized there was nothing that could have made him feel both better and worse at the same time.

The lawyer retrieved his phone from the inside pocket of his jacket as he made his way back to the courtroom. A note on the screen read: *Barclay Griffith. Text Message.* Duncan unlocked the phone and read the message. *Just heard about the verdict. Why don't you and Molly come to the house Saturday? Sit by the pool, drink some cold beer. We'll throw something on the grill.* At that moment, Duncan realized just how drained he was—mentally and physically—and relished a much-needed respite for his mind. He slid the phone back into his pocket, stuffed the files and paperwork in his leather satchel, and walked out of the courtroom. He went down two flights of stairs, out the front door, and into the muggy night.

Duncan walked the two blocks to his law office and decided against going in; he didn't want to think about the law right now. Instead, he went directly to his midnight blue Toyota Tundra, and got in. It was the first new car he had ever purchased, and he took great care of it—he would swear it still had the new-car smell despite being almost two years old.

His wife was attending a teachers' conference and would be gone for one more night, so despite his exhaustion, he was in no rush to get home, opting instead to stop by Cherry's Corner Store.

He parked his truck outside the convenience store that was a Towne staple for the last seventy-seven years. When he walked in, the ding announcing his arrival echoed in the stillness of the empty store; the smell of hot dogs left too long on the rotating spit and cherry Icee hit him instantly. He nodded to the cashier as he made his way to the beer cooler and grabbed a six-pack of Fat Tire. He gave a half smile to the dishwater blonde behind the counter as he set down the sixer for her to ring up. "Hey, Janie."

"Kinda late to be getting started, ain't it, Pheiffer," Janie replied in her country drawl and a smirk of her own.

"Never too late, never too early." Duncan took in Janie's cinnamon gum-scented breath, waived off a bag, and paid with a twenty. He received his change and dropped the coins in a jar collecting money for some charity he didn't pay any attention to. He grabbed one of the bottle openers for sale by the register and removed all six bottle caps. He put the opener back and gave the handful of caps to the cashier. "Thanks," he said as he grabbed his beer and left.

He got into his truck, rolled his windows down, and was taking a long pull on his beer when he heard a quick *whoop whoop*. Turning his head to look out the driver's side window, he saw a City of Towne police cruiser easing out from behind the building he'd just left. They were pointed in opposite directions, so their windows were adjacent to one another. "Evenin', officer," said Duncan with a tip of his bottle.

"Shit, Pheiffer," the officer said before giving Duncan the bird and driving off. For the first time in what seemed like days, Duncan laughed. He drank the rest of his beer, put it back in the space from where he had removed it, and grabbed another; condensation already forming on the bottles. He put his truck in gear, backed out, and headed home.

Home to Duncan and his wife was a small smoky-olive green bungalow with black-cherry trim in the historic section of Towne. It was in the one part of the city untouched by the population boom of the last twenty years. Every house was unique and loaded with character outside and in. Hundred-year-old oaks lined the streets and provided a charm all their own. He pulled into his driveway and followed it to the rear of the house, where he parked under a carport. He climbed the four steps to his rear door and polished off his second beer before unlocking the door and going inside.

The air-conditioned interior cooled him immediately. He dropped his keys on the table, shuffled to the den, and dropped into a leather recliner. The beer overtook the adrenalin he'd been running on, and exhaustion came on him like a wave. Grabbing a third beer, he turned the television on, and a replay of the previous day's Braves game was starting. The daylight on the re-broadcast of the game against the Pirates was at odds with the darkness outside. He was looking forward to watching a couple of innings before bed. He didn't expect sleep to come easy, so he knew better than even to try until he couldn't hold out any longer.

He awoke to find the game in the top of the fourth inning. He registered that the Braves were winning when the picture on the television froze. Several seconds later, a green screen popped up, telling him his network had disconnected and he needed to check his internet connection. He backed out of his television's streaming app and re-started it. After a few seconds, he received the same error message. He checked his phone and saw that it, too, was not connecting to his Wi-Fi. He was tired, but now he was annoyed and couldn't go to bed until he figured this out. He went to his bedroom closet and saw that his router was not receiving a signal. He mumbled a curse, grabbed the flashlight from his nightstand drawer, and went outside.

He walked around to the right side of the house, shone the light on the junction box for his cable internet, and saw the coax cable supplying his home with internet was unhooked. "What the hell?" He surveyed the immediate area with his flashlight. *Someone had to have done that deliberately*, he thought. But why? *Kids?* After a moment, he reattached the cable and slowly made his way back to the house, continuing to scan the area.

He dropped into the recliner, got the game back on, and drained the remainder of his warming beer. He reached for another—number four. He loosened his tie with his free hand, then unbuttoned his shirt at the throat. He kicked off his still-tied black cap-toed Johnston & Murphys and reclined in his chair.

He heard movement and cocked his head to the left.

A strap was suddenly around his throat and moved up under his chin. He was being pulled toward the back of the chair, neck growing taught. Duncan began to struggle, body flailing, fingers grabbing at the strap; he registered his lap growing wet from the spilled beer. To his left, just at his periphery, he noticed an object; a silvery glint in the lamplight. *Knife?* His eyes went wide, and his mouth worked devoid of speech. His thoughts turned to his wife, Molly. It was weird what went through a person's mind as the end rapidly approached, and the person knew it. He thought about Molly coming home to find him. Dead. Blood. *His* blood.

Then he thought about his client, an innocent man who was going to die in prison.

Charlie Calvin Clements was a five-percenter.

CHAPTER 2

DEPUTY CARLA MAPLES FINISHED her paperwork, leaned back in her chair, and stretched her arms above her head; it was approaching 4:00 in the morning. She had been on duty for going on twenty hours and was finally going home. The overtime was worth it, she told herself. Maybe.

The jail was quiet at this time of the morning; probably the most peaceful time of the day—if a jail can ever be described as peaceful. She got up from the computer terminal, stepped down out of the elevated command center in the middle of the booking area, and went to the break room to get her lunchbox and purse. Then, with personal things in hand, she waved goodbye to the jail staff and headed home. Carla lived outside the city limits on the far southern edge of the county, about twenty-five minutes from the jail. She was nearing home and driving down a dark county road listening to an AM Gospel station when, far up ahead, she spotted a bright light.

She turned the volume down and let up on the gas, slowing her late-model four-door compact. This stretch of road was long and straight, giving the illusion that she was driving in place, the bright light not getting any closer. She accelerated a little bit, then took her foot off the gas when she got within a quarter mile of the light. As she neared, she realized it was a fire. More to the point, it was a vehicle fire. She pulled to a stop within about thirty feet of the massive fireball, got out, and was met immediately with a wall of immense heat. She also registered just how loud the fire was. Squinting into the brightness, she removed the flip-style cell phone clipped to her hip and dialed three numbers before hitting send.

"Towne County 911, please state your emergency," said a female voice.

"Sarah, this is Carla, I'm on County Road 51 just north of the South End Baptist Church, and there is a vehicle on fire in the roadway."

"Ok, Carla, I'm sending a fire crew out there now. Can you tell what kind of vehicle it is?" asked Sarah Freeman, third shift dispatcher for Towne County.

Carla squinted and shielded her eyes, "No. No, it's too bright."

"That's ok. Can you tell if it's a car or a truck?"

Carla could hear the dispatcher hammering away at her keyboard as they spoke. She walked around the vehicle's passenger side, still keeping her distance. "It's a truck. A pick-up truck."

There was silence on the line except for the machine gun sound of the dispatcher's keyboard prompting Carla to wonder what required so much typing. "Can you see if there is anyone inside?"

Carla turned her head away from the flame and made a face that showed she wasn't sure she had heard the question correctly. "Inside? The truck? You mean like a person?"

"Yes. Can you tell if anyone is inside the truck?" the dispatcher asked in an even tone.

"I, I don't know," replied Carla easing on around the front of the truck, trying to peer inside. As she approached, she held up her right arm to shield her eyes from the brightness and heat of the flames. She made her way to the driver's side window and gasped. "Sweet Jesus," she said in a whisper.

"Carla, stay with me now. Do I need to dispatch an ambu-lance?"

Carla began to shake as she turned from the window; she brought the phone down and hugged it to her chest.

"Carla? You there?"

A few seconds passed, then: "I'm here, Sarah...Negative on that ambulance."

CHAPTER 3

TOWNE, ALABAMA, IS LOCATED in the eastern and slightly southern part of the state, approximately twenty miles from the Georgia border. The area was first settled in the late 1820s and was incorporated as a city in 1839. Upon incorporation, it needed a name, so the city's leadership suggested the terrifically unimaginative name of Town. Someone suggested they add an *e* on the end to lend it an air of sophistication, and the name was adopted. Being the first incorporated city in the area, the county that would eventually encompass Towne was given the same name.

Towne was not a large city, but it was growing rapidly, and with growth came the requisite criminal element: mostly drug crimes with a few property crimes and thefts sprinkled in. The homicides were few, but when one occurred, the bad guy was caught and convicted.

❋   ❋   ❋   ❋   ❋

Barclay Griffith's cell phone went off just after 5:00 in the morning. Refusing to open his eyes, he reached to his nightstand knocking off a book before finally locating the nuisance. "Hello," he said, trying his best not to sound like he'd been sleeping.

"Hey Barclay, sorry to call you so early, but I need your help in trial this morning."

Still in a fog, he pulled the phone away from his ear to look at the screen. The caller ID read *Stacy Steen.* "Yeah, sure, but court's not for another"—he again pulled the phone away to check the time—"three and a half hours. What's the rush?"

"Judge Pullman is starting at seven o'clock sharp."

"What?" That revelation prompted Barclay to get out of bed and make his way to the den so he wouldn't disturb his wife any more than he already had.

"Yeah, he made us strike a jury on a robbery case yesterday afternoon, knowing it would likely take a full two days to try. The only problem is that he's telling us we have to finish today. He kept us in court until seven thirty last night; even Judge Arnett had his jury still deliberating when I left the office at ten thirty. I don't know what's going on around here."

"The judge's conference is at the beach next week. Word is they were able to get the hotel to make the conference rate available for the weekend before, so they're all trying to get everything wrapped up today."

" Whatever. Anyway, can you meet me in the courtroom at about six thirty?"

"Sure." Barclay hung the phone up and headed for the shower.

Not quite an hour later, Barclay was in his SUV on the way to the courthouse.

✳ ✳ ✳ ✳ ✳

Barclay was thirty-two years old, just north of six feet tall, with emerald green eyes and hair on the blonde side of brown. He was the oldest child of Grover Handley Griffith, III, and grandson of Grover, II, and so on. The Griffiths were the proverbial big fish in the small pond.

There was a Griffith among the first settlers to call Towne home, and the story was that it was a Griffith who gave the city its name; however, many believed the story originated with and was perpetuated by a Griffith—most likely by the original Grover Handley Griffith—to dubious authenticity. In addition to the naming story, it was also the eldest Griffith that started the tradition of Griffiths as members of the Towne County Bar Association. Barclay was carrying on said tradition not as a shareholder in the family firm of Griffith & Griffith, as his father was constantly pushing for, but as an assistant district attorney.

"Mr. Griffith," said Judge Pullman. "What brings you to my courtroom so early?" Henry Pullman was short and squat with bad skin and a bulbous nose—he reminded Barclay of a Weeble. He wore his black rob unzipped over a golf shirt and khaki pants; Stacy Steen was sitting at the prosecution table with paper everywhere.

Barclay said, "I heard that the judges on the third floor had lost their minds, and I wanted to see it for myself. It would appear that my information was spot on."

"Why Mr. Griffith, whatever do you mean," asked the judge—a smile creasing his lips.

"Oh, I don't know, Judge—court before the cock crows, maybe?"

"Lady Justice does not wear a watch, my dear boy."

"It's because she's blind."

"Touché, counselor."

"Actually, I'm just here to meet with Ms. Steen about the good reverend this morning."

"No need, Griffith. She's doing a fine job." He looked at Stacy and said, "You're doing a fine job, sweetheart." Then back to

Barclay: "The jury will convict within...twenty minutes. Half-hour tops. You can tell your boss the case is in good hands."

"Judge, I asked him to be here," said Stacy. She was rising and smoothing her skirt as she spoke.

"Whatever for, may I ask? You don't need him looking over your shoulder."

At that moment, the door to the courtroom opened, and all three turned to see the defense attorney walk in.

Jim Shelby wore dated ties tied too short and suits that looked slept in; he survived—barely—on appointed work. He stopped mid-stride and said, "What?" His eyes worked between the three of them. "Were you all discussing my client? You know that's ex parte communication and highly improper."

"Calm Down, Jim. We weren't discussing the case," said the judge. "We're wagering how long the jury will take to convict Mr. Ross. Anything less than thirty minutes is already taken, so you'd better have a hell of a closing if you expect to win...the bet, I mean." Everyone laughed; everyone except Jim Shelby.

"Judge—"

The judge cut him off with, "The jury will be in the box in fifteen minutes. So everyone be ready to start." With that, the judge was gone.

In the rear hallway where the judicial offices were, Barclay asked Stacy, "So, what's up?"

"Shelby says his guy is going to testify this morning, and being that this is my first A felony case, I don't want to screw it up. So I want you to watch and ensure I don't miss anything on cross."

"The judge is right, you know. You'll be fine. I believe I prepped this case for grand jury. The facts are solid. Didn't he admit to being in the van with the guys who went in and robbed the McDonald's?"

"That's right."

"And weren't his fingerprints found on some of the money?"

"Yes, but that's what worries me. I can't imagine what he will say to explain this stuff away, but he's got to come up with something."

"Oh, I'm sure Shelby has something cooked up. That guy can't stand to lose, and he's a terrible lawyer, so you can probably expect something pretty ridiculous. So for that reason alone, I'm willing to stay."

"I appreciate it."

"I'm happy to help. But Stacy, you need to understand that this is *your* courtroom, and this is *your* case. You can't afford to appear nervous or timid in there. Not in front of the judge and certainly not in front of the jury. You're a young female, so older male jurors are going to see you as their daughter, or...well, you know." Stacy visibly reddened. "And the women, well, some are going to judge you on your clothes, your hair, your makeup...you get the picture." She nodded. "In either case, they won't be hearing what you are saying unless you make them listen to you. It's not right, it just is, and you cut through all of that mess by being strong, assertive, and confident. You have to show all twelve people on that jury that you're not there because it's a sorority mixer. You're there because you're a damn good lawyer and because that asshole at the defense table committed an armed robbery."

Stacy replied, "You're right. I just...I get a little intimidated in front of the judge."

"Look, you haven't tried a bunch of cases yet, so that's understandable, but the quicker you can flip that switch, the better off you'll be, I promise you. Some judges will screw with you as long as you let them."

"Got it."

"Good, now get back in there and shove this case up Shelby's ass."

❈   ❈   ❈   ❈   ❈

Having called the court to order at precisely 7:00, the judge said, "Mr. Shelby, do you wish to call any witnesses?"

"Just one, your honor. I call my client, the Reverend Kevin Ross, to the stand."

The Reverend Kevin Ross stood five feet tall and wore a purple six-button suit, a yellow shirt, and a purple tie. He took the witness stand and swore an oath to tell the whole truth and nothing but. Then, craning his neck to look at the judge, he began to tell his story.

"You see, your honor, what had happened was, uh, I needed a ride and this van done pulled up, and they told me I could get in. So they drove me to McDonald's against my will. Before they got out, they asked me if I wanted some food. I told them, no, and then they put these masks on, held up guns, and went inside." The defendant shrugged. "A few minutes later, they come running out, jump in the van, and hauled ass."

"Mr. Ross, please watch your language," said the judge. "And let your lawyer ask you a question before you start talking, okay?"

"It's Reverend Ross, Judge," Ross shot back.

"Uh-huh. Then please watch your language, *Reverend* Ross."

"Well, I ain't had nothing to do with no robbery. I ain't go in that store, and I *ain't* get any of that money."

Jim Shelby broke in, "Now, Reverend Ross, you heard the government present evidence that your fingerprints were on some of the cash identified as having been stolen from the restaurant. Can you explain to the jury how that happened?"

"Why yes, I can." He faced the jury and said, "You see, when they came running back to the van, they slid open that big door and threw the money at me. I knew what they had just did, and I didn't want no part of it, so I threw my hands up in front of me like this"—Ross crossed his arms in front of his body with his palms facing outward—"and all that money hit my hands, so, as you can see, that's how my prints got on that money."

Several jurors were trying to stifle a laugh at his explanation. Barclay leaned forward and whispered to Stacy, "I think you've got this." He patted her on the shoulder and slipped out of the courtroom.

❊   ❊   ❊   ❊   ❊

Barclay took the stairs down to the second floor, where his office was located. In the years since smoking had been banned in the courthouse, the back stairwell had served as an improvised smoking chamber and held onto the atrocious smell of nicotine as a drowning man clings to a life preserver. Barclay would rather avoid taking this route, but it was convenient. The office of the district attorney was not officially open for business yet, so he had to enter from the rear hallway using his keycard, and the smell of freshly brewed coffee hit him instantly. The first person he saw was Gary Roosevelt, whose office was just inside the door.

"Well, hey, Rosie. What's got you here so early?" Gary Roosevelt was the Chief Investigator for the District Attorney. He was tall, thin, and looked like he had swallowed a basketball. He was in his early sixties with salt and pepper hair shorn close and a brush mustache. A retired Robbery-Homicide detective from the Towne police department, his primary role was to chauffeur the DA from place to place. Still, the keen investigative skills never left the man.

"I guess you haven't heard."

"Heard what?"

Taking his feet off his wood laminate desk, he rose from his chair and said, "Come in and have a seat." Barclay walked in and sat, the smell of Mentholatum pungent. Rosie took his seat and moved his white NYPD coffee mug aside. He leaned forward, resting his clasped hands on the desktop. "It's about Duncan."

"What about Duncan?"

A pause. "He's missing, and it doesn't look good."

"Missing? What do you mean missing?"

"Deputy Maples was on her way home from the jail early this morning and called in a vehicle fire in the southern part of the county. A fire crew responded to the scene, but the vehicle was too far gone. The tag was still legible, though. It was Duncan's."

Barclay shook his head and tried to make sense of what he was hearing. "What time was this?"

"About four-thirty this morning."

"Any idea where he might be?"

Rosie leaned back in his chair, took a deep breath, and exhaled. "Barclay, there was a body in the car. It was pretty badly burned, so an on-site identification was impossible. The ME's office has the body and will conduct an autopsy later today." After a few seconds, "Barclay, I'm sorry."

Barclay stood up, then sat back down. Crossed and uncrossed his legs. "Do they have any clue as to what happened?"

"All we know for certain at this point is that his truck was found burning in the middle of the road and the truck contained a body."

The room went silent for some time as Barclay sat forward, elbows on his knees, and studied his hands. "Has anyone been to his house?"

"The police sent a patrol officer by there, but no one answered the door. The fire scene is their focus right now, so I sent Stubbs to the house for a more thorough look around. If Duncan is missing…well, we don't have time to waste."

Barclay leaned his head back and stared at the drop ceiling, the low hum of the fluorescent lights the only sound in the room. He then took in the small office. A deer head and a large-mouth bass adorned the wall behind the desk, and both looked to Barclay too small to mount. Leaning forward, he asked, "Why is this office involved at this point?"

"The sheriff called Maggie as soon as they determined who owned the truck. Duncan served her and this office well, and since leaving, he has always done right by us, so she immediately offered our assistance." Rosie cleared his throat before continuing. "No one was closer to Duncan than you, but he was a friend to all of us, and we are going to do what we can to find out what happened." Rosie leaned back in his chair and rubbed his face with his big, rough hands. "It's going to be one hell of a day."

"Does Molly know?"

"Not yet."

"I'll tell her."

"Barclay, you don't have—"

"I said I will tell her." Barclay braced himself to stand when Rosie's phone chirped.

"It's Stubbs," he said, looking at the screen. "What have you got?" he said by way of greeting. "Hmm. Okay. Okay. Let me call you back." Rosie tossed his phone on his desk and said, "House is locked up tight, and the blinds kept him from seeing inside."

Rising from his chair as if in an ejector seat, Barclay said, "I have a key. Tell Stubbs to stay there, and I'll meet him in fifteen minutes."

"Barclay," said Rosie getting up from his chair to give chase, but he was already out the door before Rosie made it around his desk.

❊   ❊   ❊   ❊   ❊

Barclay arrived at Duncan's house in less than ten minutes. As he pulled up to the curb, he observed Dennis Stubbs sitting on the covered front stoop, smoking a cigarette. Stubbs was the oldest investigator in the district attorney's office by a couple of years and had served as Rosie's partner while on the police force. An old-school cop, he wore his jet-black hair slick with Vitalis and looked at you through hooded eyes. The man was a chain smoker's chain smoker and had the voice and visage to prove it. He seemed to light one off another from the time he got out of bed in the morning until the time he went down at night, and he wore Old Spice like he owned stock in the company; you shake his hand, and you smelled like your grandfather the rest of the day. Stubbs rose as Barclay approached and extinguished his cigarette by pinching just behind the burning ember, dropping it into the bushes, and pocketing the butt.

"Barclay, man, I'm sorry," said Stubbs extending a hand—his voice as smooth as twenty-four-grit sandpaper.

"Thanks." Barclay took Stubbs' hand in his, and they shook.

"We're going to get the bastard that did this. You know that, right?"

"Yeah, I do," replied Barclay, and he meant it. Pleasantries aside, it was time to get to work. "So, anything outside the house?"

"Nothing that jumps out. Why don't you take a walk around the outside as well? You spent more time over here than I did." Barclay set off around the house.

Completing the circle, Barclay had not observed anything worth noting.

"Let's check out the inside," Barclay said as he fished his keys from his pocket. Immediately upon opening the front door, the coppery scent of blood assaulted their noses. For once, he appreciated the vapor trail of Stubbs' Old Spice bath.

Compartmentalization was critical to doing your job as a cop or prosecutor; otherwise, you'd go mad. This ability to compartmentalize allowed them to investigate the possible murder of a close friend and do so as if they were investigating a crime involving a stranger.

Entering through the front door, the two men found themselves in the home's formal living room. It was a wide, but shallow room with hardwood floors, floral wallpaper, and a brick fireplace that Barclay knew was never used. It was sparsely furnished, which made it easy to see that whatever violence occurred in the house had not visited this room. The air-conditioner clicked on, disturbing the quiet stillness.

The old house's floorboards creaked as they made their way through the living room and into the kitchen. Duncan and Molly had recently completed an extensive renovation of the dated kitchen. It looked like something that belonged in a restaurant—gleaming stainless-steel industrial appliances dominated the space. Barclay observed different fast food bags and cups on the counter, a telltale sign of a man living alone for a week while entrenched in a murder trial. Good eating and proper sleep habits often went to pasture while you were in trial, and Duncan was no different. Moving slowly and taking in every detail, Barclay and Stubbs moved through the kitchen, which flowed on into the den, and it was there where the source of the stench was discovered.

Against the far wall sitting at an angle facing them, approximately twelve feet away, was a leather recliner. Their eyes immediately went to a massive spray of blood on the curtains and wall beside the chair. The blood had begun to solidify and took on the appearance of strawberry preserves.

Barclay stiffened. His jaw clenched, his breathing pattern grew deeper, and the rage he suddenly felt made its way to the surface. He shook his head slowly, turned, and walked back toward the front door.

Stubbs let out a long breath he seemed to have been holding before saying to the empty room, "I'll call it in."

❊   ❊   ❊   ❊   ❊

Within half an hour, Duncan's house met all the requirements of a crime scene: yards of yellow police tape, half a dozen black-and-white City of Towne police cars, three unmarked detective cars, a crime scene unit van, two news vehicles with requisite reporters and camera crews in tow, a flurry of police activity inside the house and out, and the curious neighbors congregating in the street.

Wayne Drummond was assigned to the case as the lead detective, and he was in the living room talking to Barclay and Stubbs. He sat in a chair belonging to the kitchen table while Stubbs and Barclay sat across from him on a couch. Drummond was in his early forties with reddish brown hair and matching goatee—gray leeching into both. His reputation was that of a thorough and squared-away detective. He wore a navy sportcoat, gray slacks, a light blue shirt, and a well-worn tie that was fashionable when Bill Clinton was president.

The detective was recapping the brief interview. He was looking at his notebook when he said, "Barclay, you used a key to enter the home, and both of you conducted the search?"

"That's correct," responded Barclay.

Still looking down at his notes, Drummond said, "And as soon as you saw the blood in the den, you did not proceed any further into the house."

"Correct."

He seemed lost in thought when he finally flipped the notepad closed. To Barclay, he asked, "Any ideas what this could be about?"

"Not a clue," said Barclay shaking his head as he rubbed his palms on the tops of his thighs.

"There was no evidence of forced entry at any of the three doors leading in from the outside. Do you know who all had a key to the place?"

"As far as I know, I'm the only one. Neither Duncan nor Molly had family here, and I live just two streets over, so it made sense that I have it. They have our key as well."

"Did they typically keep their doors locked?"

"They weren't fanatical about it, but you don't prosecute as long as he did and not lock your doors."

Drummond nodded. "I know he was involved in the Clements case—you think that has any connection?"

"Honestly, I don't know. We discussed the case a few times leading up to the trial, and I know he felt pretty good about it. He didn't mention any bad vibes from the family or anything like that."

"Well, if he felt good about it, maybe Clements did too, and after the verdict, his family decided to make their displeasure known."

Stubbs jumped in and said, "If that's the case, they acted awfully quick. He was dead within four or five hours of the verdict, and that's just based on when his body was found. It could have been a couple of hours before that."

Drummond looked at Stubbs, then back to Barclay, and said, "What does this do to the trial?"

Barclay shrugged. "This is new territory for me. I don't guess the verdict will be disturbed, but the sentencing phase will almost certainly be put off, probably for several months. He'll need a new lawyer, and they'll need time to get up to speed."

Drummond thought about that and said, "This could be related to any of a few hundred cases he prosecuted. Hell, I can think of more than a few nasty ones I worked that he prosecuted." He groaned at the expanding scope of the investigation and made a note to see if anyone Duncan prosecuted had recently been released from prison. He turned his attention to Stubbs. "Do you have any thoughts?"

"Only that whoever did this caught Duncan by surprise," answered Stubbs.

Drummond narrowed his gaze and asked, "What makes you say that?"

"There doesn't appear to have been a struggle. Blood is confined to the area of the chair, and the floor lamp beside the chair is still standing upright. Same for all five beer bottles between the wall and the chair. Doesn't appear there was any kind of a struggle. Sure the killer could have righted those items before he left, but why?" Stubbs shook his head and said, "No, whoever did this had the element of surprise. I bet Duncan never knew what hit him."

Drummond flipped his notebook open and began to write. Experience told Barclay and Stubbs the interview was over, and they stood. Drummond rose with them, head down, still writing. "Rosie told me you're going to notify his wife?" Drummond said as he finished writing and looked up at Barclay.

"Yes. It'll be better hearing it from me."

"When are you going to speak with her?"

"She's traveling home today, so I will wait until she gets in. No need for her to be driving, knowing this is what's waiting for her."

Drummond wrote something in his notebook and it closed.

"Has the ME gotten a positive ID on the body yet?" asked Barclay.

"Not yet. That's another reason we need to speak with his wife—to find out who his dentist is so we can get his dental records. ME said that should be pretty definitive."

"I'll find out and let you know."

The three men made their way to the front door, and as Detective Drummond opened the door, he said, "To spill that much blood and then set fire to the body...I don't know."

Barclay: "We're going to find the person responsible. Believe that."

CHAPTER 4

ARE THEY SURE IT'S him?" asked a visibly shaken Molly Pheiffer. Sitting on the edge of a gray cloth mod chair in Barclay's den, she was wringing her hands and twisting the handkerchief Barclay had given her when she reacted to the news of her husband's disappearance and likely murder. She had cried little, though Barclay knew the tears would come.

"We need the name of Duncan's dentist...to make the identification," Barclay told her, trying to be as delicate as possible. Seeing the confused look on Molly's face, Barclay continued, "For his dental records. To identify the body."

"So it might not be him," said Molly sitting up a bit straighter and with a voice filling with hope. Her gaze flitted between Barclay and his wife Brittany, who sat across from her on the matching sofa.

"Molly, while they don't know for certain that the body they found inside Duncan's truck was him, well, I believe everyone would be surprised if it turns out to be someone else."

Molly buried her face in her hands and sobbed silently but visibly as her entire body began to shake. Brittany Griffith moved toward Molly in a single graceful stride, knelt on one knee, and embraced her. Molly reacted by putting her arms around Brittany and began to cry—loudly now.

❀ ❀ ❀ ❀ ❀

Brittany entered the study and observed Barclay. His back was to her as he leaned against the door jamb staring out the open French doors leading to the brick patio bordering the swimming pool. It was raining one of those clean southern summer rain showers that pop up without warning—no thunder, no lightning, and hardly a cloud in the sky. He was still in his suit sans jacket with his shirtsleeves rolled up past the elbow. She could see that his right hand held one of their heavy old-fashioned glasses that contained about an inch of an amber liquid and a single large cube of ice. She stood at the study's entrance watching him for a moment when he spoke.

"I remember the first time I met Duncan. I remember it as clearly as I remember what I had for lunch yesterday." Barclay spoke without turning to face Brittany. "I had been at the DA's office for all of a week, and I remember thinking how glad I was no longer being the new guy." He took a drink from his glass before speaking again. "You know, he was the only person in that office who didn't treat me differently because of my last name."

Barclay faced Brittany and pointed at her with the index finger of the hand holding the glass when he said, "Everyone in that office thought I was coming to work there to get some trial experience under my belt before going to work for my father. I don't believe anyone there took me seriously. The rich kid coming to slum it for a while." Hearing him speak, Brittany registered that this was not his first drink.

Barclay turned back toward the open doors and said, "But not Duncan. Hell, I don't even know if he made the connection with the great Griffith family name at first, but it wouldn't have mattered. Not to him." A long pause before continuing, "Oh,

I'm sure someone told him soon enough, but it didn't make a difference. He was just good people." He began to shake his head. "And a great lawyer and we tried the hell out of some cases. Whether it was simple dope possession or one asshole killing another asshole, when we entered the courtroom, everybody knew what the outcome was going to be. Even the jury knew it, and they didn't even know who the hell we were." Another drink. "We had a great thing going until he was poached from the office. Several months after he left, he told me I was the only lawyer in the office who didn't try to make him feel guilty for joining 'the dark side.' Maggie didn't, of course, but I was the only assistant not to. As much as I hated to see him go, I was happy for him. He was stepping into a great opportunity, and he deserved it. He was finally getting paid what he was worth."

After a long moment of silence, Brittany crossed the lush carpet in the mahogany-paneled room and hugged Barclay from behind, her arms sliding under his. Barclay reached up with his free hand and put his hand over hers, pressing them against his chest. Brittany freed her right hand, grabbed the glass he was holding, and finished off the remainder of the liquid.

"Blanton's?" she asked.

He did a half-turn. "Dang, woman. You're pretty good."

"Just pretty good?" she said cocking an eyebrow.

Brittany had an unlikely combination of ice-blue eyes (almost translucent) and copper-colored hair, which she referred to as auburn. On their first date, he mentioned he had never dated a redhead. She corrected him, he quoted Mark Twain: "When red-headed people are above a certain social grade, their hair is auburn." She didn't laugh. He never brought it up again.

She had a smattering of freckles across the bridge of her nose that bunched together when she laughed, which Barclay saw as her best feature. She was five-foot-ten and moved with an athlete's grace and confidence. Brittany kissed his cheek and moved toward the bar in the corner of the room. "More Blanton's?" she asked over her shoulder.

"More Blanton's," he replied with the enthusiasm of a kid asking for more vegetables. He was still staring through the open doors with arms crossed, watching it rain.

He turned and met Brittany, who was coming back with his bourbon. He sat in the ox-blood leather desk chair and pulled her down. She sat across the chair in his lap.

"How's Molly doing?" he asked.

"She's asleep in the guest bedroom. She cried for a solid hour before I convinced her to lie down." She absently played with Barclay's hair with her right hand. "This is so awful."

Barclay's phone buzzed. He swiveled the chair—wife in tow—so he could reach the cell phone on the desk. "Hello."

After being on the phone for less than a minute, he hung up and tossed the phone back onto his desk. Though Brittany could hear the voice on the other end, she could only make out snatches of the conversation. All she knew was that the call had been about Duncan.

"Who was that?" she asked.

"Detective Drummond. They ID'd the body."

"Duncan?"

Barclay nodded.

"That was quick."

"Turns out the father of one of the patrol officers on the fire scene was Duncan's dentist. He got right on it."

"Honey, I'm sorry," said Brittany, still stroking his hair.

"Yeah, me too."

CHAPTER 5

T HE WEEKEND CAME AND went without any significant movement in the case. Using dental records, the medical examiner positively identified the burned corpse as that of Duncan Pheiffer. Getting a dentist into the office on a Friday afternoon is typically like, well, pulling teeth. However, Duncan's dentist was the father of a detective with the PD, so the records were turned over without issue. Finding an ME on a Friday afternoon can be just as difficult, but given the potential victim in the crime, one was rounded up. Due to the state of the body, a cursory inspection of the remains yielded little, and the medical examiner, Dr. Leonora Bevilacqua, was reluctant to make any determination before she cut the body, which wouldn't take place until Monday due to staffing and scheduling issues. The manner of death, in this case, was an easy call. You didn't need specialized training to know this was a homicide. Cause of death, on the other hand, would have to wait for the autopsy, and no amount of cajoling could get Dr. Bev—as she was known—to render even an educated guess. Nonplussed at the interruption of her day off, she returned to her yard work.

The investigators from the district attorney's office were going through the cases Duncan prosecuted, whether as the primary prosecutor or as second chair. In an effort to make the number more manageable, they only examined the cases he tried before a jury that resulted in a conviction and only looked into guilty pleas if the case involved a class A felony. They would consider expanding their parameters if that did not yield any leads. The TPD had sent over two officers to assist in this portion of the investigation. These officers were tasked with investigating the status of inmates Duncan put away to determine whether or not the inmate was still incarcerated or had been released. Included in their investigation were all visitor and phone logs of the inmates.

The City of Towne Police Department worked diligently through the weekend. They dutifully collected evidence and delivered it to the appropriate places. TPD did not utilize an in-house forensics lab, so they forwarded all the evidence needing forensic examination to the Alabama Department of Forensic Sciences. Despite ADFS not being open to receiving evidence on the weekend, it was arranged for someone to meet members of the TPD Crime Scene Unit to take custody of the evidence. The fire evidence went to the Fire Debris Division; the blood-stained material went to Forensic Biology/DNA; when the autopsy was completed, the specimens collected would go to Toxicology for testing. In addition to the two TPD officers assigned to assist the DA's investigators, two detectives were assigned to examine the cases Duncan had handled as a defense attorney. Due to the attorney/client confidentiality concerns, Barclay got a search warrant and a court order signed by Judge Arnett, allowing the detectives access to Duncan's client files. Barclay wanted to ensure that it would be a solid case when they got the killer, and none of the evidence would get thrown out on a technicality. He had delivered the warrant to the judge a mere twelve minutes before he was set to leave for the judge's conference.

❈ ❈ ❈ ❈ ❈

The police released the house to Molly; however, she opted to spend the weekend at Barclay and Brittany's house. Molly did not feel she would ever be able to step back inside her and Duncan's home. Brittany had taken the lead in making the funeral arrangements, and Barclay spent most of the day Saturday cleaning up the violent mess. Barclay managed to clean the blood from the hardwood floor and painted the blood-stained wall.

Sunday saw everyone in better spirits; time was the elixir. Even at the visitation on Sunday evening, Molly held herself together remarkably well. The crowd that showed up to pay their condolences warmed her heart and made her proud of her husband. Being with friends, staying busy, and the adrenaline of the moment kept her together for the time being, but that would all go away at some point, most likely after the funeral Monday afternoon.

✼   ✼   ✼   ✼   ✼

Monday morning started as any other for Barclay Griffith. He awoke at five o'clock, got in his Crossfit workout, showered, shaved, and was on his way to work by 7:15. Approaching downtown, he was lost in thought about Duncan when he was brought out of his fog by the sound that signaled the start of a bad day: the familiar sound of a police siren.

Barclay glanced in his rearview mirror, now filled with the light bar of the TPD cruiser. He found the next empty parking lot—a chicken finger restaurant that didn't open until lunchtime—and pulled in, not bothering to find a parking space.

The cruiser pulled in behind him, and the officer got out, lights still flashing, and approached the driver-side window, which was already down. Not quite to the window, the officer said, "License and regis—oh, hey, Barclay." The officer re-moved his aviators.

"Officer," he replied with an embarrassed smile. "I guess I was speeding?"

"Yeah. But don't sweat it, dude. I'm not even supposed to be on, but I caught a drunk on the tail end of my shift. Just dropped him at the jail, and I was headed to the PD to turn in the paperwork."

"And here I am holding you up even longer."

"Ain't no problem, brother." Knitting his brow, the officer said, "Hell of a thing about Duncan."

"Yeah. I just…it still doesn't seem real."

Leaning both arms on the edge of the window, the officer leaned in a bit and said, "It's the damnedest thing. I saw him outside of Cherry's early Friday morning. He was drinking a beer in his truck. Didn't know who he was until he turned around." Shaking his head, he continued, "I must have been one of the last people to see him alive."

"You tell the detectives about this?"

"Oh yeah. I came on shift Friday night and heard about what happened. I typed up a statement before going on patrol and left it for Drummond."

"Good deal. Sorry again about the speed; I guess I had my mind on other things."

"Eh, like I said, don't sweat it. I totally understand." The offi-cer slapped the top of the SUV once and sent Barclay on his way.

❈   ❈   ❈   ❈   ❈

The Towne County Courthouse was a stone structure in the gothic style and stood four stories tall. The first floor housed security, the clerk's office, and a courtroom that served as storage. The second floor housed the district attorney's offices and the courtroom used by the district court judge for misdemeanor and small claims dockets, while the third and fourth floors held the four courtrooms—two on each floor—that were utilized by the Circuit Court judges for felony criminal and civil cases. Unseen from the outside was the courthouse basement, which held a café and numerous storage rooms. It was the original courthouse built in the late 1800s, and while the outside looked the same these hundred-plus years, the inside had been renovated at least half a dozen times through the years.

Barclay parked in the parking garage adjacent to the courthouse and entered via the rear employee entrance. To get to his office, he had to pass by the receptionist, who sat behind a glass partition separating the small lobby from the actual workings of the office. Anyone wishing admittance had to be vetted, approved, and buzzed in by Valerie Hall. She was friendly but also did cantankerous exceptionally well, allowing her to handle lawyers, defendants, and everyone in between with equal proficiency.

As he passed by, he said, "Good Morning, Val."

Without bothering to look up from her cell phone, she replied, "Morning, Barclay." Then, just as he began to push through the door entering the attorney section, Valerie spun in her chair and said, "Oh, hey, Mr. Kingery wants to see you. Said to tell you as soon as you got here."

"Gee, thanks." He pushed on through the door and made his way directly to the office of Maggie Gamble's chief assistant, Richard Kingery, or as he was referred to around the office, King Dick. Kingery had heard about the moniker and believed it was a term of respect paying homage to his skills as a litigator honed in the trenches of the courtroom. It wasn't.

This portion of the DA's office was a maze of cubicles that housed the legal assistants to the ADAs and smelled of hand sanitizer and cheap, flowery perfume. While each ADA had their own office, the legal assistants were relegated to a cubicle farm. Barclay noticed that many of the cubes were empty and offices dark. Except for a ringing phone, the place was quiet. The week of the summer judicial conference was a popular vacation time in the office since courtroom work would be near zero.

"Morning, ladies," said Barclay as he made his way to the chief assistant's office. He received a half-dozen responses in kind from Cubicle Land.

Each legal assistant was assigned two ADAs, except Kingery, who had his own dedicated assistant whom he treated poorly. He was forty-eight and maintained an old-school mentality regarding legal assistants or secretaries, as he referred to them, and he worked his like no one else. Standing at six-foot-five and exceeding two hundred and seventy pounds, he was an imposing figure who knew it and used it.

Barclay knocked on the open door and said, "You wanted to see me?"

Kingery, staring at the computer screen on his credenza, swiveled around in his chair to face Barclay. He was a fastidious dresser—always in his suit coat with his tie knotted to his fleshy neck. He had a double chin that reminded Barclay of a bullfrog in mid-croak. His smooth face lent him a feminine quality that looked oddly unnatural.

Kingery cleared his throat, gestured to a chair in front of his desk, and said, "Have a seat."

Barclay made a show of looking at his watch before moving in and sitting down; he saw Kingery's jaws clench. "So, what's up?" he asked.

"Playing Matlock today?" asked the chief assistant.

"What?"

Pointing at Barclay, Kingery said, "Your suit."

Looking down at his suit, Barclay said, "This is poplin. Matlock wore seersucker."

A pause. "No matter," Kingery responded with a wave of his hand. Then, leaning back in his chair, he said, "Maggie hired a new prosecutor, and he's starting today."

"This is an odd time to hire someone. Bar exam results won't be published until September. Veteran lawyer?" Barclay was aware that Maggie was looking to bring on a new lawyer to replace one who had taken a job with the U.S. Attorney's Office and that she was looking for a recent law school graduate. New lawyers were cheaper, tended to be more loyal, and she could train them how she wanted it done—no bad habits to break.

"Not exactly." Kingery was now examining his fingernails. He had a standing appointment for a manicure every two weeks and was unaware anyone knew, whereas the truth was, everyone knew. This thought popped into Barclay's mind as he sat across from him. "He passed the bar last summer, and he's been clerking for the Chief Justice over the past year. His clerkship has wrapped up, and he needed somewhere to land."

Barclay's eyes narrowed, and he said, "What does this have to do with me?"

"Maggie and I thought it would be best for you to train him."

"Maggie thought, or you thought?"

Kingery gave an exaggerated shrug and said, "Maybe I brought it up, I don't remember, but we both discussed it, and she agreed that you would do a fine job bringing the new kid along." Kingery's eyes grew cold. "Besides, his daddy is a partner in a big civil firm in Birmingham, so you two should have a lot in common. You can discuss trust funds and sailing." He couldn't keep the sneer out of his voice.

"I'm not sure anyone in my family has ever even been on a sailboat, *Dick*." Barclay put extra emphasis on the last word, and he saw Kingery's jaws clench again.

Richard Kingery, a sixteen-year veteran of the district attorney's office and a TPD cop for eight years before that, openly disliked Barclay. He resented Barclay's family money and even more the fact that he had been wrong about him. When Barclay was hired, Kingery let it be known to anyone who would listen that he did not believe Barclay would be there for the long term. The fact that Barclay had not left and was also having a great deal of success drove him crazy.

As the second-in-command, Kingery did not carry the caseload that the other prosecutors in the office did. He cherry-picked the few cases he did prosecute, choosing only higher profile cases that had evidence by the bucketloads. Kingery was quick to let it be known that he did not lose, but he was much more taciturn regarding the cases that he pleaded down or gave sweetheart deals on rather than face the prospect of a not-guilty verdict. He had poached a number of Barclay's cases through the years in the name of experience, but Barclay knew it was more about keeping him out of the spotlight. Barclay wasn't bothered by it at first; however, when he saw how Kingery was disposing of some of Barclay's best cases—allowing defendants to plea to lesser offenses, offering time served on homicides, and sometimes dismissing the cases outright—he went directly to Maggie about it. She privately admonished Kingery and told him that anytime he wanted one of Barclay's cases, she would have to sign off on the transfer. This enraged the elder prosecutor.

"Yes, well, the new guy is Clayton White, and he is waiting for you in your office. Bring him along quickly, will you? Not sure just how long he will slum it with us. I'm guessing he'll be fine until he sees some blood. That's when the job gets a bit too real for his type." Kingery swiveled his chair to face his credenza, signaling the meeting was over.

Barclay stood and spoke. "You going to the funeral?"

Kingery, who had begun typing on his keyboard, stopped and slowly turned his chair to face Barclay. "Why would I do that?"

"Because he worked in this office and did a great job while he was here."

With as much contempt as he could muster, Kingery said, "He ceased meaning anything to me when he became a defense attorney." He swiveled back to face his computer screen. This time the meeting *was* over.

❊ ❊ ❊ ❊ ❊

"Hey, Peggy. How are you holding up?"

Peggy was Barclay's legal assistant. A slight woman with a spiky bottle blonde hairdo, he had worked with her and only her his entire career. Legal assistants were reassigned on a not quite regular basis but often enough not to be considered unusual, yet through all the fruit basket turnover, he had managed to hang on to her. She had also worked as Duncan's assistant and was as proud of Barclay and Duncan as she was of her own children. Having raised Duncan from a baby prosecutor, she was happy for him when he told her what he was leaving to do; she had cried a little, too.

"I'm doing ok," she said, wiping her nose with a tissue. "After you called and told me what happened, it was all I could think about this weekend. I just can't believe Duncan is gone." She stared at her lap as she spoke.

"Yeah, me neither."

Looking up, she said, "Why are you here, anyway? I didn't expect you in with the funeral this afternoon."

Leaning on the cubicle entrance, he said, "I just had to get out of the house. Try to get my mind on something else, even if for only a little while. Besides, I wanted to speak with the detective and get an update on the investigation. Easier to do that here than at home."

"Who's working the case?"

"Drummond."

"Well, if something ever happened to me, that's who I'd want on the case." Peggy had been doing this long enough to know all of the TPD detectives and know them well.

"By the way, I just found out that Maggie hired a new prosecutor."

"Oh?"

"Yep. And I was just given the task of training him. Looks like you get the chance to turn out another superstar." She smiled a sad smile. He turned to leave, then stopped. "Let me know if you want a ride to the funeral." Peggy nodded and turned away. As he walked away, he heard her begin to cry.

❊   ❊   ❊   ❊   ❊

Barclay's was your prototypical government office: industrial carpet and wall covering, wood laminate desk and bookcase, metal filing cabinet, and outdated computer. On the walls of his office hung two Matt Sesow paintings and a three-foot by four-foot CS Fly photograph of Geronimo and his sons. He also had a sofa in his office and was known to take the occasional power nap when reading transcripts or case files lulled him to sleep.

Clayton White was sitting on the couch in the shape of a question mark; his head hung over his phone. Wearing a gray windowpane suit with a crisp white shirt and green patterned tie, he was typing into his phone when Barclay walked in and introduced himself. Clayton stood up to accept Barclay's handshake while simultaneously putting his phone in his pocket. Barclay sat his messenger bag down and dropped into his office chair. Clayton was twenty-six, an inch or so shorter than Barclay, with longish brown hair, brown eyes, and a doughy appearance. He had retaken his seat and was now sitting upright at full attention.

"So, do you want to be a prosecutor, or is your father making you do this? And no Sunday school answers. If you're lying, I'll know it."

The question caught Clayton off guard. After a moment, he said, "I want to be a prosecutor. I've wanted to be a lawyer for as long as I can remember, and, honestly, I want to try cases." Then, settling into the couch and crossing his legs, he said, "The thought of a career shuffling paper doesn't interest me in the least. This is where I want to be."

"Good answer—and no alarm bells...yet. I can only guarantee that you won't get bored working here, and you'll know soon enough if this is really what you want to do."

"How about you? Would you say this is your dream job?"

"Right in with the questions. Well, my dream job is to be the third base coach for the Atlanta Braves."

Clayton laughed and said, "My dream job is to be a bullpen catcher. Doesn't matter where just somewhere warm in April and October."

"I like it," said Barclay. Then he leaned forward, elbows on his desk and said, "Seriously, though, someone once told me that your ideal job is one where your talents and your passions intersect. So, based on that, I don't know if this is my dream job, but it's unquestionably the ideal job for me.

"This job has a way of picking people for it, not the other way around. As I said, you'll discover soon enough whether you're right for the job or not." Not wanting to get so *old guy* right off the bat, he slapped his hands on his desk and asked, "Have you eaten breakfast?" Clayton shook his head. "Good, I'm hungry. Let's go downstairs."

❈ ❈ ❈ ❈ ❈

The Courthouse Cafe was located in the basement. It was a small space of only six tables that were little more than card tables covered with plastic red and white checkered tablecloths; the place smelled of bacon grease and toast. Barclay and Clayton sat at one of the tables, each with a plate of bacon, fried eggs, cheese grits, and a cathead biscuit. They were the only people seated at a table, but most of their business was to go, so the traffic was steady. Barclay saw Clayton surveying the no-frills space and said, "This place isn't much to look at, but it's good, and the food is made fresh every day. I've eaten all over this country, and I'm yet to find a better biscuit." After drinking some coffee, Barclay said, "Tell me about yourself."

Clayton swallowed, wiped his mouth, and said, "What do you want to know?"

"Where are you from?"

"Born and raised in Birmingham."

"How did you wind up in Towne?"

"After law school, I knew I wanted to do trial work, but I was offered a clerkship with the Chief Justice of the Alabama Supreme Court. It wasn't the path I had in mind, but it was too good of an opportunity to pass up. My dad went to law school with Mrs. Gamble, so when my clerkship was up, he reached out to her. She mentioned she had an opening, I interviewed, and here I am." He drank some coffee before continuing, "I know this is a fairly young office, and unlike most DA's offices, you don't have to wait a couple of years before being given the tough cases. Looked like the perfect place to start a career."

A lady came to the table and topped off their coffee. "Thanks, Sarah."

"You're welcome. You fellas need anything else?"

"No, ma'am." When Sarah was out of earshot, Barclay leaned across the table and said, "Not a fan of the half-cup refill. I have my sugar, cream, and coffee ratios perfect based on the initial full cup, and the half-cup refill just throws it all out-of-whack."

The pair ate in companionable silence when Clayton said, "I really want this to work out. What's the single best piece of advice you can give me about being a prosecutor?"

Barclay put his fork on his plate and finished chewing. He drank some coffee and wiped his mouth with his napkin. He cleared his throat and said, "Always remember the hero rule: do the right thing for the right reason. It's something that my father has ingrained in me for as long as I can remember, both through words and actions. My great-grandfather gets the credit for coming up with it, but I'm sure he got it from someone else. Either way, it's what my family has lived by for damn near a hundred years, and it rings especially true for a prosecutor. We are the only ones in the courtroom who took an oath to seek justice—whatever that may be. The judge is the umpire. They are there to call balls and strikes, rule on motions and objections. The defense lawyer? Well, the defense lawyer has a singular goal: to do whatever they can to get the desired outcome for their client, and they won't let the truth, the law, or the facts get in the way of a good defense." Barclay sipped some more coffee and said, "The best defense lawyer a defendant has is often the prosecutor. Don't ever forget that."

Clayton appeared to be soaking in what Barclay was telling him. The mood had turned more serious, and Clayton could tell that was something Barclay took to heart. Clayton said, "One other question. Do you ever worry about your safety? About someone you prosecuted or their family coming after you? Like seeking revenge or something?"

Barclay shook his head and said, "Not really. I suppose it's there in the back of your mind at times, but you have to understand that most of the bad guys look at it as a business. They know I'm doing my job and that it's not anything personal. If they go after anyone, it's *their* lawyer. Screwing with a prosecutor or their family is not smart, and even the dumb ones understand that."

"What about your wife? Does she worry?"

"Not especially. She did a little when I started, and I actually had a defendant call the house once."

"Called you at home? Was it a threat?"

"No. His trial was coming up, and he called me to tell me about his life and what would happen if he were convicted, trying to get me to feel sorry for him. He even cried. Britt was a little shaken up by the call; she felt it was an invasion of our home. It pissed me off more than anything. I lit into the guy and called his lawyer. I also let the judge know about it, and she jacked him up at sentencing because of it." Clayton didn't look convinced.

Barclay continued, "Look, as a prosecutor, you aren't exactly dealing with a bunch of Mensa members, and they are far from the best that society has to offer, so that possibility is always out there, but I wouldn't get too hung up on it. I've never known anyone to have an issue outside of the occasional family member running their mouth after a guilty verdict. But even then, they've cooled off by the time sentencing rolls around."

The conversation lagged as they finished their breakfast, and the only sounds they shared were those of the muffled food orders.

Breakfast finished, Barclay rose from his chair and dropped a ten-dollar bill on the table as a tip. Then, as they made their way to the elevator, Clayton asked, "Say, did you know that lawyer that was killed this weekend?"

CHAPTER 6

I T WAS LATE IN the afternoon, and the crowd of people in
The Crafty Lefty was well on their way to getting drunk.

The Crafty Lefty was a beer bar owned by Barclay's
brother Grover Griffith IV (or Ivey as he was known outside his
family because of the roman numerals after his name). The bar
had two dozen televisions and an embarrassment of craft beers.
The décor was exposed brick, pine floors, and near-century-old
reclaimed timber from barns razed throughout the South. The
bar was Ivey's pride and joy; it was handmade from old, rough-
hewn wood and was the perfect final touch to his vision. Grover
started The Crafty Lefty with signing bonus money he received
from his short stint as a professional baseball player. He was Alabama's Mr. Baseball his junior and senior years of high school
and was taken in the second round of the Major League Baseball draft by the Seattle Mariners. As a result, he received a high
six-figure bonus when he signed his contract and wisely socked
it away, save for buying a new pick-up truck.

Grover's baseball career had been on the fast track after two
successful minor league seasons. He had been invited to his first
spring training, and while he was not going to begin the season
on the big league roster, a late-season call-up wasn't out of the
question if he performed as expected. Unfortunately, in his final
start in spring training, he was hit in the face by a line drive. He

suffered a concussion and cracked orbital bone, which ultimately ended his promising career before it had a chance to start.

With baseball no longer an option, Grover needed a way to occupy his time, which baseball had filled for as long as he could remember. He toiled in his uncle's billboard company the first couple of years after baseball, running the construction side of the business. It took him that long to come to grips with his lifelong dream coming to an end and to realize that he had the rest of his life ahead of him. Baseball offered him a freedom he had yet to replicate post-career, and he wanted something more than what he was getting in the billboard business. He took into account his love for beer, sports, and hanging out with friends, and the idea of The Crafty Lefty was born.

The sobriquet *crafty lefty* denotes a left-handed pitcher who doesn't get by on raw power, describing Grover's pitching style to a tee. Mix in that he wanted his bar to specialize in serving craft beers, and the name was a natural fit.

The patrons in the bar—currently closed to the general public—had all come from Duncan's funeral. A mixture of Duncan's friends from the DA's office, the defense bar, and law enforcement gathered to celebrate Duncan's life one final time in a way that he would have certainly approved of. What had started as a reasonably quiet affair had morphed into an alcohol-induced celebration of the life of Duncan Pheiffer. It had taken on the air of that post-funeral row that happens when the pent-up emotion between a person's death and their burial has a chance to finally be released. The emotionally charged collective exhale of the bereaved. Molly Pheiffer and Brittany Griffith were absent from the group, having gone back to Brittany's house after the funeral.

Barclay had set this up, and Grover was happy to do it. "Thanks again, Grove," said Barclay, sitting on a bar stool swirling around a pint glass that was a quarter full of beer.

"Glad to do it, B." Grover, with longish tousled blond hair, a three-day beard, and wearing a chambray shirt with the sleeves rolled up past his elbows, was busying himself with washing and drying pint glasses when he slung the towel over his shoulder, looked out at the crowd and said, "I hope I have this many friends show up when I die."

"You and me both." Barclay finished off his third pint in the last forty-five minutes or so. A burst of laughter rang out from one of the larger pockets of revelers, which caused Barclay to look back over his shoulder. He saw Stacy Steen approaching the bar with an empty beer glass and a slight tilt in her walk.

She set the glass on the bar a little harder than intended and said, "Ivey, your brother here is a brilliant prosecutor."

Barclay looked down with an embarrassed grin. "You think so, huh?" replied Grover as he pulled a fresh pint glass from behind the bar, filled it with beer, and swapped the full beer for the empty glass.

"Yep," Stacy replied. "He's ten times the prosecutor than King Dick. That asshole."

Barclay threw his head back and let out a laugh he could no longer contain. And it felt good. He said, "Oh, Stace. You have a bright future in that office." He reached for the fresh pint that Grover had set out for him and took a long drink. "I never heard how your trial with the good reverend came out."

"The jury convicted the shit out of him. Probably took them longer to choose a foreman than it did to find him guilty."

"Very nice," said Barclay. Holding his glass up, he said, "To the good reverend." They clinked glasses and drank.

Stacy said, "Can I ask a personal question? Just something that's been bugging me."

Barclay and Grover exchanged a glance, and Barclay said, "Sure."

"Well, Barclay, you're the oldest, right?"

"Yes," replied Barclay nodding slowly.

Stacy pointed to Grover and said, "Then why is Ivey the fourth and not you?"

"It's because I was named after the song *A Nightingale Sang in Berkeley Square*. You see, our Mom was a big fan of Bobby Darin, and his version of *Berkeley Square* was her favorite. So even though the title is *Berkeley Square*, she always thought he was saying *Barclay Square*." Grover laughed, and Barclay continued, "She had her mind set that if she ever had a son, she would name him Barclay. When she was pregnant with me, my father wanted a 'fourth,' but she insisted on Barclay, and he was so in love with her that there was no way she wasn't getting her way."

"That's so sweet," said Stacy placing her hand on Barclay's forearm.

Grover cleared his throat, looked up at Barclay from a bowed head, glanced at Stacy's hand on Barclay's arm, smirked, and made his way to the end of the bar to serve some customers.

"You know, I never got a chance to thank you for your help in that trial," said Stacy.

"I didn't do anything, Stace."

"Yeah, you did. Just being there meant a lot. And showing that confidence in me. It's just that"—she paused—"well, I appreciate it."

"Don't worry about it." They were silent for a bit when another burst of laughter erupted somewhere in the bar. Barclay said, "Come on. Let's go over and see what those yahoos are making so much noise about."

They got up and walked over to the table that was the source of all the commotion. Some folks were sitting at the table, and about twice as many were standing around it. A rosy-cheeked detective from the PD was telling a story about Duncan. It was one that Barclay was very familiar with because he was there. It was during Duncan's first felony preliminary hearing.

"So," the detective began, "I was the case agent on this sex assault case where the victim was caught by her father in the act of giving the defendant a blow job. She was embarrassed and told her father that the defendant made her do it.

"When we went to interview the guy, he was scared shit-less. He showed us a video of the two of them on his cell phone. He filmed the act, and it was clear she was into it. She kept looking up and smiling—really playing to the camera." He took a drink of something with clear liquor in it and said, "She was lying her ass off to her dad, but he was pissed and refused to believe his daughter was a willing participant. He was some local big shot, so what was I going to do about it?" He nodded his head at Barclay and said, "We talked about it beforehand, and there was no way we were going to let this kid go down for this. So we figured we'd give her father a good dog and pony show before exposing his little angel as a liar on the wit-ness stand. In her statement, she claimed the defendant said to her, quote 'bitch, suck my dick' end quote." The alcohol-lu-bricated collective laughed, which emboldened the detective to continue. "Right in the middle of the direct examination of the *victim*"—the detective made quote marks in the air when he said *victim*—"Duncan stops and asks the judge for a break. Well, you all know Judge Arnett. He's half asleep up there, so it takes Duncan two more tries to get the judge's attention. He looks at Duncan like he has three heads before taking a ten-minute recess."

Stacey Steen jumped in. "Wait. Why was Judge Arnett doing a prelim? He's a circuit court judge."

"Hell if I know," said the story-telling detective with a shrug.

Barclay spoke up. "Because Judge Maclendon is a chicken shit who binds everyone over to the grand jury, and we couldn't take the chance on this case getting past the prelim. I told Arnett what was going on and asked him to step in for this one."

"Anyway," the detective said with a bit of exasperation, "Barclay, Duncan, and I all go into the hallway behind the judge's bench, and Duncan starts in with: 'Dude, I can't say those words in court.' Barclay and I look at each other, then back at him, and Barclay asks: 'What words?' Duncan says: 'You know.'" The detective is now talking through his laughter. "He says: 'You know, bitch and dick.'" The whole crowd, Barclay included, erupted into laughter. "So Barclay tells him: 'Well, you kind of have to say it because that's what she said he said, and the judge needs to hear it. He won't hold it against you. He understands what's going on.'"

The detective is belly laughing at this point. He says, "Duncan doesn't say a word. He just turns and walks back into the courtroom like someone kicked his dog. Judge Arnett comes in, and the direct examination continues. It's clear Duncan still does not want to address the issue because he begins asking some random, rambling questions. Finally, after several minutes, Barclay clears his throat to get Duncan's attention. Duncan looks over at us, and Barclay nods at him. Duncan walks directly in front of the victim, clears his throat, and, after a pause, yells out: 'SUCK MY DICK!'" Everyone around the table exploded into laughter, beer spewing. "Judge Arnett about falls backward out of his chair since he was almost asleep again, jumps up, and bangs his gavel before running out of the courtroom."

When the laughter settled, it was as if the somberness of the occasion suddenly hit them all, and nobody knew quite what to say. Finally, Barclay said, "Come on now, y'all know Duncan wouldn't want everyone crying in their beers. So drink up and enjoy yourselves. Tomorrow it's back to work." Barclay walked back over to the bar and heard the conversation picking back up.

Grover was walking in from the kitchen with a rack of clean glasses when Barclay took his seat back at the bar. "Want another?" Grover asked Barclay.

In answer to the question, Barclay slid his glass across the narrow bar.

Grover swapped the empty pint glass for a full one and said, "The police any closer to figuring out what happened?"

"Nope. I talked to the detective before the funeral, and they still don't know much. The ME was able to determine that he was killed prior to the fire being set. The lungs were singed by the fire but smoke-free, which tells them he wasn't breathing. We don't know how he was killed, but if it were a gunshot, you'd expect to see a defect in a bone somewhere—hole in the skull, something like that."

"Did the neighbors hear anything?"

"Nothing. We figure Duncan never saw it coming or was restrained or gagged somehow."

"If he was killed at his house, why the fire?"

Barclay gave a slight shrug as he shook his head and said, "Maybe it was an attempt to destroy evidence." Barclay drank a swallow of beer. "Or maybe it was one final coup de grace. One last fuck you." Barclay was watching the convivial crowd reflected in the mirror behind the bar.

"What are you going to do about it?"

Barclay blinked and looked at Grover. He said, "What do you mean?"

"Come on now, B. You and I both know you're not just going to sit back and watch from the sidelines."

Barclay eased off his stool, leaned back against the bar, and shrugged his shoulders. "I don't know." Barclay emptied his glass.

"Bullshit. You always have a plan—for everything. Even before you know you need one."

"I've got to think this is somehow tied to his last case, Grove. It has to be. I've turned it over in my head a thousand times, and I can't make anything else make sense. I don't know much about the case against Clements, but my gut says there is something there." Grover slid a pint glass to Barclay, who turned back around and looked at it as if it had just materialized. He took a drink and said, "Good stuff. What is it?"

"Westbrook One Claw Rye out of Mt. Pleasant, South Carolina. Came in this morning, and it seemed right up your alley."

Barclay stared into the beer for a few seconds, then pushed off the bar. As he was about to rejoin the fray, Grover asked, "Whose case was it? Duncan's last trial?"

Barclay finished taking another drink from his glass before responding, "King Dick's."

CHAPTER 7

BARCLAY WOKE UP TUESDAY morning a little dehydrated and a little hungover. He finished off the remainder of the bottle of water on his bedside table as he padded to the bathroom to get ready for work.

He wasn't at his desk thirty seconds when his desk phone rang; he could see on the caller ID that it was DA Maggie Gamble's executive assistant. Barclay punched the button activating the speakerphone and said, "Hey, Sandy. What's up?"

"Maggie wants to see you," she replied.

Maggie Gamble was the third district attorney Sandy Maxwell had been the gatekeeper for, and she would also be Sandy's last. Sandy was in her early sixties, overly tan, and had what could only be described as big hair. On her desk sat a countdown clock ticking away the days, hours, minutes, and seconds until her retirement date—a gift from the other office assistants after she announced she would be leaving. Though free of the clutter of paperwork, her office and desk were awash in the detritus one collects over so many years. The pictures of her family served as a timeline of sorts: her children went from kindergarten photos directly to portraits of her children as adults with their families.

Barclay entered the anteroom that was Sandy's office and was hit with the pungent odor of potpourri. He looked at Mag-

56

gie's closed door, then back to Sandy and asked, "Any idea what it's about?" Sandy gave him a look that said he should know better than even to ask; Sandy knew everything that went on in the office. Barclay was about to knock when Sandy said, "Just go on in."

Maggie's office was spacious and had a masculine feel to it. Immediately to the left of the door was a sitting area with a sofa against the door-side wall, two cloth wingback chairs opposite the sofa separated by a mahogany coffee table that held a vase of fresh flowers, which gave the office a pleasant, welcoming feel. Behind the couch was Maggie's brag wall covered with certificates, awards, and other forms of recognition collected over her thirty-six years as a prosecutor.

The role of most elected district attorneys was that of administrator more than it was courtroom prosecutor; however, Maggie struck a balance between the two, never straying too far from the courtroom. She was reviewing recently closed cases when Barclay walked in, causing her to look up.

She wore a Burberry skirt and jacket buttoned over a French blue dress shirt and Ugg scuffs. She was sixty-one years old but looked a decade younger. She stood just over five-four with the palest green eyes—the color reminded Barclay of an old Coca-Cola bottle—shoulder-length silver hair that was not fussed over, and she wore a minimal amount of makeup. She was not a physically imposing figure by any stretch, but she had personality in spades. Her beauty and elegance saw her opponents— politically and in the courtroom—underestimate her, which was one of the reasons she had been as successful as she had in a male-dominated field. She was carrying a Tervis Tumbler of sweet iced tea, her self-proclaimed vice.

Maggie Gamble began her career as a prosecutor in 1986, just over a year after graduating from law school. She immediately jumped in with both feet and rewarded her boss with guilty verdict after guilty verdict. The southern debutant exterior belied the pitbull persona that showed up in court. She had a measured way of speaking to a jury that made you listen and assured you that whatever she said was of the utmost importance—and they trusted her. She was as loyal as she was tenacious and was rewarded after six years as an assistant district attorney when she was named the elected district attorney's chief assistant. She was Alabama's first female chief assistant district attorney and would become Alabama's second female sitting DA. As the Towne County District Attorney, the office took on her persona. Those that weren't serious about being a prosecutor did not last long, while those who were, were shown loyalty in return. She backed her employees with the same tenacity that she used in a court of law as well as the court of public opinion. Defense lawyers were sometimes left with their feelings hurt, but to a person, they all believed she was doing a great job and wanted her and her staff on the case should they ever be the victim of a crime.

She moved toward the sitting area and said, "Hey, Barclay, how have you been?"

Barclay stood in front of a chair and waited on Maggie before he sat. He said, "I've been doing ok. Trying to stay busy."

Maggie made it to the other chair, and as she sat, she said, "Please, have a seat." She crossed her ankles to her left and smoothed her skirt. "How's Molly holding up?" Barclay placed his tall Styrofoam cup of coffee on the low table and caught a hint of her perfume—it smelled faintly of citrus. After he sat, he crossed his right leg over his left and said, "As well as can be expected, I suppose. She's been spending a good deal of time with Britt; I think just not being alone right now is helping. She is starting to prepare for the upcoming school year, and I think the more involved she gets with that, the quicker she will begin to heal."

Maggie nodded, drank from her Tervis with a script letter M on the side, then said, "How is Clayton working out?"

"He's doing a nice job. Hasn't had a ton of work to do, but he asks questions and seems eager to learn."

"Well, make sure he starts trying some cases. At least let him take a witness or two. He needs to learn, and it doesn't need to be a long time before he starts. Hell, give him a dog and let him lose it. Be good for him." Barclay laughed at her last comment. "What? Not everyone is like you."

He said, "I was terrified at my first trial, believe me. There isn't anything that can prepare you for it; you just have to jump right in. But, not to worry, I will ensure he gets thoroughly baptized."

Maggie leaned forward and set her cup on a coaster. She sat back and said, "Barclay, I'm going to retire at the end of my term, and I want you to run for DA when I do."

Barclay drew back a bit, eyes going wide. After a moment, he started to speak, then stopped and shook his head.

"Is that a no?" asked Maggie with a single raised eyebrow.

"No. No. It's absolutely a yes, but you've got to know this is a bit of a shock."

"Well, it shouldn't be too surprising. After all, I've been at this for nearly four decades."

"I guess I mean that I never saw you retiring. I doubt anyone has envisioned that day coming."

Maggie laughed and said, "Barclay, I'm not a robot."

"You know what I mean."

"I understand, but it's just time. I'd go now if I could, but I'm not sure I could sell the Governor on appointing you. Not with Richard's name in the mix." She shook her head. "No, that's just too much to risk. Don't get me wrong, he has been very loyal, and you know I appreciate that very much, but," she leaned in, causing Barclay to lean in as well, and in a lower voice, she said, "can you imagine him in charge of this office?" They both leaned back in their chairs, and Barclay just looked at Maggie, who gave him a look that said she was right, and he knew it.

Barclay said, "Have you told him?"

"Not yet. I wanted to speak to you about it first to get your thoughts on running."

"What are you going to tell him?"

"That I will not seek another term as district attorney, and I will support you in the next election as my replacement."

Maggie was the most direct person Barclay knew, but this response caused even him to straighten. He said, "Maggie, I'm not questioning your judgment, but are you sure that's the right approach to this?"

"Questioning my judgment is exactly what you're doing." Barclay was about to speak when she raised her hand and said, "But a good leader should welcome it...from time to time." She grabbed her tea glass, drank from it, and settled back into the chair. She said, "I agree he's not going to like hearing that, but he's a grown man, and we're all professionals here. My duty is to the people of this county, and that's why I am making this decision."

"The election is over a year away; do you expect him to stay around after you talk to him?"

"I expect him to stay, but if he wants to leave, so be it."

Their conversation was interrupted by Maggie's desk phone ringing. Sandy's voice came from the phone's speaker: "Sorry to interrupt, but Judge Arnett is on the phone for you."

"Tell him I'm in a meeting."

"Yes, ma'am."

"Now, where were we? Oh yes, as for Richard quitting, I don't expect him to. He's going to run for this office—that you can bet on—and running as the chief assistant of the outgoing district attorney will be a nice feather in his cap. I sure wouldn't give that up."

"When are you going to tell him?"

"I haven't decided. I'd like to wait as long as possible because I don't want to make it any more strained between the two of you than it already is."

Barclay gave her a look to which she said, "What, you think I don't know what goes on in my own office?"

※   ※   ※   ※   ※

While Barclay was meeting with Maggie, Clayton walked into Barclay's office to ask a question. Seeing the office empty, he turned to leave, almost colliding with a tall, wiry man in the doorway. He had a substantial beard and longish dark hair underneath a well-worn baseball cap, too dirty to make out the logo on the front.

"Can I help you?" asked Clayton.

"Who are you, and why are you in Barclay's office?" asked the bearded stranger.

"I'm Clayton White. I'm a new assistant DA."

"Oh. Ok, well, I'm Detective Mike Wise. I work in narcotics. Do you know when Barclay's going to be back?"

"No idea. I didn't even know he was gone."

"Hmmm. Maybe you can help me, then."

"Sure. I'll do what I can. What do you need?"

Detective Wise looked around, then backed Clayton into the vacant office. In a quieter tone, he said, "Barclay has this los-er on probation that he wants revoked. The defendant crashed his car and killed a kid while on a three-day meth bender. The judge let him skate with probation on the DUI manslaughter so he could go to rehab. It's not jail, so the guy bounced after only two days inside. The court refused to act, so Barclay wants to get his probation revoked. As part of his probation, he has to call in every day to see if his color is up." Noticing the confused look on Clayton's face, the detective explained, "When someone is put on probation, and a condition of probation is random drug screening, they are assigned a color. Then they call in every day, and if their color is called, they report to probation and give a urine sample." Clayton was listening intently and nodding his head to what the detective was saying. "Anyway," the detective continued, "the asshole's color came up, and now we have a urine sample. Unfortunately, it's clean, but only me and the probation officer know that right now—well, and you, of course. You're in this now." Clayton drew back. He didn't like the sound of that. "I was coming here to see what Barclay wants me to put in it so we can revoke him." Detective Wise produced a sealed cup of what looked like urine and shook it at Clayton, who flinched.

"What?"

"I need to know what drugs to put in his sample to make it dirty. We have to get this guy revoked."

"You can't do that."

"What are you, an Eagle Scout? What did you say you were hired to do?"

"I was hired as a prosecutor. An assistant district attorney."

"Well, listen here, Mr. ADA, sometimes this is how it's done. Do you want that asshole driving on the roadway with your family when he's all whacked out on drugs?"

"Of course not, but—"

"Exactly. This is for all the people that man could kill when he finally decides he has to have his meth before he gets behind the wheel of a car. Look, since Barclay's not here, maybe you can help. If we wait much longer, the missing urine will look suspicious. I still have to go back to the narcotics unit and get the drugs from impound, so we need to make this quick."

"You just add drugs to the urine?"

"What? No. I get the drugs, give them to one of my CIs, and then have them piss for me. There's no way to know whose urine it is, am I right?"

"I don't know about this."

"You need to grow a pair, kid. Ok, I guess we can throw some meth in there. I mean, that won't be hard to believe. What about some marijuana? I mean, everyone smokes weed, right?"

"Uh…"

"Yeah, good call, kid. Thanks."

Detective Wise turned to go, and Barclay appeared in the doorway. Barclay looked at Wise and then Clayton and said, "What's going on here?"

Clayton pointed to Detective Wise and said, "This detective wants to—"

Detective Wise interrupted Clayton and said, "I just came in to ask what drugs you wanted me to put in that DUI probationer's urine."

"Oh, yeah?" replied Barclay as he eased past the two men and settled into his desk chair.

"Yeah, but Clayton here helped me out."

"What?" exclaimed Clayton.

"Yeah, Clayton was a big help," said the rangy detective as he clapped Clayton on the shoulder.

Clayton winced and dipped his shoulder to break Wise's grip as he said, "Now, wait a minute."

Looking at Clayton, Barclay asked, "And just what advice did Clayton offer?"

"He said to use meth—of course, that was obvious—but then he said to add in marijuana because"—he looked at Clayton—"how did you say it? 'Because everyone smokes weed these days.'"

"Barclay, you gotta believe me—"

Clayton was interrupted by Barclay, Wise, and three other prosecutors outside the office door, erupting in loud laughter as if on cue.

Clayton looked around at everyone and stammered, "What?"

"Dude, he's messing with you," said Barclay. "Hazing the new guy."

"Man, the look on your face. Holy shit, you were awesome," said Detective Wise, still laughing.

The crowd by the door dispersed but could still be heard—laughter and voices fading as they went on with their day. Clayton dropped onto Barclay's couch, still trying to figure out what had just happened. Barclay clicked through emails on his computer.

Detective Wise turned to leave when he caught himself. "Say, Barclay, have you shown our friend Mr. Harris to Clayton?"

"Not yet," said Barclay, not taking his eyes off his computer monitor.

"I think you ought to show him."

Barclay looked past the flat-screen computer monitor at Clayton and then back to the screen. He said, "I'm not sure he's ready to see it."

"Eh, you're probably right," said the detective as he left the office but not before giving Clayton a wink and a smile.

Clayton did not care for Detective Mike Wise.

Barclay continued working on the computer while Clayton looked at his iPhone. The minutes that ticked by did nothing to assuage Clayton's curiosity about the aforementioned Mr. Harris. After the joke that was just played on him, Clayton was on high alert, certain this was yet another joke; he would not be taken this time. It sucked being the new guy.

Finally, Clayton said, in a casual *I know this is another joke, but I'm asking anyway* tone of voice, "So, who is Mr. Harris?"

Barclay was responding to an email, paused his typing, opened a desk drawer on his left, slid something across his desk, and went back to typing. Clayton could see that it was a manila file folder; he was hesitant to pick it up.

After a few moments, Barclay stopped typing and said, "This isn't another joke."

That was all the prompting Clayton needed as he eagerly swiped the folder from the desk. Inside was a type-written statement by a Will Harris, Jr. and two eight-by-ten color photographs in a transparent sheet protector. He was not prepared for what he saw. After a beat and just above a whisper, he said, "What...is this?"

The two eight-by-ten photographs depicted a death scene. The picture Clayton saw first was a wide shot. It showed a thin man sitting on a white couch on white carpet and set against a white wall. He is wearing dark blue Liberty overalls over a red plaid long-sleeve shirt unbuttoned at the cuffs, hands resting on his knees. In his right hand, between his index and middle fingers, is a cigarette burned down the filter, leaving a long ash that seemed to defy gravity. A highly polished four-legged red-brown oval coffee table sat in front of the couch. Everything in the picture looked perfectly normal, except the top half of the man's head was missing. It appeared as if someone started at the top of the bridge of his nose and sliced the top of his head off—front to back—with laser-like precision. The missing portion of his head was on the white wall behind the couch in a Jackson Pollock-esque splatter pattern. The gore radiated out, getting lighter as it broadcasted from the dark red center in perfect symmetry like a macabre ocean sunset.

A couple of keystrokes, a press of the laptop's trackpad, and Barclay was done answering emails. He closed the computer, turned his attention to Clayton, and said, "William Wallace Harris."

Clayton stared at the photograph, eyes moving over the picture, taking it all in. He turned the sheet protector over to view the second photograph. This picture was a front-on close-up of William Wallace Harris' head. What stood out to Clayton was the detail the picture showed of the man's face: cracked, chapped lips and mostly gray two-day beard stubble growing through his porous sun-dried skin. The bright red of the wound was quite stark. Regaining his senses, he looked up and said, "What happened?"

"His twenty-year-old son shot him with a twelve-gauge shotgun."

Looking back down at the wide shot, Clayton said, "You prosecuted this case?"

"Not yet. It's been almost four years, and the son was never arrested." Seeing Clayton's reaction, Barclay said, "Mr. Harris' son, Will Jr., told police that he was cleaning his shotgun when it went off shooting his father. Now, I don't believe that story, but we couldn't prove otherwise. I've shown these pictures to better than a hundred folks trying to see if anyone could give me anything I could use, but so far, nothing."

Clayton looked up from the picture, studied Barclay for a couple of beats, and said, "Why don't you believe that's what happened?"

"Oh, several things. By all accounts, the Harrises were gun people, and cleaning one without first making sure it isn't loaded is a rookie mistake. Also, why would his son sit on the coffee table to clean his gun? And where's the gun cleaning kit? He says he put it away after he called the police, but that doesn't make much sense. There was also something about his interview with the police. I've probably watched it thirty times, and I don't buy his story."

"Did the son give you any idea why he was cleaning his gun in the living room?"

"Oh, sure, he had an explanation for everything. He said he went into the living room because that was where his father was, and they were having a normal father-son chat, if you believe Junior. He cleaning his gun, and his father having his evening smoke. Said they had been talking for several minutes when the gun went off."

"What reason did he have to kill him?"

"That's the other part we couldn't quite nail down. Mr. Harris owned four extremely successful tractor dealerships. He started them from nothing and was very much a self-made man. His son, on the other hand, is a spoiled little shit. Mr. Harris' wife died when Junior was six or seven, and Dad made up for Mom's absence by giving Junior whatever he wanted. From the folks we talked to, Mr. Harris did not like Junior's aimless life and was getting close to cutting him off. Essentially, a bunch of hearsay that we couldn't prove."

Clayton turned back to the wide shot and continued to study it. He said, "So he's going to get away with it?"

"He has so far, but I'm yet to see the perfect crime. The key to this whole thing is out there somewhere. We just have to find it."

Nearly a minute passed as Clayton read through the two-page witness statement. After reading the statement, Clayton returned to the wide shot. He saw something he knew wasn't quite right, but he couldn't put his finger on it. "What about the fact that there doesn't appear to be any damage below his nose? I mean, if it's a shotgun, shouldn't there be a spread of pellets entering the body in a wider pattern?"

"Good thought, but no. A shotgun fired within five to six feet of the target would not give the pellets enough room to spread before hitting the target. At least not enough room to spread more than what it took to take half his head off. Junior's statement puts him within that range, so the result is what can be expected."

Clayton continued to stare at the photos as that niggling feeling scratched at his brain.

His concentration was interrupted when Barclay said, "Come on. Let's grab lunch. You look like you could use some fresh air."

❖ ❖ ❖ ❖ ❖

Barclay and Clayton had walked to The Downtowner for an early lunch and were back at the courthouse steps when Barclay's phone rang. He grabbed his phone and looked at the screen before answering.

Clayton was walking just ahead of Barclay when he heard him answer. He turned to see Barclay stop walking as he talked on the phone. Clayton stopped, too, and glanced up at the sun, wishing he had not left his sunglasses in his office. His gaze drifted and began absent-mindedly people-watching as he waited for Barclay to finish his phone call. He was marveling at the throng of smokers on the courthouse steps. Only the lure of a nicotine fix could elicit the bizarre clique of cops, lawyers, and defendants on display in the hot Alabama summertime sun.

Cops having their cigarettes lit by defendants they had arrested and would be facing in court later that afternoon; defense lawyers bumming cigarettes from cops they would be cross-examining tooth-and-nail. *The smoking fraternity*, Clayton thought.

Barclay ended his phone call and caught up to Clayton, who said, "Big tobacco can rest easy tonight knowing the American smoker is alive and well at the Towne County courthouse."

They were both staring at the assemblage of smokers, and Barclay said, "Be glad they are out here instead of in the indoor stairwells. Up until just a couple of years ago, that was where the smokers congregated, and one trip up or down the stairs meant your suit had to go to the dry cleaners."

They both began ascending the stairs when Clayton stopped and said, "That's it."

"What's 'it'?"

"The cigarette," said an animated Clayton.

"What are you talking about?"

"Your gunshot victim. I can prove the son was lying?"

"What? Who?" said Barclay, clearly confused.

"The guy with half a head. Mr. Harris."

"What about him?"

"I think I figured it out," said Clayton as he turned and ran up the courthouse steps two at a time.

Upon reaching Barclay's office, he said, "Do you mind explaining what you're talking about?"

"I have to show you," Clayton said, eyes scanning Barclay's desk. "Where is the file with the witness statement and the photographs?"

Barclay went around his desk, withdrew a file from a drawer, and handed it to Clayton.

Clayton scanned the statement, nodded a few times, then pulled out the wide shot of the crime scene. "Yep."

"What are you talking about?"

"Right here." Clayton held the photograph out to Barclay and pointed at the cigarette William Wallace Harris held between the index and middle fingers of his right hand. "See the ash?"

"Yes," said Barclay, not making the connection.

"Read the statement," said Clayton as he held the statement up and shook the paper. "Mr. Harris' son said that his father had just lit his cigarette when he—Junior—sat down in front of him to begin cleaning his gun. He said they sat there for several minutes talking as he cleaned the gun and his dad smoked his cigarette."

"Ok."

Clayton was frustrated that Barclay wasn't seeing it. He said, "How long does it take a cigarette to burn down on its own? Two, three minutes? If someone is smoking that cigarette, then maybe half that time?" Barclay gave him a look that said *out with it.*

Clayton grabbed the photograph from Barclay, pointed at the cigarette ash, and said, "See how the ash is still attached to the filter? That's an entire cigarette of ash. Also, the ashtray in the picture is empty, and there is no other receptacle to tap his ash off into, and he sure as hell didn't thump his ashes onto that white carpet." Clayton stopped to take a breath as if he was relishing this moment. He continued, "Taking the son at his own words, several minutes passed between when the cigarette was lit, and the gun fired. Therefore, the ash we see in the picture was exactly as it was when the gun went off. Now, do you see?"

Barclay jerked the picture from Clayton's hand and stared hard at it. He said, "I see the ash, but what does that prove?"

"If Mr. Harris' son really did fire that gun from the distance he said, the pressure wave from the muzzle would have blown that ash away. No way that long ash stands up to the blast wave that would have trailed the shot from the muzzle of the shotgun."

Still staring at the photograph, Barclay spoke as if to himself: "So the muzzle had to have been closer to Mr. Harris. Positioned between the cigarette and Mr. Harris' head."

"Exactly."

"Huh."

※　※　※　※　※

Barclay called Judge Arnett's office. After three rings, Judge Arnett's assistant answered, "Hello, Barclay." The phone system had caller ID for all intra-courthouse calls.

"Hey there, Delta. How is everything on the fourth floor?"

"Oh, you know. Same as every other day around here."

"I heard Judge didn't go to the conference."

A snort. "He went down there on Saturday, and I was looking forward to a week of him being gone. He was up for Judge of the Year, and when he found out 'that asshole McHenry' was going to win, he just came home." She sounded sufficiently dejected. "Judge is in his office right now as we speak."

Laughing, Barclay said, "Good for him. I agree McHenry is an asshole. I'm guessing he got his buddies to get him this award to springboard his campaign for Chief Justice of the State Supreme Court."

"Did you need anything? Or did you just call to make my afternoon?"

"I need to meet with him. Is he available?"

"He is, but give him about an hour. He's still in a bad mood about the award, but I picked up his favorite lunch from Harper's, so his corned beef and potato salad sandwich should have him in better spirits by then."

An hour and fifteen minutes later, Barclay and Clayton walked into the judge's office, where Delta was on the phone. She had curly light-socket hair, wore a lot of purple, had a big personality, and was perhaps the most powerful person in the courthouse. You did not want to find yourself on her bad side.

The reception area had the requisite government-on-a-budget look. A plastic coffee maker with a stained carafe and generic non-dairy creamer sat on a side table, while a cloudy freshwater fish tank whose fish count was down from six to two sat wedged in a battered bookcase. The space was sparsely furnished with a couple of tall fake plants and a real fern whose best days were behind it, and the walls were adorned with some mass-produced pastel floral prints that were never really in style. The odor of fingernail polish remover dominated the small space.

Barclay sat in one of the two empty chairs while Clayton walked over to the wall beside the judge's interior office door. He was reading the framed article about Judge Arnett becoming Towne County's first black judge when Delta finished her phone call and said, "Judge is on the bench."

The two prosecutors walked down the back hall to the public corridor so they could enter the courtroom from the front entrance. Barclay and Clayton entered Judge Arnett's courtroom, the largest in the courthouse, and saw that it was empty save for two lawyers speaking to the judge at the bench; they sat against the rear wall and waited.

Judge Malcolm Arnett was Towne County's most tenured of the current judges, and he embodied the truism that if neither side was happy, the judge had made the correct ruling. A former Green Beret, he had the disposition to match...when he wanted to. He was not tall but not short either, and had a paunch brought on by age. He was toilet seat bald with salt-and-pepper hair and matching mustache and sideburns that always seemed in dire need of a trim. Practicing in front of Judge Arnett could be both maddening and intimidating if you did not know how to take him. He was far and away Barclay's favorite judge in the courthouse. He appreciated how the judge could temper an over-eager prosecutor or defense attorney and the way he handled both victims and defendants. He always seemed to know the right thing to say or do in a given situation.

Barclay waited for the hearing to wrap up and the lawyers to leave and spoke: "Judge, may we approach?"

The judge, writing in a file, looked up and motioned them to the front. When Barclay and Clayton reached the judge's bench, he finished writing and closed the folder.

Barclay said, "Judge—" The judge interrupted him by holding a finger up and re-opening the file. He had seen Judge Arnett do this a number of times. As a power move to show who was in charge, he would wait for the lawyers to begin speaking before interrupting them and going back into a file. After about a minute, the judge put down his pen, again closed the file folder, and looked up. "Now, what do you gentlemen need with me?"

"I'd like to talk to you about Duncan—about the case he tried before you last week."

"What about it?"

"Nothing specific, really. Just trying to determine if there may be any connection between that case and his death."

"Oh, sure, absolutely. Whatever I can do to help. Let's talk in my office."

❈ ❈ ❈ ❈ ❈

Judge Arnett entered his office, removed a stack of paper from one of his two guest chairs, and plopped it down on the corner of a desk already awash in paper. "Have a seat," he said without looking at either of his guests. He walked over to a small table that held a humidor, grabbed a cigar, and turned to Barclay, holding it out in an offertory gesture. Barclay, hands in pockets, shook his head. He then made the offer to Clayton, who also declined. Cigar and lighter in hand, the judge ambled over to the wall of windows and cranked one open. He bit the end of the cigar and spit it out the window. He lit the cigar, puffed a few strong puffs, and exhaled out the window.

"Now," he said, half sitting and half standing on the windowsill, "What would you like to know?" Then he flicked something off his tongue, probably tobacco, onto his office floor.

Barclay and Clayton sat across from the judge in curved back leather chairs. The chairs were distressed by age in a way that gave them character, not in a way that said they needed to be replaced. Judge Arnett's office décor had not changed much since he was sworn in over thirty years ago, save for a few coats of paint on the walls and three new carpet installations. Going into his office was akin to going back in time—but not too far back. The place was timeless and smelled of Murphy's Oil Soap and cedar.

The lone decorative blemish in the office space was the Anita Arnett original oil painting hung prominently on the wall behind the judge's desk. Anita was the judge's wife, and she was an artist about like Barclay was a pianist, but that did not stop her from painting. Every one of her paintings was of a young slave depicted in some modern setting, and in each one, the slave was composed the same way: young, shirtless, skinny, and wearing tattered gray capri-length pants. In the painting on the judge's office wall, the subject of the artwork was giving a closing argument to an all-white jury. Barclay actually owned one of her paintings which he bought at a silent auction to raise

money for victims of Hurricane Katrina. The Arnetts organized
the fundraiser, so Barclay felt obligated to buy something. He
ended up paying five thousand dollars for *the slave* riding to vic-
tory in the Kentucky Derby. The painting was still in the tube,
just as it had been when he received it, and he had no plans of
ever displaying it. He was sure the paintings were some sort of
social commentary, but he was either too dense or too white to
understand it. The paintings were awful but seeing one was like
watching a car wreck in slow motion. You knew it was going
to end badly, but you didn't dare look away. He was lost in the
painting when Clayton nudged his arm.

"Huh, what?" asked Barclay finding Clayton's face. Clayton pointed to the judge, and Barclay looked at him.

Judge: "God awful, I know."

Barclay: "Sir?"

"The painting. I know it's ugly. You ain't gotta stare at it."
Two more puffs. "I asked what you would like to know. About
that case."

The judge's position at the window made talking to him
from the chair awkward, so Barclay stood up and joined him.
Looking out the window and down at the street, he asked the
judge, "Do you think the trial last week got Duncan killed?"

"You don't waste any time, do you?" said Arnett.

"I don't have it to waste, sir."

Arnett stood up and peered out the window. "I liked Duncan. He was a hell of a trial lawyer." Laughing, he said, "I
wouldn't have given you a plug nickel for him making it six
months after that damn sex assault prelim." He drew on his cigar before speaking again. "'Suck my dick.' Goddamn, that was
funny." His laughing caused a mild coughing fit. He cleared his
throat and spat out the window. "That sonofabitch would try
any damn thing."

He pointed at Clayton with the hand holding the cigar and said, "That's what makes a good trial lawyer, son. When the other side knows you'll try the case without hesitation, cases get resolved." Turning back to the window, he continued, "If they don't get resolved?" He shrugged. "You just try the damn thing, convict their asses, and I send 'em to prison. Simple as that. Word gets around, and cases get settled. You can't reward these folks for dragging their cases out and taking them to trial when the evidence is stacked so decisively against them. There has to be a benefit for taking responsibility for your actions and saving the time and expense of a trial, or we would have to try everything."

Turning back to face Clayton, he said, "I can handle that through sentencing, but you, you gotta be willing to try the case. If you're competent, the cases that should work themselves out will work themselves out. Always have and always will."

Barclay had heard this spiel from the judge before, and he agreed with it, but now was not the time. He said, "Judge, about the case."

"Oh, yeah, uh, no. Nothing I can think of about that case that jumps out at me. I wasn't surprised to see him convicted, but it wouldn't have shocked me if they had let him go."

"How did the defendant's family take the verdict?" asked Barclay.

"How do you think? Momma and sister just sat there hugging each other and crying." Judge Arnett turned to Barclay and asked, "You think maybe they had something to do with this?"

"Maybe," said Barclay, but he said it in a way that told the judge he didn't believe it. "Just asking the question, you know."

"Yeah, I know." Silence engulfed the office the way the judge's cigar smoke used to before the non-smoking revolution took hold. The only sound that could be heard was the judge puffing on the cigar.

Eventually, Barclay asked, "Is that one of your Mexican see-gars?"

The judge took a vacation with his wife to Mexico every winter and always came back with a couple of boxes of Cuban cigars. He would remove the labels, mail them to himself, and bring non-Cuban cigar labels to slip onto the cigars for transport back home. That way, if his luggage were checked at customs, the customs inspectors wouldn't know he was transporting contraband. He referred to those as his *Mexican see-gars.*

The judge rolled the cigar in his fingers and looked up at Barclay. He raised his eyebrows and flashed a big grin.

CHAPTER 8

"HOW WAS WORK?" BRITTANY asked, walking into their spacious bedroom as Barclay changed out of his suit. She took in the scent of his cologne.

"It was work," replied Barclay laying his suit pants over the back of a chair.

Brittany walked over to the chair, picked up the pants, and then picked up Barclay's coat off the bed and hung them both on a hanger. She brushed the suit coat with her hand and started toward the closet. She said, "You find out anything more about Duncan?"

"Not really, no." Barclay was moving around the bedroom in his after-work routine of shedding his work clothes in favor of more comfortable attire. He removed his watch, setting it along with his pocket detritus in a leather tray on his night-stand. Everything had its place in the Griffith house; that was all Brittany. It took a while, but she had, in her words, house-broken Barclay.

"What do you think?" asked Brittany as she watched him.

"I honestly don't know. I have to think it was related to that trial, but I also don't have anything to back it up. I know it was a case that had worried Duncan for a while. He was convinced his guy wasn't guilty."

"Don't all defense lawyers believe in their client's innocence?"

Barclay shook his head. "Not Duncan."

"Maybe his guy's family didn't like the outcome and blamed Duncan."

Barclay shrugged his shoulders as he pulled on a pair of Lululemon shorts, "It's possible, but I can't make it work. The whole thing was just too clean."

"Too clean? I thought you said there was blood all over the place."

Barclay sat on the settee at the foot of the bed and said, "What I mean is that it was too clean from an evidence standpoint. No fingerprints, fiber, DNA, nothing of real evidentiary value—at least not that I know of right now. No, this was planned far in advance. Had to be. No way a spontaneous murder could be committed and not leave something behind."

Changing the subject, Brittany said, "How's the new guy working out?"

"He's doing ok. Saying the right things for now, at least. I'm trying to get him up to speed as quickly as I can, but it's only been a couple of days."

"That's a sexy look; you know that?"

Barclay stood up, looked at himself in the mirror, and took in his appearance. He wore a white undershirt, athletic shorts, polka-dot dress socks, and gray wool open-back slippers. He flashed a look that was more of a leer. "You like that, don't you?"

She rolled her eyes and turned to leave the bedroom. "Dinner is almost ready."

❖　❖　❖　❖　❖

It was nearing 11:00 now, and Brittany had gone to bed. Barclay didn't bring work home often—usually only when he was preparing for a trial—but he did his best not to let it interfere with their time in the evening.

After dinner, Barclay logged into the office's case management system via VPN and downloaded the Clements case file, complete with photographs and forensic reports. Preferring to work with paper so he could make notes and highlight information of interest, he sent the case summary, detective's narratives, and individual reports to his home printer. The trial transcript, which the court reporter emailed him, would be reviewed on his computer due to the voluminous amounts of paper required to print it.

Barclay sat in his wood-paneled study with a glass of Willett rye whiskey and the case file on his desk in front of him—the pages still warm from the printer. The room, smelling of sandalwood and whiskey, was dark except for the desk lamp, and classical music played softly in the background. He wasn't a huge fan of classical music—it all sounded the same to him— but it was a pleasant enough noise to work by. Songs with lyrics distracted him, and the classical pianos and strings helped his mind relax, so Beethoven it was. Or was it Bach?

Barclay had a general idea of the facts of the case against Charlie Calvin Clements by virtue of the osmosis that happens simply by working in the district attorney's office. Prosecutors in the office seem to have a rudimentary knowledge of the more significant pending cases, regardless of to whom they were assigned. Before cracking open the case file, Barclay mentally ran through what he knew about the case.

He knew that Charlie Clements was accused of killing Veronica Lane. She was killed in her home in the middle of the day; the investigation unable to derive a motive. A murder in Towne is always news; however, a young woman murdered in her home in broad daylight gave the local and state media something to sink its teeth into. The mere idea that Towne citizens weren't safe inside their homes in the light of day was the subject of discussions from church Sunday school, to PTA, to the Rotary Club, to the supermarket checkout lines. In short, it was on the minds of everyone everywhere.

Comfortable with the basic framework of the case, he uncapped a blue felt-tip pen and wrote *St. v Charlie Calvin Clements* and the date across the top of the fresh yellow legal pad. He topped off his Willett, leaned back in his chair, and began to read.

CHAPTER 9

THE CRIME OCCURRED IN the decade-old neighborhood of Rock Creek, an expansive, treeless, cookie-cutter neighborhood where cost—not aesthetics—drove the design decisions. It was, by and large, a well-kept neighborhood with a man-made creek ringing the property. It was a community made up of four home styles repeated dozens of times, with only the door, fascia, and shutter colors expressing the owners' individuality, and even those weren't very individual. The homes were not large, but they all had front porches, two floors, and a garage. The homeowners ranged from newlyweds to retirees and everything in between.

On a Friday afternoon in March at approximately 2:55 p.m., the Towne police department received a call on the 911 emergency line regarding a possible residential burglary. TPD patrol officer Dwayne Manley was dispatched to 619 Sandy Creek Drive to investigate, arriving less than three minutes after the emergency call was received. The caller stated she was the next-door neighbor and gave her name as Nancy Gibbons.

Ms. Gibbons was a retired schoolteacher. She was petite, wore her gray hair to her shoulders, and had a dour expression that belied her personable nature. Dressed in blue jeans and a bright yellow L.L. Bean fleece pullover, she jogged down her driveway at the sight of the police car and met Officer Manley as he rounded the front of his car. "Oh, officer, thank you for getting here so quickly," she said, wringing her hands together. "I think something may be terribly wrong." She spoke in a teacher's voice: clear and concise, firm but warm.

Officer Dwayne Manley, a slim, athletic-looking black man with a close-cropped hairstyle, spoke into his shoulder mic as he approached the house and held up his right index finger to the neighbor. He had worked for the Towne Police Department for twenty-six months; he was a professional cop with a knack for bringing calm to turbulent situations. Finished speaking into his radio, he said, "Hello, ma'am. I'm Officer Dwayne Manley; may I please have your name?"

"Nancy. Nancy Gibbons."

That was the name dispatch had given Manley. He said, "Ok, Ms. Gibbons, why don't you start by telling me what happened." He rested his forearms on the bulky duty belt around his waist as he spoke with her. Manley was not tall but had to look down to make eye contact.

"Yes, well"—she turned to point at the house next door—"my neighbor's sister, Roni Lane"—she turned her head back to the officer, still pointing—"I mean Veronica—her name is Veronica, but she goes by Roni—she lives there and watches her niece and nephew after school. They're in elementary school and ride the bus home in the afternoons, and she always meets them at the bus stop. Always. But today, just before three o'clock, I heard a faint knock on my door. So faint that I wasn't sure I heard it until I heard it again." She had taken her hand down from pointing and was back to wringing her hands together; she continued speaking at a rapid clip. "After the second knock, the doorbell rang twice. I opened the door and saw the two children standing there—Joseph, the oldest, he's ten, and Jenny, she's seven. I thought it was odd that they would be standing there with all of their school stuff—you know, back-packs and lunchboxes—so I said, 'well, hey there,' and Joseph, the oldest child, said, 'where's Aunt Roni?' and I thought that was odd because she always met them at the bus stop. Always." She turned her head back to the neighbor's house and then back to Officer Manley. "I told them I didn't know where she was and told them to come inside, and I would find out." A gust of wind kicked up, and she hugged herself—partly for warmth and partly for comfort. Children could be heard laughing in the distance, which drew her attention.

Officer Manley noticed her chill and asked her if she wanted-ed to continue in the house, and she shook her head *no* as she looked back to Manley and said, "The children are inside, and I don't want them to hear us talking." Manley nodded. Nancy continued, "After I let the children in the house, I fixed them a snack and walked next door to see if everything was ok. I knocked on the door, and it swung open a little bit. I rang the doorbell and pushed the door open a little more before poking my head inside and yelling for her. I didn't get a response." She gripped Manley's right forearm and said, "I'm so worried that something has happened."

Manley's radio squawked, and he said, "Do you know if the children went inside the house?"

"Oh no. Their mother was adamant. The children knew if Aunt Roni was not at the bus stop, they were to walk to my house."

"You said a moment ago that Ms. Lane always met them in the afternoon, but was there ever a time when she was late?"

"No. Never," Ms. Gibbons said, shaking her head. "She lives there. She works overnight as a nurse at the hospital and typically gets home after the children have left for school but before Pam leaves for work. Roni sleeps until it's time to get the children from the bus. There have been a couple of times when she ran errands and thought she might be late to the bus stop, but she would call and ask me to keep an eye out for them. She always ended up making it home in time, though."

"And she didn't call you today?" said Manley as he pulled up his duty belt. This was a habit by most patrol cops whether it needed adjusting or not. Nancy shook her head *no*. "You mentioned that Ms. Lane is your neighbor's sister. Is that the Pam you just mentioned?"

"Yes, sorry. It's Pamela. Pamela Rogers. She's divorced. After the divorce, Roni moved in, and since she works nights, she watches Pam's children after school. It's a good system. They usually eat dinner together before Roni goes on duty at 7:00." A cat walked up and rubbed itself against Ms. Gibbon's leg. She bent down to pick it up and said, "I'm sorry for prattling on like this."

"No, no, that's good. The more information you can give us, the better. Where is Ms. Rogers now?"

Holding the gray and white cat in the crook of her arm and rubbing its head, she said, "I called her right after calling the police. She was in Birmingham meeting with one of her clients. She is on the way home now."

"When does Ms. Rogers leave for work in the morning?"

"It depends on her schedule, but she stayed in Birmingham last night." Nancy Gibbons put a hand to her mouth. "I'm so sorry. I should have told you this earlier. The children spent the night with me last night."

"Was that unusual?"

"Oh no. Well, it didn't happen often, but occasionally Pamela's work takes her out of town overnight, so they would stay with me, and I would get them off to school."

"Anything unusual about last night or this morning?"

Nancy shook her head as she appeared to be thinking about it. After a few seconds, she said, "No. No, nothing at all."

"There are no cars in the driveway. Could Ms. Lane be running errands, as you said earlier? Maybe forgot to close the door?"

She was slowly shaking her head and had a skeptical look on her face. She began slowly, "I guess it's possible, but…sure, I guess that's possible." A beat, then: "She parks her car in the garage. They both do. It's unusual in this neighborhood; most garages are too cluttered for two cars." She was rambling now, and Manley was about to interrupt her, dial her back in when she said, "I guess when you don't have a man in the house cluttering up the garage." She put a hand to her mouth. "Oh my, I shouldn't be saying things like that…what if something bad has happened?"

"Ok," said Manley looking at the Rogers house, "I'm going to go take a look." Nancy stood with her arms wrapped tightly around herself as she watched Officer Manley approach her neighbor's residence.

❊   ❊   ❊   ❊   ❊

Officer Manley crossed the Rogers' front yard and traversed the three steps up onto the small porch in a single stride. He found the frosted glass front door ajar and spoke into his shoulder mic to inform dispatch that he was entering the home.

The door whined as it was pushed open, and Manley moved inside. The house was not large, maybe eighteen hundred square feet spread over two floors, so the officer could see almost the entire first floor from where he stood.

The front door opened onto the living room, which flowed into the kitchen. The house had a pleasant smell; Manley noticed a plug-in air freshener by the front door. The living room consisted of an off-white couch with patterned club chairs on either side, creating a square space. In the middle was an old coffee table that a designer might refer to as distressed. On the wall to the right was a flat-screen television with cords and cables hanging down and disappearing behind a table directly underneath that held a cable box, DVD player, and several children's DVDs, along with a juice box and a baseball glove holding a baseball.

Manley's rubber-soled shoes were silent on the faux hardwood floors and the quiet house—save for a ticking clock—set him on edge. As he moved around the couch and into the kitchen, he saw a rust-colored smear on the floor. He immediately knew what it was, and his hand instinctively went to his holster. Scanning the floor, he saw more blood moving toward the kitchen and to the backdoor, which he noticed was pulled to but not closed. There looked to be partial bloody handprints on the doorframe and the edge of the door itself, with smears of blood near the doorknob. He scanned the floor in the opposite direction and saw a sporadic blood trail leading to the stairs and to the second floor.

With his right hand resting on the butt of his gun, he eased up the left side of the staircase—back against the wall—his left hand automatically going to the handrail before he stopped himself, not wanting to touch anything in the house that could be a source of evidence. The stairs let out an audible pop as he stepped on each tread. The second floor was carpeted and appeared to be where the children spent most of their time. Toys and books lined the walls of the short hallway, forming a walking path between the rooms. The blood trail led him to what he assumed was the master bedroom.

The scent of cinnamon hung in the air, and from the doorway, he saw a red Yankee Candle burning on a dresser adjacent to an unmade bed. His mind inexplicably flashed to his own bed, and he made a mental note to start making his bed before leaving the house lest someone see it in such a condition. Easing into the bedroom, he saw no signs of a struggle other than what appeared to be blood making a trail to the bathroom—like a line of ants on the way to a picnic.

Whatever happened appeared to have occurred in the bathroom. There was considerable blood on the white marble countertop and inlay sink, the light blue painted walls, the white tiled floor, and the porcelain bathtub. Manley backed away from the doorframe and exited the bedroom.

After a quick sweep of the other two upstairs bedrooms and the Jack-and-Jill bathroom, he went downstairs and into the front yard, where he called in what he had seen. As he finished his radio call, he saw Ms. Gibbons holding and petting the cat; she was staring intently in his direction. He gave a slight shake of his head.

Officer Manley keyed his shoulder mic and reported what he observed to dispatch. He spoke in an even, measured tone despite his pulse racing and his gut churning—not because of the violence in the house, but because of the adrenaline dump from being the first on the scene of what he expected would be a big case.

Within minutes of his call to dispatch, a second patrol car arrived on the scene, followed by a third which pulled up before the officer in the second unit was out of his car.

Manley and the other two officers who arrived on the scene went to work establishing a perimeter by stretching police tape—retrieved from the trunk of the third patrol unit—around the house beginning at the front curb and encompassing what they believed was the entirety of the homeowner's property. The first detective arrived just as one of the uniformed officers was tying off the yellow *Do Not Cross* police tape to the home's mailbox at the curb, completing the circuit.

For the next several hours, numerous detectives and the lone Towne PD crime scene technician scoured the house for clues and evidence inside and out. Crime scene investigators placed evidence markers and took photographs. Blood swabs were collected, and physical evidence was bagged and removed.

A detective was questioning Pamela Rogers in the backyard, hidden from the three news cameras that had since descended on the Rock Creek residence. No, she had no idea who would do such a thing, and no, she had no reason to believe her sister had any enemies. "Roni is a nurse, for goodness' sake. Her job is to help people. Who could have a problem with that?" Pamela was a closet smoker, but this was not the time to be worried about someone catching her in the act. She fished a cigarette out and looked in the empty pack. She stuck her finger inside and fished it around as if trying to catch a cigarette hiding. Frustrated, she crumpled the empty container and dropped it in a terra cotta planter filled with dried-out potting soil, a few green sprouts, and numerous cigarette butts.

"Did your sister live with you?"

She had the cigarette to her lips, lit it, and nodded as she took a long drag. Exhaling, she said, "Yes. After I got divorced, I couldn't afford after-school care for my children, so Roni moved in to help out. She worked nights and was free to watch the children after school. It was a good setup for both of us."

The detective wrote in his notebook. They spoke for a few more minutes; then, having gotten what he felt was all he would get from Pamela Rogers, the detective released her. He let her know the police would likely be at the house for a few more hours and asked if she had somewhere she could spend the night. Clearly agitated, she stated she would find somewhere for her and her children to go.

The detective said, "I'm sorry to have to discuss this with you, but if you need the name of someone who can come in and clean up, I have a couple of options for you."

"Clean up?" asked Pamela.

The detective cleared his throat. "Yes, ma'am. The blood and everything."

"Oh, God." Then Pamela, who had yet to show any emotion other than anger and annoyance, began to cry.

❊ ❊ ❊ ❊ ❊

The last detective left just after 11:00 p.m. When law enforcement was gone, the last remaining officer took the police tape down, threw the mass of yellow plastic in the trunk of his car, and departed the scene.

The investigation into Veronica Lane's disappearance began at a furious pace. Despite the vast amount of blood at the scene, the fact that her body was not found in or near the house left the hope she was still alive. That hope—no matter how slight—energized the investigation that was running, quite literally, around the clock. It also saw the community of Towne come together as the citizens scoured the county en masse looking for Veronica Lane.

The first days of the investigation turned up no viable leads, nor did it see any significant movement in a case that weighed heavily on the dogged investigators. However, three days after her disappearance, the investigation received a much-needed shot in the arm: Veronica Lane's Hyundai Sonata was found ablaze in the cul-de-sac of a rundown trailer park out in the county. The energy that so revitalized the investigators assigned to the case was short-lived when nothing of evidentiary value was discovered in the vehicle or at the fire scene. To veteran detective Wayne Drummond, everything pointed to Ms. Lane being dead, but until he had a body or at least more evidence than he had now, he would continue to work under the assumption that she was still alive. Detective Drummond was only human, after all, and that determination began to wane. The emotional bounce from the discovery of her car, followed by the emotional ebb of learning the vehicle yielded nothing of significance, was a real gut punch to the usually steady detective.

The investigation into Ms. Lane's background revealed little. She was a lifelong resident of Towne and worked as a nurse at the local hospital after receiving her nursing certificate from the local community college. She was well-liked, moderately active on social media, and, according to her sister, she did not have a bustling social life which her sister quickly defended as the result of her overnight shift work at the hospital. "Who can go out on a date when you're working while the rest of us are going out or going to bed?"

The few leads the police had were run to ground, and a month into the investigation, they still had nothing. As the investigation moved from one month to two to three to four, the attention the case received inside the police department dissipated. While not completely ignored, the case was no longer being actively worked. It was still assigned to Detective Drummond, and as the occasional lead came in, he ran it down, but absent some catalyst, the case sat dormant. The information coming in all but dried up while new cases continued to come in the door, dictating their attention be re-directed from the Lane case.

Drummond had done this long enough to know that it did not take much to turn a case, but it did take something. He had submitted a lot of evidence to the Alabama Department of

Forensic Sciences, which he knew would take time to analyze—probably months. Perhaps the answer was currently inside an evidence bag sitting on a shelf at an ADFS lab, just waiting for a scientist to perform their magic and coax the submitted item to reveal its secrets.

And that is exactly what happened.

❀   ❀   ❀   ❀   ❀

Almost a year to the day the Towne Police Department descended upon the home of Pamela Rogers, Detective Wayne Drummond received a certificate of analysis and corresponding report in the mail. He received dozens of these in the mail every month, so seeing the envelope in his office mailbox did not generate any manner of emotion. However, that changed as he slid his finger under the envelope's flap, pulled out the report, and unfolded the papers. He let out a celebratory howl as he read the document. The bed sheets and comforter from Veronica Lane's bed were among the items seized and submitted to the lab. DNA was discovered on the fitted sheet from the bed. They had a name: Charlie Calvin Clements.

A quick check of Charlie Calvin Clements revealed he was a black male in his mid-thirties with a criminal history. He had a couple of prior misdemeanor marijuana offenses and a felony conviction for possession of marijuana. He also had a conviction for assault stemming from an argument at a cookout. Drummond tracked down the lead detective on the assault case and learned that Clements was not the initial aggressor, but while the victim was trying to engage in a fistfight, Charlie Clements grabbed a steak knife off a picnic table and stabbed the victim in the ribs. Initially charged with assault in the first degree, Clements ended up pleading guilty to assault in the second degree in exchange for a probationary sentence. A deeper dive into his criminal history revealed a burglary charge when he was seventeen.

The DNA, the prior assault, and the prior burglary were all Drummond needed to start buzzing about the case again and send Charlie Calvin Clements to the top of the suspect list with a bullet.

The detective set out to locate Clements and to get him in for questioning. He couldn't put out his usual feelers for fear of spooking his quarry and sending him into hiding. Drummond first checked with his probation officer to get a last known address and last known employer. Clements had completed his probation on the assault just over two years ago, so he wasn't optimistic about the accuracy of information that old, but it would be a place to start. His last known address was his mother's house, but his last known employer was a local lawn service company, and Drummond knew the owner. This particular lawn service liked to hire people on probation because they were folks typically ordered to have a job as a condition of probation and could generally be counted on to show up for work. The people working for him knew that if they failed to show up, Ricky Bream of Bream's Landscaping would call the probation office and report them. The way Bream figured it, he gave these convicted criminals a chance few were willing to provide them, and he paid well, so he did not feel the slightest compunction about turning them in.

Drummond knew going to the mother's house would be risky and all but guaranteed that Charlie Clements would find out the police wanted to speak to him, so he called Ricky Bream.

Bream told him that, yes, Charlie did work for him for a time and was good at his job, but he left shortly after his probation ended. No, he did not know where Charlie went to work from there. However, the guys on the crew always discussed wanting to get on at one of the tier-one suppliers for the Kia plant in west Georgia. And no, he would not tell anyone that Drummond had asked about Charlie Clements.

Drummond's next call was to a retired west Georgia detective he knew from working cases in the past and who he knew was currently head of security at the Kia plant. After the perfunctory "How the hell are you?" and the "When are you going to retire and make some real money?" Drummond got down to why he was there. The retired detective said he would make some calls, and if this guy worked at one of the suppliers, he would find out.

Drummond received a call back the following morning. Charlie Calvin Clements was working on the line at a tier-one supplier making front and rear bumpers. Drummond called the head of security of Clements' employer, introduced himself, and told him he needed to speak to a line worker. He also stressed the need for secrecy at this point; no one needed to know who or why someone was asking about Charlie Calvin Clements. After being on hold for several minutes and listening to the repetitive recruitment pitch singing the praises about working at Mobis—health, dental, and vision insurance; paid vacation; life insurance; 401K—the security guy came back on the line: "Yes he is here today, and yes I will have him in my office when you arrive."

❊   ❊   ❊   ❊   ❊

Just over half an hour later, Detective Drummond pulled into the multi-acre parking lot of the auto supplier. He parked in a *visitors* parking spot near the front door and entered the gleaming reception area filled with natural lighting. On the wall behind the large, gleaming reception desk hung a massive picture of four smiling Mobis employees—a tall youngish black man, a middle-aged white woman, a young Asian man, and a grandmotherly black lady—standing on the manufacturing floor, arms around each other in a pose, wearing polished hard hats and safety glasses with ear plugs hanging by a cord around their necks. "Mobis Means Family," boasted the caption. He wondered if they were actual employees or if it was a stock photograph hanging in all their plants.

On either side of the picture hung a seventy-inch flat-screen television running a soundless commercial about all things Mobis. The temperature was quite cool, and the place still had the new building smell even though it had been open for over a decade. He approached the reception desk, manned by two women—one blonde and one brunette—who he guessed were in their mid to late thirties, and both wearing royal blue Mobis cardigans and headsets for answering the telephone.

They both smiled at him as he approached, but it was the brunette that spoke. "Welcome to Mobis. How may we help you today?" Something about the whole scene, the choreography and the perfectness of it, creeped him out a bit.

"I'm here to see John Simpkin, head of security. He's expecting me."

With unnatural exuberance, Brunette said, "I will be happy to get him for you. May I say who is here to see him?"

"Sure," was all Drummond said, having a bit of fun with the perky receptionist.

A few seconds passed, the joviality not faltering, before Brunette said, "May I have your name, please?"

Unflappable, thought Drummond as he pulled out his badge and gave his name, title, and where he worked. The corner of Brunette's smile twitched as she said, "Just one moment, please." *Almost had her* thought Drummond.

Six minutes later, John Simpkin appeared at a side door that blended into the wall. He approached Drummond, and the two shook hands and exchanged introductions. Simpkin was on the short side with a flat-top haircut. He was thin and wearing khaki pants with a two-way radio clipped to one side of his waist, and a phone clipped to the other. In addition, he wore a red golf shirt with *Mobis Security* stitched on the left chest and *Simpkin* stitched on the right chest. The head of security smelled strongly of cigarette smoke, and the years of nicotine had tinged his white hair.

Simpkin had Drummond sign in and get a visitor badge to wear around his neck. Simpkin then escorted Drummond back through the door he had just come through and guided him through a maze of corridors to a sizable interior office. As they walked, Simpkin asked what all of this was about, and Drummond apologized, telling him that he wished he could say, but he could not—at least not yet. The head of security, not used to being kept in the dark inside his own building, nodded with thinly veiled annoyance.

Though Drummond was thoroughly turned around once they reached the office, he knew the scent of the Marlboro Man would serve as an olfactory breadcrumb trail to the exit. Inside the office stood a fat man with a shaved head and a gray mustache, also wearing khakis and a red golf shirt, and he, too, had a two-way radio and cell phone affixed to his hip. Sitting on a tan leather couch was a man wearing navy blue slacks and a light blue short-sleeved button-up shirt with a dark blue patch inscribed with Mobis in white stitching on his left chest. He held a battered blue hard hat upside down in his lap with a pair of safety glasses inside and ear plugs dangling around his neck. Drummond flashed to the picture on the lobby wall and blinked. *Well, shit,* he thought. Wonder what ol' Mobis is gonna think about one of their poster employees being questioned in connection to a murder? Then, *Mobis Means Murder.* He had to keep himself from chuckling at that last thought.

Simpkins held out a hand and said, "This is Charlie Clements."

"Mr. Clements, my name is Detective Wayne Drummond with Towne PD. I need to ask you a few questions about a sensitive matter and would prefer to speak at the police station. You can ride with me, and I will bring you back to get your car when we're done. Sound good?"

Clements' eyes darted around the room at the three white men staring at him. He swallowed and said, "Do I have to?"

Casually Drummond shrugged and said, "Well, no. I suppose you don't *have* to, but it sure would help us out." Clements didn't respond, so after a few seconds, Drummond spoke in a cheerful voice, "What do you say? Have you back in no time."

"Can I just come by after work? I don't want to lose any hours."

"Oh, come on now, Mobis means family, right? I'm sure they won't dock your pay for helping the police." Drummond looked at both security men in the room and said, "Am I right, guys?"

Simpkin, a retired homicide detective with the Atlanta Police Department, didn't miss a beat. He said, "Oh, sure. Don't worry about it, Mr. Clements. We will mark your time down as administrative leave. Won't count against your annual or sick time. You'll get full credit for your scheduled hours today."

"See," said Drummond, "Mobis *is* family." He was getting a lot of miles out of that caption.

Clements slowly rose from the couch, all six-foot-four of him, and slowly walked out ahead of Drummond. Drummond shook hands first with the fat security guy, then with Simpkin. As he shook Simpkin's hand, he whispered to the head of security, "I'll call you." Simpkin nodded and winked his understanding.

❊   ❊   ❊   ❊   ❊

The twenty-five-minute drive to the Towne police station passed in silence—not so much as the radio playing. In the Mobis parking lot, as they were getting into Drummond's car, Clements asked if the detective could tell him what this was all about, but Drummond told him they would discuss everything back at the station. Drummond allowed Clements to ride in the front seat wanting the suspect to feel both at ease with the ride up front and unnerved with the silence and lack of information.

Drummond parked in the rear lot of the police station and used his key fob to enter through the employee entrance; he held the door open for Clements and fell in behind the suspect. Drummond guided Clements to the room that housed the TPD detective bureau and on to his desk. Though the room had recently been renovated to remove asbestos, moldy floor and ceiling tiles, and old, battered desks and furniture, it was still very much a no-frills room. The room smelled of old paper and floor polish. Twelve metal desks lined the walls, and all were empty save for two. On a bank of filing cabinets sat an old clock radio providing background music. The faux wooden rectangle flashed 12:00 in green digital numbers and was rumored to have been put in place circa 1992 when it was tuned to the local classic rock station; it had not been changed or turned off since. Currently, the tinny sound leaking from the speaker was

The Allman Brothers riffing and singing about a black-hearted woman being cheap trouble.

In addition to the music, other sounds in the room included an oscillating fan and the arrhythmic sound of a detective hunting and pecking—pounding, really—with his sausage fingers on a plastic computer keyboard. The only other person in the room was a detective on the telephone. Drummond assumed he was on hold because the man neither spoke nor appeared too focused on the call.

Drummond grabbed a folder from a desk drawer and told Clements he could leave his hard hat and other work gear on his desk. Clements set his stuff down, and the pair left the office and found an interview room. The room had barely enough space for a metal table and two chairs. It also contained a video camera mounted above the door facing the interior of the room.

"Have a seat, Mr. Clements. Is there anything I can get you before we start? Water? Coke? Anything?"

Clements, taking his seat, gave a slight shake of his head and a quiet "No." The hiss of the automatic air freshener in the top corner of the room sounded as it injected an apple-scented chemical into the air. The noise drew the brief attention of both the room's occupants.

Drummond sat and scooted his chair up to the table. He opened the folder he retrieved from his desk and pulled out a single sheet of paper: an Explanation of Rights Form. He pulled a pen from his shirt pocket, clicked it, and wrote the date and time in the designated spaces in the top right corner of the document, as well as the location of the interview: TPD.

He then began asking Clements some preliminary questions to fill in the form's appropriate blanks.

"What's your full name, Mr. Clements?"

"Charlie Calvin Clements."

"And how old are you?"

"Thirty-two."

Drummond asked for and received Clements' date of birth, the city he was born in, and his current address. Clements also told him that twelfth grade was the furthest he had gotten in school and that he could read and write. The form filled out, Drummond said, "Alright, Mr. Clements, I am going to read you your rights, then have you read them back to me, ok?" Clements nodded. "This is just to ensure you can read and understand what it says. If you don't understand, now is the time to ask any questions, ok?" Clements nodded. "This interview is being recorded, so I need you to answer verbally. Did you nod yes to both questions I just asked you?"

Clements said, "Yes."

"Alright, now I am reading from this form: 'I have been advised that I must understand my rights before I answer questions.'" Looking up from the paper, he asked, "Do you understand that portion?" Clements nodded. "I need you to answer out loud, Mr. Clements."

"Yes."

Drummond then read the rest of the paragraph. It contained the standard Miranda warning explaining Clements' right to remain silent and the right to a lawyer even if he cannot afford one. It also states that if he agrees to answer questions, he can stop at any time and speak with an attorney. "Do you understand everything I just read?"

"Yes."

"Ok. Now I need you to read it back to me." Drummond slid the page across the table and turned it so it was right side up for Clements to read, which he did with no trouble.

Taking the page back, Drummond asked if he had any questions, and Clements said he did not. Drummond said, "Ok, now the next portion—and then we will be done with this and ready to talk—is the waiver of your right to remain silent. It says, 'The above rights have been read to me and by me. I understand what my rights are. I am willing to answer questions and make a statement. I do not want a lawyer at this time. I understand and know what I am doing. No promises or threats have been made to me, and no pressure of any kind has been used against me.'" Drummond again spun the page toward Clements and said, "Will you please read this aloud?" Clements did so.

"Ok, now, Mr. Clements, are you willing to speak with me today? If so, I need you to sign right here." He pointed with his pen to a line next to the word *signed* below the last paragraph on the page, then laid the pen down on the paper.

Clements picked up the pen and said, "Maybe I need to speak to a lawyer first."

"Well, Mr. Clements, that is certainly your right to do so, and it is completely up to you." A pause, then, "Just know that if you do ask for a lawyer, then our conversation ends right now. I told you back at your job that I would explain what this was all about when we got back to the station, and here we are. I am ready to talk to you. Are you ready and willing to talk to me?"

Clements didn't say anything. Instead, he just stared at the piece of paper on the table in front of him.

"Look," Drummond began, "it says right here," he pointed with his pen at a line in the first paragraph, "that you can waive the presence of an attorney and speak to me now and at *any* point during questioning you can stop and ask for a lawyer. So you see, this way, I can tell you what this is all about, and if you don't wish to talk to me, ask for a lawyer, and the conversation is over. Does that sound fair?" Clements nodded. "Ok then, before we begin, I need you to sign your name."

Clements thought about it a few more seconds before tentatively taking the pen and signing his name in neat penmanship. Drummond then took the page back and signed in the space marked *witnessed* and listed the date and time of the signing.

"Ok, Charlie. Is it ok if I call you Charlie?" Clements nodded. "Thank you, Charlie. You see, I wanted to talk to you about Veronica Lane." Drummond looked for a reaction to her name, but he did not see one. "Do you know her?" Clements shook his head *no*. "I need you to speak up, Charlie."

"No."

"Hmmm. Ok." Drummond opened the file and flipped through a few pages before speaking again. "If you don't know her, then I guess you've never been in her house? Would that be an accurate statement?"

"No."

"No, that's not an accurate statement?"

Clements looked confused and said, "No, I ain't never been in her house."

Drummond moved some papers around in the folder and removed a full-page driver's license photo of Veronica Lane. He placed it on the table in front of Clements and said, "Maybe you just don't know her name. Do you recognize her? She look familiar at all?" Clements only gave the picture a passing glance before saying he did not recognize her, but Drummond thought he saw a flicker of…something.

"Here's the deal, Charlie; I don't believe you." This drew a look from Clements. "That's right," Drummond continued, "I think you're lying to me. So I'm giving you a shot right now to come clean here. I want you to think long and think very hard about how you answer my next question." He paused for a ten count before saying, "How do you know Veronica Lane?"

"I told you, man. I ain't know this bitch you talkin' about."

This was as animated as he had gotten up to this point.

Drummond stood up, chair scraping across the linoleum before falling backwards to the floor with a clatter, slammed his palm on the aluminum table, and yelled, "Then how…the fuck…did your semen get on her sheets?"

Clements would not meet Drummond's gaze. He focused instead on a spot on the table. The silence stretched to nearly a minute before he finally spoke: "Imma take that lawyer now.

Drummond shrugged and said, "Well, if that's how you want to play it." He gathered the loose papers on the table and put them in his folder. He made for the door, and without looking back at Clements, he said, "Wait here."

Back at his desk, Drummond dropped the folder on his desk and flopped into his chair. He powered up his computer and logged into the live CCTV footage from the interview room. It was not at all unusual for a suspect to speak to themselves when they were alone, and more than a few times, they said something incriminating. That done, he rubbed his face with his hands and then rubbed his hands together. *Where to begin?* He needed to find a connection between Veronica Lane and Charlie Calvin Clements…unless this was a purely random act. *Was this a case of a burglary gone wrong, or was she targeted specifically? Was Pamela Rogers the target, and Veronica Lane happened to be in the wrong place at the wrong time?* The detective felt the first positive momentum in the case in almost a year, and he did not want it to dissipate by getting bogged down overthinking, so he began gathering information.

He placed a quick call to John Simpkin and requested the employee records for Clements for his time at Mobis. Simpkin told him that as much as he wanted to help, that would be a tall order absent a more official request—a subpoena was really what he needed. Drummond told him that he didn't think he was quite at that point just yet, but if Simpkin could just tell him Clements' start date, that could be very helpful. Simpkin was able to supply him with that information—albeit unofficially. The next phone call was to Ricky Bream.

The call was answered after the first ring. "Ricky Bream."

"Hey, Ricky, Wayne Drummond here." He could tell from the background noise that Bream was standing outside.

"Hey there, Wayne Drummond. You calling about Charlie again?"

"I am, actually. Can you send me his personnel file? Or at least his dates of employment with your company?"

"Sure thing, Detective. You know I always cooperate with law enforcement. Is there anything specific you're looking for?"

"Not really. At least not right yet. I'm trying to put together a timeline of sorts."

"As soon as we get off the phone, I will call my office manager and have her send those dates to you. You need anything more: personnel file, job responsibilities, anything, let me know, and you'll have it."

Having completed the phone call, Drummond sat at his desk thinking. *Got to keep moving forward.* He pulled a fresh reporter-style notebook from the top desk drawer and flipped it open to the first page. In his neat script, he wrote *CWC Timeline* at the top of the page with a blue felt-tip pen and underlined it. Next, he opened the folder he had carried into the interview room and began flipping through the papers contained inside. He made a bullet point on the first line and wrote *DOB* (date of birth) *February 27, 1989.* On the following line, he made another bullet point and wrote *July 2006 - Burglary.* Below that another bullet point and *December 2015 - PG* (plead guilty) Assault 2 - 10 years suspended - 5 years probation. He skipped a couple of lines on the page, then made another bullet point and wrote *December 2020 - Completed Probation*. Next line, another bullet point, then *January 5, 2021 - Began work at Mobis*. Next line, bullet point, then *October 7, 2021 - Veronica Lane Murdered*, which he underlined twice.

Just then, his computer chimed, letting him know he had a new email. It was from Ricky Bream's office manager with dates of Clements' employment. He then returned to the list and inserted a bullet point in the space he left blank and wrote *March 8, 2015 - January 2, 2021 - Worked at Bream Landscaping*. He tapped his pen on the notebook as he studied the words on the page. *Nothing*. He knew there was something there; he just needed to find it.

His mind then moved to what he knew any defense attorney worth his salt would do, and that is attack the fact that Veronica Lane's body was never recovered. He wasn't too worried about that because people didn't completely fall off the grid in this day and time, but he still needed some manner of proof. He flipped to the next page in his notebook and made notes about what he needed to research. First, he would run her social security number to make sure there was no activity with it since the date she went missing. He also needed to run her credit history to make sure no credit cards, loans, cell phone plans, apartment lease agreements, or anything else had been done which could suggest she was alive and well, living someplace far away from here. The way he figured it, by the time they were done with the deep dive into her background over the last year plus since she had gone missing, if the defense was indeed going to be "we don't even know that she's dead," then the case would be in pretty good shape.

He had a sudden thought. He picked up the phone and dialed Bream's number. One ring. Two rings. Three rings. "Come on," he said through gritted teeth.

"Ah, Detective Drummond. You should be getting the information you requested any minute. I spoke with my—"

But the detective cut him off and said in a rush, "No, I got the information. Thank you for that. You mentioned in our last phone conversation about job responsibilities. I need to know two things: Did you or do you have a customer by the name of Pamela Rogers in the Rock Creek neighborhood and did Charlie Clements service that yard?"

There was a pause as Bream thought about those questions. "We do handle the landscaping for that neighborhood. The homeowners pay annual dues that cover their lawn maintenance, and we have that contract. Have had it since the neighborhood first began." He stopped talking as if something interrupted his train of thought. Then he said, "Why does that name sound so familiar? That's the lady whose sister went missing, right?"

"That's the one."

"Yes, yes, yes. I remember now. When it happened, I remember that it occurred at one of our customer's homes. As a matter of fact, I'm almost positive we sent a card in the mail offering our condolences."

"Ok. Did Charlie handle her yard?"

"Now, that I have no way of knowing without—wait. Are you saying he did something to Ms. Rogers' sister?"

"We're just running down some leads, Mr. Bream. Please don't speak about this to anyone."

"Of course not, Detective. I will look into Charlie's work history myself and let you know." Ricky Bream let out a breath before continuing. "That Charlie was such a hard worker, one of my best. I had no idea he was capable of such a thing."

"Now, Mr. Bream, as I said, we are simply following up on some information we have received. We are a long way from accusing anyone of anything." Drummond hated lying to the man, but he had to keep this quiet for a little longer until he had something more concrete.

The clock rolled toward 4:00, and a half-hour or so had passed since he left Clements in the interview room; Drummond went back to check on him. Sticking his head in the door, he asked, "Can I get you anything?"

"When can I get out of here and back to work?"

"Soon." Drummond left Clements alone once more in the small echoey space of harsh fluorescent lighting as another apple-scented *hiss* emitted from an upper corner of the room.

❊   ❊   ❊   ❊   ❊

The case was right there in front of him, ready to be wrapped up. Sure there would be more to do before the case could go to Grand Jury, let alone a trial, but having told Clements of the DNA evidence, getting paper on him and taking him into custody was critical. If he were to be released, Drummond knew he would run.

The detective eyed the clock and thought, *good luck finding someone after hours on a Friday to sign an arrest warrant.* This had to happen soon. Then his email dinged: Ricky Bream.

It read:

> Detective,
> Charlie Clements worked as a member of one of my six lawn crews before being promoted to crew leader. He was assigned to oversee the crew in the sector containing the Rock Creek subdivision. The houses in Rock Creek have small yards, so the men on the crew operate independently once inside the neighbor-

hood. They can get in and knock out the entire neighborhood in a day. As for who specifically cut the grass at Ms. Rogers' home, I have no way of knowing because it is up to the crew to figure out who cuts which yards. That said, I imagine that at some point over the nearly two years he was head of that particular crew, he mowed her lawn more than a few times. Again, that is just a guess. Hope this is helpful.

Ricky

Wayne Drummond read the email twice and wasn't sure how to take it. On the one hand, it wasn't as definitive as he hoped, but on the other, it placed his suspect in Veronica Lane's neighborhood and likely at her house—or at least in her yard—on numerous occasions. That connected the dots as to how he could have known her. He dashed off a quick reply to Bream's email asking for the names of the other members of Clements' crew. Perhaps they could provide some insight, but those interviews would have to wait. He quickly but methodically organized his thoughts and formulated his pitch for what he knew would not be an easy sell to the DA's office regarding a warrant for Charlie Clements' arrest. An arrest in the Veronica Lane case would be an absolute bombshell, and no one, especially the DA, wanted to be wrong on this.

Detective Drummond called the district attorney's office and asked for Barclay Griffith, who he knew to be more aggressive and less concerned with whether or not they would win the case. Barclay always told Drummond that if he believed a crime occurred and evidence existed to prove a particular person was responsible, then it was his obligation to present it to a Grand Jury—eighteen citizens randomly selected—for a determination of probable cause.

But the detective did not get Barclay at 4:38 in the afternoon. Instead, he got Richard Kingery. King Dick. This guy had political aspirations oozing from every orifice of his body and would not come within a yottameter of a case he wasn't guaranteed to win.

Except this one, apparently.

Drummond couldn't believe what he was hearing from King Dick. Not only did the guy give the ok for the arrest warrant, but he wanted the case himself. He wanted to prosecute it. Sure, Drummond thought, win this, and you can write your own ticket, but lose, and your ticket becomes as valuable as one containing last month's losing Powerball numbers.

❖   ❖   ❖   ❖   ❖

After his conversation with Kingery, Drummond walked back into the interview room and had Clements stand up, turn around, and place his palms together behind his back. The ratcheting sound the cuffs made going on was music to the detective's ears. He escorted the suspect-turned-defendant wordlessly out of the interview room and to the jail, where he was photographed, fingerprinted, given an orange jumpsuit, and placed into a cell.

CHAPTER 10

BARCLAY LEANED BACK IN his chair and rubbed his eyes; he checked the time on his phone. He'd been at it for almost two hours and had not come across anything to suggest nefarious behavior by either the police or the prosecutor in the case. He stood to move around, think, and drive fatigue from his brain.

Barclay knew Kingery well enough to question why Kingery opted to handle this case himself. You didn't need to be a grizzled veteran of the DA's office to see the case would be high profile; however, there were holes. Having finally read the case file, Barclay agreed with Kingery's decision to issue the arrest warrant, and also, like Kingery, he would have had no problem prosecuting it himself. But he and Kingery weren't alike. There was a myriad of differences between the two professionally, but perhaps the largest was how aggressive they were with their cases. If Barclay believed in a defendant's guilt, he would take on the case with little regard to whether or not he could actually win. Kingery, on the other hand, was a political animal with his eyes on the big office, so he was decidedly risk-averse.

Still, the risk of losing didn't seem all that great to Barclay, and he could see Kingery weighing it out and deciding the prospect of a conviction and the attendant benefit far outweighed the prospect of losing. Maybe there was something there, but

Barclay couldn't make it work. At least not enough to spend any more time on it right now.

He knew the devil was in the details, so it was time to dig into the trial transcript.

❊ ❊ ❊ ❊ ❊

Initially given a court-appointed lawyer, the Clements family, through a barbecue fundraiser, passing the plate at the local AME Zion church (more than twice), and other various and sundry means of raising money, was able to pay the fee to hire Duncan Pheiffer to defend his case. This was met with more than a little disappointment by Richard Kingery because the appearance of Duncan made the job of convicting Clements more difficult.

The case against Clements was largely circumstantial; the only physical evidence Kingery could put in front of the jury was the DNA evidence from the semen-stained sheets on Veronica Lane's bed. However, that evidence was bolstered by yet more circumstantial evidence. Since Forensic science cannot date when a blood stain, semen stain, or other biological evidence is deposited, establishing a timeline can be difficult. However, Veronica Lane was universally described as a neat freak, and her closest friends all agreed she would never go to bed on soiled sheets. This information allowed Kingery to argue that Charlie Calvin Clements left his semen on those sheets on the day of her disappearance.

The theory that Kingery presented to the jury was that Clements became aware of Veronica Lane through his employment with Bream Landscaping. He was in her neighborhood twice a month every month for nine months, and as the leader of the crew, he was the one who made the yard assignments. Kingery's

theory entering the trial was that Clements could no longer resist an urge that had undoubtedly been festering for a number
of weeks, if not months; finally, the temptation was too much to
resist. Whether the result of a well-thought-out plan or merely
a crime of impulse and opportunity, Clements entered Veronica Lane's home—either by invitation or by force—and sexually
assaulted her and murdered her and removed her body, and
disposed of it.

Kingery advanced this theory in his opening statement to the
jury laying out what he believed the evidence would show as the
trial unfolded. The first witness he called was Officer Dwayne
Manley, who confidently took the stand in his sharply pressed
navy blue uniform. His testimony began with the call from dispatch sending him to the Lane/Rogers residence. Then he told
the jury about his interaction with Nancy Gibbons before describing in meticulous detail the carnage he observed inside the
home. By the end of his direct examination, Kingery had done a
masterful job of engaging the jury and guiding Manley through
his testimony in a most effective manner. The officer did his part
by testifying clearly, concisely, and with authority; he presented himself as an officer the jury could not help but believe and
trust.

What also made Officer Manley's testimony so compelling was that there was very little Duncan Pheiffer could ask
on cross-examination. Manley's testimony consisted only of his
observations at the scene, leaving next to no fodder for the defense attorney, so by the time he stepped down from the witness
stand, the momentum and attention gained during direct went
largely unchecked and remained in the state's favor. The trial
could not have gotten off to a more impactful start.

Kingery could try a case as well as anyone; the man was
an expert presenting the evidence for maximum impact. *Start*

strong, end strong, and bury the minutia in the middle. That is how you presented your case, he knew, so following the strong Manley, he presented Nancy Gibbons to the jury. Not every witness was a homerun hitter—not every witness was intended to be. A good trial lawyer strategically placed impactful witnesses for optimum effect while sprinkling in the foundational witnesses. Ms. Gibbons told the jury how the typically reliable Veronica Lane was not at home to receive her niece and nephew from the bus the day she went missing and how she called the police as a result. She came off as the nervous grandmother she was. Despite not having anything of significant evidentiary value to offer, she injected the proper emotion into the case.

Duncan Pheiffer made quick work of his cross-examination. He did not want to come across as beating up on someone's grandmother, and she had not said anything he did not know to be true, nor did she say anything harmful to his client.

After Ms. Gibbons testified, the court broke for lunch. A further advantage to the state by sending the jury away on such a somber note.

After the lunch break, Kingery called some law enforcement witnesses that dealt with evidence collection and crime scene photos. These foundation witnesses only existed to admit evidence later in the trial. He was a veteran enough prosecutor to know jurors aren't necessarily their most attentive after lunch, so he opted for non-critical witnesses on the chance he had some sleepy, less focused, post-lunch jurors.

As a result of the officers' bland and technical, albeit necessary, testimony, Duncan Pheiffer passed on cross-examining the officer responsible for photographing the crime scene. He had only a single question for the evidence tech: "Did you find any fingerprints belonging to Charlie Clements?" To which the crime scene investigator said, "No." The defendant did not agree with his attorney's strategy on either witness believing he should be asking more questions. He expressed his displeasure verbally, just loud enough to draw looks from the jury and the judge, neither of which helped his case. The judge asked Pheiffer if he had any further questions for either witness, to which Duncan replied, with a hand on his client's arm, that he did not. Duncan would later explain to the defendant that he had nothing more to ask and could only risk potential damage by questioning a witness simply because he could. "What was there to ask the witness when all they did was take a couple hundred photographs or bag and tag evidence?" Duncan had said to his client. "We got what we needed from the evidence guy. Your prints were nowhere to be found. That is a very compelling point in our favor that we can now argue in closing."

Kingery wanted to end the day with the testimony of the victim's sister, so, having some time to fill to make sure her testimony was the last for the day, he called two more chain witnesses. These were witnesses whose involvement in the case was simply that they took evidence from one person or place and moved them to somewhere else. These were necessary but not-so-sexy witnesses that populated every criminal trial. These witnesses never made the television screen in courtroom dramas. Again, Duncan did not ask any questions on cross-examination.

The last witness of the day was Pamela Rogers—the victim's sister. She detailed her relationship with her little sister; she told the jury how, after her divorce, Roni moved in with her to help with the children. She described her sister for the jury as only a big sister could. She also spoke of how she paid monthly dues to her homeowners' association and that a portion of those dues went to pay for landscaping which she knew to be handled by Bream Landscaping. The fact that Ms. Rogers was so clearly a strong woman made the emotional cracks show even brighter;

by the end of the direct examination, the testimony of this broken woman was brutal to hear.

Duncan did ask Pamela Rogers some questions on cross. He established that since she worked during the day—when the landscapers would have been at her house—she had never seen his client, Charlie Clements, prior to his arrest. She had never seen him at her home. Her sister had never spoken to her about his client. Ms. Lane never said anything about being scared of Mr. Clements, nor did she ever speak of Mr. Clements at all—good or bad. He also asked her if she knew the last time the victim had washed or changed her bedsheets, and she replied that she did not. Cross-examining a victim or a member of the victim's family can be a tricky proposition, and Duncan handled it well. He scored some points while remaining respectful of what she had been through.

The morning of the second day of the trial saw less impactful—but no less critical to advancing the state's theory—witnesses take the stand. The day began with Ricky Bream testifying to the defendant's employment with his business and that he was promoted to supervisor of the crew that serviced the victim's home. On cross-examination, Duncan established that Charlie Clements was a good employee who had risen through the ranks going from crew member to having his own crew. It was also established that the defendant had a clean work record, meaning no customer complaints or work-related disciplinary actions. Bream also admitted on cross that he was disappointed when the defendant quit his job.

Following Ricky Bream was a parade of Bream Landscaping employees who all testified that, as their supervisor, the defendant made a point to personally handle the yards in the cul de sac where Veronica Lane's house was located. They also stated that when the crew was disbursed into the neighborhood to commence work, they were alone without supervision until lunch and after lunch until the last yard was completed. The implication was that the defendant was free to do as he wished, and no crew members were around to see.

On cross-examination, the defense strategy was to establish that none of them had ever seen the defendant interact with the victim—or any customers for that matter—in any way. That they had never heard him mention the victim by name or otherwise, that the defendant was a good supervisor, that they all liked and got along well with him, and that he was a hard worker.

The state then called the human resources director for Mobis to establish that the defendant was not at work the day of the crime—it was a scheduled day off.

The second half of the day began with an analyst from the Alabama Fusion Center. She testified to running the victim's name, date of birth, and social security number through a laundry list of services (she named and went through each one for the jury) and came up with zero hits after the day she went missing. Veronica Lane had not opened a credit card, bought a house, rented a house or apartment, earned taxable income, made any purchases, or entered agreements requiring a credit check. Moreover, she had not filed a state or federal tax return for the year 2021 or beyond. Kingery used the analyst's testimony to establish that Veronica Lane had completely fallen off the grid after October 7, 2021. The implication was clear: Veronica Lane was dead.

Duncan asked a few questions on cross to establish that the analyst could not say with any certainty that Veronica Lane had not voluntarily left to start a new life under a completely new identity. He had to walk a tightrope here. Solely arguing that the state had not even proven she was dead or that a crime had even occurred was risky. The amount of blood found inside the house, coupled with the difficulty for any person to exist without leaving the slightest digital footprint in this day and age, made that argument difficult to sell with a straight face, so he did not expend much energy on it. He only wanted to raise the question and did not want the state's theory to go completely unchecked. *And who knows*, Duncan thought, *all I need is one juror to hang it up and cause a mistrial.* In a case like this, you threw out a lot and hoped something stuck with at least one juror who could not, in good conscience, vote in favor of guilt for whatever reason.

The next witness called by Kingery was the DNA analyst from the Alabama Department of Forensic Sciences. The analyst was the antithesis of what one might expect of a DNA forensic scientist: he was a young, stylish guy who made his off-the-rack suit look custom tailored for him, far from the bookish scientist stereotype. After spending several minutes reviewing the analyst's impressive education and professional credentials for the jury, the court granted the state's motion establishing him as an expert in DNA analysis.

He first had the analyst explain to the jury what DNA is and how people can leave samples of it in the world in which they live. Next, the analyst discussed how the sample is tested from a given piece of evidence and how it is compared to a known standard. The first item of substance Kingery had the analyst testify to was that the blood at the crime scene belonged to Veronica Lane. This wasn't a contested issue by the parties, but it needed to be established for both the jury and the court record. Then Kingery got down to the primary reason the analyst was on the stand. The witness explained how semen contains DNA and how semen was found on a bed sheet collected by the Towne Police Department. He went on to explain how the test was done in this specific case and since he did not have a known standard to compare it to, he entered it into the national Combined DNA Index System—CODIS for short. He explained that CODIS is a repository for known standards taken from individuals. When an unknown sample is submitted into the system, the system scans the millions of known standards until a hit is found or until it is determined that no match exists within the database.

In this case, a match was found: Charlie Calvin Clements, the defendant. After a CODIS hit is made, the next step is to get a search warrant for a DNA standard from the offender, which was done in this case. This standard is then tested against the evidence, in this case, the semen sample from the bedsheet, and a subsequent match was made. Knowing he had the jury in the palm of his hand and knowing he was about to deliver what he felt was the kill shot, Kingery stood at the railing in front of the jury box. Without taking his eyes off the jury, he asked the analyst, "What is the certainty that the semen left on the bedsheet belonged to the defendant Charlie Calvin Clements?"

"The chances that more than one person shares this DNA strand is one in four hundred trillion," said the analyst.

Kingery let that number hang in the air for a few beats before asking, "What is the approximate population of planet earth?"

"More than seven billion people currently inhabit the planet."

"So, there aren't even enough people currently on earth for there to be a second match?"

"That is correct."

"No further questions."

Duncan stood up for cross-examination and asked the analyst, "You don't know when that semen sample was left on the bedsheet, do you?"

"No."

"In fact, you have no way of knowing that, correct?"

"That is correct."

"For all you can possibly know, it could have been left the day of the incident we are here about, or it could have been left a year earlier, correct?"

"That is correct."

"You also can't tell the jury, can you, sir, how the stain got there."

"No, I cannot."

"It's possible, is it not, that the semen came to be on the sheets not as a direct ejaculation from the person you say it belongs to but by way of transfer from Ms. Lane's underwear."

"Transfer is one possible explanation," the analyst responded. "However, given the amount of semen found on the bed sheets, I would say transfer is highly unlikely in this case."

Duncan objected to the latter portion of the witness's answer as unresponsive, meaning that the answer was not in response to the question asked. The judge overruled, saying, "Just because you didn't like his answer doesn't make it objectionable." To be called out in front of the jury like that was not good, and Duncan knew it. Wishing he had just one more question to ask to end on a better note, Duncan reluctantly sat down, not wishing to do any more harm, and passed the witness.

Kingery was smart enough to leave the judge's rebuke of Duncan hanging in the air and offered no re-direct. The witness was excused, and the court took its second break of the afternoon.

The time was nearing 4:00, so during the break, Kingery informed the court that they had only one witness left to call, the case agent Detective Wayne Drummond, and his testimony would take quite a while. He asked the court if they could break early for the day so as not to interrupt the testimony when the clock struck 5:00. The judge discussed getting the detective on the stand and dispensing with the introduction and other preliminary matters so they could jump right into the meat of his testimony when court resumed in the morning, but ultimately the judge allowed the state to start the witness fresh at 8:30 the next day. For scheduling purposes, the judge asked Duncan if he intended to call any witnesses, to which Duncan replied that he was not entirely decided on the matter. When the jury returned from its break, they were dismissed for the day.

Detective Drummond was on the stand when the jury entered promptly at 8:30 the following morning. The detective dressed for his time in the spotlight. He wore his dark blue trial suit, a white French cuff shirt with skull and crossbones cufflinks, and a bright blue tie. He was sworn in and introduced himself to the jury. He said he was the case agent, meaning he was the detective in charge of the investigation.

Over the course of the next two hours, Kingery painstakingly took the witness through his investigation, allowing him to explain to the jury how the investigation unfolded and, ultimately, how the police developed Charlie Calvin Clements as a suspect. In the middle of his direct examination, Kingery closed the chain of custody on all the evidence with Drummond since he was the final person to handle each piece.

As his direct examination wrapped up, the discovery of the DNA evidence was discussed, leading to the report from ADFS regarding the CODIS hit matching the DNA evidence from the semen on the bedsheet. That led to the defendant being picked up at work and brought to the police station for a formal interview. After establishing that the defendant was read his rights and the signed Waiver of Rights form being admitted into evidence, Kingery asked the detective if he asked the defendant if he knew the victim.

"Yes, I did."

"And what was his response?"

"He said, 'I ain't know this bitch you talkin' about.'"

Kingery let that hang in the air before asking the detective if he presented the defendant with the fact that his DNA was found on the victim's bedsheet.

"Yes, I did."

"And what was his response?"

"Objection!" yelled Duncan. "Approach, your honor?"

The judge waved the lawyers forward and covered his microphone when they reached the bench. Duncan spoke sotto voce so as not to be heard by the jury. He told the judge that Clements asked for a lawyer at that point and to allow the jury to know that would be improper and prejudicial. The judge looked at Kingery, who responded that he was only asking the witness what the defendant said, but yes, that would be his testimony—that the defendant asked for a lawyer. The judge sustained the objection without seeming to give it much thought. Kingery figured that would happen, but he knew he had made his point with the jury. And so did Duncan, who was, by now, quite angry.

Back at the counsel table, Kingery stated, "No further questions."

When Duncan told the judge his cross-examination might take a while, the judge called for a mid-morning break.

On cross, Duncan began by saying, "Let's see if I have this right, Detective, the only reason you ever suspected my client did something to Ms. Lane was because a forensic scientist told you a semen stain on a bedsheet belonged to him?"

The detective squirmed a bit because he did not like the characterization, but Kingery had beat it into his head to only answer the question asked, so he said, "Initially, that is cor-rect."

"So the answer to my question is yes, you only suspected him after a forensic scientist told you a semen stain on a bed-sheet belonged to him?"

Clearly annoyed, Drummond gave a terse, "That is correct."

"And is it fair to say that you only arrested him in this case because he denied knowing Ms. Lane?"

"No, that's not correct. I had other evidence." The detective ticked off what he found out about his yard work at the victim's house and the fact that he wasn't at work the day Ms. Lane disappeared and thus did not have an alibi. He also mentioned that he learned Ms. Lane was a neat freak, so they were going off the belief that the stain was left that day.

"So, Detective, you're assuming, then, that any sex that may have occurred as recently as that morning was non-consensual?"

This seemed to jar the detective. After a beat, he said, "Well, yeah."

"Why?"

"Why?" Drummond's tone suggested it was a stupid question.

"Yes, why? You do understand the question, don't you, De-tective?"

Drummond's face flushed, and he just stared at the lawyer.

Duncan stared back for what seemed like minutes, but was probably less than thirty seconds, before saying, "Do you need me to repeat the question?"

"No."

After several more seconds passed, Duncan said, "Your honor, would you please instruct the witness to answer my question?"

Judge: "You need to answer the question, Detective."

Drummond looked at the judge, then Duncan, then, with

his face steeling with resolve, he said, "I just put two and two together. A gruesome scene, such as it was, did not exactly seem congruous with consensual intimacy."

"What time did the sexual encounter occur?"

"I don't know."

"What time did the 'murder' occur?" Duncan used air quotes when he said murder.

"I don't know."

"So, you deduced that a sex act occurring at...well, you don't know when it occurred, and a crime that occurred at... well, you don't know when that occurred either...must invariably be linked. Is that about right?"

Drummond shifted in his seat and audibly exhaled before saying, "I believed them to be linked, yes."

"What if the sex were consensual? Would that change your mind at all about there being a connection?"

"I don't have any evidence the sex was consensual."

"What evidence do you have that it wasn't?"

That question scored a direct hit, and everyone in the courtroom knew it. Drummond didn't answer, but he didn't have to. Duncan went back to the first question in this sequence. "Let me ask my question this way, Detective. If you knew the sex was consensual, would that change your opinion, at all, regarding the person she had sex with being responsible for committing this violence against her?"

Staring at Duncan, the witness said, "No."

"No? Are you serious now?" Kingery objected to the second question as argumentative, and it was sustained. Duncan moved on, getting animated now. "So you're sitting there, under oath, and looking at this jury and telling them that whether the sex was consensual or not had *zero* bearing on your investigation?"

"That's correct."

"How many murders have you investigated that occurred after a consensual sex act?"

Drummond gave the question some thought before saying, "None."

"But you have investigated homicides after sexual assaults and rapes, correct?"

"That is correct."

"So this case, if the sex were consensual, would be a first for you. Is that correct?"

"I don't believe the sex was consensual." Kingery could not show it in front of the jury, but he was frustrated with Drummond bordering on angry. He was saying to himself, *Just answer the question.*

"Detective, do you absolutely refuse to believe that it's possible my client and Ms. Lane had consensual sex that day or any day?"

Drummond shrugged, which had Kingery about out of his chair, ready to strangle his own witness.

"Come on, Detective, you know you must answer out loud so the court reporter here can take down your answer."

This time Drummond broke eye contact with the lawyer. He looked down at his lap and said, "I guess I never considered it."

"But you do believe it is possible, correct? I mean, you don't have any reason to believe otherwise, do you?"

"I suppose," was all Drummond said.

Duncan had made his point, so he moved on. "The fact is, Detective, you don't have any physical evidence linking my client to the crime, do you?"

"His DNA was in her bed," the witness answered confidently.

"Ok, so you have evidence my client had sex with Ms. Lane, we've established that, but my question is, what physical evidence do you have that Mr. Clements was responsible for whatever harm befell Ms. Lane?"

"Physical evidence? None." Drummond's tone now was much less confident than when he testified on direct or even at the level with which he began answering the defense lawyer's questions.

Duncan paused here and reviewed his notes. Not because he needed to check them but because he needed time to think. His opening salvo had far exceeded his expectations with how well it went; he eviscerated the detective on the sex issue. The question he needed to answer, and quickly, was whether to stop here or press forward. The seconds stretched on before the judge interrupted, "Any further questions, Mr. Pheiffer?"

"One moment, Your Honor," said Duncan. He did a quick mental review of what was testified to on direct. He felt he diffused the major bomb in the case—the DNA—as best he could. There were other issues, but nothing he had not addressed through other witnesses who previously testified. The fact of the matter was that this was a largely circumstantial case, and he felt as if he negated the one real piece of physical evidence tying his client to any crime that may have occurred. So he made the calculated decision to let his brief but effective cross-examination stay where it was, and he sat down after letting the court know he had no further questions.

Kingery couldn't get Drummond off the stand fast enough, so he was quick to tell the court he had no need for re-direct.

With that, the state rested its case.

After lunch, the defense would call its only witness: the defendant, Charlie Calvin Clements. Since he was in custody, he had to wear ankle chains in court but no handcuffs. The court made sure the jury could not see his leg irons under the table where he sat as that may prejudice the jury against him, so he took the witness stand before the jury was led into the courtroom. When the jury was seated, he stood, raised his right hand, and swore to tell the whole truth and nothing but the truth.

It did not take long to get the first true bombshell of the case: the defendant told the jury that he had an ongoing sexual relationship with the victim. He stated that he met her one day when he was cutting her grass, and she brought him a cup of ice water. She would usually come outside and speak to him when he was working on her street when one day, a few weeks after they first met, she invited him inside, and they had sex. The defendant told the jury that he liked her and she liked him, but because of their respective work schedules—she worked nights, and he worked days—they never saw each other outside of their occasional trysts.

He further stated that their arrangement, as he referred to it, continued after he left the landscaping company, albeit less frequently. He admitted that he did have sex with her on the morning she went missing but was adamant that she was alive and well when he left her house just after 10:00 that morning. When asked why he did not come forward with this information when he found out she was missing, Clements stated that he knew what would happen if the police found out a black man had sex with a white woman who went missing from her home later that day.

"And what did you believe would happen?" asked his lawyer.

"Exactly what did happen," he said. "I knew they would say I had something to do with it."

Duncan nodded at his answer and asked why he lied to Detective Drummond about knowing Ms. Lane, to which the defendant replied, "For the same reason I just said." Again Duncan nodded at this answer.

Knowing that the prosecutor would ask about the prior felony assault conviction on the defendant's record, Duncan asked him to explain the facts of the case, and Clements did so. He talked about not instigating the fight and only taking the plea because they promised him probation if he did so.

"Charlie, did you do something to Veronica Lane after the two of you had sex?"

"No, sir."

"Was she alive when you left her house?"

"Yes, sir."

"Did you have *anything* to do with Ms. Lane's disappearance?"

"No, sir."

"Do you know anything at all about what happened to Ms. Lane after you left her house?"

"No, sir."

"Thank you, Charlie. Now, the prosecutor is going to have some questions for you. You answer his questions truthfully, ok?"

Charlie Clements nodded *yes*.

Kingery was up and out of his seat before Duncan had taken his, and he jumped right into his cross-examination, not allowing the judge an opportunity to ask if anyone needed a break. He said, "Let me see if I have this straight, Mr. Clements, you cut the victim's grass, and at some point, she lured you into her house so she could have sex with you. Is that about right?"

"It's not like that. We became friends, and one day she asked me to come inside, and I did. We were talking, one thing led to another, and we had sex."

"Well, now, that sounds like a letter to the Penthouse Forum. You're quite the lucky guy."

"Objection," said a rising Duncan Pheiffer.

"Sustained," said the judge.

"Did you care for this woman, Mr. Clements?" asked Kingery.

The defendant shrugged and said, "Sure."

"That didn't sound very sincere. Did you honestly care for her, or was it just about the sex with you?"

"Nah, I liked her."

"How often did y'all text one another?"

"She ain't have my number."

"You didn't give your number to a girl you were sleeping with and said you care about?"

Clements shook his head *no*.

"You have to speak up," said Kingery. "For the court reporter."

Leaning forward, speaking directly into the microphone, and enunciating each word, he said, "No. I did not give her my number." Kingery had seen this many times before. When a witness grew frustrated, they often exaggeratedly leaned into the microphone mounted on the witness stand to give their answers.

"But you cared about her."

"Yes. I told you that."

"When did you find out something had happened to her."

"I don't know. Whenever it was on the news, I guess."

"So when you learned something bad had happened to a girl you cared about, I assume you went to the police and told them you had been with her that morning."

Clements sucked his teeth and, leaning into the microphone, said, "No."

"You never went to the police to see if you could help them determine what happened to this woman you cared about?"

"No. I told you I knew they would try and pin it on me, which they did."

"So, you weren't willing to assist the police in finding this woman you cared about because you were afraid of what might happen *to you*."

A shrug from the witness stand and an admonition from the judge to speak his answers. Then the defendant said, "Yeah, I guess."

"Do you have any evidence, other than your word here today, that you had a consensual relationship with this missing woman?"

Again he sucked his teeth, leaned into the microphone, and said, "No."

"And just to be clear, today, in front of the jury, is the first time you have told this story, correct?"

Leaning into the microphone, he said, "Yes." Then, as Kingery walked back to the counsel table, Clements said, "It's the truth." Kingery ignored the witness.

"Again, to be clear, Mr. Clements, you were in the victim's house the morning she went missing."

"That's right."

"You had sex with her."

"Yes."

"You say the sex was consensual, but we only have your word for that, correct?"

"I guess so."

"And as you've already testified to, you have a previous conviction for a violent assault, correct?"

Again leaning into the microphone, he said, "Yes."

"In fact, you were on probation for that violent assault when you first met and allegedly began a sexual relationship with Ms. Lane, correct?"

"Correct."

"But you didn't have anything to do with Ms. Lane's disappearance."

"No," he said directly into the mic. It was Kingery's turn to nod at the answers Clements was giving.

For the next several minutes, Kingery asked Clements about the morning of October 7, 2021. Clements stated that after he had sex with Ms. Lane, he left sometime before lunch and went home. It was his day off, so he sat around his apartment. No, he did not go anywhere the rest of the day, nor did he see anyone. Yes, the jury has only his word that he was at home all day and never left.

Appearing to have wrapped up his cross-examination, Kingery headed for the counsel table. Then, as if just remembering something, he looked up and said, "Oh, not only did you not try and help the police when you found out something happened to her, you lied to the police about knowing her when they spoke to you, correct?"

Into the mic: "Correct."

"And you referred to her as a 'bitch', correct?"

A shrug, then into the mic: "Correct."

Kingery told the court he had no further questions for the witness, and the defense rested its case. The judge adjourned for the remainder of the day so the lawyers could prepare for closing arguments to begin the following morning.

❉   ❉   ❉   ❉   ❉

The short fuzzy-headed bailiff led the jurors into the courtroom at two minutes past nine in the morning, ready to hear closing arguments.

The state began, and Kingery laid out what the charges against the defendant were: capital murder for intentionally causing the death of Veronica Lane and doing so while committing a rape.

He then went through the elements of the offense charged, what he needed to prove to them beyond a reasonable doubt, and how he had done so throughout the trial. He discussed witness testimony, exhibits, and other evidence that established the defendant's guilt. He reminded the jury that each one of them had taken an oath to follow the law, and following the law and the facts left them with only one choice: guilty.

Kingery sat down, and Duncan Pheiffer stood to deliver his closing argument.

Duncan began by reminding the jury that his client came into the trial cloaked with the presumption of innocence, which was a piece of evidence they should consider in his favor. Then, he attempted to hammer home the fact that it wasn't up to the defendant to prove his innocence. Instead, the burden is on the state of Alabama to prove the defendant's guilt; to overcome the defendant's presumption of innocence. "Hold them to that!" he said.

He went on: "The *only* thing the state has proven to you beyond a reasonable doubt is that my client, Mr. Charlie Clements, had sex with Veronica Lane on October 7, 2021." He paused before going on. "They haven't proven to you to any acceptable degree that the sexual encounter was anything more than an act between consenting adults.

"They want you to convict this man of the most serious crime in our country based on supposition and innuendo and just plain guesswork. Folks, that just isn't enough. Not to convict a man of capital murder!" His voice seemingly rose with each sentence spoken. He let the words hang in the air as he reviewed his notes.

He recapped the testimony of each of the state's witnesses. He talked about what they had testified to and how not a single witness had implicated his client as a rapist, much less a murderer. "And that is critical because, without a rape, there can be no capital murder. Period."

Finally, in a controlled tone of voice, he reminded the jury of what was at stake. He implored them to take their time, considering all the information they had been presented with over the last four days. To go into the jury room, find reasonable doubt, and render a verdict of not guilty for Charlie Calvin Clements so he could get this nightmare behind him and move on with his life.

Duncan sat down, and the judge asked the jury if they needed a break before hearing the state's rebuttal argument. The tension in the air was thick, and the jury wanted to press on.

Kingery stood up, strode confidently before the jury, and said in an even tone, "Your job is not to look for reasonable doubt, as Mr. Pheiffer told you moments ago. No. It's to look for the truth." So began his rebuttal argument.

He attempted to attack, point by point, what defense counsel discussed in his closing. He told the jury where Duncan was misleading them regarding witness testimony and why he was misleading them: "Because the truth is not good for Mr. Clements. The truth demands a guilty verdict, and he knows that." He flipped a couple of pages on his yellow legal pad and said, "He is hanging his hat on you all believing the sexual encounter with 'that bitch,' as he called her, was consensual." Kingery held up a blowup photograph of the crime scene showing all the gore in sharp detail and said, "Does this look like post-coital bliss to you?" Some of the jurors were visibly affected by the poster-sized carnage.

Kingery pressed on. "Or does this look like the work of a deranged rapist and murderer? The defendant presented no witness or evidence corroborating his story of a long-term, semi-regular sexual dalliance between him and the victim, Veronica Lane. Not one person, text message, email, Facebook message, anything over the course of some eighteen months that this alleged relationship was occurring that would prove what he wants you to believe...that's because it did not exist. His story is one of convenience. A Hail Mary, if you will, to try and avoid responsibility for his heinous actions."

Kingery walked up to the rail of the jury box, letting silence fill the room—the ticking clock above the heads of the jury sounding like a gong in the stillness of the moment—before saying, "The defendant's lawyer asked you to find him not guilty so he could, quote, get on with his life. Well, you know who can't get on with her life? Veronica Lane. And it's because of that man"—he jabbed a finger at the defendant without looking at him—"Charlie Calvin Clements. He raped that poor woman, savagely murdered her, then took her body and put it somewhere it would never be found." Another long pause as he searched the faces of each individual juror. A sob from the gallery penetrated the silence, but Kingery dared not break the bond he was certain he had with the jury. He said, "Be Veronica Lane's voice and hold him responsible. Find that man guilty of raping and murdering Veronica Lane."

Kingery sat down at the counsel table, signaling he was done, and the judge called for a twenty-minute break.

Upon returning to the courtroom, the judge spent forty-five minutes charging the jury. He explained the law: the standard of proof to find the defendant guilty, the elements of the crime charged, and all lesser included offenses. Among the additional legalities explained to the jury was the verdict form and how they should fill it out once they had reached a verdict.

The jury retired to the jury deliberation room just before noon and opted to begin deliberations immediately and work through lunch. The jury's foreperson sent a note requesting food be brought in so they could continue to deliberate without breaking—they were making progress. Sandwich boxes were brought in for lunch, and pizza was provided later that evening for dinner. Finally, at 11:38 p.m., the jury announced they had reached a verdict.

Twelve solemn souls made their way to their seats in the jury box; each of the eight men and four women—nine whites and three blacks—looked as if they were carrying a thousand-pound weight on their backs. After being seated, the foreperson stood at the judge's request and handed the jury form to the bailiff, who then handed it to the judge. Guilty of capital murder.

CHAPTER 11

B ARCLAY SAT BEHIND HIS desk, scrolling through his computer and viewing his case assignment queue in the office's electronic case management system. He was conducting his weekly review of new cases assigned to him as well as transferring cases to Clayton for the young prosecutor to cut his teeth on.

During this process, he saw a name that stopped him cold. He immediately clicked on the defendant's name, which took him into the details of the case. Being a newly assigned case, he expected the information in the system would be scant, and he was right. The only information contained therein was the charging affidavit which set out the probable cause for arrest and the arrest warrant.

The warrant revealed the defendant's race and date of birth which all but confirmed what Barclay was hoping against hope would not be true.

❀ ❀ ❀ ❀ ❀

He put together driver's license photos for each name in the file, had criminal histories pulled, and, half an hour later, Barclay found himself inside an interview room on the third floor of the Towne County Jail. The room had a gray linoleum floor with mustard yellow cinderblock walls and smelled of sweat and stale cigarettes. There was a small square metal table and two metal chairs in the six-foot by four-foot room. Finally, after waiting for almost ten minutes, the heavy metal door to the room opened, and a young black man in an orange jumpsuit—hands cuffed in front and attached to a chain at his waist—shuffled in, chains rattling, eyes to the ground. Once inside the room, the inmate lifted his head and met Barclay's gaze.

"Aw, fuck," said the inmate turning to leave, the guard blocking his way.

Barclay, seated at the table facing the door, looked past the inmate to the guard and nodded his head once. The guard backed out of the doorway and locked them in. Barclay said, "Have a seat."

"I'm glad you're here, Barclay, man, you—"

"I said have a seat," interrupted Barclay nodding his head to the empty chair.

The inmate closed the short distance to the chair in two shuffles. With his hands bound, he leaned into the back of the chair, grabbed it with both hands, and backed it out from under the table so he could sit. Once the chair was out, he made his way around the chair and dropped onto the seat—chains rattling. His shoulders slumped; he kept his head down, not wanting to look Barclay in the eye. He could feel Barclay's stare boring into him.

After a long minute—the silence interrupted by muffled shouts from a nearby cell—Barclay slid the file toward the inmate just short of the table's edge.

"What the hell happened?" asked Barclay in an even tone.

The inmate, Prentice Watkins, looked up with tears in his eyes and then dropped his gaze back to his lap. After a moment, he just started shaking his head and said, "I'm sorry."

Barclay met Prentice Watkins almost seven years ago—Prentice was twelve years old and playing basketball for the YMCA; Barclay, twenty-five and recently licensed to practice law, was his coach. Prentice wasn't the tallest kid in the league or on the team, but he was probably the toughest. He battled in the post with players six inches taller and won many more battles than he lost. Barclay had taken an interest in Prentice that season and that interest went beyond the basketball court.

He could tell that the kid's toughness had its roots in more than just wanting to be a great basketball player. He came to learn that Prentice's father, a small-time drug courier, was shot and killed when Prentice was only two years old, and his mother was a crack addict turned prostitute who had been arrested so often that she was on a first-name basis with most of the city and county patrol units. Prentice lived with his Aunt Rai—he called her Aintie Rai. Barclay had gotten to know her that first basketball season. She was his mother's sister and had pretty much raised Prentice. She worked two jobs and put him into basketball to keep him occupied and to get some of his pent-up energy out. She was a small-framed woman with a big heart who was just what Prentice needed: a disciplinarian who, despite her lack of free time, managed to stay on top of his school and extracurricular activities. Aintie Rai, as Barclay also referred to her (at her insistence), was not always available to get him to and from practices and games, so Barclay committed to helping out when needed. He became somewhat of a big brother to Prentice, spending time with him even after the season ended.

Barclay and Brittany, still only dating at the time, took him to a couple of Atlanta Hawks basketball games that winter and a couple of Braves games over the summer. Barclay coached basketball for three more seasons until his schedule became too unpredictable to continue to do so.

Over the subsequent years, Prentice was developing a nice mean streak on the basketball court and, other than a few minor instances, was staying out of trouble. But, working in his fourth year at the district attorney's office, Barclay knew full well what awaited Prentice if he wasn't careful. Growing up in a single-parent home was tough enough, but he knew the added element of living with an aunt who worked two jobs and was rarely home before 10:00 at night left too much unsupervised and unoccupied time for Prentice, and that worried him.

Even after Barclay stopped coaching basketball, he kept up with Prentice and his Aunt Rai as much as possible, but over time the contact diminished. He and Brittany still took Prentice to Atlanta a couple of times a year for various sporting events, but he could tell Prentice was drifting away little by little. In spite of it all, Barclay always made sure Prentice and his aunt both knew that he was available anytime if they ever needed anything. He was never shy about reminding Prentice to stay out of trouble and what his messing up would do to his aunt. She was trying her best to provide for Prentice and make sure he had what he needed to make it through high school, but there was only so much she could do.

The last time Barclay had spoken to Prentice was when he had seen him at a local gas station two years ago. The two had talked for close to fifteen minutes just catching up. Prentice had recently graduated high school with no real plans for the future. He was still living with his Aunt Rai and assured Barclay that everything was good. The two exchanged cell phone numbers, and Barclay told him to call if he needed help finding a job or just wanted to hang out and talk. Prentice had grown into a strong young man, and Barclay worried about him, especially now that he did not have the structure of school in his life.

Barclay stared across the dimpled, dented metal table at the top of Prentice's head with a knot in his stomach. He took an audible breath and said, "Prentice, please look at me and tell me what happened. I can't help you if you won't talk to me."

Prentice bent his head further down and wiped his eyes with his bound hands. He looked up and stared at Barclay with red-rimmed eyes. He said, "I was with some guys who hit a dealer's crib." Then he said quickly, "But Barclay, man, I didn't know what they was gonna do. I swear."

Barclay slowly leaned forward, shaking his head, then, without warning, slammed his hand on the metal table, causing Prentice to jump in his seat—the sound echoed like a gunshot in the small cinderblock room.

Barclay yelled, "How could you be so stupid?" The guard's face appeared in the small glass opening in the door; Barclay saw this and shook his head slightly. He then stood up and turned his back to Prentice as he walked around the small room. Looking back at him, he said, "Do you honestly think I'm that dumb? You do realize I deal with this same boneheaded shit on a daily basis, right?" Pointing at the file, he said, "I read the case file. It's all in there: how y'all were sitting around smoking weed and decided to roll a dealer because you all knew there would be a lot of cash there." He walked up beside Prentice, placed his left hand on the edge of the table, bent down, and whispered in his ear, "Do you have any idea how fucking stupid that was?" Straightening back up, he continued, "But dealers don't call the cops, right? Isn't that what y'all discussed? Well, you're right...most of the time. Only this one was *really* pissed off and did call the cops. Now you're staring at twenty years minimum in big boy prison for what? A few hundred dollars? Hell, you were stopped with the guns and cash not a mile from the dude's house. Real fucking brilliant." Barclay walked back to his side of the table, sat in his chair, and said, "I want you to tell me everything." Prentice had his head down only slightly and averted Barclay's gaze. Barclay tilted his head to the side, trying to look Prentice in the eye, and tapped a finger on the table to get his attention. "Hey," he said. "Everything, you hear me?" Prentice looked up, and Barclay continued, "I am *not* going to allow you to do this to your aunt, do you understand? You have one shot here, and then we are done because if you still want to live your life like this, then there isn't anything I can or will do for you, understand?"

The room was quiet again. Prentice stared at Barclay for a moment, then leaned forward—his rattling chains breaking the silence. "We was just sitting around this guy's house, and they ask me who my local contact was and—"

"Local contact?" asked Barclay. "What do you mean?"

Prentice took a deep breath and let it out. He leaned forward, looked around as if seeing who could hear him, and, in a low voice, said, "I run drugs and cash back and forth between here and Montgomery. I work for a guy there, and he has a guy who sells for him here. I deliver the inventory, pick up the proceeds, and take it back to Montgomery. That's *it*."

Barclay's head dropped. He shook it as he said, "Jesus, Prentice."

"I deliver and pick up once a week. These guys I was with, they know what I do and knew it was about time for me to do another pickup." He shrugged and said, "They figured there would be a lot of cash at his place since it was almost time to make another run."

"Whose idea was it?"

"Pooh Bear."

Barclay reached for the file and slid it back to himself. He flipped through it until he found what he was looking for. The page had a photo of a male with dreads and a criminal history, along with known aliases. He spun the folder around to Prentice and said, "This Pooh Bear?" Prentice leaned forward for a better look, then nodded. Barclay spun the folder back and said, "Alright, go on."

Prentice said, "They needed me to show them where the guy lived, so I rode with them."

"What the hell were you thinking doing this?"

Prentice gave a weak shrug and said, "I don't know."

Prodding Prentice on, Barclay said, "So you agreed to take them to the house. What happened then?"

"I told them I wasn't getting out of the car. The guy sees my face, I'm dead for sure. I figured if nobody could put me there, they'd chalk it up to a snitch who just seen or heard something, or maybe they'd see it as two dudes getting lucky hitting a stash house."

Barclay's phone buzzed in his inside coat pocket. He pulled it out, looked at the screen, and returned the phone. He motioned for Prentice to continue.

Prentice said, "So we get in the car and drive to the house. We ride by real slow one time to see if anyone else is there. It looked pretty quiet, so we turned around, drove back to the house, and stopped at the curb. Pooh and Swish jumped out all quick and shit and ran up to the front door."

Barclay flipped through the case file again and showed the page he found to Prentice. "This Swish?"

Prentice nodded and continued talking. "They knock on the door all casual like and this girl answers. Pooh and Swish bust through the door and slam it closed. Next thing I know, they running out with a backpack, the backpack I make the pickups and drops with. They said it was just sitting on the table begging to be took." Prentice shrugged, causing his chains to rattle, and said, "Then we just booked out. Got down the road a bit and got lit up."

Barclay sat there, taking in what he had just heard. There were no glaring holes in the story. He asked, "Who do you work for? I need a name."

Prentice's eyes went wide. "You want me to give him up?" Shaking his head, he said, "That detective asked me that earlier. No way I can flip on this. He'll have me killed for sure."

"You don't get it. Your life is worthless right now. The police, court, prison, those are the least of your worries. One of his couriers steals from him? That will not go unpunished. You know that as well as I do."

Prentice wore the weight of the situation like a piano around his neck. "If I give you a name, you gonna tell them?" Prentice asked and motioned his head toward the hallway indicating the police.

Barclay looked in the direction Prentice had indicated. After a moment, he looked back at Prentice and said, "You be straight with me, and that name stays between us."

Prentice leaned back and looked at the stained drop-tile ceiling. He let out a loud breath. He began to shake his head and dropped his gaze back to his lap. One minute passed. Then two. His chains rattled as he attempted to lift his hands. In a low voice, he said, "Malik Traylor."

Barclay concentrated on the name. He said, "I've heard that name before."

"But Barclay, man, something wasn't right about that night. We was stopped too damn quick."

"What do you mean?"

"Man, ain't no way that dude called the police that quick. He would have called Malik first and seen what he wanted him to do. I mean, like you said, dealers ain't real quick to be calling the cops." Shaking his head, he said, "Naw, man, no way."

Barclay read the arresting officer's report twice, so he knew the facts, but he scanned the report again to make sure. Eyes still on the report, he said, "Says right here that he made the stop because the car fit the description of the BOLO: dark red Honda Accord with three black males."

"But that's what I'm sayin'. No way that BOLO goes out that quick."

✻   ✻   ✻   ✻   ✻

Barclay's first stop after leaving the jail was Clayton's office, which was empty. He then went to the office's sad excuse for a law library, where he found Clayton working on a laptop computer. The room contained a large, heavily scarred blonde wood conference table and several matching and equally nicked-up wooden chairs. It also had floor-to-ceiling bookcases on three walls and two computer terminals on a desk under the windows. The bookcases were lined with outdated legal tomes that, to Barclay's knowledge, had never been used since he had been working there. This room was referred to as the library because every law office had to have a library. In reality, it served primarily as the lunch table for those who ate at the office since it had a large flat-screen television on the wall and a cable hookup. Being later in the afternoon, it was empty except for Clayton and some fast food ketchup and salt packets that the day's lunch gang had left behind. The television was on and tuned to a baseball game—two American League bottom dwellers—volume muted.

Barclay sat down directly across from Clayton, who, being lost in a case file, was startled by his appearance. Clayton said, "Oh, hey. You need something?"

"Yeah," said Barclay sliding Prentice Watkins' arrest warrant across the table to him. "I need you to get me the nine-one-

one tape for the victim's call and all of the dispatch and radio logs from that night for the patrol officer who made the arrest. Just ask for the CAD info for this case."

"CAD?"

Barclay waved a hand at Clayton and said, "They'll know what I'm asking for. This case is fairly recent, so they may ask why you want all this stuff now. Just tell them I am asking for it."

"Sure thing," said Clayton, writing on a yellow legal pad. "But, who do I call about all of this?"

"Don't call. This request needs to be made in person to make sure it gets done. Go to the police station and tell the desk sergeant what you need. Tell him you need it ASAP."

"Do you want me to wait on it?"

"Yes. I'm going to try and meet with the arresting officer this afternoon, and I need that first."

"Ok. Anything else?"

Barclay shook his head and said, "Just call me when you have it in hand."

❊   ❊   ❊   ❊   ❊

It was just after 4:30 in the afternoon when Barclay's office phone buzzed. When he answered, the voice on the other end said: "There's an Officer Stoddard here to see you."

"Ok. Send him on back."

Barclay, his shirtsleeves rolled up and his tie knot loosened, met the officer halfway between reception and his office. He extended his hand: "Barclay Griffith. Thanks for coming by."

"Rick Stoddard," the lean, redheaded officer said with a return handshake.

As they walked to Barclay's office, Barclay half-turned and said, "You look familiar. Have I had you in a case before?"

"You sure did. A dope case maybe eight months ago. I made the stop and found a bunch of weed in the car's center console."

"That's right. They gave you consent to search the car." Stoddard nodded proudly.

They entered Barclay's office, and he gestured for Stoddard to take a chair as Barclay made his way behind the desk. He said, "So, you going on duty or off?"

Stoddard was wedging into the chair, the chair arms protesting against his duty belt. He looked down at either side of the chair and said, "Shift starts at six tonight, but I was upstairs in a motion hearing when I got your message about meeting, so the timing worked out." He was looking up now, having gotten himself situated.

Barclay told him he wouldn't keep him long. "Don't worry about it," said Stoddard. "I'm getting comp time for coming in early, so you have me as long as you need me."

Barclay started looking through the records Clayton had pulled for him. He was doing this to ensure he knew the details and to allow Stoddard to stew for a minute or two. Barclay was absently flipping pages when Stoddard spoke up: "What's this about? We have a case coming up or something?" Barclay glanced up at Stoddard and returned to the stack of paper. "Because I haven't received a subpoena or anything."

Barclay dropped the paper on his desk and leaned back in his chair. "I want to talk about a stop you made a month or so ago." Not seeing recognition on Stoddard's face, he continued, "Maroon Honda Accord? Ended in three arrests for armed robbery?"

Stoddard relaxed, and again pride showed on his face. "Oh, hell yeah. That your case?" he asked, pointing at Barclay.

"Yeah, it is, actually. I have a few questions about it." Barclay grabbed the warrant and pretended to scrutinize something. "Why did you make the traffic stop?"

"I heard the BOLO go out on the radio, and damn if they didn't roll by not a minute after that. Pure luck, really. Good for me, bad for them." A pause. Stoddard's brow furrowed, and he said, "I put it in my report. Don't you have it?"

Barclay closed the file folder and tossed it on his desk. "I just have the warrant." More silence.

Stoddard: "I'm sorry. Is there a problem?" He leaned forward in his chair, causing his shiny leather duty belt to groan.

"That's what I'm trying to figure out. You see, I pulled the radio logs from that night—"

"Why did you do that?" Stoddard interrupted, his friendly demeanor fading.

Barclay shrugged a casual shrug and said, "Just want to be prepared." Leaning forward, he said, "Does that bother you? It seems to bother you?"

Leaning back and trying to appear unfazed, Stoddard said, "Doesn't bother me, man. Whatever you want to do."

"Good. Now, about that night, tell me what happened. From the beginning."

Stoddard exhaled, gave a half eye roll, and said, "I was on routine patrol in the Westgate community, and as I was approaching an intersection with a four-way stop, dispatch put out the BOLO. I sat at the stop sign listening to the radio call. I recognized the address of the location of the robbery and knew it was nearby. I sat at the stop sign for just a few seconds to get my bearings, and then I turned right onto the cross street when I saw the Honda approach the intersection, maybe fifty yards ahead. It was approaching from the left. At that point, I sped up to the intersection and turned right to follow them. Once I was behind them, I activated my blue-lights, and they pulled over."

"About how far ahead of you was the car when you turned your lights on?"

A shrug, then: "I don't know. Maybe thirty feet." A shrug, "Maybe forty feet. Could've been more. I didn't measure."

"It's not a trick question, Officer. I'm just trying to get an idea of how it all went down. So, they pulled over immediately?"

"Pretty much. I mean, I never thought they wouldn't. Nothing like that."

Barclay said, "Tell me what you did next."

"Well, I verified the make, model, and tag number with dispatch, and then I got out and approached the car."

"How many people did you see in the car?"

"Three. Just like the BOLO said."

"Did you know the nature of the crime they were supposed to have committed?"

"Yeah. Armed robbery. That was part of the BOLO."

"Do you know why they tell you the nature of the crime?"

"Look, I know I don't have a ton of experience, but this feels an awful lot like a cross-examination. Is there something I should know?" Officer Rick Stoddard was beginning to squirm in his chair.

"I'm just walking you through that night. That's all. Better we do this now, here, than on the witness stand for the first time. Don't you agree?"

Shrug. "Yeah, I guess."

Barclay leaned far back in his chair and propped his feet on the corner of his desk. "Alright, officer, now back to my question: do you know why they tell you what crime the occupants of the car are suspected of committing?"

Stoddard's eyes flicked to Barclay's size twelves and then back to his face and said, "So we know what to be prepared for when we make contact."

Barclay pulled his feet off the desk and rolled his chair to the edge of the desk in one fluid motion. He pointed at Stoddard and said, "Exactly. Because if they are armed, you need to know that, right?" Stoddard nodded slowly. "And you knew in this instance that the occupants had at least one gun, right?" Again Stoddard slowly nodded. "Hell, for all you knew, all three of them had a gun, right?" Nod. "And you didn't know what kind of gun, did you? Could have been a pistol, a shotgun, or a fuckin' Mac-10, right?"

Officer Rick Stoddard had gone from eager to guarded and was now venturing into defensive territory. He said, "What's your point?"

Barclay held his hands palms up and said, "Why didn't you wait for backup?"

"What do you mean?"

"You knew these guys were accused of robbing someone at gunpoint, and you were outnumbered three to one, so why didn't you wait for backup?"

After a few seconds, Stoddard said, "I didn't want them to get away. I figured waiting on backup to arrive would give them a chance to drive off. To escape."

"But you had them stopped. You were parked, what, three or four feet behind their car? They didn't bail out of the car when you pulled them over, which, if they were going to run, that would have been the time they'd have done it. So, no, running wasn't a real threat, not at that point." Stoddard didn't say anything, so Barclay asked a follow-up question: "Did you even call for backup, Officer Stoddard?"

The fair-skinned officer's face had flushed, and he was staring past Barclay. He refocused on him and said, "Huh?"

"You didn't call for backup, did you?" Stoddard looked down and shook his head. Barclay continued: "I read the dispatch and radio logs, Officer Stoddard." Barclay picked the logs up and flipped a couple of pages to where he had made some highlights. "Let's see, at 1:07 a.m., you radioed a 10-38 to dispatch." He eyed Stoddard over the paper and asked, "What's a 10-38, officer?" Barclay knew the answer but wanted to hear Stoddard say all of this himself.

Stoddard cleared his throat and said, "That's the code for calling in a car tag."

"You call in a 10-38 with the tag number, a description of the car, and the number of occupants, correct." Stoddard again nodded. "Then it says here that you called in a 10-39 at 1:09 a.m." Again flicking his gaze back to Stoddard, he said, "What's a 10-39?"

"It's telling dispatch that I'm initiating a traffic stop." Stoddard's voice was devoid of emotion as if reading the phone book out loud.

Eyes back on the paper, Barclay said, "Says here you then called in a 10-27 at 1:14 a.m." He looked at Stoddard over the paper, leaving the next question unasked.

Stoddard said, "I'm running the driver's license."

Barclay bobbed his head at this as if this was new information to him, and he found it quite interesting. "Say, you know what time that BOLO went out, Stoddard?" The officer shook his head *no*. "1:21." Barclay bore his gaze into Officer Rick Stoddard, who blinked twice before looking away.

After being silent for more than a minute, Stoddard said lazily, "What's your point?"

"What's my point?" Barclay was trying hard to maintain his composure. He stood up from his chair and closed his office door. He sat beside Stoddard, angling the chair so it faced the officer. Stoddard twisted in his seat to meet Barclay's gaze. Barclay leaned in, elbows on knees, and said, "Let me tell you what I think happened: You're on routine patrol in what passes for the bad side of town for a city this size. You stopped somewhere in the area for your dinner break. Maybe you surfed the internet on your in-car computer, or maybe you were talking to your girlfriend on the phone. Don't know, don't care. Anyway, you see this older model car roll by containing three people. You have a pretty good idea that it's three black dudes, and you figure they're probably ridin' dirty if they're out at this time of night. You fall in behind them at a decent distance, so you don't spook them, and you watch and wait for them to commit a traffic violation, only they don't commit one. How am I doing so far?" Officer Stoddard gave nothing away with his expression. Barclay continued, "See, you don't know it yet, but they just committed a robbery and no way are they getting popped on a traffic stop. Your cop gut tells you they have something, so instead of letting them get away, you pull them over for nothing more than being from the wrong part of town." Stoddard opened his mouth to protest this last statement, and Barclay held his hand up. "Save it, Officer. If you had a reason to pull them over, you wouldn't have had to go with the BOLO story. So, you have these three guys pulled over, you run their tag and all three names through dispatch, and you come up with nothing. You had to be expecting at least one warrant, right? You probably run some bullshit by them about why you stopped them. Probably ask a bunch of questions to see if you can shake anything loose."

Barclay's office phone beeped, and Peggy's voice sounded through the speaker: "Barclay?" Stoddard turned his attention to the phone on the credenza.

"Not now," Barclay responded curtly and without taking his eyes off Stoddard. Back to the conversation: "Were they not acting nervous? They'd just committed an armed robbery, not three minutes prior to being stopped by the cops. They had to know they were busted, and you know nervous behavior is grounds to press them a little bit more. Probably could have gotten them out of the car with that." Barclay stopped and stared at Stoddard, getting nothing back. "In the end, though, you held out long enough, and the BOLO came through. I bet you about shit your pants when you realized you had the guys right in front of you. Word of caution for next time? It's best not to let the suspect hear the call through your radio. Bad guy hears that, and he wants to shoot the cop who aims to bring him in. This could have gone really bad for you, my friend."

The first signs of worry crept into Stoddard's face. He spoke pensively and said, "So, how are you going to handle this?"

"First of all, I need you to tell me this is how it went down—at least something close to that. Honestly, I just need you to admit the stop was bullshit, and you used the BOLO as cover once you heard it go out." Stoddard exhaled audibly and began to rub his palms on his pants. Barclay continued, "Look, you seem pretty sharp, and you're obviously enthusiastic about your job. I don't want to see your career end before it even starts, and I can't move forward until I know for certain that the case has to go away." Still sensing reluctance, he said, "I promise you I will see to it that the case goes away without this coming to light. Either that or you don't admit anything, and I will jam you up on this right now.

"I'm done fucking around on this, Officer Stoddard. You pulled some shit that I hate, and, quite frankly, the easiest and cleanest way out of this is to burn you with it. Whether or not you get burned on this deal is totally up to you." Barclay stood up and went to the window behind his desk, watching the foot traffic below. As 5:00 loomed, the businesses were emptying out. Barclay saw older men with briefcases and younger men with messenger bags and backpacks. There were ladies in heels and ladies in post-work tennis shoes. Almost all of them walking to the three-level municipal parking deck serving the small but parking-starved downtown. The Flagon and Snake was coming to life with the after-work crowd, while the park across the street, bustling during lunch, sat empty save for those passing through on their way home. The weather was perfect, and Barclay's thoughts went to what he could throw on the grill for dinner. He had narrowed the options to chicken wings or steak kabobs when Stoddard cleared his throat, ready to speak.

Stoddard said, "You know, you seem to be missing the fact that I was right." His tone was lacked confidence.

Barclay half turned and said, "What?"

"About them being up to no good. About them having committed a crime. I was right about that." His voice grew more assertive as he spoke.

Barclay's jaw muscles grew taught, and his face burned. He sat on the front corner of his desk in front of Stoddard and said, "That's not the point. You've got to understand that there's enough bad shit going on out there that you don't have to resort to this type of thing. As cops and prosecutors, we have to be above that—at all times. There has never been a bad guy worth my good name and character, and I suspect the same can be said for you. You get caught lying to a judge or jury, and your career is over; you can never testify again. That's how important it is, and I *really* need you to understand this." Stoddard would not meet his gaze.

Finally, Barclay said, "Look, man, I'm going home. It's beautiful outside, and I'm not going to sit here and beg you to do the right thing. I stand up, put my coat on, and leave this office, you and I are done, and I suggest you put together a resume because I will destroy you with this." More silence before Barclay eased off the corner of the desk, saying, "View this as your one and only mulligan, alright? Don't lose your career before it even gets started." Sixty seconds passed as the two men just stared at one another. "Fair enough," Barclay finally said and he grabbed his cell phone off the desk, slid his laptop into his bag, and plucked his coat from the hook behind the door.

"Wait."

CHAPTER 12

I T WAS A RARE cool summer morning in Towne. The humidity was down, and the cloud cover was up; the combination of the two made it a windows-down ride to work for Barclay. Standing outside The Downtowner with coffee in hand, he made a phone call: "Hey, Fitz, you around this morning?"

"Yeah, Boss," replied the familiar baritone.

"Good. Can you meet me in my office...say nine o'clock? I have a project for you."

"See you at nine." Fitz hung up without saying goodbye, which is what Fitz did when the conversation was over.

Barclay slid the phone into his pocket and drank from his Styrofoam cup sans lid. *You could still get a great cup of coffee for a buck*, Barclay thought as he stood on the sidewalk watching the square come to life. He also thought about Prentice and the plan he had hashed out the prior evening that he hoped would get him out of the mess he had made for himself. After another minute, he made the walk to the courthouse at the center of the square. A light rain began to fall.

Barclay was going through his email, reading and answering recently filed motions, when he heard a knock. He looked up and saw Winston Fitzsimmons pushing through the door. "Fitz, how are you," he said, closing the file and standing. "Please, have a seat." He waited for Fitz to sit before he returned to his chair.

Winston Fitzsimmons, the office's best investigator in Barclay's mind, was six-four, solidly built, and at forty-two, he was the youngest investigator. He was also the only one who had not retired from the police department or the sheriff's office. He lacked the investigative experience the other three investigators had, but he made up for it with the tenacity that had long since left the others; a tenacity fostered growing up on the tough streets of Prichard, Alabama, just outside of Mobile. If you needed a witness found or wanted to make sure someone showed up to court, he was your guy. Fitz was hired to balance out the other three personalities, and he did that perfectly. Maggie had assembled a good crop of investigators, and when and if it were ever Barclay's decision to make, he would make Fitz his chief.

Fitz was the office's only black investigator and the only college graduate out of the bunch. He had a criminal justice degree from the University of South Alabama, where he played tight end. After college, he served as a police officer with the city of Mobile before becoming an investigator with the state Securities Commission.

Maggie first met Fitz when she prosecuted a white-collar case where his work as an investigator with the securities commission had proven to be the linchpin of a highly complex case. Within a month of the conclusion of that case, Fitz had filled what Maggie had termed "a fortuitous opening."

Winston Fitzsimmons' three constants are that he always wore a suit when he was on the clock, he called everyone at the office "boss" (if he liked you), and he almost always stashed a thumb-sized amount of Red Man in the lower right side of his cheek. Barclay once saw him on the witness stand for the better part of an hour with a chew in his mouth and never spit; he could hardly pay attention to the testimony because he kept waiting for what would never come.

"So, Boss, what do you have for me?" Fitz's eyes sparkled at the prospect of anything other than listening to the same old war stories from the office's three other investigators, which he was usually doing until some actual work came along.

Barclay leaned back in his chair and said, "Malik Traylor. You know that name?"

Fitz spit into an empty Diet Coke bottle, leaned back, and looked at the ceiling for five seconds. He tilted his head forward and said, "That name sounds familiar."

"Dope dealer down in Montgomery. We've had a couple of his boys here on distribution charges."

Fitz nodded a faint recognition. "Didn't his name come up in that Watson murder last year?"

Barclay pointed a finger at Fitz and said, "That's him."

"What's he done this time?" Fitz grunted.

"Well, he's actually a victim...of sorts." Seeing the confused look on Fitz's face, Barclay continued, "One of his boys got rolled sometime back, and one of the doers is a kid I know. I say kid, hell he's nineteen now, but I've known him since he was twelve. His name is Prentice. Good kid, but this wasn't a terrible shock given his background. I busted my ass as long as I could to try and see him past all of this, but..." Barclay's voice trailed off.

"What about Y-O?" Fitz interjected, then spit. Y-O was a reference to the Youthful Offender Act that allowed people who committed crimes under twenty-one years old to face a much lighter punishment and sealed their record.

"He's charged with armed robbery, and you know Y-O is next to impossible to get for that. Besides, after a discussion with the arresting officer, it appears to have been a bad stop." Seeing Fitz's face perk up, Barclay waved his hand and said, "Long story. The case is going away, but I still need to square things with Malik."

With a quick, humorless laugh, Fitz spit, then said, "Shit, your boy's probably better off inside."

"I agree, and I told him that. Problem is that he's going to be getting out as soon as I go see the judge, so I'm holding off on that until I have a face-to-face with Malik."

"And that's where I come in?" the silky radio voice asked.

"Exactly. I need you to arrange it. If I go down there, you know what'll happen. You can make him...understand."

Leaning forward in his chair, Fitz said, "You got it. I will have you two talking in a day or two, depending on how hard them boys want to act."

"Appreciate it." The two men stood, and as Fitz turned to the door, Barclay said, "And Fitz. Keep this quiet, will you?"

Fitz winked and spit.

❊　❊　❊　❊　❊

The shiny black Crown Victoria sat on Marlyn Street at the intersection with Otis Lane in the Smiley Court housing project in west Montgomery. Fitz had the car pointed south, which gave him an unobstructed view of Malik Traylor's crew: seven black guys ranging—as best Fitz could tell from sixty yards away—from early teens to early twenties. There were two late model Dodge Chargers—one painted metallic green and the other metallic purple, both with shiny thirty-inch rims—and both were serving as the crew's office.

After leaving Barclay's office that morning, a phone call to the Montgomery Police Department's narcotics department got Fitz the location of the crew's hangout spot. He was also told not to expect to see Malik Traylor, and so far, an hour into the sit, MPD had been right.

Smiley Court was a typical housing project: the same duplex replicated many times over, clotheslines in every yard, more weeds than grass, and a rundown basketball court, all amid a dense fog of hopelessness. No trees were spared in the building of the housing project, so it was a scorching place to be in the summertime.

Fitz had gotten a few looks his way when he first pulled up to his current spot but had largely been ignored. The foot traffic through the area had been light; he only remembered seeing one person outside of the crew wander through. Nevertheless, Fitz knew it was only a matter of time before he was paid a visit.

At 4:18 in the afternoon, almost four hours into the sit, a member of Malik's crew made his way over; the movement caused Fitz to look up from his book. Seeing the man approach, he marked his page with the flap of the dust jacket and set it on the passenger seat. Then, not looking away from the person walking toward him, he reached down, grabbed a Diet Coke bottle, unscrewed the cap, and spit.

"Fuck you want?" asked the man at the driver's side window. He was in his early twenties, dressed in a blue Kevin Durant Oklahoma Thunder jersey and denim shorts that went past his knees and were too big in the waist; he had to hold them up as he walked. He had four gold teeth in the middle of his mouth and a thick gold chain around his neck.

Looking around the man at his window Fitz shrugged and said, "Who said I want something? I'm just sitting here reading my book." He motioned to the passenger seat.

Gold Chain leaned into the open window and said, "We know you a cop, a'ight. You ain't gonna see shit, cuz shit ain't gonna happen long as you're sitting here. We ain't stupid."

Looking straight ahead through the windshield Fitz said, "Look, man, I don't care what y'all are doing out here; this isn't even my jurisdiction." Pulling a business card from the breast pocket of his shirt and holding it out to Gold Chain, Fitz said,

"I'm an investigator for the DA over in Towne County. I need Malik to meet with one of my prosecutors." Gold Chain didn't take the card. Instead, he straightened up and laughed a sarcastic laugh while grabbing himself. Fitz waited him out, then said, "You done?"

"Man, Malik ain't gonna meet with no cop."

Fitz rolled his eyes and said, "Hey, dumbass, I'm not a cop. I'm a—"

"You work for the DA. You a cop." He shrugged his shoulders at the last statement as if to say, "You can't argue with that." Then: "Malik don't talk to no cops."

"You remember Malik's boy getting rolled over in Towne?"

"Yeah, so?"

"It's about that."

"Shit, they done caught them niggas. Malik gonna handle it."

"Malik know you're telling his business to a cop?" Gold Chain made a face that was equal parts confusion and worry. Fitz continued, "I need you to have Malik call me to set a time and place for a meet. It needs to be today or tomorrow. Doesn't matter which, but it's got to happen soon."

A young kid wearing a white t-shirt, basketball shorts, and flip-flops at least two sizes too big was riding a girl's Huffy bicycle with a basketball under one arm. Gold Chain and Fitz paused their conversation as they watched him pass.

Fitz was watching the kid on the bike in his rearview mirror when Gold Chain said, "Look, nigga, that ain't gonna happen. Now get the fuck outta here." He punctuated the statement with a hard slap to the roof of the car.

Fitz calmly crooked a finger at Gold Chain and signaled him to lean in. When he did, Fitz's left hand shot up and grabbed the thick gold chain, twisted it once in his fist, and yanked down, pulling Gold Chain's head and shoulders through the open window. Fitz flashed a look to the crew to see if they were alert to what was happening; he did not want them coming over to his car. He put his mouth to Gold Chain's ear. "Look, nig*ga*," he placed heavy emphasis on the second syllable of the last word. "You said yourself that as long as I'm out here, you're not going to transact any business, and I got news for you: I'm not leaving here until I hear from Malik. Now, what's Malik going to think when you go to him holding light for today and tomorrow and the next day and on and on as long as I have to sit right fucking here? Huh?"

Gold Chain's hands were braced outside the driver's side door. Either because he couldn't move or, most likely, because he didn't want to risk breaking his chain, he did not try to pull away. Breathing hard, Gold Chain said, "Alright. I'll tell him you want to talk."

"Smart man."

❖ ❖ ❖ ❖ ❖

At 9:00 the following morning, Barclay pulled into a Mc-Donald's parking lot located not a half mile from the entrance to Smiley Court; his Audi as inconspicuous as a sailboat in a desert. The inside smelled like cooking grease and syrup. He saw Malik sitting in a booth and slid in opposite the drug dealer.

Malik Traylor was a good-looking guy in his late twenties. He wore a Kelly green Polo with a white undershirt and a silver necklace that looked like a bicycle chain. He also wore a large diamond stud in each ear. His hair was cut close and meticulously outlined; his face was clean-shaven.

"Mr. Griffith. It's a pleasure," Malik said.

"I doubt that." Then, looking at the table, Barclay said, "What's with all the food?"

"I didn't know what you'd want, so I ordered one of everything on the menu."

"You're quite the host, but I'm cutting back on my intake of crap. By all means, you feel free, though," he said with a wave of his hand.

Malik laughed and slid the pancakes toward him. After a bite, he said, "So, what is it that's so important that you needed to cost me half a day's take yesterday? Must be big for you to come down to these parts in that shiny ride." He shrugged as he continued, "I mean, unless you enjoy hanging out in the projects."

"One of my best friends growing up lived right here in Smiley Court."

"Who was that?"

"Andre Roberts." Seeing the lack of recognition, he said, "He went by Rabbit."

"Damn, you knew Rabbit?" A confused look crossed Malik's face. "Wait, you're from Montgomery?"

Nodding, Barclay said, "Yes, I knew Rabbit, but no, I'm not from Montgomery. Rabbit lived in Towne before moving here. We went to school together from kindergarten through fifth grade when he moved down here. It seemed like we were on the same football and basketball team every year." Barclay looked out the window and said, "I didn't see him again until four years later when our high schools played each other in football. Dude had gotten big." Looking back to Malik, he smiled and said, "I remember—oh, must have been our junior year—they came up to Towne for a football game, and he brought this tape he made. See, he started this rap group that called themselves The Smiley Court Gangstas, and they were just God-awful, but he just knew that was going to be his ticket out."

Malik laughed and said, "Yeah, I heard about them. Of course, I was just a kid, but I looked up to Rabbit and those guys."

"He was a good guy in a bad spot. The last time I saw him was about two years ago when he was a witness in a murder case I prosecuted. He was dead a month later."

"Yeah, he was shot by his uncle, right?"

"Yep. His uncle shot at someone else and missed, the bullet went between two houses, and Rabbit walked right into it. He walked up between the houses where the bullets passed and saw his uncle holding the gun. Told him: 'You fuckin' shot me,' and dropped dead right there."

"Damn, man."

"Yeah."

The two men sat in silence for the better part of a minute, Malik eating his pancakes and Barclay staring out the window. Malik spoke first, "So, back to this meeting. Your investigator didn't have to sit on my corner all day. He could have just told them you needed to talk to me."

"Ah, come on now, Malik. If Fitz hadn't done that, would you and I be sitting here this morning?"

Malik, chewing on a bite of pancakes, tilted his head to the side, conceding the point. The straw turned orange as he drank from his extra-large McDonald's cup; Barclay glanced over at the soda fountain: *Fanta.*

"I'll get to the point," said Barclay, "I'm here specifically about Prentice Watkins."

"Who?" Malik asked with a twitch of a smirk.

"Cut the crap, Malik. Like my investigator told your guy yesterday, I'm not interested in that angle. I want to square things up by him and make sure you never talk to him again." Barclay dropped an envelope on the syrup-laden plate of pancakes. "You don't take his phone calls, and you don't talk to him...ever."

Malik, clearly annoyed at the envelope in his plate and eye-balling Barclay, picked up the envelope by a corner and dropped it on the table. He opened it as it lay there and saw cash inside. He pointed at the envelope as he looked up at Barclay.

"It's five thousand dollars in cash. That more than makes up for the eight hundred and change they got from you in the robbery."

"Eight hundred?" said Malik, clearly surprised. "Shit, man, he had five times that much for sure."

"That's interesting because they had a little over eight hundred on them within a few minutes and a mile or so of the robbery. Sounds to me like your boy saw an opportunity to pocket some extra cash and blame it on the robbery."

Malik looked out the window adjacent to their booth and banged his fist on the table. "That motherfucker's a dead man."

"Hey," said Barclay pointing to himself. "Really?"

"Huh?" said Malik looking back to Barclay.

"Dude, you really want to be talking about killing someone right now...at this table?"

Malik eyed Barclay for a moment, then said, "Naw, you cool man."

"Seriously?"

Malik shrugged, then focused back on the cash. "What makes you think this squares anything? I mean, if I don't do something about this, people will think they can do this to me anytime they want to." Shaking his head, he said, "No, man. Them three niggas gotta pay."

"Look, you're in this business for one reason: money. And I just made you whole plus some." Barclay sat back in the booth and looked over at the entrance as an elderly couple walked in:

the man in a plaid long-sleeve shirt, jeans, and a John Deere cap, she in a flower print dress. He was holding the door for her, and Barclay liked that. Leaning forward, Barclay said, "I will make sure Prentice goes away...at least for a while. You can say whatever you want about him not being around anymore, and by the time he comes back, no one will remember."

"What about them other two boys?"

"What about them?" said Barclay with a shrug.

Malik laughed and said, "Damn, you cold."

"Whatever. You just leave Prentice alone, alright? And if I hear otherwise, you'll be the one who needs to leave town, like forever, because you will become my personal mission. Understand? He so much as stumps his toe, I'm holding you responsible."

"Man, please. You ain't never gonna have nothing to put me away with."

"With your reputation, do you honestly think that's going to matter?"

After a few seconds of eye contact, Barclay slid out of the booth and was almost to the door when Malik spoke: "Hey, man, why you doing this?"

Barclay turned and said, "Doing what?"

Malik held up the envelope of cash and then said, "Why Prentice?"

Barclay studied his shoe tops, then looked back to Malik and said, "You've got a little brother, right?"

"Yeah. So?"

Barclay shrugged and left.

CHAPTER 13

T IM AND MEGAN POPE were spending the weekend in Portland, Oregon. Though they had lived in Tacoma, Washington, for more than three years, this was the first time they had taken the two-and-a-half-hour trip down Interstate Five into Portland, and they were excited.

This was the couple's first getaway without their children since they had moved to the Northwest. Megan had it all planned out: they were staying at the historic Benson Hotel downtown, and they would have lunch on Saturday at the Library Taphouse—Tim was an unabashed lover of all things beer, and in Portland, Megan could think of no better place. Dinner Saturday night would be at The Urban Farmer, then brunch Sunday morning at Pine State Biscuits. The rest of the time would be filled with wandering the streets of downtown Portland—together—and simply doing whatever presented itself. Though only a quick trip, the couple would enjoy spending a couple of days at a leisurely measure free from schedules and the frenzied pace that is two working parents and children with an active extra-curricular calendar.

Prior to moving to Tacoma, the Popes had lived the previous two years in Towne. Tim was an airplane mechanic in the United States Air Force and was currently assigned to the Joint Base Lewis-McChord in Tacoma after having been stationed at Maxwell Air Force Base in Montgomery. The couple had two elementary school-aged children, so they opted to live in Towne, which afforded a better public school system.

It was mid-morning, the sky was overcast, and the temperature had barely broken sixty degrees. With no sun and a noticeable breeze, Tim and Megan were forced into light pullovers as they walked from their hotel toward Powell's Books. Holding hands and each holding a coffee, Tim and Megan moved up Tenth Avenue toward Burnside Street as they took in the sights and sounds of the City of Roses.

Megan leaned on Tim's shoulder and said, "Isn't this great?"

"Yes," Tim said with a squeeze of her hand. "It is." The couple walked a half block more, when he said, "I've got to tell you, I'm not sure what to do, not having anything to do." There was a smile in his voice, and Megan laughed.

The traffic was moderate on a Saturday, and they stopped at the intersection of Tenth Avenue and Stark Street, waiting on the light to change. The breeze kicked up, causing them to squeeze together while they waited. The light changed, and they got the signal to go. Though the car traffic wasn't heavy, there were plenty of pedestrians. Tacoma is the largest city that both Tim and Megan had lived in, so seeing all the Portlanders on the move caused Megan to wonder where everyone was going.

She said, "I think I could get used to this."

At six-foot-three, Tim looked down on most folks, and few more so than his diminutive wife. Still walking, he looked down at her and said, "Really? This is fun to visit and experience, but I'm not sure I would like to live in this. Give me a house with a yard on a quiet street, and I will be quite happy."

"They have that here, too, silly."

"Yeah, I know. It's still a little too fast-paced for my liking." They made their way toward the next intersection—Oak

Street—and Tim tossed his empty cup into a trashcan. "So, tell me about this bookstore we are about to see. Is it like a Books-A-Million or Barnes and Noble?"

"It's like both of those…combined…and on steroids." She laughed, then said, "It's seventy thousand square feet of space and the largest privately owned bookstore in the world."

"Gee, you sound like their spokesperson." She elbowed him in the side, and he gave an exaggerated *oomph*. They arrived at the intersection with Oak Street and were again waiting on the light. The density of the automobile and pedestrian traffic picked up noticeably as they were closing in on Burnside. Tim asked, "You think they have a Sci-fi section inside?"

She looked up at him and said, "I bet they will have every Sci-fi book ever written."

"Well then, by God, this I gotta see."

❊　❊　❊　❊　❊

The corner entrance of the bookstore said nothing of the size of the inside, and the red and white marquee-style sign announcing you were entering Powell's Books welcomed you into a four-level wonderland of new and used books. Megan was an avid reader and was as excited about this as she was for Tim visiting his beer utopia just two blocks west of here. They both paused steps inside the door as they surveyed what was before them. The place reminded Tim more of a collegiate bookstore than a Books-A-Million-style retail space. Grabbing maps—because you needed a map—they each went their separate ways: Tim staying on the street level going to the Science Fiction section and Megan going up a level for books on the Pacific Northwest; neither in a rush, as they browsed while they walked.

The Pacific Northwest section was to the immediate right of the elevator, and Megan had been there long enough to pick out three books she wanted to buy. She was holding them in the crook of her arm when the ding announcing the elevator's arrival caught her attention. Instinctively she looked in the direction of the sound and saw a lone female exit the elevator car.

The girl who got off the elevator was of average build with chin-length blue-black hair, wearing dark jeans and a red Trail Blazers hoodie. The girl turned right off the elevator and looked up, making eye contact with Megan; the girl stopped in her tracks. A look of recognition showed on her face, then vanished just as quickly. The girl put her head down and her hood up as she blew past Megan toward the stairwell exit, where she slammed the bar on the door and was gone leaving Megan staring after her.

❖ ❖ ❖ ❖ ❖

Sitting at the thick wood-slab bar inside the Library Taphouse—beers on the bar and books at their feet—Tim hoisted his pint glass and said, "To the city of books."

Megan laughed and met his glass with hers. The smell of beer and the hum of a multitude of conversations in the busy restaurant relaxed them.

"I have to say," said Todd with his beer at his lips, "I never thought 'visit bookstore' would make a to-do list visiting a city, but that place was neat." He drank down some of his beer—a local porter—and set it on the bar.

He was surveying the multitude of beer taps, already deciding which beer he would order next, when the bartender—a youngish-looking guy with a hipster mustache curled at the ends and kind eyes—appeared, offering to take their food order.

Tim ordered the fish and chips along with another beer. "Anything local."

When Megan did not respond to the bartender, Tim noticed her staring into her beer. He said, "Do you know what you want to eat?" No response. "Megan?"

"Huh?" she said, looking up at Tim.

Cocking his head to the bartender, he said, "Do you know what you would like to order, or do you need some more time?"

She shook her head as if trying to clear it. "Sorry, yeah." She absently viewed the menu and said, "Uh, the turkey Reuben." The bartender turned away, and Megan added, "And another beer, please."

Orders placed, and the bartender gone, Tim said, "What's up?"

"It's weird." Hooking a thumb over her right shoulder, she said, "I'm pretty sure I saw someone I knew back there."

Tim leaned back on his backless bar stool and looked past her. "Where?"

"At the bookstore."

"Someone from Tacoma?"

Megan, looking down at the bar, shook her head. Then meeting his gaze, she said, "From Towne."

"From Towne? Who was it?"

"Do you remember Pamela Rogers? We worked together at Bishop and Barnes."

Tim thought for a moment and said, "I think so. She was an accountant, right?"

"That's right. She was one of the CPAs. Anyway, I'm fairly certain I just saw her sister, Roni."

He shared her surprise. "This is a long way from home. Did you speak to her?"

Megan shook her head. "No. It was...odd. She got off the elevator, we made eye contact, and then she practically ran to the emergency exit."

"Are you sure it was her?"

"Not a hundred percent, I suppose, but I feel like I know her well enough that I would recognize her."

They were interrupted by the bartender delivering another round. Megan continued, "You know, I remember Roni having longish white-blonde hair always in a ponytail, and the girl in the bookstore had short dark, maybe even black hair."

Tim shrugged. "Maybe it wasn't her."

"I always thought she had a distinctive face: her and Pamela. They had deep-set eyes and angular features with hollow cheeks and a squared-off nose. Honestly, I believe I saw Pamela in that girl's face before I recognized her as Roni."

Their attention got diverted when a group of guys who appeared to be regulars came up to the bar receiving a boisterous greeting from the bartender. Space at the bar was at a premium, and Tim and Megan kept these four gentlemen from sitting together, so they agreed to each move down a seat. The regulars bought them a round for their troubles, and Megan and Tim briefly engaged them in conversation. They explained they were visiting from Tacoma—where it so happened one of the four guys grew up—and after exchanging a few more pleasantries, they focused on their respective groups.

"So," Tim said, trying to refocus on the conversation, "did she recognize you?"

Her voice gaining conviction, she said, "That's the other thing. I believe she did. At least it looked like it. Anyway, I think that's what makes this whole thing so weird—her reaction to seeing me." She ran her finger up her beer glass, through the condensation. "You know, when we made eye contact, it was as if she saw a ghost. She looked, I don't know, almost scared."

❈   ❈   ❈   ❈   ❈

The rhythmic buzz of Megan's cell phone woke her at just after 5:00 in the morning. The combination of having been in bed for less than four hours and the quantity of beer and cock-tails in the last nineteen or so hours caused her to wake with a start. Heart pounding, she had no idea where she was. The Benson Hotel room curtains made for a very dark room, aid-ing her confusion. She finally located her phone, but not before knocking her watch and the clock radio to the floor.

"Hello," she said in a thick tongue.

"Megan?" replied a female voice, the antithesis of Megan's.

"Hello?" repeated Megan.

"Megan, this is Pamela Rogers." Not receiving an immedi-ate response, she said, "Oh no. The time change. It's what, ten after five out there? Oh, Megan, I'm so sorry; I didn't even think about that. Just call me back later." The call ended, and Megan instantly fell back asleep.

Almost four hours later, Megan was wearing a white terry-cloth robe she found in the room's closet and was blow-drying her hair when it hit her. She turned off the hair dryer, walked to her side of the bed, and began looking around.

Tim was sitting up in the bed leaning against the headboard, remote in hand, watching SportsCenter. Without taking his eyes off the television, he said, "What are you doing?"

"Looking for my phone." She picked up the clock radio and put it on the nightstand, and continued searching, picking up the sheets to look on the floor beside the bed.

Tim finally looked at her. "What are you looking for on the floor?"

"I just remembered that I got a call this morning from Pamela, and I guess I didn't bother putting the phone back on the table when I hung up. I found the clock on the floor."

Tim leaned over and gave a cursory scan of the immediate area.

Megan lifted the cool white sheets and found her phone down towards the foot of the bed. She scanned the call list and said, "Five-oh-eight."

"What?"

"Pamela called at five–oh-eight this morning." Phone in hand, she flopped onto the bed. "Ugh, I don't feel so great."

Smiling, Tim slid over and ran his hand up her bare thigh. "It's because you're getting old. Been a while since we've done that."

She brushed a few strands of damp hair from her eyes, leaned against the headboard, closed her eyes, and let out a resounding exhale. "Yeah, well, I guess I can't rally like I used to." She peered over at Tim with one open eye, and said, "But we had fun yesterday, didn't we."

"That we did," he said, a devilish grin on his face. After a moment, he gave her a playful push and said, "Now finish getting dressed so we can grab brunch."

"Don't be ugly. You haven't even gotten out of bed yet." She got out of bed, walked over to the window, and threw back the curtains bathing the predominantly beige room in sunlight. She enjoyed watching the city come to life on a lazy Sunday morning. She heard Tim get out of bed and pad into the bathroom. The shower turned on.

She pulled the phone from her robe pocket and dialed Pamela's number.

"Oh my gosh, girl, I am so sorry for the early phone call," Pamela said when she answered.

"Don't worry about it. Tim and I are visiting Portland, and we had a late night, so sleep was not hard to come by. How have you been?"

"Been doing okay; just busy with work and children. You know how it is."

"That I do," said Megan wincing a bit at her nagging headache. She left the window and sat in the upholstered chair in the corner, putting her feet up on the ottoman.

Pamela said, "So, how long has it been? Three years?"

"Has it been that long? We did so well keeping in touch for a while after we moved, but then life got in the way."

"Tell me about it. How are you liking it?"

"We love it. The landscape and the people are so different from anything we knew before coming out here. This has been a great opportunity."

"How are the children doing?"

"Great. You know how kids are; they adjust pretty fast. Much quicker than mom and dad." They shared a laugh. "So, Tim Jr. is starting seventh grade and playing football this fall. Landon will be going into the fifth grade, and he's really gotten into karate, and Gracie has just started gymnastics. We found a great gym for her in Seattle. It's a bit of a drive, but so worth it."

"That's great, Megan. I'm so happy you all are doing well. We sure do miss you and Tim."

The shower turned off, and Tim danced into the room with nothing on. Megan is unsuccessful in suppressing a laugh as she says, "That's so sweet. We miss y'all too." Tim continued with suggestive moves, and Megan cleared her throat to regain her composure and said, "Are Joey and Jenny keeping you busy?"

"Of course they are. Always on the go, something you know all about."

"That I do." Megan, smiling, mouthed the word *stop* as Tim, still naked, danced toward her.

Pamela said, "Here I am rambling, and you on a getaway. I got your voicemail last night. Did you have anything specific you needed? I can't imagine this was a social call, or at least I hope not, given that you're on a date weekend and all."

"Yeah, well, it was the weirdest thing. I saw your sister up here yesterday. At least, I think it was her. Her hair was dark and much shorter, but I'm pretty certain it was Roni. Anyway, it bothered me not knowing for certain, so I wanted to ask if she was out here."

No response.

After four seconds, Megan said, "Pamela? You still there?"

A timid voice responded, "Yeah," Pamela cleared her throat, "I'm here."

More silence.

"Pamela?"

"Where did you see her?" asked a voice devoid of emotion.

"At a bookstore in Portland." Megan sensed something was wrong.

A sob broke the silence. "Tell me about it."

"What?"

"Tell me about seeing her."

"Pamela, what's wrong?"

"Just tell me." Pamela's voice had taken on an edge.

Megan quickly told of her encounter with the woman she believed to be her sister. She recounted the strange way the woman reacted at seeing her and reiterated her belief that the girl was Roni Lane.

After several seconds of silence, which Megan was not going to break first, Pamela said, "Megan, Roni's dead."

Now it was Megan's turn to be silent. Finally, she said, "What?"

"Roni's dead. She was murdered almost two years ago."

"Dead." It was part statement and part question.

"She was murdered."

"What? How?" was all Megan could think to say.

"They don't know how, exactly. She was never found, but they just convicted the guy who did it."

❈   ❈   ❈   ❈   ❈

As soon as she ended her call with Megan Pope, Pamela Rogers called the only person she knew in law enforcement: Barclay Griffith, a client of her accounting firm. She explained to Barclay who she was and how one of the firm's partners gave her his cell number. She apologized for the weekend intrusion and quickly explained it was about her sister's murder.

Barclay had met her before during various visits with his accountant and seeing her at Chamber of Commerce events. He relayed that he knew who she was and assured her that the call was no intrusion at all. After explaining the reason for her phone call, she got his attention.

Not quite an hour later, Barclay and Winston Fitzsimmons arrived separately and were seated at Pamela Rogers' glass-topped kitchen table, each with a cup of coffee in front of them that neither had touched. Upon entering the house, Barclay could not help but steal a couple of glances around the home's interior, having only seen it through the lens of the crime scene photographer. Barclay was wearing jeans and a golf shirt, his casual dress contradicting Fitz, who wore a tan and light blue windowpane suit with a sky blue shirt and tangerine tie. Pamela was dressed for house cleaning, which she was doing when she got the call from Megan; cleaning supplies sat on the counter. The house smelled of lemon wood polish.

"Okay, Pamela, I want you to tell me everything that your friend told you," said Barclay leaning on the tabletop.

"Her name is Megan."

"Yes, I'm sorry." Then in a softened tone, he said, "Tell me everything that Megan told you about seeing Roni."

Pamela wrapped her hands around the still-full cup of coffee, trying to absorb its remaining warmth. She stared into the caramel-colored liquid and said, "Do you think it could be her?"

Barclay reached over and placed his hand on her wrist. "That's what we're here to find out, but first, I need you to tell me everything Megan told you."

She nodded and proceeded to tell Barclay and Fitz what Megan had relayed over the phone, alternating her gaze between the two men who returned her eye contact, only listening, not taking any notes.

When she was done, Barclay leaned back in his chair and looked over at Fitz, who returned his gaze, betraying nothing of what he was thinking. He looked at Pamela and said, "Let's talk about what we know to be fact." Pamela gave a barely perceptible nod. "First, it was her blood in the house—a lot of it. Secondly, her body was never recovered—"

Pamela jumped in: "But the jury convicted Clements for killing her."

Barclay responded with an even voice in an attempt to keep Pamela calm. "That's true, but we simply can't ignore the absence of a body when we have a potential sighting of the victim." Pamela opened her mouth to speak, and Barclay put a hand up and said, "That doesn't mean the jury got it wrong, okay?" He was nodding to her in hopes of getting feedback that she understood. She nodded slightly. "That said, we have to look into this and do it quietly. Until we know something more substantive, we cannot let word about this get out, okay? The Clements family getting wind of this could open up a huge can of worms." He paused to allow what he said to sink in. "I need Megan's phone number."

Pamela's tear-filled gaze drifted off to nowhere. She remained silent as tears spilled from her eyes, trailed down her face, and splashed onto the glass.

❖   ❖   ❖   ❖   ❖

"What do you think?" Barclay asked Fitz as they sat on a bench under a large shade tree outside the venerated Local Burger Joint. LBJs, as it was known in localese, was a walk-up burger spot that had been serving up the same burger from the same griddle to generations of Towne citizens. It was only open for lunch and stayed busy; there was a line before it opened, and they invariably had to cut the line off at closing. This was the first place they passed after leaving Pamela Rogers' house, so they stopped in to parse out everything they had learned in the last few hours. They spotted someone they knew toward the front of the line and got them to order a chocolate milkshake and a bottle of water each.

Fitz considered the question as he fish-hooked the tobacco from his mouth and threw it into the bushes. He took a drink of water, swished it around, and spat. "Honestly, Boss?" The question was rhetorical, but Barclay nodded anyway. "I think it could be the girl."

Barclay took in the people and the cars coming and going from the small structure and the parking lot around it. The gardenias ringing the business gave off a pleasant smell in the warm air. "I do, too," he finally said, followed by a curse through clenched teeth.

A few moments passed—Barclay bobbing the straw up and down in his shake, thinking, and Fitz sitting back, legs crossed, eyes hidden behind a pair of aviators waiting on marching orders. An angry metallic crunch broke the silence and drew the attention of the prosecutor and investigator. The source of the interruption was one car backing out of a parking spot and into another vehicle doing the same. The two drivers—one male, one female—did not get out immediately but did get out simultaneously and converged on the contact point.

Barclay shook his head. "People, man." Fitz laughed a low chuckle. "Alright, here's the deal," he said, leaning in, "I need you to dig up everything you can on Veronica Lane. I'm going to call Megan Pope and then get with the forensic scientist who tested the blood at the scene and identified it as Veronica's." Fitz nodded, and the pair rose to leave. "I know this goes without saying—"

"But you're going to say it anyway."

"This is between us."

Barclay was at the driver's side of his SUV, and Fitz was at his back, unlocking the driver's door to his sedan. Barclay turned, and across the roof of the gleaming Crown Vic, he said, "There's something here, Fitz. We just need to find it."

* * * * *

"Megan Pope?"

"Speaking."

"This is Barclay Griffith. I am an assistant district attorney with the Towne County DA's office. I'm calling about Veronica Lane." Barclay paused to see if Megan would say anything. Hearing nothing, he continued. "I spoke with Pamela Rogers earlier today. She called me after she spoke with you this morning, and I'm following up. She gave me your cell number; I hope that's okay."

"Yeah, sure. That's fine." Megan's tone of voice was one Barclay heard often. No one liked speaking with the police or a prosecutor, whether they did anything wrong or not.

"Do you have a few minutes to talk, or would you rather I call back later?" Barclay was home in his study, leaning back in his desk chair, bare feet on the desk crossed at the ankle.

He could hear her muffled voice talking to someone and, based on the background noise, guessed she wasn't indoors. After a few seconds she said into the phone: "No, this is fine. Just on the road headed back home." Her voice was losing its skepticism.

"Washington state, right?"

"The very one."

"I love it up there in the Northwest. I've been to Seattle a couple of times and Portland once. Drove along the Oregon coast down the one-oh-one; absolutely beautiful. Now, I love our sugar-white sandy beaches on the Gulf Coast, but what you have out there is special."

The small talk continued for another minute or two until Barclay felt Megan becoming more comfortable talking to him. He could hear the angst in her voice when he brought up her encounter in the Portland bookstore. To put her at ease, he assured her this was not an official investigation, and nothing was being recorded or written down. He was merely following up on the earlier meeting with Pamela Rogers and how, as a prosecutor, he had a duty to seek the truth no matter what it was or where it led.

"And if that *was* Veronica Lane I saw?" she had asked him when she finished her narrative.

"Then we have a problem," he responded matter-of-factly. He went on to ask some questions about the brief meeting. When he asked her what gave her the initial impression that it was Veronica Lane she was seeing, she told him about the distinctive facial features shared by the sisters. Barclay immediately saw Pamela in his mind's eye and knew exactly what Megan was referring to; his pulse ticked up a notch. He asked a few more perfunctory questions to see if anything substantial shook loose. Nothing did.

"What can you tell me about Ms. Lane?" asked Barclay.

"What do you want to know?"

"Let's start with how well you knew her."

"I knew her well enough, I guess. Pamela and I frequently talked at work; ate lunch together most days. Outside of her children, Roni was the topic of conversation with her."

Barclay was about to ask another question, when Megan said, "Why aren't you asking Pamela about this? I mean, it's her sister."

"I like to get an unfiltered view of a person. Close friends and family members tend to give a sanitized version of those they love; dress them up or leave out the warts."

Barclay could hear Megan Pope thinking. He let the silence drag on before he added, "This information isn't for any purpose other than background. No one else even needs to know we spoke."

"I'm not worried about that. It's just...I don't know. When Tim and I moved away, Pamela and I grew apart, you know, over time and before this morning, we hadn't spoken since, well, it's been a while, and then to hear that Roni is dead..." Emotion was filling her voice. "This has just been a lot, Mr. Griffith."

"I understand. Take your time."

He heard her take a deep breath before saying, "Pamela worried over Roni."

"How do you mean?"

"Their father died several years ago, and Roni took it particularly hard. She was still in high school, and I think Pamela saw it as her responsibility to help her mother and be a second parent. You know, fill that void. Roni went through a bit of a rebellious stage as a result. 'You can't tell me what to do,' 'You're not my mom.' That sort of thing. Honestly, I think Pamela still sees that as her role to a degree, whether she admits it or not."

"Was there anything specific Pamela was worried about?"

"Yes and no. I think she had a general worry—a parental worry. But she was quite concerned about Roni's future. Making sure she set herself on a path where she could make a future for herself."

"Why was she so worried about that?"

"Roni is a nurturer, Mr. Griffith, a caregiver at heart; she wanted nothing more than to help people. Because of that, she always wanted to be a nurse, and Pamela believed she would be wonderful at it. After their father died, Roni got into a pretty dark place. Pamela never said anything specific, but I got the impression she may have gotten into drugs. Her grades got worse, and she skipped school more than she was going. She started in about not going to college, and that was when Pamela had enough. She told me she wasn't going to watch her sister throw her life away. It's like she believed in Roni more than Roni believed in Roni. Does that make sense?"

"Absolutely."

"It took some time, but Roni got things in order, went to the community college, and got her LPN. I don't think Roni knows this, but Pamela paid for part of her tuition."

Barclay could hear admiration and wistfulness in her voice. The weight of it all beginning to hit. She sniffed, and Barclay wondered if she were crying.

She continued: "After graduation, she was hired as a nurse at the hospital. Despite everything, she ended up with her dream job. To see the two of them…those women were thick as thieves."

Megan caught herself and made a noise Barclay couldn't decipher before continuing. "Well, they were very close when I moved out here, and, as far as I knew, any demons Roni had fought were behind her. Pamela was so proud of her little sister."

There was a long pause. Because of the gravity and tone the conversation had taken on, he thought it almost rude to ask another question. He was processing what he had heard, thinking about what he needed to know, and determining what he would ask next. The lull was long enough to cause Megan to ask Barclay if he were still there. He said he was.

Barclay: "From what I gathered from Pamela, you didn't know Ms. Lane had been killed?"

"No. No idea. I felt awful and even a little embarrassed about that."

"Pardon me for asking this, but how did you not know? You and Pamela seemed pretty close."

"We were. She was my best friend in the office, but it was a work friendship." She was quiet, thinking, then said, "She was divorced with a couple of children. I don't believe the father was in the picture, so when she wasn't at work, she was busy being a single mom, you know. For one reason or another, we never socialized after hours."

Barclay asked more questions to better understand Veronica Lane. Some Megan could answer, but most she could not. After a few more minutes, the conversation abated.

A few seconds of silence as Barclay gathered his thoughts. He could hear the radio droning on in the background, and then a car horn honked. Finally, he said, "Alright, Megan, I want you to do something for me. I want you to close your eyes and think about the instant you made eye contact. Without thinking about it, was it her?"

One second passed, then two. "Yes."

❊   ❊   ❊   ❊   ❊

The lunch hour was approaching, and Judge Pullman's Monday status docket was winding down. Court had started at 9:00 a.m. sharp, and there had been a steady parade of defendants and probationers going before the bench for the better part of three hours. Barclay had begun the docket handling cases and gave way to Clayton after only handling four files; this was part of Clayton's education. It was also a perk of being the senior prosecutor in the courtroom.

Barclay loved most things about being a prosecutor, but he detested status and review dockets; it was boring and mindless minutia. He could take only so many failed drug tests and people behind on their court-ordered payments. Making it worse was Judge Pullman's need to have a heart-to-heart chat with every defendant that appeared before him and stretch what should be a thirty-minute rocket docket to a three-hour marathon.

Once Clayton had taken the reigns of the docket, Barclay sat at a table tending to other business: answering emails and catching up on the previous evening's sports headlines.

"Only three more defendants, and we're done," said Clayton, relief evident in his voice.

"Good. I'm hungry," said Barclay.

"Who's next, Mr. White," said Judge Pullman impassively. He was looking at his laptop, which was a good sign. It meant he was also losing steam.

Clayton eyed the top file in his hand, called the defendant's name, and went back to work at the bench. Barclay wrapped up what he was working on and began to get everything organized and ready to leave the moment the last defendant was seen.

The din of the courtroom had grown quiet as the mass of humanity was whittled down to near zero; the door to the courtroom opened with a *whoosh*. Barclay, who was on his phone reading an article about a Major League Baseball trade involving a team in rebuilding mode sending their only superstar to a National League East contender, turned and looked behind him, afraid he would see a defendant late to court. Instead, he saw Fitz making his way to the front of the courtroom.

Fitz approached the table, leaned over Barclay's shoulder, and said in a low voice: Drop by my place tonight around 8:30 and come thirsty.

❋   ❋   ❋   ❋   ❋

Winston Fitzsimmons lived in a newish two-bedroom townhouse with all the trappings of bachelorhood. He had a well-kept, but no frills landscape on the outside, and on the inside was a well-worn leather recliner and matching sofa, empty wall space, a huge flat-screen television, Klipsch home theater system, and no tchotchke whatsoever.

Barclay knocked at 8:30 sharp and was greeted by Fitz, who had traded in the day's suit for jeans and a faded New Orleans Saints t-shirt extolling their 2009 Super Bowl win; his casualness an incongruity to the normally fastidious investigator. Barclay had traded his suit for a navy summer-weight sport coat, yellow v-neck t-shirt, and jeans.

The two shook hands—Fitz's beefy paw swallowing Barclay's hand, which wasn't small. "Come in, come in," Fitz said. "I've got something that you'll appreciate."

He led Barclay through the den, down the hall, and to the guest bedroom. He stood to the side of the door and motioned for Barclay to look inside, ala Vanna White. Fitz had transformed the bedroom into a study with mahogany walls and a built-in bookcase spanning one wall containing not so much as a magazine. He had installed stylish thick shag carpet and two-leather club chairs in the middle, a round end table between them. Another huge flat-screen television hung on the wall opposite.

"Fitz, this is great. Seriously, this is awesome," said Barclay as he dropped into one of the chairs.

Fitz laughed and said, "Check this out." Barclay stood and watched as Fitz opened what Barclay assumed was an armoire but was, in actuality, a bar.

"Alright, this is where I am hanging out after work. Every day."

Fitz grabbed a bottle and handed it to Barclay, who read the label. Barclay said, "Okay, where the hell did you get this?" It was a bottle of George T. Stagg bourbon.

Fitz said, "You remember that case where that father from Kentucky killed his three children, drove down here, and tried to sink his car in Towne Lake to dispose of the bodies?"

"Yeah. That was a while ago, right?"

"Three years or so. Anyway, they just convicted the sonofabitch, and the lead investigator sent this to me as a thank you for our help catching that asshole."

"Wow. The most you ever got from me is some beers and barbecue."

Fitz laughed and said, "Want to break the seal with me?"

"Does a bear have hair?"

Bourbons poured and both men sitting in a chair, Fitz opened the doors on the middle table and pulled out a heavy square crystal ashtray and a box of cigars—Fuente Fuente Opus X. He placed the ashtray on the table with a thud and offered the open box of cigars to Barclay who took one and said, "Smoking inside now?"

Fitz retrieved a small remote control from inside the table, pointed it skyward, pressed a button, and a green light came on beside a vent in the ceiling. "Had this ventilation system installed. Does a nice job removing the smoke."

The two smoked and sipped in silence for a few minutes—each savoring both the cigar and the bourbon—before Barclay spoke: "I'm guessing this invitation wasn't simply about three hundred dollar bourbon and a thirty dollar cigar."

Speaking around the cigar in his mouth, Fitz said, "It's about Veronica Lane."

Another puff, then Barclay pulled the cigar from his mouth. "What did you find out?"

Fitz pointed at Barclay while holding the cigar and said, "There's definitely something going on there."

"What do you mean?"

"Well, first, I searched our system to see if we ever opened a file on her. Nothing. Then I did an NCIC search—nothing there either; looked like this girl was clean. Clean as a fucking whistle. Yes sir," he said with a nod, then took a drink of Stagg, followed by a couple of puffs on his cigar.

"Now, Fitz, I know you didn't ask me here to tell me you didn't find anything."

Fitz, who was facing the blank television on the wall, cut his eyes at Barclay and smiled—cigar clenched in his teeth.

❊   ❊   ❊   ❊   ❊

A pall of gray-white smoke was accumulating at the ceiling, and the first glass of bourbon was working through Barclay's system, relaxing him—loosening his mind up for freer thinking. Barclay grabbed the bottle of Stagg and filled each empty glass with an inch of the amber-colored liquid. Setting the bottle on the table between them, he moved his chair to face Fitz. After he was seated, he said, "What did you find out?"

Fitz took two puffs of his cigar, then leaned forward, resting his elbows on his knees. He said, "Your girl was being investigated for stealing from the hospital's drug dispensary. Morphine, Oxy's, Xanax, you name it."

"How long ago was this?"

"The investigation started several months before she was *murdered*."

"Wait, she was still working for the hospital at the time of her disappearance. How far had they gotten with the investigation?"

"Pretty damn far. Word is, they were in the process of getting an arrest warrant when someone put the kybosh on it."

Barclay, "Who stopped it? The cops?"

"Nope. According to my guy over there, word came down from on high."

"On high? What does that mean?"

Fitz gave an exasperated look. "From the DA's office."

"Did you get a name?"

Fitz puffed his cigar a few times before responding. "Your boy Kingery."

If this surprised Barclay, he didn't show it. He just sat back in his chair, staring at the bottle of bourbon—thinking.

Fitz grabbed his iPhone off the small table, worked his thumb over the screen, and Dave Brubeck's *Take Five* filled the room. Fitz thumbed the volume lower and said, as much to himself as to Barclay, "Too damn quiet in here. Can't think." He laid the phone down. "I talked to Peters in narcotics. It seems the hospital noticed some drugs missing during an internal audit and, through their own investigation, developed Ms. Lane as their primary suspect in the thefts. Their in-house counsel met with Maggie about it, and she got the TPD narcotics unit involved.

"Peters got the hospital to hold off firing her so they could make their case. He said they were on her for over eight months. They had video of the thefts and everything; the case locked up tighter than Dick's hatband. Turns everything over to our office to present to the grand jury. Then one day he inquires about the status of the case, you know, 'when's grand jury?' that type of thing, and he's told there is no Veronica Lane scheduled for grand jury."

When Fitz paused to puff on his cigar, Barclay said, "Was he told the case wasn't set, or was he told that there was no case at all?"

Fitz bobbed his head and said, "He was told that there was no defendant by that name with a case pending grand jury and, after some digging, found out there was no case, period. No paper trail that he could find. It was as if the case never existed."

The pair sat in silence. Fitz enjoyed his smoke and his drink while Barclay ignored his as he thought. Finally, Barclay stood, placed his cigar in the heavy crystal ashtray, and walked over to the window. Peering out into the backyard, he said, "What's the connection between her and Kingery?"

"Don't know that there is one." Fitz drained the remainder of his bourbon and said, "Look, Barclay, I'm just riffing here on this Kingery stuff. Maybe there's something there, maybe not. Give me some time to nail it down."

Landscape lighting illuminated the manicured rear lawn, and Barclay saw the eyes of a small animal glowing back at him. He turned back to Fitz and said, "I have a feeling that you're on to something with this; we just have to find that connection. Once we have that, well..." Barclay's voice trailed off as he retreated into his thoughts. After a few seconds, he said, "I suppose before we do anything, we need to nail down this Oregon sighting. Unless Roni Lane is alive, this whole line of investigation is moot."

"Yeah, but if she is alive...ho-ly shit."

CHAPTER 14

THE C. L. RABREN Laboratory in Montgomery is a single-story eighties-era flat-roofed brick structure that houses one of only two autopsy labs in the state. Though the building's exterior had not aged gracefully, its interior had recently undergone a comprehensive renovation and rivaled any medical examiner's office in design and technology.

When Barclay and Clayton arrived at the ME's office just before 10:00 in the morning, they had their choice of parking places. There were only three other vehicles in the parking lot: two white Chevrolet Malibu sedans and a full-size white Ford van—all with the ADFS logo on the front driver and passenger doors.

Barclay and Clayton shrugged into their suit coats as they approached the lab's entrance. Despite the early hour, the air was heavy with heat and humidity to the point that they broke a sweat traversing the small parking lot; the blast of cool air when they opened the door was a welcomed respite. Upon entering the lab, a receptionist sat to the left of the entrance behind a glass partition. The public portion of the lobby reminded Barclay of a loft apartment building with a lot of glass, exposed brick, and wood beams. The reception area belied the hospital-like setting just beyond the double doors leading to the office's inner workings. It smelled like industrial cleaner and faintly of fresh paint.

The receptionist, Carol Bolling, was a humorless woman of indeterminate age. She had served in this role for decades but looked oddly young. She had a short, man's style haircut that was mostly gray and wore large eyeglasses that she had had so long they were back in style; the kids would call them retro. She wore a chain attached to her glasses, but Barclay could not recall a time he had ever seen her without them on her face, which was set in a perpetual scowl that did not invite casual conversation. He had also never seen her without the white cardigan sweater with the ADFS logo embroidered on the left chest. The cuffs were filthy and were covered in tiny lint balls.

"Hey, Ms. Bolling, how are you today?" said Barclay in his most disarming smile and voice.

"Fine," was the curt reply that was her nature as she stared back expressionless.

Barclay gave it a few seconds trying to force her to say something more, but she didn't, and he knew she wouldn't. He had been here and spoken to her at least two dozen times, yet she always acted as if it were her first time meeting him. He knew from talking to other folks that she was the same with everyone who visited. He cleared his throat as he glanced at Clayton, then to Ms. Bolling, and said, "Yes, well, we are here to see Dr. Bev." Ms. Bolling's eyes narrowed, then Barclay said, "I mean Dr. Bevilacqua."

She looked down and scanned the counter in front of her as if looking for something stating that they were supposed to be there. Without looking up, she said, "Is she expecting you?"

"Yes, she is."

"Very well. Sign in," she said, sliding a clipboard under the partition toward them. She looked at Clayton for the first time and said, "Both of you." Barclay signed them both in and handed Clayton one of two visitor badges attached to the clipboard. "Dr. Bevilacqua currently has a case in suite two."

Signed in and badges affixed to their lapels, Barclay and Clayton were making their way through the double doors and into the inner sanctum of the lab when Carol Bolling spoke in her authoritarian voice: "Have a seat, and I will let her know you are here."

Barclay, a hand on the door, said, "We know where we're going."

The grim, unblinking countenance behind the window invited neither argument nor disobedience. Barclay and Clayton dutifully retreated to a couple of chairs to wait.

❈　❈　❈　❈　❈

They had barely gotten settled when the receptionist told them that Dr. Bevilacqua was available. Barclay didn't notice Ms. Bolling speaking with anyone, so he wondered if what he had just experienced was a weird flex by the receptionist. He glanced back at her as he reached the doors, and he could swear he saw the ghost of a smirk as he pushed through.

The narrow hallway had silver-gray walls and a gray-blue tile floor with can lights in the ceiling providing ample illumination throughout the corridor. Four offices—two on each side of the hallway—housed the lab's investigators and, at the end of the hallway, were two sets of double hollow stainless steel doors. Above the doors on the left was the number *one*, while the number *two* was above the doors on the right.

Clayton grabbed Barclay's arm and stopped in the middle of the hall. He said, "What did that lady mean about the doctor having a case?"

"Means she's cutting a body," Barclay said with raised eyebrows, an expression of giddiness. Barclay started toward their destination, and after a moment, Clayton followed.

Suite two was twelve hundred square feet of bright light and stainless steel. The walls and floor were a surgical green color, and everything from the cabinets to the shelving units to the two autopsy tables gleamed in the harsh lighting. The room was maintained at sixty degrees, which caused both Barclay and Clayton to shiver slightly, still being a bit damp with sweat. A body occupied the table farthest from the entrance; Clayton let out an audible gasp. The smell was ever-present: a combination of the metallic scent of blood and the stench of death. It was pungent, it was invasive, and it had a way of adhering to you—both physically and mentally. Barclay had been present for more than a dozen autopsies, and he still had not gotten used to the smell. Clayton let out a gagging noise.

Barclay turned to look at him when the door on the opposite wall opened, and a thin man wearing scrubs and earbuds danced into the room. He almost made it to the occupied table when he saw movement out of the corner of his eye and stopped, clearly startled. Reaching for his heart with his right hand and pulling the earbuds out with his left, he gave a nervous laugh. "Damn, Barclay, you about scared the shit outta me."

Laughing, Barclay said, "What's up, Willie?"

Willie Raines was five-foot-eight with a head shaved smooth, skin the color of cappuccino, skinny tattooed arms hanging from his blue scrubs, and a genial personality contagious to anyone in the same room. He had been an autopsy tech for seventeen years and had seen just about everything.

"About to have a heart attack, is what," the tech said, still catching his breath.

"Sorry about that. Dr. Bev around?" asked Barclay.

"You just missed her. She went to her office."

"Alright, man. We'll see you."

Willie gave a head nod and put his earbuds back in before shifting his focus to the pale nude body on the table.

❊   ❊   ❊   ❊   ❊

Barclay found the medical examiner's office and knocked on the doorframe.

"Well, hello there, Barclay," said Dr. Leonora Bevilacqua in slightly accented English. The longest-tenured medical examiner in the state stood behind her desk and motioned with her hands for the two men to enter. "How long has it been, dear?"

"Better than a month of Sundays for sure." He smiled and said, "You look amazing as always, Dr. Bev. How a man hasn't made an honest woman out of you yet, I do not know."

"Who said I want to be an honest woman?"

Barclay laughed and introduced her to Clayton.

The copper-haired Dr. Bevilacqua was fifty-four years old and tall, standing almost six feet. She has a full, curvy figure and is exceedingly unpretentious, which made her a great deal of fun to be around—especially after hours.

Her office could be best described as organized chaos. Every available surface was covered with stacks of papers, forensic reports, and autopsy photos. On the wall behind her desk hung a medium-sized corkboard flanked by two floor-to-ceiling bookcases. A mass of subpoenas compelling the doctor's appearance at various trials or hearings was pinned to the corkboard. Her bookcases were filled with forensic texts and thick white three-ring binders.

Dr. Bev liked to travel, and one of the slate-gray walls of her office chronicled her adventures in pictures: her in the foreground with the Eiffel Tower in the background, the exact composition with the leaning tower of Pisa, London's Big Ben,

Stonehenge, the Washington Monument, Cinderella's castle at Disney World, and several others.

Barclay noticed a picture that hadn't been there the last time he had visited. It was the medical examiner on a knee surrounded by penguins. He commented on it, and she told him it was taken a few months ago in Antarctica—she had now visited every continent.

She came to Alabama by way of North Carolina, Canada, and Italy. Her grandparents moved their family, including a young son—her father—from Italy shortly after World War II and wound up in the Canadian province of Quebec, where she was born. After graduating high school and college, she received her M.D. from the Université de Montréal. She was then accepted into the Wake Forest School of Medicine's forensic pathology residency program in Winston-Salem, North Carolina. After completing her residency program, she was hired as Alabama's first female medical examiner more than twenty-two years ago.

The small office was uncomfortably cold, and the small space heater under her desk was both slightly warming the room and adding a hum of background noise. Her office had the faint fresh paint smell of the lobby accented with eucalyptus from the hand lotion she habitually applied post-cut.

Introductions made, she looked at Clayton and said, "You ever see an autopsy?"

Clayton shook his head *no*.

"Fantastic. Willie is prepping a body for Dr. Monroe. You ought to go check it out." Clayton stared at her, then at Barclay, then back again. "Seriously, you need to see one. I believe that fellow was killed in a car wreck. Should be a good one to watch."

Barclay said, "Go ahead; I'll grab you when we're done here. Just go back to where we saw Willie. He'll get you squared away."

Clayton left the office looking like he was being sent to the firing squad.

Barclay leaned out of the office and, seeing Clayton turn toward the autopsy suite, said with a laugh, "You're so bad. That boy may quit after this."

"Ah, bullshit. If he can't handle that, he isn't cut out to be a prosecutor—pun *intended*." Barclay laughed. "Now, down to business. I've got a very interesting blood report for you."

"Is my theory correct?" asked Barclay.

"I read back through the original analysis of the blood found at the scene and didn't see any indication of anything unusual."

"Oh," said Barclay, disappointment evident in his voice.

She held up a finger and said, "But," as she grabbed the red file folder off a stack of blue folders, opened it, and took out a report. She laid the folder and report in front of her and looked at Barclay. He just stared back before giving her a look that said *well, are you going to tell me?* She allowed herself a teasing smirk.

"So you did find something," said Barclay.

She eyed the report and squared the edges of the paper with the folder. She looked up and said, "Just so I understand, you wanted to know if someone could have survived the amount of blood loss observed at the crime scene, and, if not, is there a way to tell how old the blood is assuming it was not freshly spilled? That about right?"

Barclay nods. "Pretty much. Yes."

"Well, best guess—and this is only a guess—there were somewhere between two and three liters of the victim's blood in that house. In my opinion, without immediate medical attention, it is unlikely that a person losing that much blood could ultimately survive. It wouldn't be impossible, but I believe it to be highly unlikely."

"The investigation did not turn up any ER or hospital visits from a person with an injury type consistent with that amount of blood loss," said Barclay. "The detectives reached out to every hospital, ER, and doc-in-the-box from Mobile to Huntsville and from here to Atlanta. Nothing even close."

"If the person lost that amount of blood on the day of the incident and did not receive medical attention, again, I don't believe they would have survived."

Barclay tapped his lips with steepled index fingers in thought. After several seconds, he pointed those fingers at Dr. Bev and said, "Let's assume the person who that blood belonged to is alive, and let us also assume that she did not require medical treatment. In other words, let's assume that the blood loss did not occur the day of the crime."

Dr. Bev's chair squeaked as she leaned back. "Well, to answer your second question, we can't date blood other than to say how old it's not." Seeing the look on his face, she said, "When blood leaves the body, nitric oxide levels in the blood begin to drop and become almost nonexistent after forty-two days which, as a rule of thumb, is the expiration date of blood. Does that make sense?"

"It does."

She continued, "As I stated earlier, I examined the original blood report and did not see anything significant. So, one thing we could theoretically rule out is that the blood had been frozen prior to being splashed around the house; that would have definitely stood out to even the most inexperienced criminologist. As for the nitric oxide level, that's not something we look at as a matter of course." Her computer made a blip noise, and she cut her eyes to her computer monitor, then back to Barclay.

She consulted the contents of the red folder in front of her—flipping pages and scanning. She said, "Based on your phone call, I had the blood re-examined. This time, I did it myself."

She tossed the report on her desk and said, "Two things: the nitric oxide levels were normal, and the blood sample contained glycerol." She eyed Barclay as if gauging his understanding of what she was saying. Barclay knew enough not to speak and allowed her to continue at her own methodical pace. "Care to guess what that means?"

"Well, I'm guessing the nitric oxide levels being normal means that the blood was not particularly old." Barclay stopped here, eyeing Dr. Bev for feedback on his statement. She nodded once, and he continued, "I have no idea what glycerol is or what it means that you found it in the blood."

She enjoyed playing teacher and her demeanor showed as much. "Glycerol is a cryoprotectant. On a hunch, I ran a Glycerol Colorimetric Assay, and there it was." Another pause and stare. Not seeing the light come on, she said, "I believe the blood had been frozen."

Barclay sat up and forward and said, "But you just said that if it had been frozen, it would have easily been detected."

"It would have been...unless a cryoprotectant was added prior to its freezing...which it was...glycerol." Another pause as Barclay was trying to fit it together. Not seeing it click, Dr. Bev continued, "As I said, there was too much blood to have recently left the body and the owner of the blood to have survived. So, assuming the blood was drawn, say a pint at a time, it would take a while to stock up on the amount found at the scene, and the nitric oxide levels were too high for it to be old enough to have been collected that way. You follow?"

A tentative nod.

"Only one conclusion I can reach," said Dr. Bev. "I believe the blood was drawn, glycerol added, and frozen."

❄ ❄ ❄ ❄ ❄

Barclay and Clayton shed their suit coats when they left the Rabren building. Stepping outside, they were greeted with the machine gun sound of Jake brakes from the nearby interstate. The hot, humid air of the Alabama summer made it feel like they were breathing through a wet rag, the heat helping the color back into Clayton's face.

"How was it?" said Barclay.

"It was...interesting."

"Well, now you've seen one more autopsy than most prosecutors. Consider yourself lucky."

Lucky was not the word Clayton was thinking of at the moment.

They got into Barclay's Audi, and he cranked the air conditioner to the maximum. The two prosecutors sat in the white noise of the rapidly cooling air—Barclay staring ahead, thinking.

Finally, Barclay spoke more to himself than to Clayton. He said, "We need to take another look at Lane's computer." He clicked the fan speed down a notch to use the phone. He called the East Alabama Computer Forensics Lab using the car's hands-free setting.

The interior of the SUV was filled first with the ringing of the phone Barclay was calling and then with an impatient male voice: "Yeah."

"Gus, it's Barclay. Listen, I'm leaving Montgomery now and headed your way. Be there in, oh," he consulted his watch, "fifty minutes or so—"

Gus cut him off, "Sorry, Barclay, but you know I go to the gym during lunch."

Barclay started to speak before Gus cut back in: "Besides, I'm slammed. I've got all this stuff in the Pheiffer case to get done." Barclay could hear papers shuffling. Then Gus said, "A cell phone and four computers—all belonging to the vic."

Barclay mentally rolled his eyes at the term *vic*. Gus was a computer guy who watched a lot of cop shows and thought that was how the cops really talked. Then he said, "Clayton and I will grab some lunch. You go lift or run or do yoga or whatever it is you do, and we will be at your office at one-thirty. Have the report you prepared from examining Veronica Lane's computer with you."

"Veronica Lane. What's she got to do with this?"

Barclay told him, ended the call, and backed out of the parking space. To Clayton: "You like hot dogs?"

CHAPTER 15

THE EAST ALABAMA COMPUTER Forensics Lab is housed in an old shotgun house located less than a half mile from the courthouse. Its ramshackle exterior belied the clean, modern interior. It housed critical evidence in criminal cases and tens of thousands of dollars worth of computer equipment, so the derelict appearance served as an additional security measure to the already impressive security system installed on the property.

Barclay turned into the gravel driveway two minutes early, pulled around to the rear of the house, and parked. He and Clayton got out of the SUV; their ties pulled loose from the neck, collars unbuttoned, and cuffs rolled up to the elbow. Barclay held a small round key fob to a sensor by the back door, releasing the door lock with a series of quick beeps.

The EACFL was one of four such regional forensic computer laboratories in Alabama. Alabama's district attorneys started the labs due to the influx of digital evidence and no central agency to analyze it. Maggie Gamble came up with the spark of the idea and became its chief proponent when other DAs did not see any value in the concept. She fought tooth and nail for the project, which was now a feather in the state's cap as they were among the first such labs in the country and perhaps the most respected. Most wanted the first lab to be in Montgomery—the capital—or

Birmingham—the state's largest city—but Maggie would not relent, which is why it ended up in Towne. Since then, three other regional labs have opened across the state, and countless crimes were solved and criminals convicted as a result.

The air inside the house was frigid; the thermostat was kept at sixty-two degrees to keep the massive amount of computer equipment and servers from overheating. The interior of the house was one big room with four workstations, a bathroom, and a kitchenette. The walls were lined with locked Faraday cages containing computers, cell phones, tablets, and other devices either waiting to be examined or picked up by law enforcement after an examination had been completed. The constant hum of computer fans filled the room with a low white noise, and the place still smelled like a new building despite being renovated more than four years prior. Gus was standing in front of the sixty-inch flat screen mounted to the wall, still sweating from his workout and drinking a protein shake from a Blender Bottle. He was watching a strong-man competition.

His attention turned to Barclay and Clayton. He turned up the bottle and finished the shake. As he walked to the sink to rinse the bottle, he said, "Give me a second to shower."

They heard the shower turn on, and Barclay located the remote for the television and, not finding a baseball game, changed the channel to a news station. Clayton followed Barclay's lead and sat in one of the four overstuffed fabric chairs forming an informal meeting area.

"What are you thinking?" asked Clayton.

"What do you mean?"

"What are you thinking about regarding Veronica Lane's computer?"

"I'm thinking we missed something." He muted the television and placed the remote on the round coffee table. Barclay sat forward, elbows on knees, and said, "The entire Lane investigation was approached as a homicide. Now that the homicide is in question, I believe looking back through the examination of her computer with a different mindset may reveal something that was missed the first go round."

Clayton nodded the way people do when they don't know what else to do. After another minute or so of silence, they heard the shower turn off, and two minutes later, Gus emerged from the bathroom, finger-combing his wet hair. He wore a light blue golf shirt with the EACFL logo on his left chest, khaki pants, and flip-flops. Gus Petropolous was mid-forties, had dark hair, dark eyes, a slightly olive complexion, and was short for a man. He was barrel-chested and looked more puffy than muscular; he had smallish hands, which Barclay always noticed when they shook. He had a *computer-guy* personality that made non-work-related conversations a bit on the awkward side, and he had a way of making you feel pretty dumb when you spoke with him on a professional level. He walked to the sitting area and greeted Barclay and Clayton, who rose to meet him. Barclay, who didn't offer to shake hands, introduced Clayton to Gus.

Gus said, "How was Chris'?" This drew a look from Barclay; Gus, expressionless, said, "You always eat at Chris' Hot Dogs when you're in Montgomery for lunch." He then pointed at Clayton and said, "Besides, he's got chili sauce on his tie." Clayton and Barclay looked at Clayton's tie, and Clayton said, "Damn," and Gus went to his workstation. He grabbed the report he did on Veronica Lane's computer and a notepad and came back to the chairs. He sat and motioned for the other two to do the same.

"So," Gus began, "I'm running a bit late for the meeting because I went ahead and pulled the report and looked through it before I went to the gym. Based on what you said on the phone, I believe there's something here." He was looking at the report through bright blue framed half-moon reading glasses and flipping through it as he spoke. He laid the report in his lap, took off his glasses, looked at Barclay, and said, "Our conversation earlier actually jogged my memory about something, so I found it fairly quickly. Your girl had been planning this for quite a while—at least eight months prior to her disappearance."

Barclay responded, "Ah, shit."

Gus continued: "It was right at eight months to the day she went missing that the first searches showed up on her computer regarding blood storage. I also found where she ordered the"— he raised his readers and scanned his notes—"the glycerol. She ordered the glycerol, bags for the blood, blood draw kits—all the supplies she needed to do this—within days of those initial searches."

Barclay said, "Well, I think we can quit calling this a murder or even a kidnapping." He blew out a breath as he leaned back, eyes toward the ceiling.

Clayton said, "How was this missed before?" This caused Barclay to slowly bring his head forward, first looking at Clayton and then at Gus.

Barclay knew Gus well enough to see the anger that was likely lost on Clayton. Gus said, "Who are you again?" Then to Barclay, "Who is this guy again?"

"New prosecutor. He's learning. Asks a lot of questions; sometimes good ones."

"And sometimes bad ones," said Gus staring at Clayton, who shrank back into the chair a bit. "But to answer the question, I saw this stuff when I did the exam. It's in the report." To Barclay, "She was some kind of a nurse, right?"

"Yes."

"I remember seeing this and thinking it probably had to do with her job." Back to Clayton, "My job is to extract information from a computer or other digital devices—cell phone, iPad, whatever—and report my findings to the case agent leading the investigation. What he does with that info is up to him, and I never heard back regarding anything in the report." Jabbing a finger at Clayton, Gus said, "Perhaps you should ask the case agent that question."

"Anything else in the report jump out at you?" asked Barclay.

Gus shook his head. "No, but as I said, I was looking for something specific based on what you told me on the phone. I will give it a more thorough read later today."

When Barclay and Clayton left the house, the near one-hundred-degree heat felt good after the meat locker they had just left, but only for about fourteen seconds.

CHAPTER 16

WINSTON FITZSIMMONS' SEDAN SAT idling in a *Law Enforcement Only* parking space in front of the Towne police station. Barclay, Fitz, and Gus Petropolous sat inside the car, waiting for Detective Wayne Drummond to arrive. Fitz sat in the driver's seat, head laid back, eyes closed; Barclay sat in the front passenger seat, leaning his head on his fist, elbow propped on the door, and staring out the windshield; Gus sat in the back seat behind Barclay, engaged with his iPad. It was late afternoon, and the super-heated August air kept the car's air-conditioner from reaching its maximum cooling potential. A satellite radio classic rock station played lazily in the background.

The trio had been there for ten minutes—preferring to wait for the detective in the car rather than the station lobby. Although they could have waited for Detective Drummond in the station, neither Barclay nor Fitz was in the mood to small talk inside with Gus in tow. Used to working alone and with electronic devices that didn't talk back, small talk with Gus bordered on uncomfortable. Barclay learned early on not to engage Gus in conversation unless there was something specific to discuss.

"When is this detective supposed to be here?" asked Gus, not hiding his annoyance. "I have other cases to work on, you know."

This elicited only the slightest reaction from Barclay, drawing no more movement than a blink. Then, after a beat, he said, "Shouldn't be too long."

The sound from the back seat said that Gus did not care for that answer. He clapped his iPad case closed and said, "Where's that new guy? Why isn't he here? He should be here learning something."

Barclay's first thought was that it was none of Gus' business, but he answered anyway. "Dentist."

Fitz cocked an eye at Barclay and said with a chuckle, "Oh, man. I hate the dentist."

Barclay: "Everyone hates the dentist."

Gus: "I was almost a dentist."

"No shit," deadpanned Fitz closing his eyes. Barclay shook his head. *Figures.*

Several more minutes passed as Barclay observed the comings and goings of the police station. The foot traffic in, out, and around it belied the small-town feeling that pervaded Towne. His thoughts then turned to Duncan and the first time they had made the trip to the police department.

They were taken there by assistant district attorney Tyler Franklin—a lifer at the district attorney's office. Former military, he came to the office after having previously served as a JAG officer at Maxwell Air Force Base in Montgomery. He still maintained a military-like appearance: flattop, square chin, heavily starched shirt, tie always knotted tightly. That was his physical appearance. But, behaviorally, he left his military bearing at the Air Force base.

It's said that prosecutors secretly want to be cops, and no prosecutor embodied that greater than Ty. Among his favorite things to do is to introduce neophyte prosecutors to the Towne PD Special Operations Unit and their war room which contained all the resources necessary to fight the burgeoning drug trade and the violence that invariably followed. He liked doing this because it allowed him to show off in front of the newbies just how close he was with local law enforcement. He also figured that since he liked it so much, surely anyone else would.

The Towne PD special ops division had its own structure located behind the main police station building. It was a single-story brick building originally built as a storm shelter but had since been refurbished to create offices, interview rooms, a conference room, and a storage room for all of their toys.

When Ty, Barclay, and Duncan arrived, the detectives in special ops were in the middle of a taser training class. Seeing this and observing some of the officers volunteering to be tasered, Ty decided it was a good idea to jump in and get tasered himself. Duncan, being new, felt like what better way to earn the respect of the cops whose cases he would soon be prosecuting than to get tasered, so he did.

There was no way Barclay could allow Ty and Duncan to get tasered and be left out. So one of the detectives fixed the taser leads to Barclay's belt on either side of his waist.

Another two detectives flanked Barclay and interlocked arms; he was nervous. He can still remember how the two- or three-second wait for the taser to fire felt like minutes. How, suddenly, his body went into full spasm as his muscles locked up, straining against but held upright by the two detectives on either side—fully aware of the rapid tick, tick, tick sound of the taser as fifty-thousand volts of electricity surged through his body.

The *ride* only lasted five seconds, but that was plenty long enough for Barclay to respect the hell out of the taser and what it was capable of. There were no lasting effects, for as soon as the electricity quit flowing, the pain was gone; the only lasting reminder of the event was the photograph that hung on his office wall—a photo taken by Duncan.

Barclay jumped at the sound of Detective Drummond rapping on the driver's side window with his college ring. In response, Fitz rolled down the window peering at the detective through a squinted left eye. Drummond wordlessly signaled them to follow him into the building as he moved toward the entrance.

❖ ❖ ❖ ❖ ❖

As the group climbed the stairs to the fourth floor, Drummond said over his shoulder, "We're going to meet in the chief's office."

They made their way down the hall and into the chief's office suite—the low din of hard sole dress shoes on the well-worn carpet and the swish, swoosh of men in suits announcing their arrival. They walked past the chief's personal assistant, a stern-looking schoolmarm of a woman, everyone except Drummond nodding in greeting and receiving an unblinking stare in return.

Walking into the chief's office was like stepping back in time. Faux wood-paneled walls and orange shag carpet spoke of a time before Barclay and Gus were even born. Fitz was the first to speak. He said, "This is like being back in my grandmother's living room...in 1976." Then raising his nose in the air, "I swear I can smell Hai Karate in the air."

Casting a glance around the room, Drummond said, "Yeah. The chief had the opportunity for an update when they refurbished the rest of the building, but he chose to keep it this way. He wants to send the message about old-school police work. Working with what you have and not needing a lot of spit and

shine to solve cases and catch the bad guys. 'This is a police station, not a goddamn casino.'" Drummond shook his head. "He
tried to shit-can the whole refurbishment, but thankfully, the
city wouldn't hear it." He pointed at Barclay and Fitz, "Y'all
remember the condition this building was in before. Mold in the
ceiling tiles, the electricity that would go out if someone farted,
and an air conditioner that only worked when the temperature
outside dropped below sixty." He signaled them to follow him
into the attached conference room and said, "The AC unit was
so old they could no longer find parts for it—had to machine
the damn things when parts were needed."

The conference room sat in stark contrast; it was as new
and updated as the rest of the building. Seeing the looks of the
other three men in the room, Drummond said, "The city updated this space over the chief's objection. They hold press conferences in here as well as other meetings with important officials,
and they weren't going to continue to do all of that in the Brady
Bunch living room."

The conference room had the same blue-gray theme that
ran throughout the rest of the building. But, aside from a fresh
coat of paint and new carpet, the room's trademark was the
new window that ran the full height and breadth of one wall
providing an elevated and unobstructed view of the city. The
view attracted the newcomers like moths to a flame. Towne was
far from a metropolis, but the view was impressive.

As the men began finding seats around the table, there was
a light knock on the open door, and in stepped a woman who
looked to be in her late twenties. She wore a tan skirt just short
of the knee, a navy blouse, and a lightweight canary yellow
sweater with three-quarter sleeves. Her ponytail was up in a
messy twist keeping her blonde hair off her neck. She carried
a silver MacBook under her left arm and walked in, taking the

empty chair next to Drummond. She brought a scent of fruit and spices to the table that did not go unnoticed by the men in the room.

Drummond stood as she sat, and he said, "This is Tina Crump. Tina, this is Barclay, Fitz, and Gus." He pointed to each man as he said their name. "Tina is our resident computer expert. I asked her to join us when you mentioned what you wanted to discuss." Tina nodded her greeting as she opened her computer. "Now," Drummond said as he leaned back in his chair, "why don't you explain exactly what you would like to know. I'm sure this will make much more sense to her than it did to me."

Barclay said, "What we have to discuss is sensitive. I don't want this information leaving this room." He looked from Tina to Drummond and said, "Is she…um, does she understand… uh, is it ok if she hears this?"

Tina spoke up, and any notion of her self-confidence eroded instantly. She said, "Uh, Barclay, was it? Uh, I'm a police officer. They give me a badge, a gun, and real bullets. I can even shoot a bad guy if I need to, so yeah, uh, my delicate ears can hear whatever it is you want to talk about."

Barclay's face reddened, but he had a job to do, and he wanted to make sure it was done right. "I apologize if I offended you, Ms. Crump, but that is not what I meant. I didn't know if you were simply the office IT person, and I don't believe it appropriate for non-law enforcement to sit in on this meeting." Tina gave a nod in response to show she accepted his explanation, but she still had her hackles up. All eyes were on Barclay, who said, "In fact, what we are about to discuss does not leave this room." He then made eye contact with each person at the table to underscore the importance of his statement.

Having made his point, he continued, "We believe Duncan's case may be related to the Veronica Lane case."

That was enough to sit Drummond up straight. "And just how are they related?"

Drummond was the case agent on the Veronica Lane case, same as Duncan's case. As the case agent, he led the investigation and maintained the case file. Detectives did not particularly care to hear what Barclay was about to say. He knew this was a delicate area but decided it best if attacked head-on. "Wayne, I didn't say they *were* related, only that they *may* be related. Now, I'm going to lay it out for you, and all I ask is that you let me explain everything before you ask any questions." Drummond nodded, and Barclay continued. "The long and short of it is that we believe Veronica Lane may be alive."

"What?" said Drummond.

Barclay put both hands up and said, "Just give me a few minutes to explain, and then I will answer your questions." That placated Drummond for the time being, but Barclay knew he had better get to the point quickly. He explained to the two police officers about the possible sighting of Veronica Lane at the bookstore in Portland. About Megan Pope recognizing Veronica and the recognition she believed she saw in the woman's eyes. He also told them about his visit with Dr. Bev and explained the presence of the cryoprotectant in the blood, what it is and what it does. He refrained from spelling out the implications of the newfound blood information, not wanting to insult their intuitiveness as police officers. If they had questions, they would ask. He acknowledged the connection between the two cases was tenuous. "However, if Veronica Lane is alive, we can't simply ignore it—not after what happened to Duncan. Never mind the fact that would also mean an innocent man is facing the needle."

Wayne Drummond opened his mouth to speak but said nothing. A heavy silence followed as the five people in the room sat staring at one another—Barclay, Fitz, and Gus because they were waiting on the detectives to respond, while Drummond and Crump were silent because they did not know what to say.

Finally, Tina said, "What does all of this have to do with me?"

Barclay said, "I attended a capital litigation conference last fall, and while I was there, I ran into an old law school buddy who is now a prosecutor with the Los Angeles County District Attorney's Office. We were catching up, and he mentioned a case he prosecuted, and, quite frankly, I had forgotten about it until yesterday." The loud ping of a new email notification sounded from Tina Crump's computer. She apologized, tapped a couple of keys, and closed the laptop. Barclay continued, "The case was a straightforward DV homicide. The husband killed his wife because he wanted her gone and did not want to go through the hassle or expense of a divorce—you know the drill.

"When the police searched his house, they couldn't locate a computer. They knew he had a laptop because friends of the family they had interviewed mentioned seeing it, and during the search, they found a receipt from Best Buy showing the computer's purchase. The husband said the computer belonged to his wife and didn't know where it was or what she had done with it. The investigation turned up one of the husband's girlfriends whom he had met online. She gave them the website, and through a subpoena, the company gave the police all the IP addresses associated with the husband's account."

Drummond looked at Crump and said, "IP address?"

"Internet Protocol address," she said. "It's a set of numbers that act as a unique mailing address for your computer. It's how your computer communicates with websites."

Drummond looked to Barclay for clarification, and Barclay

said, "I don't know all the ins and outs, but basically, she is correct—"

"Basically?" Tina cut in.

"Poor word choice. Essentially, if you are connected to a wireless router, the IP address that will show up is that of the router and not the computer."

"How is that helpful?" asked Drummond.

"In Sean's case—that's my buddy in LA—in his case, there were four IP addresses associated with the account. One was the wireless router at his house, another was the router at his workplace, a third was at the Starbucks around the corner from his office, and the last one, I think, was a fast food place a block or two from his office where he was known to eat three to four times a week."

"Fast food four times a week?" asked Fitz. "How much did this guy weigh?"

"That he didn't tell me," Barclay said, "but they were able to use the IP addresses to establish his presence on the site. Or at least that someone using an account created in his name was accessing the website at those locations. This after he adamantly denied visiting any such websites." Barclay then leaned up and placed his elbows on his knees, hands clasped, and said, "I say all of that to ask this question: how much value could there be in the *Find Veronica Lane* website data?"

Drummond rocked back hard in his chair. He turned to Tina and said, "What do you think?"

"What's this website he's talking about?" she asked.

Barclay said, "After Veronica went missing—within a week, I believe—her family created the website findveronicalane.com where they displayed photographs of Veronica, posted videos of her family asking for the public's help locating her, and listed the secret witness phone number. The site also posted case updates, potential sightings, that sort of thing. Her mother mentioned seeing something similar on one of the true crime shows she watched. Seems like a cousin or something who worked at a web design firm got the site up and going for them. I'm not sure how much traffic it generated or how much good it did, but it gave them some semblance of peace of mind at the time."

Tina was working through this in her head, and no one said anything as they let her process this information. Finally, Gus said, "I already told you what we could do." He said this in a most disinterested voice. He had very little patience for the non-computer literate. He viewed anyone who knew less about computers than him as computer illiterate. He was also not thrilled to be at this meeting with this female police officer, who surely did not know as much as he did. *Why were they asking her to get involved? He had already told them everything they needed to know.*

Tina flashed a look, and Barclay said, "Gus mentioned the possibility of seeing the IP addresses of everyone who viewed the site."

"If Gus is so smart, then why do you need me?" said Tina, not trying to hide her annoyance.

"Computer people," mumbled Fitz shaking his head. This drew looks from both Tina and Gus.

"Look, I know Gus is very good at what he does, and the fact that Wayne brought you in on this lets me know that he has a great deal of respect for your ability. This could wind up being a big damn deal, so I want more than just one person generating ideas and leads." Taking his voice down a notch, Barclay said, "We need the login information and access to all the website data. We also need someone to go through it. Between you and me, I'd rather you deal with Ms. Lane's family than Gus." Gus gave Barclay a look he didn't see but knew was there. He'd deal with Gus later; he needed Tina on board, and he needed that now. He leaned back and said, "Besides, it would be best if this line of inquiry came from the police. For a lot of reasons, this does not need to come back on the DA's office or me until we have it all figured out."

This seemed to mollify Tina for the time being. She said, "That could potentially be hundreds if not thousands of different IP addresses."

Barclay said, "I thought about that. But what if you look at it from a broad view—see if you notice any anomalies? Anything that jumps out at you and then go from there."

Tina gave that some thought then nodded and began typing on her computer.

❋   ❋   ❋   ❋   ❋

Barclay, Tina Crump, and Wayne Drummond assembled in Barclay's home study the following evening. The French doors were open to the patio, and the room smelled faintly of tobacco and bourbon. He asked if he could get them anything to drink. The two officers replied, "Sure," as he closed the study's mahogany pocket doors. He went to the stainless mini-fridge set into the bookcase, then joined them in the sitting area in the corner of the room. On a wooden serving tray on the square leather-topped coffee table, he set down two bottles of beer, a Lemon-Lime Gatorade, a bottle of water, and three koozies. Tina grabbed one of the beers and a koozie while Drummond snatched up the Gatorade. Barclay took the second beer and a koozie and opened the bottle with his wedding ring. He held out a hand to Tina, who surrendered her beer for him to open in the same manner.

Barclay and Tina sat in soft forest-green leather chairs around the coffee table while Drummond chose the matching sofa. Barclay muted the large wall-mounted television with a remote he scooped up off his desk and then set the remote on the tabletop.

Barclay and Tina were dressed casually: he was wearing jeans, an untucked white golf shirt, and loafers without socks, while she wore skinny jeans, white Tretorns, and a faded green t-shirt from a brewery in Nashville—her hometown. Drummond was still in his work clothes—khaki pants and a blue button-down.

Tina said, "What's with all the cloak and dagger stuff?"

Ignoring her question, Barclay said, "First of all, I appreciate you doing this at my house. I know it's asking a lot to give up your Friday night." Then to Tina, "Why the cloak and dagger? We need to be discreet about this and—"

"And just what are we doing exactly?" said Tina.

"Hopefully justice," said Barclay fixing his gaze directly on her—holding it there until she broke eye contact. Then, when she didn't respond, he continued, "As I was saying, we need to be extremely discreet about this, and that means not meeting at the police station or my office. Maybe I'm being a bit paranoid, but so be it.

"The point is *if*, and that is a big if, *if* Veronica Lane is still alive and given what we found out about the blood evidence, then this took a hell of a lot of thought and planning, and the fewer people that know about this, the better. I asked Dr. Bev to sit on the blood results for a while, and she said she'd withhold her report until I gave her the go-ahead."

Tina: "But isn't that potentially exculpatory evidence for the guy convicted of killing this woman? Clements, right?"

Barclay: "Yes and Yes"

Tina: "So he is entitled to the results of the blood test, correct?"

Barclay: "He is, which is exactly why we need to work through this quickly but also thoroughly. The way I see it, letting this out now without investigating it could hurt Clements by giving whoever actually is responsible for this a heads-up to fix what needs fixing. I also don't want to mention anything about it until we have Ms. Lane located and in our custody, if that's even possible. She is the thread holding this case together; pull on it, and the case likely unravels. We need to be the ones to pull the thread and not have the person she's involved with tie it off. That would not be good for her or us."

Tina: "Person? You think she is only involved with one person?"

Barclay shrugged. "That's my guess. Like Ben Franklin said: 'Three may keep a secret if two of them are dead.'"

Drummond had uncapped, drank, and recapped his Gatorade three times throughout this exchange. Barclay wanted to take it from him and throw it out the window. He settled instead for a look. Drummond did not receive the message as he uncapped, drank, and recapped once more.

"So," Barclay said, looking at Tina, "what did you find out?"

Tina reached for her iPad and flipped the cover open, bringing the screen to life. Ignoring it, she said, "In a nutshell, that we...or you rather, may be onto something." She drank from her bottle, settled back into her chair, and said, "There wasn't a great deal of traffic on that website, and it only averaged maybe twenty or so unique visitors per day at its peak. As you could guess, the overwhelming majority of those visitors were from Alabama."

Drummond uncapped, drank, recapped, and belched under his breath, causing Tina and Barclay to look at him. He returned their gazes.

Tina continued, "There were a few hits scattered through-out the country, which is also to be expected. People find their way to a website for any number of reasons. Curiously, though, when I mapped the IP addresses, the only cluster of visits outside Alabama was in the northwestern part of the country. More specifically in and around the Portland area."

This got a reaction from Barclay, but Drummond didn't flinch. *Had he heard what she just said?* Barclay noticed him eyeing the baseball game on the muted television. He was a more than competent detective, but sometimes Barclay wondered. No cop wanted it proven that he had arrested—and God forbid convicted—an innocent person, so he knew getting Drummond fully on board with this off-the-books investigation would be at least a minor challenge. After all, no detective worth his salt ever made an arrest without fully believing they had the person responsible, so re-opening a closed case after a jury validated the work with a guilty verdict was not something any detective was naturally inclined to engage in with any great enthusiasm. However, no cop Barclay ever met wanted an innocent man to sit in jail either. He knew Drummond would come around if the evidence were there.

"The site went live on the twelfth, and the first hit in that area was the morning of the thirteenth from a Starbucks in Mil-waukie," said Tina.

"Wait, I thought you were telling us about site visits from the Northwest?" Drummond said.

"I am."

"Milwaukee is in Wisconsin," Drummond said as he gave Barclay a look that said *this girl doesn't even know basic geography.*

"What? Oh, yeah, sorry. It's Milwaukie, Oregon. Spelled with an I-E." Barclay thought he saw the slightest look of contrition cross Drummond's face. Tina continued, "It's across the Willamette River from Portland, about a ten-minute drive. All told, there were a hundred and twelve total hits from in and around Portland over the next month. Four came from that same Starbucks in Milwaukie, two from a Thai restaurant also in Milwaukie, two from a coffee shop in Beaverton, and the rest from various places in the city of Portland. Including thirty-seven from Powell's Books, where you told us she was spotted."

Barclay stood up, grabbed a baseball bat from the corner, and began to walk around with the bat on his shoulder.

"What's with that?" asked Tina, pointing at him with her beer bottle.

Barclay glanced down at his hands gripping the bat and said, "It helps me think." He walked to the open French doors and stood there looking outside. Then, after about forty-five seconds, he spun to face the two police officers. "That's got to be her. I mean...wait, how do those hundred-some-odd hits from Portland compare to hits from other areas outside Alabama."

Tina examined her iPad, scrolled several times, and said, "The next highest concentration is New York with forty-two hits which I attributed to national news outlets. The next highest after that is six, and there are several of those from all parts of the country."

Drummond asked, "How did she know about the website?"

Barclay said, "What do you mean?"

Slouched into the sofa, Drummond said, "I mean, how did she know about the website? Y'all are awfully quick to assume it was her, but we know she didn't speak to anyone in her family about it, so how did she know the site existed?" That question seemed to take a bit of air from Barclay but not Tina.

She grinned and said, "I had that same thought and made a couple of phone calls." Barclay raised an eyebrow while Drummond remained disinterested. "I went back through the Towne Tribune's online archives, reading the case stories. I started with the first story printed the day after she was reported missing, which would be the eighth. The *Trib* printed stories daily, as you can imagine, and the story on the thirteenth mentions the website."

Drummond still seemed unmoved. He met Tina's glance with a shrug. She continued, "I know one of the IT guys at the *Trib* who gave me the site stats for the day of the thirteenth so I could look at the number of hits on that particular article the day it was published. Included in that information were the IP addresses for each hit. Any guesses about what I found out?"

"No one reads the *Trib*?" droned Drummond.

Barclay pointed his bat at Tina and said, "Someone accessed that story from a Starbucks in Milwaukie."

"Bingo," said Tina.

*   *   *   *   *

Barclay and Tina polished off their beers. Barclay fetched two more from the office fridge, and Drummond asked for a water this time which Barclay gave him but not before uncapping it and tossing the lid into the trashcan.

"You still need the girl." Drummond's words broke the revelry.

Tina drank some beer while Barclay walked back to his desk, sat on it, and said, "He's right. Without her, we can only prove that someone in the Pacific Northwest was keeping close tabs on this case."

Tina shrugged and said, "I can keep going if you'd like."

"You have more?" spoke Drummond—his tone a mixture of disbelief and disappointment.

Tina looked between the prosecutor and the detective and

said, "Well, yeah." The two men exchanged glances then turned their attention back to her. She took that as her cue to continue. Setting her bottle down, she said, "After researching the website traffic, I felt we were really onto something, but I also figured we needed that one more thing to absolutely nail down it was Ms. Lane we were tracking." She stood up, iPad in hand, and said, "I took a chance and asked Ms. Lane's mother if she had received any phone calls from numbers she didn't recognize. Specifically, if she received any hang-ups." She paused for effect before saying, "She did."

Drummond said, "Of course she did. It was a high-profile case, at least around here, and they went on television, radio, and the internet asking for help locating their daughter. That'll bring the weirdos out of the woodwork every time. How could you possibly glean anything from that?"

If Tina was frustrated by Drummond's continued negativity, she didn't let it show. She said, "All pleas for information directed callers to a police tip line. Neither she nor anyone else in the family released their cell number, so I thought any odd calls or unknown numbers could be very helpful."

Barclay liked her approach—both in the investigation and with Drummond.

She said, "Mrs. Lane, the mother, mentioned that she did, in fact, get three or four hang-ups shortly after her daughter's disappearance. She had recently begun getting calls from telemarketers, so she quit answering her phone if she didn't recognize the number. After her daughter had gone missing, though, every phone call could be important, so she never let a call get past the second ring. Of course, she had the occasional telemarketer during that time, but she also remembered a few hang-ups during those first few days as well, which she also attributed to telemarketers, so no red flags for her there."

"Let me interrupt here," said Barclay. "Did her mother ask you why you wanted to know all this information? I'm curious how you explained the sudden interest first in the website and then the phone calls she received."

"Funny you should say that. I had the same thought. I didn't want to alert her to what we were up to, so I went to the person who created the website. You were right about it being a cousin. I told him what I needed and that it needed to be kept confidential, and he obliged. As for the phone information, I just told her we were investigating Duncan Pheiffer's murder, which included looking back at every case he handled. Veronica's was the last case he worked on, so we wanted to start with that one."

Drummond took this opportunity to ask Barclay where the bathroom was. He excused himself but not before telling them, "Go on without me."

With Drummond out of earshot, Tina said, "What's up with him?"

"We are dissecting and essentially reinvestigating one of his old cases right in front of him. He'll be fine."

"If you say so." Tina took a drink of her beer and said, "I asked Mrs. Lane to pull her cellphone bill for the timeframe covering the hang-ups. I asked her to mark every phone number she knew and write down who the number belonged to. She was pretty certain all of the calls occurred during the month of October, and she is not a high-volume cell user, so that made for an easy search. She identified nine phone numbers she didn't have in her phone's contacts list. Of those nine phone numbers, five appeared one time while one number appeared four times."

Drummond had not closed the pocket doors all the way when he left the room, and Barclay could hear him and Brittany talking in another room.

Tina continued, "I was fairly certain what the five individual numbers would turn out to be, but I had someone in the department run a quick check on them. Sure enough, they all came back as owned by telemarketing companies. The one number that appeared four times is a burner."

"Of course it is," said Barclay.

"Hold on, now."

"What do you mean? Aren't those prepaid devices essentially anonymous? I mean, that's why people use them, right?"

"Well, they are anonymous...to a point. When you go to, say, Verizon, for example, you have to submit to a credit check, sign a contract, et cetera, but with a prepaid phone, you simply walk into your local Walmart or wherever, pay cash, and walk out with your phone. No paperwork, no record, no anything that says who bought that phone."

"So where does that leave us identifying the owner of that phone number?"

"You first need to understand how these burner phones work. I won't go into the technical aspects, but principally these prepaid cell phone providers are MVNOs which stands for Mobile Virtual Network Operators. They lease network space from the big boys—Verizon, AT&T, T-Mobile—instead of creating their own network.

"So, for our purposes, you just need to know that they still ping towers and connect to towers like any other cell phone and—"

Barclay interrupted: "And they leave the same digital footprint as any other cell phone."

"Correct."

"That's all well and good, but how do we find out which network that number is on so we can track it?"

"Way ahead of you," said Tina. "I've got a buddy who works with AT&T—we met at a training in Quantico about cell phones and cell tower mapping. I sent him the number and had him look into it. Turns out it's a Boost Mobile device that uses the Sprint network."

Barclay stood up off the edge of the desk, anxious, gripping his bat with both hands. "Great. Now, all we need to do is get with the Sprint folks and…" He saw a growing smile on Tina's face. "You're way ahead of me." Tina nodded. "Right," said Barclay.

Barclay flopped down into the empty chair opposite Tina and said, "Is it good?"

Tine shrugged slightly but had a look on her face that said: *Of course. What else would you expect?* It was her turn to stand up now. She held her hand out, and it took Barclay a beat to realize she wanted the bat. He handed it to her, and she grabbed the handle with both hands. Then, just as quickly as she grabbed it, she pulled a hand away and made a face.

It was Barclay's turn to smile. "Pine tar."

"And why?"

"It's a game-used bat. My brother pitched in the minors, which means he was never in the lineup to hit; however, once, in an extra-inning game, his team ran out of position players. He pitched in relief, and since there wasn't anyone left to pinch hit for him, he had to swing the bat himself. He hit a walk-off bomb, and this is the bat."

As Barclay was talking, Tina was examining the bat. She said, "Why is there a different name on the bat?" She was referring to the player's name burned into the barrel.

"Ah, well, being a pitcher, he didn't have his own bat, so he had to borrow one."

Still looking at the bat, Tina said, "This name sounds familiar."

"It should. He's playing in the big leagues now. He was the American League Rookie of the Year and a three-time All-Star."

That was enough baseball talk for Tina. She handed the bat back to Barclay and said, "What were we discussing? Oh yeah, tracking Ms. Lane's cell activity." She finished off the last of her beer, set it on the coffee table, and said, "We've got her."

※   ※   ※   ※   ※

Drummond walked back into the room. Then, seeing Barclay and Tina silent and staring at him, he asked, "What?"

Barclay: "It would seem that Tina, here, has found our girl."

Tina: "Well…maybe I overstated that. What I found is her digital footprint—I think." She grabbed her messenger bag and withdrew a MacBook Pro. She went to the desk, sat in the oxblood desk chair, and said, "Let me just show you what I found."

As Tina flipped up the screen on the laptop, Barclay and Drummond stood behind her, flanked on either side. Her finger dragged across the touchpad as she clicked through her files until she found the file she was hunting. She pulled up an excel spreadsheet that made little sense to anyone except Tina. She began explaining what they were looking at without waiting for them to ask.

She said, "This is a report of the carrier records for the subject number that we believe belongs to Veronica Lane. It shows the call activity associated with this number and the cell tower information. I also have the text activity, but we will start with the call data." She pointed at the screen and said, "First, let me explain the information contained in each column, and then I will explain how it applies in our case." She glanced up first at Barclay over her right shoulder, then at Drummond over her left and said, "Good?"

Both men said, "Good."

Tina continued: "Ok, so the first column contains the subject number. That's the number these records are associated with. These next columns show the date the call occurred, the time the call was initiated or received, the duration of the call, and whether the call was incoming or outgoing. Next, we have the phone number that was called, followed by the phone number that made the call. Now, the last two columns are the ones we are most interested in right now. They show the cell tower sites."

Up to this point, the information they had been looking at was easy for Barclay and Drummond to recognize. These last two columns, however, not so much. Rather than speaking, though, they both let Tina continue to explain.

"Alright," she began, "this next to last column shows the originating cell tower while the last column shows the terminating cell tower. In other words, the cell tower the phone connected to when the call was received and then the cell tower the phone was connected to when the call ended."

"Where did you get all this?" asked Drummond.

"Friend of a friend," she said, not taking her eyes off the screen. Then she turned to Barclay and said, "You will need to subpoena these records if you want to use them for anything official. What I have was turned over as a favor and could get my contact in some trouble if Sprint finds out."

Barclay said, "Your favor probably saved us a month or more getting this information—not to mention saving us the exposure a subpoena would have opened us up to."

Drummond said, "How does this information help us?"

Tina: "The information in each cell gives us the latitude and longitude of the cell towers in question. Using the lat and longe, I mapped the phone's activity." She went back to manipulating the touchpad. After a couple of clicks, a map popped up on the screen; you didn't need to be a cartographer to recognize the significance immediately.

"Holy shit," said Barclay.

"Holy shit, indeed," said Tina.

※   ※   ※   ※   ※

The map before them revealed a trail from Towne, Alabama, through Mississippi, Missouri, Nebraska, Wyoming, Idaho, and on into Oregon. The phone's activity began with a text the night of Veronica Lane's disappearance, followed by a series of calls and texts—mostly texts—across the midwestern United States, with the first phone activity in Milwaukie, Oregon appearing six days later on the thirteenth.

"This is great, right?" said Barclay. "Now all we have to do is track the phone, and it will lead us right to her."

Tina said, "Well, not exactly. First of all, simply knowing what cell tower the phone is pinging off of only gives us a general area which could be a radius of several miles in size. You see, the system is designed to connect a phone to the strongest signal to create the best call quality. That strongest signal is almost always the closest tower. If it isn't the closest tower, for whatever reason, then it attempts to access the next closest tower, then the next closest, and so on." She again turned to look first at Barclay, then Drummond to gauge their comprehension. Both men wore expressions of concentration.

She continued, "The information we have is good to identify general locations and is typically more useful to prove where someone is not rather than where they are."

This time Drummond spoke. "I know we've tracked people using their cell phones before in real-time." He recounted a particular instance when he was part of a team that went out to serve a drug trafficking indictment. They had used an SUV on loan from the State Bureau of Investigations loaded with hardware and software that allowed them to track the drug trafficker in real-time. It ultimately led them straight to the suspect, who was driving around in his car, believing that being on the move would keep him safe from being found.

"Cell phones can definitely be used to triangulate a person's location, but that involves coordinating with the cell company and additional equipment and information we don't have and probably can't get without shining a big ol' light on what we're doing."

"But—"

Holding up her hand at Drummond and interrupting him, she said, "That phone is no longer in use." That pronouncement hit both Drummond and Barclay like a bucket of ice water. "I believe she is now using a different phone."

Drummond was the first to speak. He said, "So all this talk about cell towers and maps was bullshit."

Barclay said, "That's enough, Wayne."

"No. No, it's not. She comes in here running her mouth about 'we know this, and we know that,' and in the end, we aren't any closer to finding this woman or even proving that she isn't really dead and that Charlie Clements isn't exactly where he's supposed to be."

After a few seconds of silence, the sound being sucked out of the room by Drummond's outburst, the detective said, "Fuck this. I'm out of here." He stopped as he got to the door, turned around, pointed back toward the desk, and said, "Y'all can keep on doing whatever it is y'all are doing, but I'm going to keep doing what I do: catch bad guys...not release them."

"Hold up," Barclay said, anger edging into his voice. "First of all, Tina is only doing what I asked her to do. And all she did was get us in just over twenty-four hours what would have otherwise taken us a month or better. So to say anything to her other than thank you is what's bullshit."

Drummond cut his eyes to Tina and then back to Barclay. Barclay continued, "Secondly, we have a forensic blood report that we will have to turn over to Clements' attorney sooner rather than later, and the information it contains is not good for us. Either *we* can investigate and get to the bottom of it, or they can. I don't know about you, but I prefer it be us."

Barclay could see Drummond's posture relaxing. He pressed on. "Come on, man, if you can't see what all of this cell phone information is showing us, then you're either stupid or blind, and I've known you long enough to know you're not stupid— you're a hell of a cop. Now, based on your dating history, you may well be blind, so I don't know." That last statement got a smirk out of Drummond.

Barclay was still standing behind the desk. He gestured to the sitting area where the meeting began and said, "Now, let's all just take a deep breath and talk this through."

☼　☼　☼　☼　☼

They made their way back to their original seating arrangement—Tina a little slower than the other two, still stinging from Drummond's rebuke of her work. Seeing this, Drummond offered an apology. While it wasn't oozing with feeling, Tina knew it wasn't easy for him to do and accepted it with a nod.

Barclay eased up to the edge of his chair and said, "Unless either of you can offer an alternate explanation, I don't believe there is any doubt that Veronica Lane is alive. I believe we can also safely say that she was a willing participant in this scheme. We need to find her, find out why she did it, and find out who is in on it with her…easy, right?"

Tina quietly cleared her throat and looked between the two men before saying, "I have some more information."

Drummond: "Of course you do."

Barclay pointed at her with his chin and said, "What have you got?"

"I went through the call and text history of the phone, and calls were placed to seven different numbers, but she only texted one number. As for the calls, one was her mother's number which we already knew. Five were various businesses. After looking up each number, I'd say these calls were typical of a traveler seeking information: restaurants, hotels, a Walmart. The final number she called was also the only number she texted." Seeing Barclay open his mouth to speak, she said, "All I know is that it's a Boost Mobile phone, same as our girl. Probably bought them at the same time if I had to guess."

Drummond began to speak, but Tina held up a hand to stop him. "No, I don't have anything more than that…yet. I didn't want to over-ask until I knew for certain we were onto something."

Barclay gave it a beat to make sure she was done speaking. Then, he said, "Not to state the obvious, but that's our guy. Figure out the owner of that number, and we may crack this thing wide open."

"Sorry to jump around on you," said Drummond, "but you mentioned earlier that she's using a new phone?"

"I remember," Tina deadpanned.

Drummond said, "Again, sorry about that, but my question is, how do you know?"

"I suppose I don't know that for certain, but the last activity on that phone was on October fourteenth. So either she got a new phone or hasn't used a cell phone at all since that day—

which doesn't seem likely. I'm guessing she got a new phone when she reached her destination."

"I don't guess we can access the texts sent from that number?" asked Drummond.

Shaking her head, she said, "No. Not without the device itself. Get me that phone, though, and you will likely have the answers to a lot of your questions."

The three of them sat in silence. Tina had nothing left to add, and Barclay and Drummond were uncertain what to ask. Finally, Tina said, "So, what's our next step?"

Barclay stood from his chair with the aid of his bat, slung it up on his shoulder, and said, "We need to find Veronica Lane."

CHAPTER 17

BARCLAY ENTERED WICKED' WICH just before noon. He scanned the distressed-wood interior of the sandwich shop until he found what—or rather who—he was looking for: Lucas Jackson. As he made his way to the rear of the restaurant, he stopped at no fewer than six tables, saying his *hellos* and *howzit goings* before finally making his way to the butcher block table for two that already had one chair taken.

Lucas Jackson—who goes by Luke—was seated at the table wearing a light gray dress shirt with a brilliantly colored pattern tie. He was busy typing on his phone and only noticed Barclay when he scraped his chair across the floor and took his seat at the table. Acknowledging Barclay with only the quickest of glances, he continued to type for almost a minute longer before Barclay finally said, "You typing your memoirs?"

Luke grunted, continued to type for ten more seconds before hitting a button, and setting the phone down. Barclay heard the familiar *whoosh* sound effect signifying an email being sent as Luke looked up and said, "Hey."

Barclay said, "Do you ever take a break from that thing?"

"Nope," Luke said. He picked his phone up and said, "Emailing is billing, and I can bill anytime from anywhere with this bad boy." Barclay just shook his head.

Luke Jackson was around Barclay's age and a fellow attorney. He liked to say he was six feet tall, but he wasn't. He was neither fat nor thin and had prematurely gray hair that, though longish, was always styled just right. He was recently made partner in Towne's only other white-shoe law firm: Abner Underwood. However, finally achieving his goal of becoming a partner seemed only to drive him even harder.

Luke began his legal career handling indigent criminal defense work, which was how he met Barclay. The low-paid defense work ended when the Abner Underwood opportunity came along; he primarily handles civil defense now. Barclay greatly respected Luke as an intelligent legal mind with an even temperament that kept his services in demand.

Luke said, "Don't shake your head at me like that. Cranking out billable hours is what enables me to buy you lunch."

"Oh, so you're buying me lunch today?"

"Sure. You're a low-paid public servant helping to protect our community. It's the least I could do."

"Gee, Luke, you're all heart, you know that." Just then, a waitress shows up with two baskets containing a steamed sandwich, homemade potato chips, and a pickle spear. "And you took the opportunity to order for me too."

"You and I only eat one thing here, B."

"This is true."

What Luke and Barclay always ate at Wicked' Wich was the *Wicked 'Wich*—the sandwich for which the place was named. Wicked' Wich had been open for over six years but looked decades older based on the decor. People liked to feel like they were eating at a hallowed, must-visit establishment, and that is hard to pull off with bright lights and gleaming stainless steel. They served a variety of steamed sandwiches, all of which could be made *wicked* by adding a habanero and ghost pepper cheese they had specially made, along with a proprietary hot pepper spread that was a closely guarded secret. The *Wick-ed' Wich* sandwich was by far the hottest sandwich on the menu and—according to both men—far and away the tastiest.

Barclay and Luke had an unspoken contest whenever they ate there to see who would be the last to go to his water glass. The two men began eating their sandwiches.

"I forget just how hot this damn thing is," said Barclay.

Luke smiled and said, "I don't know what you're talking about. I think it's delicious." Barclay laughed a genuine laugh. Then after another bite, Luke said, "Is there anything particular you want to discuss, or did you just want a good lunchtime sweat."

Barclay, wiping his brow with a napkin, said, "I have something to discuss with you; a favor, really." Barclay took another bite, wiped his mouth, then the back of his neck, and continued, "I need you to represent Charlie Clements."

Luke finished chewing and said, "You know I don't handle criminal cases anymore...and I damn sure don't do appellate work."

Barclay finished a bite and took a drink of water. Luke gave a low chuckle as he bit into the second half of his sandwich. Barclay realized his faux pas and chastised himself for being first.

"Actually, I just need him to have an attorney of record. I doubt he can pay you, so I will have you appointed in light of Duncan's death."

Luke waved his hand and shook his head. "You don't have to do that. We can put it in our pro bono column." Luke stopped eating, wiped his hands on a napkin, and asked, "What's this about?"

"How much do you know about the case?"

Luke thought about it and said, "Probably about as much as anybody, I guess. Clements killed a girl, got convicted, and now his lawyer is dead." Barclay didn't care for the nonchalance Luke showed toward Duncan's death, but he knew that was just the clinical approach Luke took to his work. "Save emotion for the jury," as Luke was fond of saying.

"Yeah, I guess that's the crux of it." They both took a drink of water. "After the murder, I began to look through the case file thinking maybe it had something to do with his death." Barclay waited a beat before adding, "I'm not so certain that Clements killed that girl."

This brought Luke up short as he was about to finish off his sandwich. "Say that again."

Barclay exhaled and said, "I don't believe he killed Veronica Lane." He then went on to give a CliffsNotes version of what he had discovered in the previous days: the sighting of Veronica Lane in Portland, the cell phone information, and the blood evidence.

Luke put his sandwich in his basket as he looked around, and lowered his voice. "What the hell, dude? You need to be telling this to the judge. Not me."

"Come on, Luke, you know it's not that easy. A jury of twelve found this guy guilty, and no judge is going to let a convicted murderer out of jail just because I said so. Especially not one that has any interest in getting re-elected. Besides, I need him to stay in jail for the foreseeable future."

"You need a potentially innocent man to continue sitting in jail facing a death sentence?"

"Yes."

Luke thought about this and said, "Ok. I know you well enough to know that you must have a damn good reason for this, so what is it, and where do I fit in?"

"I need to turn the blood report over to the defendant as potentially exculpatory scientific evidence. The other information

I have, the sighting and the cell phone stuff, isn't quite a sure thing, so I don't believe I have to turn that information over just yet."

"But...," Luke said, drawing out the word.

"But I have exculpatory information, and I need it to stay quiet for the time being. If you represent him, I can hand over the blood report and fulfill my duty of disclosure. I also need you to persuade him to keep his mouth shut about this and convince him that it's for his own good."

"How so?"

"We believe Ms. Lane had an accomplice, and right now, it looks as though everyone has gotten away with this crime because Clements is facing the needle. But, the moment this news leaks, guards go up, potential evidence gets destroyed, and people go underground.

"Also, if Clements was, in fact, framed for this, and it looks as if he may get out of jail, that puts a pretty big target on his back. If he dies, particularly if it happens in jail while he is awaiting a motion for a new trial to be ruled on, the interest in solving the case goes way down, which is good for the individuals who put this whole thing in motion."

"So you want me to represent him so you can turn this evidence over and, what, convince him jail is the best place for him to be? Then tell him: 'Oh, don't tell anyone, not even your parents, who are devastated by the way, about this turn of events?'"

"Yeah, I guess that's what I need you to do." Luke appeared unsure, so Barclay said, "Look, if anyone can have that conversation with him and convince him this is in his best interest, it's you. We are working as quickly as possible on this, but it has to be done very quietly if we are going to find the people responsible for this and truly exonerate him.

"I honestly believe that if word leaks out about what we have found, then the odds of us solving this are between slim and none." Barclay paused, gathered himself, leaned into the table, and said, "I have no doubt in my mind that whoever is involved in this is responsible for Duncan's murder, and I am not going to lose this opportunity to find out who it is.

"I am coming to you and telling you about what we've discovered because it's the right thing to do. I also need this handled a certain way so this opportunity does not go to waste. Both for Duncan and Mr. Clements."

Luke was tearing at a napkin as he processed everything he was hearing. "I will agree to meet with him and do what I can to keep this quiet." Barclay was about to say something when Luke held up a finger and said, "But, I can't force him to take my advice, and if he asks me to file a motion with regard to this new information, I will."

"That's fair, but keep in mind filing that motion doesn't guarantee him getting out of jail, let alone an exoneration. The blood itself isn't new evidence, and I don't know that the trial judge or an appellate court won't find that his lawyer had an opportunity to test the blood before trial. Remember that appellate judges are also elected, so you know the pressure will be on them not to cut a murderer loose. Besides, even if he does succeed in getting his conviction overturned, his time as a free man will only last as long as it takes certain persons to realize *his* freedom may threaten *theirs*."

Barclay and Luke realized that everything that needed to be said about the situation had been said. So when the pair finished eating, Luke left cash on the table and got up to go.

As they walked toward the exit, Barclay looked at Luke, then back at their table and said, "Where's your coat?"

"Didn't wear it. I walked here from the office, and it's hot outside."

"Didn't wear it because it's hot? This isn't the Sahara, Luke. And It's called a suit for a reason. The jacket is meant to be worn with the pants. Were you raised by wolves?"

CHAPTER 18

ARCLAY SAT IN HIS office—the room dark except for two lamps on either end of the credenza behind him. The sun had long since set, and he was now the only person in the building, having even outlasted the cleaning crew. In the days since Duncan's death, Barclay could concentrate on little else, and now he found himself at his desk, unsure what to do next.

He, Fitz, Drummond, and Tina Crump had seemingly taken the case as far as they could with what they knew. Their unofficial investigation had yielded some good results, and they had made tangible progress in a short amount of time, but they were in a rut.

Barclay's office overlooked courthouse square, which was all but shut down at this time of the evening. The glow of storefront neon and sodium streetlights had a very relaxing effect, and he just sat staring out the window, thinking. He watched as two people stood outside The Downtowner locking up. One of them threw their head back in apparent laughter. Three young people were on the opposite side of the square, passing through on skateboards. Barclay wondered why they weren't at home at this hour which caused him to think to himself, *God, you're getting old.* He watched as the two people from The Downtowner disappeared behind the building, and he noticed two cars parked in the entirety of the square. He was more alone than he realized in more ways than one.

He pulled his feet off the credenza and swung around to face his desk. The classical music emanating from the Marshall Stanmore Bluetooth speaker on his bookcase served as the soundtrack to his deliberations.

So many things frustrated him about this case: they had a murder victim that they believed to be alive; they had a good idea where she was but no way to locate her; the investigation they were running got off to a fast start but had since slowed significantly and was threatening to stagnate. Factor in that they were running short on time, and Barclay found himself as frustrated as he could ever remember.

He cracked open the small leather-bound notebook in front of him and began re-reading his notes on the case. He read a few lines and then closed it. As much as his mind was firing and wanting to figure all of this out, he just could not concentrate. He swung back around to look outside at the barren square— one of the two cars had left—and saw the aged crepe myrtles moving in the breeze. Then he had an idea. "To hell with it," he said to the empty room.

He went to the coat rack by his office door and dug his iPhone out of his suit coat. He saw on the lock screen that he had two missed texts from his wife. One thirty-four minutes old and one eight minutes old. Both asked when he would be home. He walked back to his desk as he typed out *At work. Home soon.* His thumb hovered over the *send* button. He considered how this was impacting his wife. He knew she supported him unconditionally. She knew what his job meant to him, and now that Duncan was the reason for his current distraction, he knew he had even more grace at home. Still, he did not want to test the boundaries of Brittany's support and understanding.

He contemplated the message. He weighed a different response. Ultimately, in the quiet dimness of the office, he prayed for her continued understanding and a quick resolution to the case and pressed send.

After sending the text message, he opened the notebook and flipped through the pages until he found what he was looking for: the mystery phone number that had been in communication with Tina after the murder.

Opening his phone and touching the green telephone icon, he brought up his phone's keypad and thumbed in the number. He stared at it for a few seconds before hitting the green *call* icon on the screen. He stared at the screen for a beat until he heard the tiny speaker emit the sound of a ringing phone, and then he activated the speakerphone function; the next ring was much louder. After the third ring, Barclay realized he was hearing something in the office, so he ended the call. He strained to listen, then, not hearing anything, redialed the number and again put it on speakerphone.

After the second ring this time, he again heard a noise. He was certain of it. Again he ended the call and strained to hear. Nothing. This time he got up and walked to his door. Sticking his head out, he looked left then right, hearing nothing. He dialed the number a third time and stood in his office doorway as the call connected and began to ring. Then, almost simultaneously with his phone ringing, he heard a faint noise.

He wasn't hearing things. There was a definite noise somewhere in the office. After the second ring, he heard it again and again; it was nearly simultaneous to the ringing of the phone he was calling. Without moving his head, he shifted his eyes to his phone screen. Another ring on his phone, another noise in the office. He began to walk toward the sound.

Another ring, another noise—louder this time. Another

ring, another noise: a ringing phone. That is what he was hearing. Then the call he was on went to voicemail—a mechanical voice with a generic voicemail greeting stating the phone number of the phone he was calling. Coincidentally—or not—the other ringing noise stopped when the voicemail picked up.

Still moving toward where he knew the ringing phone was coming from, he redialed the number. This time he did not activate the speakerphone function and instead concentrated on the ringing in the office. By the fourth ring, he located the office the sound was issuing from, and he stood in the doorway, unsure what to do. After the next ring, the call went to voicemail, and all the ringing stopped.

After nearly a minute, he looked side to side, confirming what he already knew to be true: he was utterly and completely alone. He opened his phone and redialed the number. Both his heart and stomach lurched when the loud ringing came from inside the office. One more look left then right, and he slowly made his way into the office, behind the desk, and into the credenza. He moved aside some law books, and the phone's ringtone, now unencumbered, blasted a shrill tone into the office.

Barclay reached in, grabbed the phone, and slowly pulled it out. He looked at the illuminated screen and saw his phone number staring back at him. "What have you done?"

❊   ❊   ❊   ❊   ❊

"Wait a minute," said Tina Crump from the edge of her chair. "Just wait. I need you to slow down and go over that one more time."

Barclay was a ball of energy—baseball bat on his shoulder—pacing and speaking fast. Tina's statement stopped him, and he scanned the room. It was pushing 1:00 in the morning, and he, Tina, Drummond, and Brittany were in his study—everyone sitting down except him.

After his discovery in the office, Barclay bolted to his car and raced home, calling Tina and Drummond, summoning them to his house, telling them only that he may have a break in the case. Tina was still up when Barclay called, and she answered on the first ring. Drummond, on the other hand, had been asleep. However, after so many years of getting called out in the middle of the night, he answered after only two rings and sounded as if he had been up for hours. They both agreed to come over.

Tina showed up wearing jeans and a hoodie with her hair in a ponytail; Drummond was wearing khaki cargo shorts and a rumpled TPD golf shirt—he had not bothered to brush his hair. Brittany was in a long bathrobe, and Barclay was still in his light gray suit pants and blue dress shirt. A large carafe of coffee sat on the coffee table, along with a carton of half and half and a container of sugar. Each of them had fixed a cup of coffee except Barclay—he didn't need the caffeine.

Barclay took a breath and began his story again: "I'm sitting in my office staring out the window as I often do. Typically it's just for people watching, a way for me to clear my head. Nighttime is even more relaxing; it's when I do some of my best thinking at work. Anyway, I keep thinking about this case, and I'm frustrated, so I finally said, 'to hell with it.' I grabbed my phone and called the mystery number."

He looked each of the three in the eyes, ensuring they were following along. He went on to tell them how he dialed the number and thought he heard something or someone in the office. He explained how he hung up, called back, and eventually tracked the phone to Richard Kingery's office.

"Was it just sitting out?" asked Tina.

"No. It was in his credenza hidden behind some books."

"Do you have the phone?" asked Drummond.

Barclay shook his head. "No. I didn't want him to discover it missing."

Drummond said, "But when he looks at the phone, he will see all the missed calls from your phone."

"Ah, but I figured out how to go into the call log and delete the missed calls."

"Look at you, Mr. Tech Guy," said Tina.

"I'm not completely useless."

Drummond looked at Tina and said, "Without the phone, this really doesn't do us any good does it?" Then to Barclay: "Why don't you just go get the phone? At this point, what can it hurt?"

Tina began to speak when Barclay put up a hand to cut her off. "I don't believe we need to do that quite yet. He's held onto it this long; I doubt he's going to move it any time soon. That said, I did manage to get some information that I believe could be useful—or at least give us something to dig into. This is the same phone he has had since day one, and he's still using it—"

It was Tina's turn to hold up a hand and interrupt. "He's still *using* it?"

"Yes. He used it yesterday." He looked at his watch and, realizing it was after midnight, said, "Well, the day before yesterday."

"Well, ok then," said Tina. "What did you get?"

"Oh, just the entire phone log. Every number called or received on that device."

Drummond: "You're shitting me."

"Nope."

"But how—"

Barclay held up his phone and said, "I scrolled through and photographed it all."

Tina: "You didn't say anything about text messages."

"There weren't any. We know texts originated from the phone we suspect is Veronica Lane's, but there were not any on Dick's phone."

"Dick?" asked Tina.

"Kingery. Long story," said Barclay. "I'm guessing he deletes them. As dumb as it is to keep the phone around, I guess deleting them is smart. Nothing is readily apparent if, for some reason, the phone was found."

"Considering he didn't even have the phone passcode protected, I wouldn't be extolling his digital acumen quite yet. And he's a prosecutor. What a dumbass."

Drummond looked at Tina and said, "But we can do a phone dump and get his deleted texts." Then to Barclay, "You gotta get that phone, man."

"You need a warrant."

Barclay, Tina, and Drummond all turned to Brittany. The surprise—either at her voice or her legal commentary—shone on each of their faces. She shrugged and said, "Well, you do."

Barclay said, "She's right. We would need a warrant to seize and search the phone, and no way in hell I'm going to a judge with this." Drummond opened his mouth, and Barclay interrupted, saying, "At least not right now."

They all sat in silence for a long moment letting everything sink in. The adrenaline was wearing off, and Barclay was beginning to crash. On the other hand, Tina seemed to be gaining whatever energy Barclay was losing. She said, "Forward me the pictures, and I will get to work on the numbers in the call log."

"Granted, I didn't study the call activity, but it sure looks as if he has only called or been called by two phone numbers, and one of them is the one we already know about."

"Well, that should make it easy then."

CHAPTER 19

THE FLAGON AND SNAKE is an English Pub and one of the oldest restaurants in Towne. It was opened in 1964 by Alastair Sands, a retired British Air Force pilot who knew the area from his time attending the Air War College at Maxwell Air Force Base in Montgomery. He was so taken with Towne that he chose it as his retirement home and fulfilled his dream of opening an English pub. It was tremendously popular from the day it opened and remains so today. His daughter Millie and her family took over the day-to-day operation when Alastair suffered a stroke in 1982.

The pub's name is a reference to the quote attributed to W.C. Fields: *Always carry a flagon of whisky in case of snakebite and, furthermore, always carry a small snake.* That quote is painted above the pub's entrance, both inside and out, greeting the pub's patrons and bidding them farewell.

The pub's exterior was the color red of those famous London phone booths with the pub's name broadcast in foot-tall three-dimensional gold letters. In addition to being one of Towne's oldest restaurants, it was also among its most recognizable. Patrons entered the pub through a century-old red door that Alastair purchased from his favorite pub in his hometown of Kenilworth, England. The bar, too, was from an actual English pub and was brought over in sections; the character and charm imbued by such authenticity were unmistakable. Barclay entered and was met by the smell of beer and fried food. He saw his father sitting alone at a well-worn wooden table in the middle of the room.

"Hey, Dad," Barclay said in greeting as he walked around the table to the chair across from his father. "You haven't been here too long, I hope."

"Not at all. I was a few minutes early, so Lilly kept me company; she was catching me up on the latest gossip. I think it's been almost two months since I've been here."

As if on cue, Lilly arrived at the table, setting a drink in a rocks glass in front of the elder Griffith, and said, "Your Chivas, Mr. Griffith. Hey, Barclay, get you anything?" Lilly was the great-granddaughter of Alastair and was the fourth generation of Sands to run the pub. Despite being born in the United States, she maintained a slight British accent owed to her mother and grandparents. She was five-foot-five inches tall with a full figure. Her dark hair always sported a shock of color streaked through—today, it was bright pink.

"Hey, Lilly. Just a water, please."

Mr. Griffith said, "Water? At The Snake? Come now."

"I'm working, Dad."

Mr. Griffith held up his glass to Barclay and said, "I'm working, too. Cheers." He took a drink, and the air at the table took on the smell of Scotch.

Barclay said, "The worst part about coming here for lunch during the week is not being able to enjoy it to its fullest. This place begs you to drink some cold beer."

"Suit yourself."

"And Scotch of all things," said Barclay. "You really should try other options. There are a lot of good whiskeys out there."

Mr. Griffith waggled his glass and said, "Chivas Regal."

Then, in unison with Barclay, he said, "The mouthwash for lovers." The two had a good laugh at Mr. Griffith's standing joke.

Grover Griffith III was tall, lean, tan, and only wore three-piece suits—he wore his wealth very well. He combed his thinning silver hair straight back and wore stylish round tortoise-shell eyeglasses. He drank Scotch—almost exclusively—and ate red meat and potatoes—almost exclusively. He knew what he liked, and he indulged in it.

"I haven't talked to you since the funeral. How have you been?" asked Mr. Griffith, taking another sip of Scotch.

"Oh, middlin', I suppose," said Barclay leaning on his forearms resting on the table and looking absently around the pub.

"You know, I really liked that boy." Shaking his head, Mr. Griffith continued, "What in the hell possesses someone to do that to another human being."

"What possesses anybody to do any of the stupid shit they do? There's evil in the world, Dad. Every defendant I have ever prosecuted could give you any number of reasons for why they did what they did, and their reasons almost always exist in the hope of some manner of justification. Even when there is a clear-cut motive, it still just makes you shake your head, but I learned a long time ago not to try and think about it too much. To attempt to figure out *why* can drive you mad in the process."

Lilly arrived with Barclay's water, and Mr. Griffith said, "Two shepherd's pies, Lilly. Oh, and..." He raised his near-empty glass, and Lilly winked, and left. Then he said, "How is his wife doing? I can't imagine having to deal with such a thing."

"Each day is better than the last. She needs to get back into a routine and get some normalcy back in her life. School will start soon, and that will help. She has a lot of time on her hands right now, time she is using to grieve. Brittany is doing what she can to keep her occupied, but there is only so much she can do."

"Speaking of Brittany, how is she doing?"

"She's Brittany."

Mr. Griffith finished his drink. "How's work?"

Any other day and all of the good cheer shared by the two men up to that point would have been undone—in Barclay's mind—by those two words. Barclay's job did not sit well with his father. Anytime they discussed his work, there was a hint of disapproval in his father's voice.

Barclay was excited about the opportunity to become a prosecutor, and he was sure that his father would share his excitement and maybe even have some admiration for choosing such a worthy profession. Instead, his announcement was met with disappointment that he would choose "a low-paying public service job." His father let it be known that his hope was for Barclay to come work with him and eventually take over the law practice. The disappointment softened with the passage of time but had not completely gone away.

Barclay did not begrudge his father's feelings. After all, the disappointment stemmed from his wanting the two of them to work together. Barclay even left the door open to that possibility, initially believing that after a few years, he may want to go to work with his father. But, as excited as he was to become a prosecutor, he never expected the job to grab his heart as it had.

Barclay said, "Are you honestly interested in how work is going for me, or are you just being polite by asking?"

His father gave him a look and said, "Now, son, when have I ever said something just to be polite?" He was right. Grover Griffith III was not a man to waste words. There was nothing superfluous about anything he said or any question he asked.

"Funny you should ask. I had a very interesting meeting

with Maggie this week. She won't be seeking another term and asked me to run for DA in the next election."

Glass almost to his lips, Grover set the glass on the table and said, "Well hell, son, that's fantastic." He lifted his glass again, then set it down again. "What about the asshole?"

"She hasn't talked to him about it yet."

"What I wouldn't give to see the look on his face when she tells him." Grover was looking past Barclay as he said this as if picturing the exchange between Maggie and Richard Kingery. Grover then laughed to himself and took a drink of Chivas. The realization that his glass was empty seemed to bring him back. He looked at the glass then scanned the restaurant looking for the waitress. "Ah, yes," he said with a smile as Lilly approached with a fresh Chivas. Grover accepted the Scotch with his right hand as he handed the empty glass to Lilly with his left.

Grover said, "Your Uncle Jack has an offer for the billboard business."

"He's had offers before. He's not going to sell."

"He's never had an offer like this one."

"Really? Who?"

"Well, I'm handling the contracts for it, so I'm not at liberty to say, but it's a substantial offer, and I expect him to take it."

"Good for Uncle Jack. I thought about him the other day when I saw his crew prepping for a structure on the Pickens property. Can't believe he finally got them on board."

"He's been after that spot for years, and all it took was old man Pickens to die. His kids couldn't start monetizing that property quickly enough." Another sip of Chivas. "I'm pretty certain that land lease is what got the buyer to up his offer. It will be the best billboard location in the county." He cleared his throat and said, "You know, if you have any bodies to dispose of, this may be your last chance to do it."

Barclay laughed, and Lilly, who was passing by with a tray of drinks for a neighboring table, pulled up short. She said, "Wait, what? Bodies?"

"Nothing," Barclay said.

"You hush," said Grover to Barclay. Then to Lilly: "Growing up, my son here was obsessed with crime and crime shows, and he often told his Uncle Jack that he thought a billboard was the perfect spot to hide a dead body." Then, seeing the look on Lilly's face, he explained, "By dropping the body into the pipe before the head of the billboard was affixed. He said it would create a seal no smell could escape from, and the sheer size of the head of the billboard would essentially guarantee it would never be disturbed."

"This is what you all discussed at the family dinner table?" The Griffith men shrugged in unison. Lilly shook her head and tended to another table.

Grover said, "It will probably be the last board erected in Towne given the ordinance about to go into effect, and the board is going to sit relatively low, so you'll have access without much hassle."

"Will you stop it?"

Grover laughed and sipped.

"Any idea what your baby brother will do with his new-found wealth?"

The old man wiped his lips with his napkin and said, "No idea, but whatever he does, I'm sure it will make him money."

Lilly approached and set two shepherd's pies on the table. Barclay said, "Lilly, I can't stand it. I will have a beer. Boddingtons on draft." That request seemed to please Grover *and* Lilly.

※ ※ ※ ※ ※

Back at the office, Barclay sat in his chair, ruminating on his lunch with his father and the information he had learned. In his mind, he had taken a step onto a path, and it scared the hell out of him. He had never been much of a planner, nor was he particularly organized, but he did like information. When considering any course of action, he liked to garner as much information as possible. He picked his iPhone off the desktop and stared at it rubbing his thumb across the black screen. After staring at the phone for more than a few seconds, he activated the phone, scrolled through his contacts list, and made a call.

"Barclay, my boy, how are you this beautiful afternoon?"

"I'm good, Uncle Jack. How about you?"

"Everything is made for love. But, say, is everything alright?"

"Well, sure. Why do you ask?"

"Oh, it's just that I haven't heard from you in a while, and I guess in my old age, that's the first place my mind goes when I get a call out of the blue like this."

"Old? You're not even sixty." A laugh on the other end of the line. "And sorry about not being better about keeping in touch—"

"Nonsense," Jack interrupted. "You're busy. Hell, I'm busy. I'm just glad you called." Barclay could tell from the background noise that his Uncle Jack was standing outdoors. "How are things at the district attorney's office?"

"Things are good. Just busy as you could imagine."

"Of course, of course. I appreciate what you do, Barclay. Seriously. Proud to call you my nephew."

"Thank you. That's nice of you to say, and I really do appreciate it." Barclay could hear Jack having a conversation with someone.

Jack came back to the line and said, "Sorry about that. I'm out here at the Pickens property talking to a guy with the county. They're all up my ass about this structure and absolutely hate the fact they can't stop me from putting it up."

"Yeah, I wanted to congratulate you on finally securing a lease on that property. I know you've been after it for a while."

"A while? Try long before you worked here if you can imagine that." Barclay had begun working summers for his uncle's outdoor advertising business when he was fourteen and continued throughout college. He started with keeping the back of the shop clean and then worked on a crew hanging vinyls before going to law school.

"Good for you. I had lunch with Dad today, and he told me about your offer." He added quickly, "He didn't give me the details, only that you had an offer come through."

Jack inhaled and sounded wistful when he said, "Yeah, it's hard to believe that my days in the outdoor business could be coming to an end." Both men were silent for a beat then Jack said, "It's been a wild ride, B."

"That it has. Say, when is the head going up on the pipe where you are now?"

"Oh, I don't know. Within a month, probably. I need to get some things sorted before that happens, but it's going to get done." Then to whoever was there with him, he yelled, "You hear that, Tommy? This is getting done." Back to Barclay, "Bureaucrat politicians. Bunch of damn crooks is what they are. So many of these assholes had their eye on this property. I was the first to get there; they can't stand it." He lowered his voice and said, "This isn't public, but when I sign on the dotted line, I'm going to take the cash from the sale and invest in a decent size development for this property with the new owners." He laughed and said, "Man are they going to be pissed when they hear about what I have planned."

"Can't wait to hear about it. I mean it. I'm excited for you. I know you probably need to go, but can I ask a favor?"

"Barclay."

"I know, I know. I never want to assume anything, though. Can you let me know when the head's going up? I'd like to be there. For old time's sake, you know."

"Absolutely. I've been thinking about doing something special with this one. Make a real statement."

"I can't wait to see what you have planned."

"Hell, maybe the first advertisement I put up will be touting the new development going there." *Yep,* Barclay thought, *that's my Uncle Jack.*

CHAPTER 20

WHAT THE HELL IS going on?" Kingery's voice startled Barclay, who was kneeling before the open credenza.

It was after 10:00 in the evening, and Barclay had made certain the office was devoid of any activity before going into Kingery's office to retrieve the burner he knew to be hidden in the very spot he had just been busted searching. *What is he doing here?* Barclay thought as his heartbeat began to settle into its normal rhythm. Then his thoughts turned to how he could explain what he was doing in this office, hours after the last person had left for the day, crouched behind Kingery's desk, burner in hand. Options spun through his head like a slot machine, only no triple sevens emerged; he did the only thing he knew to do: start talking.

"What are you doing here?" he asked Kingery, not moving from where he was found.

The question seemed to fluster Kingery as he briefly sputtered before finally noticing what Barclay held in his hand. He stared at it and murmured, "My phone."

"This is your phone?" Barclay said, holding it out toward Kingery.

A long silence followed—Barclay holding his breath, hoping for an incontrovertible admission; Kingery's legal mind kicking in almost automatically, weighing what to say or not say. Both men sensed this was a critical moment. As the silence drew on, Barclay fought the urge to break it. He knew well the old negotiation adage *he who speaks first loses*. That would not be him.

After an interminable amount of time, Kingery jutted his chin toward the phone and said, "What do you think you have there?" To which Barclay thought to himself: *You lose, asshole.*

Barclay stood, looked down at the phone in his hand, and said, "What do I have?" He shrugged and continued, "I think this is a phone you've been using to communicate with Veronica Lane since she went missing." A few seconds passed before he continued, a slight smile creasing his lips, "You going to tell me I'm right?" Barclay tried to read his face. Nothing. "Well, ok, if this isn't your phone, I guess I'll be seeing you." He began to walk to the door, and the big man grabbed Barclay by the arm as he attempted to pass.

"Give me the phone."

"So this is your phone?"

He let go of Barclay's arm. "Of course, it's my phone. You found it in my office. Who the hell else would it belong to?"

"Huh," was all Barclay said.

It was Kingery's turn to smile, "What? You think you have something of value? You do realize that even if there were something on that phone, you'd need a search warrant not only to seize it but also to analyze it, right?" Kingery made a show of examining Barclay's person and said, "I don't see any paper, so I'm assuming you don't have the legal authority to walk out of here with my personal property." He paused, sniffed, said, "You going to tell me I'm right?" He looked quite pleased with himself, having used Barclay's previous turn of phrase against him.

Barclay began to see his out, but he was careful not to show Kingery any sign that he was relaxing. He held up his hands and said, "You're right."

"You're goddamn right I am. You don't have anything on me; otherwise, you'd have a warrant and wouldn't have had to sneak in here under cover of darkness...so to speak. Now give me the phone." Barclay handed him the phone, and once Kingery had it in his hand, he said, "You know. I've been meaning to get a new cell. This one has been acting up a bit as of late." He then popped open the back of the phone and removed the sim card. Holding the tiny object in his sausage fingers looked comical. Turning it front and back, looking it over, he said, "I will probably go ahead and shred this before I leave tonight." Then, to Barclay: "Can't be too careful these days with all the identity theft and whatnot." Barclay wasn't sure what identity theft had to do with anything, so he left the statement alone, hoping Kingery would keep talking. "And as for the phone itself, probably need to destroy it too, don't you think?" He held the phone up to Barclay and said, "It is amazing what information these phones hold. I mean, you and I both know that when you delete something on your phone, it's never really gone, right? So yeah, with the technology we have at our fingertips, these phones nowadays can tell a hell of a story."

He was taunting Barclay now. Despite all but confirming what Barclay and his folks believed to be true, it was really pissing him off, which Kingery seemed to notice. "Oh, you thought, what, that you were going to walk out of here with this"—he waggled the phone between them—"and do a full forensic exam on it? And find what? Evidence to confirm some ridiculous notion of yours that I have been using this phone to communicate with... with a dead woman?" Kingery made a noise with his mouth and said, "You disappoint me, my friend. Look at it this way, I saved you some embarrassment. Imagine actually going to a judge with such a story." He laughed and shook his head. "No. It's better this way." Then, with all humor gone: "Trust me."

❋   ❋   ❋   ❋   ❋

It was precisely 5:00 in the evening, the day before, when Barclay entered Judge Arnett's courtroom and saw His Honor, robe unzipped, eyeglasses perched on his forehead, reading glasses astride his nose, and reading from a red and blue leather-bound law book.

Barclay cleared his throat and said, "I was hoping to catch you in your office, but Delta told me you were on the bench. I need to speak with you about something of a sensitive nature."

Arnett did not react to the interruption except to appraise Barclay across the top of his glasses with watery eyes. After a few seconds, he said, "Something of a sensitive nature? What the hell's that supposed to mean?" Judge Arnett had a way of making people ask for things—especially if he thought you were asking him for a favor.

"It means you and I need to talk...outside the courthouse."

"Oh." Barclay's father, Grover, was largely responsible for Malcolm Arnett's judgeship and the judge never forgot that. It was never cause for special treatment, and the elder Griffith never asked for it. What it did mean, though, is that Barclay had leeway with the judge more than most. He could be more direct with the judge, but that was a rarity which told His Honor that this was indeed a serious matter. "I have several orders I need to get out and two briefs I've got to get through before tomorrow, so I am going to be up here a while. Meet me at Tincs at midnight."

Most people would have been shocked being asked to meet at such a time, but not Barclay. "I believe it closes at midnight, Judge."

But the black robe flowing cape-like was all Barclay saw as the judge exited the bench without another word.

❖　❖　❖　❖　❖

The Tincturist—known to the locals simply as Tincs—was the bar in the historic Dabney Hotel located a half-mile from the town square. The Dabney was the first hotel built in Towne. With the beautiful Victorian architecture inside and out, its secret rooms and passageways, and its impeccable staff, the place was a destination spot in its own right for those who wanted to take a step báck in time and experience life at a slower pace.

Tincs was all brass, dark mahogany, and gilded glass and mirrors. It boasted the finest bartenders for more than a century; there wasn't a cocktail known to man they couldn't make. Barclay arrived thirty minutes early for no reason other than having nothing else to do. He was the only customer and chatted up the bartender over a pint. Tincs was set to close at midnight, and at 11:59, Judge Arnett walked in and laid six one hundred dollar bills on the bar for what remained in the bottle of Ainsley Brae 1964 on the top shelf behind the bar. The judge asked for two glasses and to be left alone. The bartender pocketed the cash, set the bottle and two heavy Waterford cut crystal glasses on the bar, and left. The judge poured them each an inch of Scotch and said, "Now, what's this all about?"

Barclay spent the next few minutes telling the judge about his theory of the Veronica Lane case. Judge Arnett presided over the trial, so he did not get in-depth with the facts, although he did touch on a couple of the issues pertinent to where they were now. He explained finding the cryoprotectant in the blood, the sighting of a person believed to be Lane in the Portland area, and the cell phone activity and cell tower mapping.

Barclay had been doing all the talking up to this point, so the judge was on his second Scotch before Barclay took his first sip. Now it was the judge's turn to talk and Barclay's turn to drink. Judge Arnett said, "So the long and short of it is that you believe—"

"Damn," Barclay interrupted, looking into his glass.

"Good, isn't it? You know I don't drink bad liquor." The judge coughed once into his fist, then said, "As I was saying, you don't believe Clements killed that girl." It was said as a statement.

"That's right."

"How long have you had this notion?"

"A few days now." They both savored the amber liquid, the judge pouring Barclay's second and himself a third.

The judge took a slow drink and said, "Well, his lawyer is dead...." He tapped the glass on the bar a few times. "I can appoint him a new lawyer in the morning—"

"I've already handled that. I got Luke Jackson to agree to represent him and talk to him about where we are."

"He going to file a motion?"

"Remains to be seen, but I made certain he understood that it is in his best interest not to. At least for the time being."

Arnette gave a look that oozed skepticism. "And why is that?"

"Ostensibly because the longer we can keep this information under wraps, the better our chances of figuring out what the hell is going on and who all is involved. It's also a safety issue for Clements."

The judge appeared to turn that over in his head and said, "Right now, the person or persons involved believe they've gotten away with whatever it is they did, and Clements filing a motion would only serve to announce that their secret may not be so safe. Kill Clements, and who wants to investigate the possible wrongful conviction of a dead man?"

"My thoughts exactly."

Arnett had a look on his face that said he was weighing what he was hearing. He was swirling the last of the Scotch in his glass before killing it. As he poured his fourth, he said, "This information alone may not...check that, is probably not enough to overturn his conviction and set him free." He was going right down the path Barclay hoped he would. "You need to figure out who is involved in this. Only after this thing is solved will Clements be released...and safe." Barclay could hear the alcohol working on the judge. "So, any thoughts as to who is involved and why?"

This was it; what his dad called *nut-cuttin' time*. He had to lay out his suspicions regarding Kingery's involvement in all of this, and he knew the judge wouldn't like it. So Barclay drained Scotch number two, the judge refilled the glass for Scotch number three, and Barclay began to talk.

❊   ❊   ❊   ❊   ❊

"Kingery? Chief Assistant District Attorney Richard Kingery. You're shittin' me." The judge had listened thoughtfully and without interruption.

Barclay shook his head and said, "Nope."

Judge Arnett poured Scotch number five—he was pulling away. "So, let me make sure I've got this right. Bottom line is you believe this Veronica Lane is alive, and you also believe that Kingery has been in contact with her since her disappearance." Barclay nodded, and the judge continued, "You came to this belief because you called a number that was in contact with a phone that appears to be connected to Lane, and you found that phone in Kingery's office?" Another nod, another drink by both, another pour for Barclay (number four). "How do you plan on proving this?"

"That's why I wanted to talk to you. I need a search warrant for that phone."

Arnett rubbed his face with his left hand and said, "Jesus Christ, son."

"You know me, Judge. You know how I work, and you know I don't bullshit about this stuff."

Arnett exhaled and said, "I know you don't." He thought for a moment and said, "I respect the hell out of you, Barclay, and not because of who your daddy is. You're a good man and a helluva prosecutor who has always done things the right way." He tapped his glass on the bar again and continued, "This is a helluva thing we have here." He was nearing the end of his fifth Scotch, and they'd barely been there an hour. Barclay knew his window to get a search warrant from a judge with a sound mind was rapidly closing.

"We can do all of this under seal. The last thing I want to do is ruin his career over a false allegation. Don't get me wrong, I don't much care for the guy, but I certainly don't want the fallout from this to impact him in any way if I'm wrong…but I don't believe I am."

"No. It doesn't sound like it," said the judge. His voice telling Barclay he was going to issue the search warrant, but he was not happy about it.

Barclay pulled a stapled set of papers folded once lengthwise and sat it on the bar in front of the judge. He set a Montblanc rollerball with the cap removed on top of the papers. The judge scrawled his name in blue ink on the page authorizing the search and then on the page to serve as the court order. Barclay stared at the Scotch-laden scrawl on the signature lines and hoped to God no one questioned the particulars of the warrant's approval process.

"You've got your warrant, Mr. Griffith. Care to tell me your plan to get his phone without him suspecting anything?"

A smile that was more of a smirk marked Barclay's face as he said, "You sure you want to know?"

"Goddamn you, man," Arnett said, laughing. He finished off number five and poured number six. "You were right to come to me about this and that we handle it outside the courthouse." The judge pointed at Barclay with the hand holding his glass and said, "Only you and your team know about this. I hear it from someone else, I'll know one of you leaked it, and I will burn your asses, understood."

"Yessir."

Arnett and Barclay spent the next hour sitting in the dimness of a bar closed for the night and finished the bottle.

CHAPTER 21

BARCLAY SAT BEHIND THE desk in his home study, and Tina Crump and Winston Fitzsimmons were seated in chairs on the opposite side. The eucalyptus smell filling the room was owed to a candle burning on the bookcase.

"Before we begin," said Tina, "I want it on the record that I think Drummond should be here for this."

"I'm with her, Boss," said Fitz with a tilt of his head in her direction. "We're monkeying around with his case, and I know if it were me, I'd be pretty pissed about this meeting behind my back."

Barclay held up a hand and said, "First of all, we aren't meeting behind his back. I texted him that we were due for a briefing and asked if he wanted to join us—"

Fitz interrupted, saying, "This is a little more than a briefing."

Barclay continued, "And secondly, I'm not in the mood to deal with him on the phone stuff. We are seriously crunched for time here, and now my ass is directly in the jackpot with Judge Arnett over this. Besides, I can handle Wayne. I'll update him when we're done here." Tina and Fitz exchanged dubious glances. "Look, I will put this on me, ok? Now, what were you able to find out?" This last question was directed at Tina.

Tina removed some papers from a manila envelope. Eyeing the documents, she said, "I still can't believe you got his phone." Looking up, she continued, "You got soooo lucky."

"Oh, I know. It scared the hell out of me when he walked in. Thirty seconds earlier, and I would have been busted, no doubt about it, and all of this"—he waved a hand over all of the files that made up this investigation splayed across his desk—"would have been for naught. It was his hubris that allowed me to get away with such a shallow story. He couldn't see any way that he was busted."

"Well, he's flat-busted, alright," Tina said as she looked through the stack of papers. Finally finding what she was looking for, she said, "And using Gus Petropolous for the phone dump was a fantastic idea. The PD's phone guy would have run his mouth for sure. He's fresh off training and tells everyone who will listen how great he is and what an asset he will be to any investigation with a cell phone in evidence."

"He's right," said Fitz.

"Of course he is," said Tina. "But I don't have any doubt what was recovered would have been all over the PD and courthouse within five minutes of reading the first text."

Fitz said, "You don't have to worry about Gus running his mouth. He doesn't talk to anyone. And that's no exaggeration." Barclay fiddled with his iPhone, and the purr of Sinatra filled the room at a low volume.

Tina: "Well, any doubts we had regarding who these numbers belonged to are now assuaged. The number we thought belonged to Veronica Lane does—or did, in fact, belong to her. And I confirmed the other number she was in contact with belongs to the phone you found in Kingery's office."

"Text messages?" asked Barclay.

"Yes. More than a hundred to the first number, which is much fewer than I would have guessed."

"Anything good in the texts?" said Barclay.

"Good in that we can connect the two of them communicating from the day of her disappearance; however, there wasn't anything of great substance as to their plan and nothing from Kingery regarding Duncan's murder."

Barclay seemed to be weighing what he was hearing when Fitz said, "At least now we have confirmation of our working theory. Establishing the link between the two of them is big."

Barclay said, "That's true. But what about this second phone number? Were you able to find out anything?"

"It's another burner. Went live the day after the first one went dead." Just then, Tina's phone rang. "I need to take this," she said, eyeing the caller ID as she slipped outside to the back porch.

"I'd say any question that Lane was the woman seen by the Popes is also gone," said Fitz. "Looks like she made a life for herself up there."

"Sure appears that way." Barclay got up, walked to the mini-fridge, grabbed a water, and held it out to Fitz, who waved it off. He uncapped the bottle and drank. He walked to the door and scratched his back against the doorframe. The sound of the garage door opening and closing was followed by the odor of pizza wafting into the room. He continued rubbing his back against the doorframe and said, "This is all good stuff, but I'm not sure we have *it*. I think we're just going to have to get up there and try to make contact with her. See if she'll talk." Seeing the look on Fitz's face, Barclay said, "What?"

Fitz shook his head as he said, "I don't fly." Barclay thought he detected real fear in his voice.

"You don't fly?"

"Nope."

"You serious?"

"As a heart attack."

"Come on, man. What am I supposed to do with that?" Anger leached into Barclay's voice. "I need an investigator to go, and you know I can't take anyone else."

Fitz shrugged and said, "Take Drummond." Barclay met that comment with a stare when Tina walked back in, sliding her phone into her back pocket.

"What's going on?"

Both men looked at Tina, and Barclay said, "Our fearless investigator is afraid to fly."

"What brought that up?" she asked.

"I suggested going to Oregon and trying to connect with our girl."

"But she's not in Oregon."

"Say what?" Both men said in unison.

"She's not in Oregon. Well, I should say that her phone isn't in Oregon. I'm making an assumption about her, I guess."

Brittany walked in with a large pizza and sat it on the coffee table with plates and napkins. All three turned and looked at her, and she wisely extracted herself, saying, "I'm not even going to ask."

Barclay rubbed his face with both hands and said, "Ok. Can you please explain what you're talking about?"

"Sure. According to the cell tower mapping, she left Oregon end of July and headed back east. The most recent location we have for her is North Charleston."

"What?"

"It's in South Carolina."

Barclay exhaled. "I'm aware Charleston is in South Carolina. It was a rhetorical question." Exasperated, he said, "I need some food."

❊　❊　❊　❊　❊

The three of them sat in silence around the coffee table, eating pizza, only now realizing just how hungry they all were. Barclay and Tina drank beer with their pizza while Fitz drank a Coke. The food and the alcohol worked to calm Barclay's fraying nerves. He, in particular, had endured a tremendous amount over the last few weeks, and the ebb and flow of the seemingly slow-moving investigation was weighing on him.

"I don't know about you, but I needed that," Barclay said, referring to the pizza and beer. Tina and Fitz nodded their agreement, mouths full. The smell of cured meats had overtaken that of the eucalyptus candle. "Alright, now that we've all had a chance to catch our breath and relax, let's get back to this new development that Veronica Lane is no longer in Oregon." Fitz and Tina shared the briefest of glances, both feeling like Barclay was the one who needed to relax at the moment. "Alright, Tina, what's this about Lane now being in South Carolina?"

Tina finished chewing, drank the last of the can of beer, wiped her mouth with a napkin, and said, "Same as I did with the previous phone number; I requested a report on the cell tower mapping for the new number we discovered. I input the lats and longes and produced this." She pulled up a program on her MacBook Pro that plotted a path eastward across the United States and settled into a cluster of hits around northeast coastal South Carolina. "The last hit in the Portland area was July twenty-seventh. It appears that's the day she left and made her way back east."

There was something familiar about that date to Barclay. He got up and grabbed his bat, resting it on his shoulder as he paced the room. "What is the significance of that date?" he said out loud, but more to himself. Fitz was helping himself to the last piece of pizza.

Barclay leaned the bat against his desk and dropped into the overstuffed chair behind it. He began sifting through the papers on his desk until he found what he was looking for and slapped his hand on his desk. "That's it! The twenty-seventh is the day Pamela Rogers called to tell me about the Pope's seeing a person they believed to be her sister."

Tina said, "So she fled Oregon the day she was seen? That is an awfully quick reaction."

Fitz jumped in: "Actually, she was seen the day before. If I remember correctly, Pamela missed the call from the Pope's the day prior and had only learned of the sighting the day after when she returned Mrs. Pope's phone call."

Tina: "The Popes see her on the twenty-sixth, and on the twenty-seventh, she's on the road. Still a quick decision."

Barclay: "Agreed. Guess you stay pretty nimble when you are on the run like that." He clapped his hands and rubbed them together. "Good news, Fitzie ol' boy, you won't have to get on a plane after all."

"Were you going to force me to get on a plane?"

A shrug. "Guess we'll never know."

The trio spent the next hour going through the text messages and other evidence gleaned from Kingery's phone; they went back and forth about the significance of it all. Finally, the decision was made to confront Kingery with what they had discovered. This was debated—at times heatedly—but the one point they all agreed on was that the case needed movement. They had the evidence, and nothing Kingery could do could change that, so the risk seemed minimal compared to the potential gain. The final consensus was that they needed to shake Kingery up. Show him what they had and see if that would force him into doing something stupid.

That decided, they then went through the to-do list previously compiled and marked off what tasks had been accomplished and what needed to be added based on this new information. Task assignments were made, and a preliminary plan of action for trying to make contact with Veronica Lane was formulated.

Barclay found himself climbing out of the valley he saw himself in just days ago. Momentum was back, and the buzz was palpable.

❉   ❉   ❉   ❉   ❉

The following day Barclay strode into Kingery's office. It was late—after 8:00—and they were the last two people in the office. The night cleaning crew had just left, which told Barclay it was time.

The previous weeks had been tense around the office. Since finding Barclay in his office, Kingery had been more of a jerk than usual, with a shorter temper and sharper tongue when he wasn't closed up in his office. He had been the first to arrive and the last to leave every day, which was unusual. And only Barclay knew why.

Unlike the previous two trips into Kingery's office, this visit carried no sense of dread or worry. The door to the office was open; presumably, Kingery believed himself to be the only person still at the office. Barclay walked in and sat in a chair across from Kingery's desk. Kingery, who had been writing on a legal pad, looked up non-plussed, said, "Get out," and went back to writing.

Barclay didn't move, and after a few seconds of continued writing, he stopped, laid his pen down on the legal pad, leaned back in his leather executive desk chair, and said, "Why are you still here?"

In answer to the question, Barclay reached into an outer suit jacket pocket, withdrew a clear plastic evidence bag, and tossed it onto Kingery's legal pad.

"What is that?"

"Pick it up and look at it. You tell me."

Kingery looked from Barclay to the bag, then back to Barclay, then back to the bag. He leaned forward, picked up the bag, and pressed it against its contents. There it was: recognition. It was brief, but Barclay saw it because he was looking for it...and expecting it.

His composure regained; Kingery tossed it back onto his desk, leaned back, shook his head, and said, "Is this really the best you've got? You're not dealing with a moron. I'm not some shitbag off the street who you can throw some bullshit evidence at and expect me to vomit a confession." He leaned forward, picked the bag up, and almost as quickly tossed it back down. He was about to speak and caught himself. His gaze went to Barclay's chest, then back to his face. A smirk then: "This phone is bullshit, and we both know it." His voice was louder and more direct.

It took a moment, but Barclay understood why the change in tone. He said, "You think I'm wearing a wire?"

Kingery shrugged, "I don't care if you are or not. We both know this isn't my phone. I caught you in my office attempting to steal a phone a few weeks ago, but you were unable to accomplish your...*mission*." He paused before continuing. "In fact, you witnessed me destroy that phone. So, I don't know what it is you purport to have." Every word up a tick in volume and enunciation.

Barclay let a silence hang between them before speaking. He pointed at the phone in the evidence bag on the desk and said, "Are you sure that's not your phone?"

Kingery narrowed his eyes at Barclay, doubt beginning to chip away at his confident visage. His eyes flicked down to the bag-encased phone.

"You know it's your phone. I can see it in your face."

"Bullshit," was all Kingery could muster.

"You see...Dick, when you walked in on me in your office that night, I wasn't removing your phone; I was putting it back. Well, I was actually putting back a replacement phone. The real phone—your phone—was already in my pocket." Barclay wished he had a camera to capture the look on Kingery's face. He continued, "I found the number of the phone Ms. Lane was using to communicate with you when she disappeared." He nodded, "That's right. Hell of a thing, I know. Anyway, we could *not* figure out who she was talking and texting with. We had a phone number, of course, but no way to trace it to the number's owner. No matter what we tried, this mystery person remained just that—a mystery." He paused here, dragging his story out, knowing that Kingery was working a slow burn and silently cursing him, trying to move the story along. Barclay shrugged and said, "So one night, I'm up here at the office, and I decided to call the number myself. I mean, what else could I do, right? I needed to move the investigation along." Seeing the look on Kingery's face, he said, "Oh, not a formal investigation. Just me looking into who killed my friend." He pointed at Kingery and said, "You didn't have anything to do with that, did you?" No reaction. He continued, "Where was I? Oh yeah, I called the number. I don't want to bore you with the details, but I called the number and, well, I found the phone in your office, tucked way back behind some books in your credenza. I didn't take your phone that night because I didn't want to alert you to what I had found, and, as you said, I didn't have a warrant." He spread his arms and said, "And here we are."

The air was gone from the room, and Barclay sat back content to wait on Kingery to speak, and after almost a full minute, he did. "Even if all of that is true, there is no way a judge gives you a warrant for this which just tells me that anything you may have found is useless."

"If all of that is true? I assure you, Dick—"

"Quit calling me that," he said through gritted teeth.

"All of what I have told you is most certainly true...Richard. I got a warrant, but I still did not want to alert you if you went to look for your phone and it was missing, so I figured I would trade out your phone for another one of the same model, and you'd never notice. At least not until we had what we needed. I have to say, your walking in on me was serendipitous. I got your phone, but you walked out believing you had nothing to worry about, so there was no longer a sense of urgency which allowed us the time to do what we needed to do."

"Which was what?" Kingery asked, but he knew, and the bravado was leaving his voice with every syllable.

"You know *what*, Richard. Look for evidence."

Kingery said, "I don't believe you." But any trace of confidence he was trying valiantly to hold onto evaporated from his voice.

"What do you not believe, Richard?"

"Any of it," he croaked.

"Perhaps this will convince you." Barclay tossed a letter-sized manila envelope on the desk and grabbed the evidence bag containing the phone.

Kingery stared at the envelope before slowly, steadily reaching for it as if it were a bomb ready to detonate at the slightest misstep. He pinched the tiny metal clasp with his thick sausage fingers and slid the flap open. He reached in and pulled the contents halfway out of the envelope; his face immediately grew ashen. The first thing he saw was the search warrant for the phone signed by Judge Arnett. He need only see the next couple of pages to know he was looking at the phone extraction report. His phone.

"You're fucked...Dick."

CHAPTER 22

BARCLAY WAS EXACTLY WHERE he told her he would be: At Waterfront Park on a porch swing under the middle of the three covered structures on the Vendue Wharf overlooking the Cooper River. This was day three, and he was going home if she did not appear today.

Charleston, South Carolina, was perhaps Barclay's favorite southern city. The combination of history, food, and drink was unrivaled by any city south of the Mason-Dixon, save for New Orleans. Of course, he liked New Orleans, but Charleston's quieter, slower pace was more him than the Louisiana's port city's laissez les bons temps roller attitude.

It was just after 7:00 p.m., and the sun was setting to Barclay's back as he sat facing out over the water with views of the U.S.S. Yorktown and the Ravenel Bridge off to his left. The sounds and smells of tourists and locals enjoying the food and drinks at Fleet Landing were drifting his way. He had been there since 5:00 p.m., just as he had been the previous two days and just as he had said he would in his text message. The previous two days, he had sat there until 9:00 p.m., and he would do the same this evening unless Veronica Lane showed up earlier, which was looking less and less likely with each passing minute.

Five days prior, almost to the hour, Barclay, Fitz, and Tina had sat in Barclay's study, fleshing out a plan to make contact with their missing girl. The plan had been a simple one: text her. After all, it was a decision to dial the mystery phone number that had resulted in their most significant development to date: unearthing Kingery's involvement. The three of them debated the pros and cons of making direct contact until Barclay made the executive decision that texting her was the way they would go.

He texted her the following day. The text read:

> *Hello, Veronica. My name is Barclay Griffith, and I am an Assistant District Attorney with the Towne County DA Office. I don't know if you are aware, but a man named Charlie Calvin Clements was recently convicted of your murder and is facing the death penalty. I know you are alive, and unless I can prove that, Mr. Clements will die in prison. You can read about Mr. Clements' conviction online to verify my story. I have zero interest in charging you with a crime. The fact is, I'm not sure you have committed a crime. I only want Mr. Clements freed from prison, and I hope you can find it in your heart to do the right thing. I will be at Waterfront Park on a porch swing under the middle of the three covered structures on the Vendue Wharf from 5:00 p.m. to 9:00 p.m. this coming Wednesday, Thursday, and Friday. I will be wearing an orange golf shirt and khaki pants. You can find a picture of me at townecountyda.org. A very good friend of mine, Mr. Clements' lawyer, was murdered, and I believe it is related to your case. You can look up his death as well: Duncan Pheiffer. I will be alone. Approach me on the pier, and we can chat. This is my personal cell.*

The text had gone unanswered, which surprised no one. They also weren't terribly optimistic about her showing up, but they all agreed they were running out of options. No one wanted to speak about what worried them most: she dumped the phone when she arrived in Charleston, thus leaving that text floating somewhere in the ether. Barclay personally covered the expenses for himself and Fitz because he couldn't ask his office to pay for it, and he wasn't going to ask Fitz to come out of pocket for what amounted to his idea. The next day the pair made the nearly six-hour trip to Charleston and enjoyed what could be their only free night by having dinner at Hall's Chophouse and finishing the evening across the street at Proof for cocktails. Barclay enjoyed three Knuckleballs with extra pickled boiled peanuts while Fitz knocked back three classic Old Fashioneds. Neither of them spoke a word about work after crossing into Charleston County, and they wouldn't until it came time to get down to business. They stayed at the Francis Marion Hotel on King Street and grabbed coffee and biscuits the following morning at Callie's Hot Little Biscuit.

"I swear, Boss, traveling with you is bad for my health," Fitz said with a laugh as he polished off his third Conecuh sausage, fried egg, and pimento cheese biscuit.

"Ah, but a hell of a way to go, my friend."

After breakfast, they wandered around downtown and made their way to Market Street, which took them to Concord Street and on down to Waterfront Park. They reconnoitered where Barclay would be set up and looked for a spot for Fitz to camp that would have line of sight. Barclay would wear an earbud that was a speaker only. He could hear Fitz talk to him, but he could not speak to Fitz; Fitz was only there as an extra pair of eyes. He would keep an eye out for the surrounding area and alert Barclay to anything that raised his antenna.

They killed the first afternoon walking downtown, in and out of men's clothing shops. They each made purchases at M. Dumas and Sons, grabbed some afternoon coffee at Kudu, and discussed their plan. Finally, just before 5:00 in the afternoon, the swing had become available, and Barclay claimed it before anyone else could.

The first two evenings came and went without contact being made, and he was getting anxious. The first evening on the pier, he enjoyed the beauty of the Cooper River at sunset, even thinking that this would be a great place to retire. However, he appreciated the sunset less the next night because he knew what was at stake; his thoughts were fading into the realm of *what if this didn't work.*

Here he sat on Friday evening as the clock passed 7:15. He now viewed the sunset as a metaphor for his dwindling chances of cracking this case with her failure to appear. That was when he heard a female voice speak his name from behind.

❊   ❊   ❊   ❊   ❊

Hearing his name startled him the way it does when you hear your name from a voice you don't recognize—that and because he had been lost in his thoughts.

Barclay stood and said, "Ms. Lane? Veronica Lane?" She looked small and apprehensive as her eyes darted back and forth between him and her surroundings. Her hair was dyed purple, a distinct departure from her natural white blonde as seen in the now-familiar missing person photo. She was wearing dark blue skinny jeans and a faded dark-colored hoodie that was unzipped, exposing a light grey t-shirt with writing on it that Barclay couldn't read.

She said, "Are you alone? You said you would be alone."

Barclay had a decision to make, and he opted for the truth. "No. My investigator is nearby."

He had calculated wrong.

She muttered, "I knew this was a bad idea," as she pulled up her hood and turned to leave.

"Ms. Lane, wait. Please." She stopped but did not turn around. "He's only here to watch my back. With everything that has happened with this case, he wouldn't allow me to do this by myself." Barclay felt a twinge of guilt at the lie, but he was losing her. After maybe five seconds, she turned her head slightly, and he could see her purple hair falling around her face. He considered taking a gamble, believing he had nothing to lose. He gave it another beat, then pressed on. "Look, if I were here to arrest you, it would have happened already." *Now for the gamble*: "I know you came by each of the last two days." She stiffened. *Bingo*. "My investigator saw you. I would have done the same thing." That last statement was true, which was why he took the flyer. "I wanted the decision to talk to me to be yours and yours alone. You were right to be cautious, but you would also be right to trust me. I'm not the enemy here."

He could see her shoulders soften, and she turned back to him as she looked around. "Will your investigator be joining us?"

Barclay shook his head. "No."

Weighing the decision, she finally said, "Okay. But I want to keep this meeting out in the open."

"Fine by me. Why don't we walk as we talk?" They moved out from under the structure and headed south on the sidewalk bordering the river.

They walked in silence until they passed the pineapple fountain. Veronica Lane spoke first. "It's funny you asked to meet here because this has become my favorite place in the few days I've been here. It's beautiful. So peaceful at night."

"I love Charleston; everything about it. It's a favorite spot for my wife and me." He was wading in carefully. He didn't want to press too hard too quickly and lose her.

They continued at a sluggish pace, and when they neared the end of the sidewalk fronting the river, she steered them toward the last park bench and sat down. Laughter and music floated on the waterfront breeze while their silence stretched on—no way Barclay was speaking first.

She finally spoke: "I guess I should start at the beginning."

❊   ❊   ❊   ❊   ❊

Barclay sat in one corner of the wood and cast iron bench angled inward to Veronica with his left leg crossed over his right. Veronica was leaning forward, elbows on her knees and her head hanging. A man and woman walked by—she pushing an empty stroller and he with a little girl riding atop his shoulders—and Veronica watched them, head down, eyes up, and waited for them to pass before she began speaking.

"No one was supposed to get into trouble." Veronica spoke with both regret and pain. She sat up and eyed Barclay. "I was supposed to spread some blood around and get out of town. That's it. Simple. Make a mess and disappear." Her eyes were pleading. For what? Understanding? Forgiveness? Barclay couldn't decide.

She seemed to want him to say something, so he said, "What were you running from?"

She leaned back, looking toward the sky before leaning forward, eyes out over the river watching a barge approach from their right. "I met a guy," she said with a snort. "Malik Traylor."

This got Barclay's attention. "Wait, you know Malik?" She just looked at him. "Sorry. Please continue."

"We met at a party. Don't ask me what it was for because I don't remember." She pulled a thumb drive from her hoodie pocket. Barclay was watching her, wondering what she was about to do with it. She put it to her mouth, then exhaled a stream of smoke. *A Juul,* Barclay thought. "We hit it off. I knew he wasn't from Towne, but he was there often enough. It wasn't anything serious at first—I was working nights, he lived forty-five minutes away—but we clicked." Another drag of the Juul. "I even started to look into nursing jobs in Montgomery. That was until I told Malik what I was planning."

"He wasn't into you as much as you were into him?"

A long drag on the Juul this time, then she shook her head as she exhaled a plume of smoke and said, "I honestly don't know. At the time, I truly believed we had something, but looking back, I'm not so sure." They eyed a group of college-aged kids walking by laughing, two of them pushing on each other. Veronica continued: "He said he liked me where I was. That hurt me, and I asked him why he didn't want me to be where *he* was. He said he had bigger plans for me—for us. He started asking me about my access to drugs in the hospital. What was I authorized to get, what were the procedures to get them—"

"He wanted you to work for him."

"Pretty much, yes. *But,*" she emphasized, "you must understand that I saw it as us doing something together. You see, he wasn't using *me* so much as I was helping *him.*" A shrug. "At least, that's how I saw it at the time, and as I said, I liked him, and I believed that he liked me. He said it helped that I had been at that hospital so long; I had the trust of everyone there. If I moved to a new hospital, I wouldn't be as trusted, at least for a while. The idea was that if drugs were discovered missing, my current employer was more likely to believe a denial than if I were the new person." She paused here as if setting down a heavy weight before having to pick it back up to carry it farther. "It made sense—all of it." She drew on the Juul, which was empty. She cursed under her breath and said, "I need a beer."

"I thought you'd never ask. I know a good place nearby—the beer is cold, it's a little dark, and not too crowded right now. A good place to talk." She nodded her assent, and they rose from the bench and walked to the end of the waterfront walkway before turning right on Middle Atlantic Wharf, talking as they walked. "Full disclosure here: I'm aware you were being investigated for stealing pills from the hospital." Veronica pulled up short. "Hey, I already told you I'm not here to get you in any kind of trouble. Please believe that. I also want you to understand that I have been and will be honest and upfront with you." They began walking again and hung a left on East Bay Street. "To be clear, all I know is that there was an investigation. I don't know any details aside from the assertion that the thefts were captured on video." Foot traffic was still relatively light at this hour, so they strolled at an easy pace. "I assume you were aware of the investigation?"

"Not at first. Not until Kingery told me. That's where things began to sorta go off the rails." They dodged a pair of couples as they approached the next block. "Back to Malik. I agreed to his plan." She shook her head and said, "Don't ask me why. I mean, sure, I liked the guy, but still…I look back and ask myself, 'what the fuck was I thinking?' you know?" They made the turn onto Broad Street. "I started fairly small, as a test, and gradually increased what I was taking."

"How long after you started taking the pills did Kingery make contact with you?"

She gave that some thought before saying, "Six or seven months, maybe."

"How did you get the pills to Malik?"

She looked up at Barclay and said, "Are you looking to charge Malik with anything?"

"No." Barclay weighed what he should say here. He wanted to give as she was giving, keep building trust, and getting information. However, he did not want to turn all his cards over on the table. "Did you research Duncan Pheiffer's murder that I referenced in my text?"

"I did, and I'm sorry about your friend."

"Thank you. That is what, or rather who, I'm after—the person who did that. I need to know what happened and why my friend is dead. I don't give a damn about Malik's business—at least not right now." He stopped, which caused her to stop. He looked at her intently and said, "Nothing you tell me will come back on you, nor will it be used to make any case against Malik. You have my word." He searched her face for any sign that she believed him, and all he saw staring back was fear and doubt. "I need you to understand and believe that." She stared back, this time her eyes searching his, and seemed to find whatever it was she was looking for. She nodded once and started back walking. He caught up to her in three paces and said, "The bar is the next door on the right."

They entered The Blind Tiger Pub and approached the bar, ordering a pint. The smells from the small kitchen hung in the air; the sounds of a Celtic tune clung to the ceiling. Pints in hand, Barclay laid a twenty on the bar, said to the bartender, "Keep it," and made their way to a hightop in a corner of the small space. They drank from their glasses and savored the hoppy bitterness, whatever tension remained between them fading.

"I don't remember where we were," Veronica said.

Barclay thought about it and said, "I asked you how you got the pills to Malik. I need to understand as much of this as possible."

"The first time, I drove them to Montgomery. I wanted to surprise him with what I could get, and he got pissed—big time. Said he didn't want me getting stopped with the pills on me and getting arrested. He told me how he has people to move his drugs for him and that, going forward, he would send someone to get the pills from me."

"How was your relationship? Did you still feel like you had something going outside of getting him drugs to sell?" After the words left his mouth, he knew it was an unfair characterization, given the circumstances of their conversation. She bristled at his statement but answered nonetheless.

"That first delivery was an eye-opener for me. I suppose Malik cared enough not to want me to get arrested, but I soon realized there were two Maliks: the guy I met at the party and the businessman. He kept them separate and was pretty fanatical about it. When he was in work mode, you didn't bother him with anything that wasn't work-related. Nothing."

"So you continued to steal pills from the hospital, and Malik would send someone to get them from you."

"Yeah, pretty much."

"How often would there be a pickup?"

"Every couple of weeks, I'd say. There wasn't a set schedule or anything. I'd get a text saying when I'd be getting a visit, and someone would show up."

"Can you tell me about when you first met Richard Kingery?"

She nodded, taking another drink of her beer. She sucked the foam off her top lip and said, "He approached me in the hospital cafeteria during my dinner break."

"Wait, weren't you working nights?"

"Yep. Eleven P to seven A."

"So, he would have come to see you when?"

"I don't remember the exact time, but it would have been somewhere around two o'clock in the morning." A waitress came to their table and asked if they wanted to see food menus which they took to be polite but set them aside when the waitress walked away. "He introduced himself by showing me his badge. But, honestly, given the time of day he was there, I thought he was full of shit."

Barclay wanted to remark about him being full of shit *any* time of day but said instead, "What did he talk to you about?"

"Not much that time. He just introduced himself, gave me his card, and said he would be in touch. I didn't know what to think. One of the nurses I work with is married to a lawyer, so I asked her to ask her husband about him. I was able to verify that this Kingery was who he said he was."

"I'm guessing he showed back up?"

"Yeah. About a week or so later, same time and place. He said he was aware I had been stealing from the dispensary. Scared the hell out of me." She gulped down a quarter of her beer as if speaking it brought that fear front and center. "He just told me to be careful, be smart. Said he would be paying attention." She stared at Barclay. Shrugged. "And that was it. He was gone." The waitress was back now, and Barclay ordered two more beers and the Butcher's Board off the menu. She scooped up the menus and was gone.

Barclay said, "Hope that was ok. I hate taking up a table and not ordering something."

She finished off her beer and said, "Totally fine. The beer hits the spot, and if I'm honest, I could use a little food."

"Well, if you'd rather get something else, feel free to order it." Barclay sipped his beer before saying, "When did you next see him?"

"I'd say probably sometime in January or February. He came to me—same time and place as before—and said there were rumblings throughout the hospital of meds going missing from the dispensary. He reminded me to be smart about what I was doing and that he would continue to handle things on his end. He mentioned something about an exit plan, but I had no idea what that even meant. He said he would let me know my next steps but that Malik expected me to keep working."

"He mentioned Malik?"

"Yeah. I thought it was weird, too. I didn't even know they knew one another."

"And what did you do after that?"

"I kept working. I was well past the realization that I had gotten myself into something I didn't need to be a part of and seemed to be in too deep to do anything about it. A couple of weeks later, Kingery comes by my house during the day."

"Just shows up?"

"Just shows up. I'm telling you, there is something off about that guy." The beers and food arrived: smoked sausage, crispy pork belly, and duck cracklins. Seeing what was delivered, Veronica ordered a club sandwich. "Guess I just realized how hungry I really am."

Barclay did a quick scan of the interior before his eyes fell back on her. She said, "It was then that he laid out his plan. His idea was for me to fake my death and leave Towne forever under a new identity." She shook her head. "I couldn't believe what I was hearing, and all I remember thinking was how calm he was, how matter of fact. But then again, it wasn't his life that was going to be uprooted, now was it?" Anger edged into her voice. "He wanted me to start stockpiling my own fucking blood." She paused to let her last statement sink in. "It did give me at least a little bit of satisfaction to pick apart his little scheme, though."

"In what way?"

"As I said, his idea was for me to draw some blood so he could splash it around the house and have it look like something horrible had happened. I informed him that even a cursory examination of the blood would show that it wasn't fresh, which would blow his plan to shit, and no one with half a brain would believe I had been murdered. Also, it had to be enough blood. It couldn't be, say, a pint. It had to be a significant amount, or they could believe I was just badly injured and wandering around dazed somewhere."

"So the cryoprotectant was your idea?"

"Yep," she said proudly. "Wait, how did you know about that?"

"When I got word that someone thought they saw you in Oregon, I had the medical examiner go back and re-examine the blood evidence to look for anything unusual." He drank from his glass and said, "If it's any consolation, the ME was quite impressed."

"So that's how you knew I wasn't actually dead?"

"That and a few other things. The blood evidence was compelling, and what prompted us to take a closer look at everything else." He detailed their investigation up to that point: her computer internet history, discovering the burner phone, and tracking her to Oregon. It was her turn to be impressed when he detailed how they tracked her to Oregon and identified where she accessed the newspaper's website and her family's website about her case.

Her club sandwich arrived, and as she was pulling out the toothpicks holding the stacked sandwich together, Barclay said, "Why the sudden need for a plan?"

She paused, sandwich halfway to her mouth, and said, "What do you mean?"

"Well, he comes to you with what amounts to an escape plan. You clearly hate this guy—and believe me, you're not alone—so I know you did not do what he asked without finding out what was happening."

She nodded, mouth full. She finished chewing, wiped her mouth with a napkin, and said, "Kingery's story was that he had heard rumblings that the hospital was opening an internal investigation into missing meds from the dispensary. According to him, an internal audit showed some discrepancies. He told me the investigation was in the very early stages and whatever would come of it would take some time. Likely a few months since they didn't have the technology in place seen in some of the more updated hospitals. I knew from the hospital grapevine that that was an area the administration was looking into but was slow moving on it. That's a big part of why I felt comfortable doing what I was doing."

"But why did he care?"

She pointed a french fry at him and said, "Because he was working for Malik," then popped the fry in her mouth. Barclay could not hide his surprise, and she said, "Oh, you didn't know that?"

Barclay leaned in and said, "Did he actually tell you that?"

Shaking her head, she said, "Not initially, no. But I knew. At first, I couldn't figure out why he was turning a blind eye to what I was doing and why he went even further, essentially offering to make sure I didn't get caught—at least, that's how I took his message. Then it hit me: he was working for Malik." She took a bite and drank some beer. "Malik's operation runs like a business. He puts someone in charge of his divisions—as he calls them—so I assumed that Kingery was in charge of whatever business interests Malik had over here."

Barclay's right leg was going like a piston as he worked through all this. "Tell me about what it means to work for Malik."

"First and foremost, he is very loyal and demands the same. He takes care of his people."

"I'm sensing a *but*."

She swallowed the last of her beer and said, "But...you fail him, you do anything that costs him money or puts him at risk with the police, and he's done with you."

It was Veronica who signaled the waitress for more beers this time, and Barclay, leg still pumping, said, "What happens when he's 'done with you?'"

"You need to know it does not happen often because he makes it very clear what he expects before he gets involved with anyone. That said, he will essentially do whatever it takes to make sure whatever the problem that's been created cannot find its way back to him and that you pay for your mistake. He will also make certain that whatever he does sends a message to others about the consequences of failing him."

"Has he ever killed anyone who failed him?"

"I haven't personally known it to happen, but of course, there are stories."

The small space was crowding with revelers celebrating the arrival of the weekend; the music had also ticked up a notch in volume. The beers and overall mood of the bar were working their way into Barclay's and Veronica's conversation—any pretense between the two had evaporated. So many questions ran through his head. He finally settled on: "What would you say is his biggest worry?"

"His biggest worry?"

"Yeah. Or maybe I should ask...I guess what I want to know is the one unforgivable thing that one of Malik's people could do?"

"That's easy. Anything that can bring heat from the cops." The waitress dropped two full pints on the table—some beer sloshing over the sides of the glasses—and was gone just as quickly. It was now full-on Friday night at The Blind Tiger, and the wait staff was hustling to keep up.

"Really. More than taking a financial hit?"

She set her glass down, having taken an inch off the top, and said, "Oh, yeah. Well, now, I'm not talking about someone outright stealing from him. I don't believe anyone would be that stupid. Don't get me wrong, now, he doesn't like losing money, but he's not stupid. He knows people are going to skim, and others'll get busted, but he views that as a cost of doing business."

"But don't do anything to get him locked up."

"Hell no. Too many people out there ready to pounce and step in. The quickest way to lose everything he has worked for is to get sent away."

Barclay nodded, but more in contemplation than agreement. He killed what remained of the near-empty glass and swapped it for the full one. "Tell me," he began, "where does Kingery fit into all of this? How did it come to be that you had to implement this plan?"

"In the months since they suspected drugs were walking out of the dispensary, they instituted a swipe card procedure for entering the dispensary and getting medication. The hospital issued everyone a swipe card with their name and photo. You used it to unlock the dispensary, and once inside, you had to swipe again to unlock the cabinets that stored the drugs. That was it."

"I guess that's why they suspected you? Your card swipes?"

"Actually, no." She paused as the waitress began to clear the dirty dishes. Barclay took the last piece of sausage off the cutting board as the waitress took it away. "It slowed me down, for sure, until I found a workaround. You see, the swipes only documented who went in and out of the room. They still used the sign-out method to record what drugs were taken." She explained how the nurses were supposed to document what medication they were taking from the cabinet, the patient it was for, the doctor who prescribed it, and the time, date, et cetera."

"Wow. The best the hospital could come up with was essentially the honor system?" He shook his head as he drank his beer. "So, how did you become a suspect?"

"Cameras." She punctuated the statement with a humorless laugh. "Everyone knew about the swipe cards, but no one knew about the cameras."

Barclay thought about it and said, "Wait a minute. All the cameras would show is who was going in and out, which would only serve to verify the swipe records, right? Or was there a camera inside the dispensary?"

"Nope, just the outside. Only the person entering the room did not exactly match the swipe records."

"What do you mean?"

She made an exaggerated inhale and exhale and said, "Welp, I figured I could swipe another nurse's card and use that to go in and out. You know, use my card for legitimate purposes and use another nurse's card to get Malik's stuff. It was super easy. No one was used to this swipe system, so nurses always left their cards lying around. Most of the time, a nurse would get to the dispensary only to realize she had left her card at the nurses' station. It worked great—until it didn't."

"So, you didn't get busted for taking the pills." This was stated as a conclusion.

Slowly shaking her head, she said, "They were doing a random audit of matching video to card swipes. Apparently, some dumbass security consultant hired by the hospital recommended they do this from time to time. He all but guaranteed the hospital officials they would catch someone in the first couple of months, and damn if he wasn't right."

"Guess he wasn't such a dumbass after all."

"No shit." They sipped their beers in silence, leaning back in their chairs and listening to the music.

Barclay's phone chimed, signaling a text message. He fished out his phone and saw the message was from Fitz. He placed the phone on the table without reading the message and drank from his beer when Veronica slid out of her chair and said, "I'm going to the ladies' room."

Barclay wagged a finger at her and said, "Don't break the seal." She replied with a shrug, a tilt of her head, and a smirk that said *oh well*. Barclay reached for his phone and read the text.

Fitz: How's it going? I'm next door at the Brown Dog Deli if you need anything.

Barclay: Going well. I'm good if you want to head back to the hotel.

Fitz: x4

Barclay sipped his beer and finished off the last few fries left on Veronica's sandwich plate as he surveyed the ever-crowding space. An older, long-haired man was bringing in some sound equipment; Barclay groaned inwardly. He was in no mood for live music. He knew it would make conversation next to impossible—at least the conversation they were having. He needed to move it along while the sound was still at a manageable decibel.

Veronica slid back onto her chair. "Whew. I feel much better."

"Good." Barclay motioned with his head toward the front of the pub, where a guitar case and small amp were sitting unattended. "We're going to get serenaded before too long, so if it's okay with you, I'd like to finish this up and get out of here before it starts."

"Fine by me," she said and drank some beer.

"Now," Barclay began, "you said you were caught on video swiping another nurse's card. What happened after that?"

"My supervisor brought me into a room with her and the hospital's lawyer. She explained what they saw on the video and asked me to explain myself. I told them it was a mistake. That swipe cards were left lying around the nurses' station, and I must have picked up the wrong one by mistake."

"What did they say to that?"

"Well, the lawyer was totally pissed. She started in on policy and procedure and security and blah blah blah." She was animated at this telling waving her hands around. She seemed to find some humor in the lawyer's reaction.

"What about your supervisor?"

"I don't think she believed me, but she didn't have any evidence otherwise, so she let me go with a 'That's not how you were trained. Don't do it again,' for me and a, 'I will address it with the other nurses,' for the lawyer."

"That was it?"

"That was it. Like I said, the hospital didn't have any way of knowing whether or not I took something I wasn't supposed to. After I left, I thought about it and wondered if they might go back and do some more checking. I had swiped another nurse's card several times. Too many to claim they were all accidental."

"So, you called Kingery?"

"Yep. That's when I finally called him. I told him what happened, and he said to sit tight and that he would look into it. The next day he came by my house and said that the police were not involved, but an internal investigation was being prepared. In-house security was going to review more footage, and an audit of the dispensary was going to happen. I assumed I was the only one who'd been using other nurses' swipe cards, so I knew then that it was only a matter of time, and that's what I told Kingery."

"What did he say to that?"

"What do you think? He was pissed and, I think, a little scared. He said it was time to implement his plan." She stopped here—pensive. She was staring intently into her beer, looking to Barclay like she had something she wanted to say but couldn't make herself speak it.

Finally, she looked up, eyed Barclay, then dropped her gaze back to her beer. She said, "There's something I didn't tell you." Another long pause. "I found myself in some trouble after I began working with Malik. You see, I was ok with stealing pills for Malik because I had already been taking some here and there. Not to sell, though; I took them for myself. I had a bit of a problem and figured since I knew how to get a few pills out unnoticed, what would it hurt to take a few more? Anyway, I got in a bad wreck one night. I straightened out a curve and hit a telephone pole. Luckily for me, I wasn't going too fast, so other than a few bumps and bruises, I was fine. But the cops showed up, charged me with DUI, and found my pill stash in the floorboard. They must have spilled out of my purse when I crashed.

"I was scared to death; I knew I messed up bad. All I could think about was what Malik would do to me. Not a single thought to my job or career, but about Malik." She gave a humorless laugh. "He comes to see me and tells me it's handled. I ask him what that means, and he tells me not to worry about it and that I'm good. He said that this was my one chance. He made it clear what he thinks about junkies—particularly junkies that work for him." She snorted a laugh and said, "Imagine that. A drug dealer getting all high and mighty about a drug user." She drank her beer and still wasn't meeting Barclay's eyes. "I'm not stupid. I understood very well how big a bullet I dodged—literally and figuratively—so I took the pills I had collected for myself at home and bundled them with the next delivery for Malik. I haven't taken one since."

After another long pause, Barclay sensed she was finished and said, "Let me guess, Kingery made your case go away." Her eyes stayed downcast which was an answer in itself. "Malik ask him to do that?"

"Yeah." She looked up and said, "I didn't know it at the time, but Kingery told me as much when he first mentioned his *plan*. When it came time to run, he told me if I didn't go through with it, he would reinstate my old case, make sure I got busted on all of this new stuff, and make certain I went to prison."

Barclay was shaking his head. "Such an asshole," he said more to himself. "So, what day was this, and what exactly did he ask you to do?" He peered back at the musician, who was moving slowly in his setup.

"I don't know the exact day, but probably a couple of weeks before I left. He needed time to arrange things on his end."

"Wait. I don't mean to get off topic, but I'm particularly curious about one thing: how much blood did you wind up with, and where did you store it?"

"I put away eight pints. That's about twice as much as I should have given in that amount of time, but I didn't see where I had a choice. When Kingery told me his plan, I knew it had to be enough to be convincing, you know. As for storage, I kept it in the chest freezer in my sister's garage." Barclay rocked back, eyes wide. She said, "I didn't have anywhere else to keep it."

"You weren't worried about Pamela finding a blood bank in her freezer?"

"Eight pints of blood takes up less room than you think, and she doesn't ever go in there anyway. Her ex used the freezer to store deer meat, and she isn't exactly what you'd refer to as domestic, so I wasn't too worried about anyone going into it."

Moving on, Barclay said, "What did he need to arrange?"

"He promised me fifty thousand dollars in cash, a driver's license with a new name, social security number, DOB, and a car registered in my new name."

"Whoa."

"Malik pays well, and I got the impression he had been working for him for a while. And remember what I said: the worst thing you can do is bring heat on Malik. So I get busted, and suddenly both he and I are loose ends."

"You give any thought to not running?"

"Sure I did, back when he first came to me with this idea, but Kingery had all of the leverage, and he made sure I understood that. He had me believing that my only options were running, jail, or facing Malik, which he was adamant meant certain death. He also made it clear that jail wouldn't keep me safe from his reach. In reality, jail would be worse because he would know exactly where to find me, and there would be nowhere to go."

"Did you believe that?"

She leaned back in her seat. "At the time, yeah. I mean, you hear things, you know? I didn't know what was true and what was just street talk—still don't actually—but it didn't seem worth the risk. I mean, what was I leaving behind? At best, my career was over, and at worst, I was going to jail. I had *no* doubt that Kingery would make good on that threat. For all I knew, *he* would kill me if I opted to stick around. He would have plenty of motivation to keep me quiet."

Barclay and Veronica were silent for a while, she staring at her near-empty glass, and he looking around, eyes stopping on the corner of the bar where he saw the musician sitting enjoying a Bud longneck.

"You expecting someone?" Veronica asked, breathing life into the dead air between them.

"Huh?"

"You keep looking around," she said, moving her head around in demonstration.

"Oh, no, just habit, I guess. More than a decade as a prosecutor has taught me to be aware of my surroundings, I suppose." He drained the last of his beer and asked, "Can I ask a difficult question?"

It was her turn to laugh. "Seriously? With all we've talked about so far? I'd say there isn't a single question off limits at this point."

"Good point...I'm just curious, about something...your mother. And your sister and her children?"

"How do you mean?"

"A few minutes ago, you posed the question of what you would be leaving behind, and you referenced your job but not your family. What made you think you could walk away from them? And even more so, having them believe you were dead."

From the moment he met her, he had seen a tenacious, resolute woman. Now he was seeing a different side for the first time as she was biting back tears. He could see her eyes brimming, and then a single tear escaped. She blinked, soaking her eyelashes. She looked skyward as she wiped her cheek with her hand and said in a hoarse whisper, "Yeah." Barclay handed over his handkerchief, which she took and put to her eyes. She sniffed and said, "Barely an hour goes by that I don't think about them." She looked away from him, wiped her eyes again, looked back, and said, "I screwed up my life. I accept that. I didn't want to heap that on them. My momma is sick; she doesn't need to be worrying about me and my troubles." The waitress approached the table but veered away as experience told her now was not a good time. "I love my sister, but she'll be fine. She is far too busy to let me slow her life up too much."

Things had taken a turn, and guilt was tugging at Barclay, which frustrated him. Why was he feeling bad for this woman with everything she had done and potentially set in motion? "Was his intent from the beginning to get someone charged and convicted for this?"

She shook her head and said, "No way. In fact, he wanted to make sure that didn't happen; he said that would only complicate things."

"So, what are you supposed to do? Be on the run for the rest of your life? Did he have an end game?"

"Other than getting rid of me and saving his own ass? No. As for me ever coming back, I don't see that as an option as long as he's around. That assumes, of course, I don't mind going to prison, which I assure you I have no desire to do."

"No," he replied, "I don't suppose you do."

CHAPTER 23

BARCLAY WAS IN CLAYTON'S office, standing over his shoulder, answering a question about the wording of an indictment, when his cell phone rang. He fished his phone out of his pocket, checked the caller ID, and answered: "Hey, Uncle Jack." He moved from behind Clayton's desk and exited the cramped office.

"Barclay, my boy. How's my favorite nephew?"

"Your favorite, huh?"

"Let's not tell your brother." Both men laughed. "Just wanted to call and let you know that we finally got everything set, and the head is going up on the pipe a week from today. Supposed to begin assembly at seven a.m."

"Well, alright. I will do what I can to be there."

❀ ❀ ❀ ❀ ❀

FIVE DAYS LATER

Richard Kingery settled into his recliner with a bag of fast-food takeout in his lap. Wednesdays were preliminary hearing days, and the docket on this day had kept him in court all day which made for a late night at the office.

It had been almost two weeks since Barclay confronted him with his burner phone, and he had not had a relaxed minute since—the stress weighing heavy. He let a couple of days pass after Barclay accosted him in his office before buying a replacement phone, and, as an added precaution, he drove to Georgia to make the purchase. It had taken some time to convince Veronica Lane that this new phone number sending her text messages was really him. The last thing Kingery needed was for her to text his old phone while it was in Barclay's possession.

He then began to subtly backchannel the Towne police to find out if they had an open investigation into the Clements case. They did not. He had no clue what Barclay's play would be, but he took only a modicum of solace in the fact that the police did not seem to be involved, at least not officially. *He could still find a way out.*

Finally able to eat dinner, he had the television tuned to the *History Channel* and was taking the food out of the bag and setting it on his chair-side table next to the large paper cup of Diet Coke when he heard a phone signal the receipt of a text message. He knew at once which phone it was. "Goddammit."

He set the bag on the floor, rocked forward, clambered out of the chair, and went to his briefcase to retrieve the phone. The sender was listed as a phone number only—no name. Only one person had this particular number, so he did not need to risk putting that person's name in as a contact should his phone get lost or stolen. That wasn't much of a risk, however. Since the episode with Barclay and his previous phone, this new one was never out of his possession.

Their communication was infrequent, so when he heard the phone's text message alert just now, his heart raced.

Sender: *We need to meet. ASAP. Some guy from your office is trying to find me.*

He felt his stomach flip as he read the message; he waited a beat before responding.

Kingery: *Are you sure? What happened?*

Sender: *YES I'M SURE!!!! He sent a text to this number asking me to call him. We need to talk.*

Kingery: *When did he text you? Did you call him?*

Sender: *Hell no! He texted me this morning. Said he would give me three days to call him back. So we need to meet. I can be there tomorrow.*

Shit, shit, shit. Kingery's thumbs hovered over the keyboard of the pay-as-you-go Android phone.

Kingery: *Ok. When can you be here?*

Sender: *Tomorrow night. 11:30 at the Pickens property.*

Kingery gave a confused look to the phone.

Kingery: *Why there?*

Sender: *It's on the edge of town. No way in hell I am going any closer than that. I heard Old Man Pickens died so the place will be deserted and it's far enough off the highway that we'll have plenty of privacy.*

Kingery: *How do you know so much about that place?*

Sender: *My mother was their housekeeper for a while. See you tomorrow night.*

Sender: *I don't plan on staying. As soon as we meet I'm getting the hell out of there. I need to know you're going to let me leave.*

Kingery: *I sure as hell don't want you here. You can go wherever you want so long as it is far from Towne.*

Sender: *No worries there. Bring your phone.*

Kingery: *??*

Sender: *In case something happens I need to be able to contact you.*

Kingery scrolled back through the conversation, trying to make sense of everything. He had a day to figure out what to do, two days max. If Barclay didn't hear from her the day after tomorrow, there was no telling what he would do. His lone certainty was that as long as Barclay never found Veronica Lane, there wasn't a damn thing he or anyone else could do to him. He wondered if, in that logic, he had his answer.

❀ ❀ ❀ ❀ ❀

Barclay was sitting in the desk chair in his study, cell phone in hand. He typed a text message to the only phone number with which this phone had ever communicated.

The text message read: *We need to meet. ASAP. Some guy from your office is trying to find me.*

At the conclusion of the text conversation, he looked across his desk at Veronica Lane and said, "It's all set."

❀ ❀ ❀ ❀ ❀

THE NEXT DAY

Richard Kingery guided his car up the quarter-mile-long dirt driveway toward the Pickens house. His windows were down and his radio off; the only sound was his tires on the dirt driveway. The dust from the dirt road prompted him to roll up his windows and turn on the car's air conditioner. He had not slept the night before, nor had he accomplished anything at work that day because all he could think about was this meeting. Handle it correctly, and he would enjoy what he had been unable to for going on two years—peace of mind.

At this late hour, the traffic was negligible, so a drive that usually took him twenty minutes had only taken fifteen. He had allotted a half-hour to get here, so he was considerably early.

This was truly on the outskirts of the Towne city limits. So close that when he turned off the highway, he saw the rectangular green sign marking the city limits of the neighboring community illuminated by his high beams.

He also noticed the three-foot-wide rust-colored pipe rising eight feet out of the earth and the assembled billboard head sitting on the ground next to it. "Goddamn eyesore."

Overhanging oaks covered the long dirt driveway creating a tunnel of flora. He eventually made it to the end of the oaks, and the driveway dumped him out in an open field with a rutted dirt trail through the grass, which he followed to the Pickens' house. As he swung his car into the wide gravel parking area, his headlights swept across the rear of a vehicle and what appeared to be a person sitting on the trunk. His heart skipped until he realized it was Veronica Lane. "Play it cool," he said out loud in the car. He parked, turned off the car, and opened the door.

The chime indicating the keys were still in the ignition, and the car's dome light exploded into the night but was just as quickly extinguished when he closed the driver's door. He stood beside the car for a moment letting his eyes adjust to the cloudy, moonlit night before moving slowly toward Veronica, who spoke first: "He knows."

Clear of his car's hood, he stopped walking, leaving maybe ten feet between them. He said, "Knows what?"

"My God, Kingery. Everything." She slid off the trunk but did not move any closer. "He knows I'm alive, and he knows you're involved." Her movement disturbed the air between them enough that he detected the faintest trace of her familiar scent—something floral.

Kingery knew he had to be smart with how he played this. He was aware that Barclay believed—hell, he knew—what really happened. But knowing and proving are two different things, and Kingery knew that without her, there was little, if anything, that could be done to him.

She was recording their conversation for all he knew, and he was too damned smart to fall for something he had used to convict so many criminals. He scanned the area. Other than the two-story painted wood farmhouse and detached garage, he did not see anything other than trees, grass, and dirt in the moonlight. "So, he knows about you stealing from the hospital?" He was careful about mentioning any more than that. He did not want his voice on tape saying Malik Traylor's name if she was recording.

"Like I already told you, I haven't spoken to him, but if he tracked me down, I'm going to assume he knows a lot."

"Do I need to remind you of what you're risking by talking to him? I want you to think long and hard about that before you have any ideas about clearing your conscience."

She gave a mirthless laugh and said, "You don't get it, do you? I just want to be clear of all this…shit! Good or bad, I've made my choices, and I'm prepared to live with them, but I cannot and will not live my life forever looking over my shoulder. You need to handle this right fucking now."

He studied her face, her body language. As much as he was trying, he could not get a read on her. His gut told him she was scared and nervous and shooting him straight, but he couldn't afford to let his guard down. "Alright, look, without you, he's got nothing. I'm serious, he can think and even believe whatever he wants, but unless he has *you*"—he emphasized 'you' with a jab of his thick finger—"there's not a damned thing he can prove. Understand?"

He thought he saw a nod.

"I need to hear you say it, Ms. Lane. I need to hear you say that you understand. I need to hear you say that you understand you are the key to all of this, and if they don't have you, they don't have anything."

"I understand," she said with a mixture of anger and frustration.

"Good. Now—"

"Why did you do it?" she interrupted.

She could not see his eye roll in the dark as he said, "Do what?"

"Convict Charlie Clements." She let that hang, and when she did not get a response, she continued. "My god, you know he's innocent, and you're trying to send him to death row?" In her anger was confidence. "You promised me no one would get hurt. That no one else would be involved in this." She was seething now. "I need to know what you're going to do about *that*." Had he been able to see her bitter gaze, he may have been more cautious in his reproach

"Me?" It was his turn for vitriol. He knew instantly that he should be diffusing the situation, but tact had never been his strong suit. "You do know that the reason he was charged in the first place was because of you, right? If you hadn't had sex with that, that—"

"That what, huh? What were you going to call him?"

"Don't get all high and mighty on me, little lady. Like you already said, you made your choices; we all did. As a result, we had to do whatever was necessary to avoid those choices destroying us. You did that, same as me; I just had to get a little dirtier than you." He paused to catch his breath. She had a lot of nerve with everything he had done for her. "Instead of getting indignant, you should be thanking me."

She made a noise to argue, but he cut her off. He closed the gap between them as he spoke. "Just what would you have me do? Go to the court and say, 'You know Mr. Clements? The guy twelve jurors recently convicted of murder? Yeah, well, you need to let him go because—this is so crazy—the woman he was convicted of murdering is, in actuality, alive. How do I know this? Because I helped stage the whole thing, that's how.'"

Arms crossed, she said, "Sarcasm doesn't suit you...Dick."

"Don't call me that," he said through gritted teeth. He was about to continue when the click of an opening car door interrupted his thoughts. It was the passenger side of Veronica Lane's car, and the lack of an interior light meant he could not immediately recognize the person exiting. "Who's there?" Kingery was squinting, straining to see the mystery person. To Lane: "What the hell have you done?"

"Whatever it is you think she's done doesn't begin to compare to what is going to happen to you."

"Barclay? What the..." Apprehension morphed into determination. "Let me guess: you've been recording our conversation. Well, you don't have anything—"

"We aren't recording anything." Barclay's calm voice unnerved Kingery.

Regaining his composure, Kingery said, "Then what the hell is this all about? I assume you're aware of Ms. Lane here?" The cloud cover cleared, and the full moon increased the brightness enough to see Barclay nod in assent. "Then you know about her stealing drugs from the hospital? I suppose you deserve the credit for finding her so we can hold her accountable for her criminal behavior. Nice job."

Barclay shook his head, frustration evident on his face. "I told you we aren't recording, so there's no reason for histrionics." He could see confusion clouding Kingery's features, and he pressed on. "The fact is, the last thing any of us want is a record of this meeting. Well, *you'll* probably wish there was some record of it, but I assure you one will not—will never—exist."

A sharp noise cracked the silence causing Kingery alone to jump. He turned to see two men dressed in dark clothing walking toward him from either side of a smoke-gray SUV. The color drained from Kingery's face as he turned to Barclay and the girl, then back to Malik Traylor and his lieutenant, who was holding an AR-15 across his body and pointing toward the ground. Kingery's mind was racing but going nowhere fast. Confusion giving way to fear.

Barclay closed in on Kingery, which made him twitch. He said, "There's nowhere for you to go, Dick. The best thing you can do right now is to answer some questions, starting with why you killed Duncan." Kingery was not expecting that, and it showed. "You see, that's how we got here. I've been doing everything I can to figure out the who and the why of his murder. After weeks of running through it all, you're the *who* that makes the most sense, the only sense, really. Now, I need to know the *why*."

Kingery looked behind him, then back to Barclay. He steeled himself and said, "I don't know what you're talking about."

"Cut the bullshit! The only way this works out well for you is to talk."

"I don't know what this is all about, but there is a man with an assault rifle present. I'm feeling quite threatened right now." Kingery's raised voice echoed around the property.

Barclay gave a tired shake of his head and said, "For the final time, we are *not* recording this, so you can cool it with the method acting."

"Prove it."

"Prove it?" Barclay gave that some thought, then said, "You sure?"

"Yes," he said. The slight quaver in his voice belied his sanguine expression.

"Hmmm. Ok. So, if I do something I would certainly not want captured on tape, would that convince you?"

He had gotten himself in this spot, so he couldn't back down now. "Yes," he said, his confidence dissipating.

Barclay clapped his hands and rubbed them together as he looked around, his gaze alighting behind Kingery. He locked eyes with the lieutenant and gave a casual nod toward Kingery. The lieutenant looked at Malik, who nodded back. The lieutenant raised the gun; Kingery, wild-eyed, said, "What?" Barclay said, "In the foot," and the AR barked as Kingery's right foot exploded.

Kingery screamed and fell back against the front of his car, leaning on the bumper and grabbing at his foot.

"Convinced?"

"You're a goddamned maniac!" Kingery screamed as he howled in pain. "You'll fucking pay for this!"

"You think so, huh? And just what are you going to say? That me and you and Veronica Lane and Malik Traylor and"— Barclay looked to Malik, who said "Tim," which caused Barclay to do a double take, and when Malik nodded, Barclay continued—"and Tim were at the Pickens' place, and Tim here shot you at my behest? Gee, that sounds perfectly plausible. Unfortunately for you, though, we aren't recording anything, so where is your evidence? Not to mention that now you've involved your living murder victim." Kingery opened his mouth, causing Barclay to hold up a hand and say, "And supposing you keep her out, I call her in to dispute your account. Besides, what do you say when they ask you why this happened?"

Whether due to adrenaline or fortitude or whatever, Kingery ignored his foot and responded: "You think you're so fucking smart. You seem to keep forgetting that Ms. Lane here can't come back—ever—or she goes to prison."

"Hey, shitbird. You forget you're dealing with a prosecutor? No, make that *the* prosecutor. No one is going to care about a three-year-old drug case that probably can't even be proven. Hell, I'd be shocked if any evidence of that still exists."

Kingery, still resting on his car's bumper with his bloody stump of a foot propped on his left knee, managed a cough of a laugh and said, "And how will she explain her role in having her lover convicted of her murder?"

Veronica jumped in and said, "You asshole—"

Barclay grabbed her by the waist as she tried to get at Kingery. He said, "Quiet." Then to Kingery: "She was twenty-seven hundred miles away, and his arrest was a year after she left. No way to prove she knew anything about anything. It would look as if she returned upon finding out about his conviction to help set him free. Hell, the public'll view her as a victim and a hero.

"Listen, we're getting off track here. Let's get back to talking about Duncan. Why'd you do it?" Kingery's face was slick with sweat, and he was growing pale. "You need a hospital, Dick. Let us help you. You just have to answer my questions."

"What does it matter at this point? You know as well as I do that nothing can come of any of this. Nothing I say is admissible, and you obviously can't prove anything you think you know; otherwise, we wouldn't be out here."

For the first time, Barclay appeared weary. "I need to know, alright? Look, I agree that nothing comes of this. Any of it. Not you and Lane, not you and Malik, not you and….and Duncan. But, man, I just need to know."

Silence ensconced the group. All eyes were on Kingery. Kingery's eyes bouncing between everyone else.

"Fuck it," Kingery finally said. "Yeah, I killed him."

And then he told them why.

✳   ✳   ✳   ✳   ✳

He explained that a couple of weeks before jury selection was scheduled to begin in the Clements trial, Duncan called him, and the pair met at Duncan's office.

"It was late, around midnight, and when I got there, he stank of bourbon. I'm not there two minutes, and he starts in on how he knows Veronica Lane is alive, and he knows I'm involved somehow. Starts in about an email he received, but he wouldn't give me any details. He's disheveled; he's slurring his words—it was pathetic. He's telling me how this is my one shot to come clean and see to it that an innocent man doesn't go to the death chamber." He is not even trying to hide his disgust for Duncan Pheiffer. "Defense lawyers are all the same. At some point, they all drink the Kool-Aid. Can you imagine?"

To a person, everyone was shocked at what they were hearing. "Don't look at me that way, Barclay. As prosecutors, we do everything in our power to make sure monsters are locked up; put away so as not to do any more harm. That's our role in society. It's more than what we do—it's who we are."

Barclay charged at Kingery and slammed him across the hood; the audible crack of Kingery's ribs like a gunshot in the still of the night. Malik ran and pulled Barclay off him. Barclay was strong but no match for Malik, who drove him backward, saying, "Barclay, man, calm down! Calm the fuck down!"

Barclay, struggling against his captor, yelled over Malik's shoulder, "We don't convict innocent people! What is wrong with you?"

Kingery had recoiled as if trying to melt into the car. "Oh, give me a break," he said in ragged gasps. "In the course of seeking justice, sometimes we break a few eggs."

Barclay had calmed enough that he no longer needed restraining, but he was still breathing hard. He shook his head at the ridiculous idiom and said, "Do you even listen to yourself?" He could not begin to understand the man. Though an enemy to some degree, he had still respected him as a prosecutor. "You're insane," he said, much calmer. He turned and walked back towards Veronica Lane's car.

Malik to Kingery: "Keep talking."

Kingery attempted to sit up and let out a painful growl in response. He wrapped an arm around his midsection, head back and eyes closed, teeth clenched. He eventually spoke. "I left his office that night convinced he had no way of proving any of what he was saying. If he had anything of substance, any measure of proof, he would have produced it." He shook his head, unable to resist taking another shot at Duncan: "He took his best shot with a bluff, and I called it. That told me all I needed to know about him. He was weak, and I was going to convict his client. I was going to win."

Malik looked at Barclay, tensing in case he needed to intervene again, but he did not. Barclay rested against the trunk of Veronica's car. Head down, he looked beaten. The course of everything that had happened over the weeks subsequent to Duncan's death had come flooding forward. He thought about how helpless Duncan must have felt going into that trial. How utterly powerless he was to help a man he knew was innocent of the most egregious crime under the law.

Malik said, "So why'd you kill him? You knew he couldn't do anything to you? Why you have to go and do that?"

"Because he told me he had proof."

That statement electrified the air and jolted Barclay back to life. He stood up and slowly approached Kingery. Malik coolly eased between the two—just in case.

Kingery continued, "After Clements was found guilty, the jury was dismissed, the judge left the bench, and the courtroom cleared. It was just the two of us getting our things together. Actually, I was getting my things together. He was sitting there… wallowing." Barclay tensed, causing Kingery to flinch. Seeing he wasn't going to be attacked, he continued, "That was when he told me he had proof. He said it may take a while to sort it all out and determine what it all meant, but he was going to prove his client did not kill anyone, and he was going to see that everyone knew my involvement."

Barclay said, "What was his proof?"

"A cell phone. *My* cell phone."

Malik and Barclay whipped their heads around while Kingery just cut his eyes at the source of the statement: Veronica Lane.

Barclay: "What are you talking about?"

Veronica was silent, considering how to proceed. She finally spoke: "I found out that Charlie Clements was charged with my murder right before the trial started. I saw an article online from the *Trib* that jury selection was set to begin, so I sent his lawyer an email from a single-use account. I told him Veronica Lane wasn't dead, and the prosecutor knew it. That was it. I didn't sign my name. I never even logged back in to see if he responded."

Kingery cut a look at Veronica and said, "You stupid bitch." If looks could kill, Veronica Lane would have been dropped where she stood.

Ignoring Kingery, Barclay said, "Tell me about the cell phone."

She indicated Kingery with a movement of her head and said, "He gave me a pay-as-you-go cell phone the day I left.

Per his instructions, I got a new phone when I got to Oregon." Barclay thought about the report Tina Crump had gotten, and he remembered her saying the phone stopped being used shortly after Veronica arrived in Oregon, so the story had merit. "Only I didn't throw the old one away. I figured it may come in handy one day, and when I saw my email didn't seem to do anything and the trial was moving forward, I knew just what to do with it."

To Kingery, Barclay said, "What did you know about this phone?"

Speaking in a strained voice, Kingery said, "I asked him what his evidence was while we were in the courtroom. I tried to sound nonchalant about it, like I wasn't worried. All Duncan would tell me was that he now had a cell phone, and he reminded me of the email he mentioned before the trial. Of course, a random email and a cell phone would never be enough to overturn a jury's verdict, but it could sure as hell cause me some problems. I did wonder if he was lying since he had yet to produce anything resembling evidence. But what if he wasn't? I couldn't take that chance. I had to know if he really did have something." He was trying to catch his breath, all the talking taking great effort with his busted ribs. "Duncan was a lot of things, but dumb wasn't one of them. If he had anything of substance, sooner or later, he would connect the dots. I was certain of that."

Another painful coughing jag, then: "When he made his play after the verdict, I just shrugged it off and left the courtroom. I hurried to my car and waited for Duncan to leave. Just when I thought he might spend the night there, I saw him leave and followed him—first to his office, then to a gas station, then to his house.

"I parked down the street and devised a plan to get him out

of his house so I could slip in. I didn't have a plan for when I got inside. I mean, what was I going to do, beat it out of him? I knew I was screwed if he ever figured it out, and I did what so many of the folks we prosecute every day do: I panicked. I grabbed a knife from his kitchen, and I did it. I killed him."

"What did you do with the phone?" Barclay asked.

Kingery shook his head and said, "All that, and I still never found that goddamn phone. I searched his house for it that night and even went through his office. I looked everywhere, but nothing. So until tonight, I wondered if he'd been bluffing. I guess I'm glad to know I didn't kill the man for nothing."

That last statement earned a punch to the ribs from Malik, who turned and nodded at Barclay, who reciprocated. The blow caused Kingery to lose his legs, and he slid done the front of the car. He was now sitting on the ground in obvious pain.

To Veronica, Barclay said, "Why didn't you tell me this at the beginning?"

"I was scared. I got your text out of the blue telling me you had tracked me to Charleston and that someone was murdered. I didn't know how any of this fit, and when you said this lawyer was your friend, I didn't know what to do...or say."

Barclay: "Did you ever give Duncan any specifics? Any information he could actually use?"

There was pain and regret in her voice. "I thought I did. I just assumed a lawyer could figure it all out—trace the calls or something. I guess I thought if *he* figured it out, then no one could blame me. Punish me." She paused, eyes to the ground, before looking at Barclay and saying, "I'm sorry."

"Wait a minute," said Barclay. "We scoured Duncan's computer and didn't find any emails like what you mentioned. Where did you send your email?"

"I sent it to the address on his website, but I set the message to delete itself two minutes after it was read. I didn't want to take any chances it could be traced. Once he knew the truth, I figured that would be it."

Kingery made a noise and muttered, "Of course, he didn't even have the email."

No one said anything for more than a minute. Finally, Barclay spoke up. He looked at Veronica and said, "I gotta get out of here. Let's go."

They crossed paths to enter the vehicle when Kingery said, "Whose taking me to the hospital? I can't drive in this condition." Exhaustion and resignation in his voice.

"Malik's got you," said Barclay without even looking at him. Then he stopped. "I need your phone. The one you've been using to communicate with Veronica."

That energized Kingery. "What? Why?"

"Because I need it." Barclay took a step forward, held out a hand, and said, "Toss it to me."

"Fuck off."

Barclay looked back at Veronica. "Call it." She did, and they heard a muffled ring.

"It's in his car," said Malik.

Barclay walked to the driver's side and looked in, seeing the glow of the phone's screen. He pulled out a handkerchief and used it to open the door. He reached in, careful not to touch anything, and grabbed the cell phone. He was carrying it back to Veronica's car wrapped in the cloth, and Kingery said, "Why are you carrying it like that?"

"Fingerprints, you idiot."

"What are you going to do with it?" asked Kingery, anxiety spiking.

"He's yours, Malik."

"What the fuck?" Kingery was trying to stand but failing.

"What's going on?" Panic setting in.

"Like you said earlier, you made your choices. Now you have to live with them. I'm guessing Malik doesn't appreciate you putting him and his business at risk. Murder tends to bring the heat, but that's between you two."

"Come on, Barclay. Y-y-y-you can't do this to me." He was scrambling, trying to get to his feet and moving toward Barclay before falling back to the ground. "Please. I gave you what you asked for. Show some mercy here."

Barclay looked at him with as much hatred and acrimony as he could manage and said, "Now, who's pathetic?"

Barclay opened the car door and was about to get in when Kingery yelled at him, spit flying. "You're such a hypocrite." Barclay turned and faced him, saying nothing. "I gave you what you asked for. So where's the mercy, huh? Where is it?"

"You don't deserve mercy. You're getting justice."

CHAPTER 24

EIGHT DAYS LATER,
TACOMA, WASHINGTON

MEGAN POPE HAD TAKEN the day off because the lady who usually watched the Pope children during the summer was herself taking a summer vacation. Her day began in the quiet of the early morning—before her children woke—drinking a cup of coffee and reading her latest find from the Tacoma Public Library. Moments like this were rare, especially on a weekday when her routine had her at full speed from the time her feet hit the floor at 6:00 in the morning until she was out the door getting her children to school and then onto work at a local accounting firm. Her husband Tim left for work at 5:30 a.m., so she was on her own getting herself and the children ready for the day. This morning, though, she was into her second cup and fully engrossed in a novel about vampires when she heard The Heathens begin to stir.

The Heathens was very much a term of endearment for her boys, twelve and ten. They were so nicknamed because they were always at full throttle, whether in the house or on the playground. Her husband had repaired more than one hole in the wall and replaced one broken television.

She looked up at the ceiling, fully expecting one or both of them to come crashing through per the sounds coming from the playroom directly above the den where she was sitting. She used to worry about them involving their five-year-old sister in the roughhousing, but, as so often happens with the third child, she got over that quickly, knowing that she would grow up tougher because of it, which made her husband happy.

As a special treat, she took them to Shake Shake Shake for lunch—which may as well have been Disney World as far as the children were concerned—and enjoyed burgers and milkshakes. Tim met them at the restaurant, which made lunch at their favorite family spot all the more fun because weekday lunch with dad was rare.

After arriving home, stuffed from the burgers and hyper from the sugary milkshakes, the children tore out, joining the neighborhood kids for a game of who knows what. Megan and Tim settled in front of the television to catch up on their Netflix series du jour. She folded laundry, and he attempted to glue together some tchotchke broken by The Heathens two nights prior as they bounded around the house via every accessible raised horizontal surface because "the floor was lava." Laundry folded and the glue drying, the couple sat on the couch together, sock feet on the coffee table, and just a few minutes into the second episode of the afternoon when the doorbell rang.

Tim paused the show and made his way to the door. When he opened it, there was no one there. He figured he had been ding-dong-ditched by the gang of children out playing in the neighborhood when he heard the rumble of a diesel engine, and he saw a Fed Ex box truck pulling away from the curb; he looked down and noticed the Fed Ex package at the base of the door.

The box had some weight to it, and he brought it into the den, turning it over in his hands. It was addressed to both of them with no return address. He asked Megan if she was expecting anything, to which she replied she was not. He sat on the couch, pulled back the cardboard strip, and emptied the contents onto the coffee table. It was an Android cell phone attached to an external battery charger.

With the Android on the table, the couple exchanged looks, and both were hesitant to handle the phone. They were sitting there staring at the phone when it rang. This startled both Tim and Megan, who again looked at one another and then back to the phone. The caller ID showed a blocked number, so they didn't answer. The phone finished ringing, and it began ringing again almost immediately. After four rings, Tim answered and was greeted by a female computer-generated voice:

> *Hello, this is a message from Federal Express. We at Fed Ex constantly strive for excellence. To ensure our delivery routes are running at optimal performance, we routinely send test packages to randomly chosen addresses. Congratulations on being selected to participate in our quality control exercise. The only thing we ask of you is to verify that your address is the address listed on the outside of the package. If your address corresponds with the address on the box, then there is nothing for you to do. If, however, your address is different from the address listed on the package, please push one. And that is it. This phone was purchased with only enough minutes to conduct this quality control exercise and cannot be reloaded with additional minutes.*
>
> *Additionally, the wifi feature has been permanently disabled. The phones are passcode*

protected and are programmed to shut down at a specific time. Once powered back on, the phone is useless without the assigned passcode, so the phone has no resale value. We ask that you please power the phone off and discard it with your household trash. As a thank you for participating in this quality control exercise, the attached external battery charger is yours to keep. Thank you and goodbye.

The message ended, and Tim and Megan stared at the phone, then at each other, then back at the phone. "What the heck?" was all Tim could think to say.

❊ ❊ ❊ ❊ ❊

It was after 5:00 that same afternoon, and Barclay is sitting at his desk in the near-deserted Towne County courthouse. Jazz hums in the background as he sits monitoring his email for more than two hours when a chime signals the arrival of a new email to a web-based email address he created for this singular purpose; an email address that will not be used again. It was a message from Federal Express letting him know the package he sent has been delivered.

He reads the email two more times for reasons he doesn't know. He grabs the flip-style cell phone sitting next to his computer, thumbs the screen open, and dials *67 to block the number on the recipient's caller ID, followed by a phone number he has committed to memory. This is the only call this phone will make, and after six rings, voicemail picks up. "Come on," he says to himself, hoping the package isn't sitting untouched on the front porch. He dials again, and after four rings, a man answers. He pushes a button on his laptop, holds the phone's mouthpiece to the computer's speaker, and a female computer generated-voice emanates from the speaker: *Hello, this is a message from Federal Express. We at Fed Ex constantly strive for excellence. To ensure our delivery routes are running at optimal performance...*

When the recording finishes playing, he presses the *end* button, terminating the connection. He leans back and lets out a breath he believes he may have been holding for the entirety of the message. He then removes the battery and sim card from the phone and breaks the phone at the hinge where the screen connects with the keypad. He will dispose of the battery, sim card, and phone pieces separately on his way home.

❉   ❉   ❉   ❉   ❉

THREE DAYS LATER

The *team* was gathered in Barclay's study after-hours. Tina and Drummond—getting along much better these days—had called for this meeting, so they had the floor as they presented Barclay and Fitz information the detective and his computer expert had compiled on a recent missing persons case.

Drummond said, "I got the expedited blood analysis report from Forensics, and you ain't gonna believe this shit. It's got that stuff in it."

"Cryoprotectant?" asked Fitz.

"Yeah, that stuff. Anyway, it reads exactly like Veronica Lane's blood report, only a hell of a lot less blood at this scene."

Barclay said, "Huh," and reached for the report.

"That's not all," said Drummond, then looked at Tina.

Tina opened her laptop and spoke as she typed on her keyboard. She said, "I had my guy look into that phone number

like you asked, and he was able to get me the cell tower info."
She spun the computer around and said, "This is the map of
its travel." Nobody said anything as they viewed the familiar
route across the United States. "As you can see, the phone left
Towne the day before we went to arrest Kingery at his house
and found the blood in his kitchen. From Towne, it went to
Atlanta, then on to Memphis, where it sat overnight. Early the
next morning—like before the sun came up early—the phone
left Memphis and made its way over the next three days to Tacoma, Washington. We have no further tower activity after 3:32
p.m. pacific time."

"Was there any phone activity? Calls? Texts?" asked Fitz.

"Only one," she said. "A phone call was received at 3:18
pacific time that lasted fifty-eight seconds. The call pinged off a
cell tower in Tacoma."

"The number that called the phone?" asked Fitz.

"What do you think? Another burner, and unless we get
lucky, the number alone is useless."

"Huh," repeated Barclay.

"You know what I think?" Drummond asked the group.
They each looked at him but said nothing. "The cryo blood?
The trip across the country that he *knows* we can track? It's
Veronica Lane all over again. I think this smug sonofabitch is
giving us the finger. This is basically a big *fuck you* on his way
out."

Fitz glanced at Barclay, then at the group, and said, "We'll
find him. He can't run forever."

Drummond: "Yeah, well, if he expects us to believe he's
dead, then fuck *him*. This ain't over, and it won't be over until
we catch that asshole."

CHAPTER 25

ILLIAM WALLACE HARRIS JR sat in the lobby of the district attorney's office.

With Duncan's case still fresh but behind him, Barclay wanted to take one more run at a case that had stuck in his crawl for so long: the death of William Wallace Harris Sr.—the near-headless man in the photograph Barclay kept in his desk drawer.

Upon arriving at the DA's office at precisely 2:00, Will had been kept waiting for several minutes before Barclay came to greet him; he wanted to try and ratchet up Will's anxiety before the meeting began. After shaking hands and speaking with him in the lobby, though, Barclay didn't believe he had accomplished what he wanted. Will was a good-looking twenty-four-year-old single guy with a bank account that would keep him in his current lifestyle—no job required—and an unmistakable laissez-faire air about him. Barclay did not like this man.

Winston Fitzsimmons and Clayton White were already seated at the conference table when the two of them entered.

The conference room was well-appointed and rivaled that of any private law firm. Prosecutors met with victims in this room, it was the setting for press conferences by the DA, and serious plea discussions were held at this very table. Maggie

Gamble made it a point to ensure this room gave the best impression to anyone invited in.

The dark grey walls were trimmed in rich mahogany, which went along with the thick-topped mahogany conference table. The table had an ornately carved edge matching the carvings on the thick table legs. There was a matching sideboard against the wall at one end of the big table with a crystal water service set upon it. Above the chest was a large flatscreen television. One length of the wall was made of floor-to-ceiling windows. The room perpetually smelled of fresh-cut flowers and furniture polish.

Fitz was there as an investigator, and Clayton was there because he effectively broke the case, so Barclay thought it only right he should sit in. However, it was made clear to Clayton that he was only to be seen and not heard.

This time Barclay's gamesmanship had the desired effect. Will stopped walking, turned to Barclay, and said, "What's going on?"

Barclay gestured to a chair. "Just have a seat, and we'll talk about it." Barclay sat at the head of the table opposite the television; on the table lay a closed MacBook Air and a manila folder.

Will had stylishly-long brown hair held back from his face by the Costa Del Mar sunglasses perched on his head. He wore a faded green fishing shirt, khaki shorts, and flip-flops. He gave off the slightest odor of marijuana.

After his father's death, Will had sold the tractor dealerships for a nice sum and bounced between his family's house in Towne and their house in Orange Beach. His tan, though, said he was spending much more time at the beach than in Towne.

The feeling that Will would not show up was almost unanimous, but Barclay knew that as the bereaved son, he would feel the need to show up if only to keep up appearances lest he give the police a reason to re-open the case against him.

"We appreciate you coming in, Will," said Barclay once everyone was settled at the conference table. He then gestured to Clayton and introduced the new lawyer while ignoring Fitz. More gamesmanship.

Will acknowledged Clayton with a head nod, then looked down the table at Fitz, where his gaze hung for maybe five seconds as if waiting for an introduction, then at Barclay, shrugged and said, "Happy to do whatever I can to help you guys out, you know that." He glanced back at Fitz but only for a second.

Barclay said, "How would you feel if I told you that we have taken another look at your father's death?"

Will bounced his gaze between the two lawyers at least twice, then moved his head to look down the table at Fitz before catching himself and said, "Why would you do that? It was an accident."

Barclay got up, walked the length of the table to the sideboard directly behind Fitz, and poured a glass of water from the crystal pitcher. He took a drink, held the glass out, and said, "Anyone?" Clayton shook his head, looking confused, while Will said, "Naw, man. Look, if you've got something to say, just say it." Fitz remained a statue—maybe blinking, maybe not.

Barclay finished the water, pulled a coaster from its stack, and set the empty glass on top. He leaned back against the sideboard, resting his hands on the table on either side of him. He pursed his lips, looking off as if thinking about what he was going to say. Finally, he looked at Will and said, "We don't believe your story." A pause to gauge Will's reaction. Nothing. Barclay continued, "Quite honestly, your story never—"

"Story?" Will said, interrupting. "It wasn't a story. It's what happened." The relaxed devil-may-care attitude gone, and in its place, what, anger, worry? Barclay couldn't decide which.

Barclay stared impassively at Will, waited a beat, and said, "Are you finished?" Not getting a response, he continued, "As I was saying, your story never did sit well with me." He pushed himself off the table and walked slowly back to his seat. He spoke as he walked: "At the time, there just was not any evidence that suggested otherwise...or so we thought."

"Oh, what, you have evidence now?" There was an edge of defiance in Will's voice.

In answer to the question, Barclay opened the manila folder and slid two eight-by-ten glossy photos in front of Will. They were the photos from Barclay's office: the wide shot of the crime scene and the close-up of the victim's head. Will looked at the pictures without reaching for them, took a second to process what he was looking at, and said, "Ah, come on. What the fuck, man!" Will turned his head and pushed the pictures across the polished surface. He stood up and said, "This is bullshit. I'm out of here." *Anger*, Barclay thought. *Good.*

"Sit. Down." Fitz's baritone caught Will by surprise—as if he had forgotten he was in the room. He and Fitz locked eyes for maybe six seconds before Will broke off his gaze and slowly sat back down.

Changing tact—he wanted to keep Will off guard—Barclay apologized for showing him the photographs. He said, "You're right. I should have given you some warning before putting them in front of you. It's just that, you know, you asked about evidence, and well, that's what I was trying to show you."

"That was fucked up."

Ignoring the comment and ignoring the photographs still visible to Will, who kept sneaking glances at them, Barclay opened the MacBook and hit the spacebar; the TV on the opposite wall came to life. The television showed a mockup of the senior William Wallace Harris' living room. The camera was set perpendicular to the two figures on the screen: On the left side sat a female, hair pulled into a ponytail, wearing plastic safety glasses and a white lab coat, holding a shotgun. Across from her sat a faceless, bald mannequin wearing dark blue Liberty overalls over a red plaid long-sleeve shirt unbuttoned at the cuffs and holding a smoldering cigarette in the right hand resting on its right knee. The mannequin sat on a blood-stained white couch on the right. The pair were separated by a highly polished four-legged red-brown oval coffee table.

"Look familiar?" said Barclay breaking the palpable silence. He was looking at the television screen. Not getting a response, he turned his gaze to Will, who was staring down at his hands in his lap. Barclay snapped his fingers at the young man. "Hey!" Will looked up at him, and Barclay pointed to the TV.

Will slowly turned his head to look at the screen. He stared at it for a few seconds, then went back to eyeing his hands in his lap. Not picking his head up, he said, "Maybe I should get a lawyer." And like the drain plug being pulled on a bathtub full of water, the confident defiance seemed to drain from Will Jr.

"Do you want a lawyer?"

"Nah, he doesn't want a lawyer," Fitz said in his baritone. "Just a few minutes ago, he said he was happy to help. Didn't you say that, Mr. Harris?"

Will nodded, keeping his eyes down.

Barclay spoke: "You can certainly have a lawyer if you want one, but as Fitz said, you already told us you want to help. Have you changed your mind about that?"

A long pause was followed by a slow shake of his head.

"I tell you what. To make it cleaner, sign this piece of paper before we go any further." Barclay was sliding a Waiver of Rights form in front of Will. Barclay produced a fat Mont Blanc rollerball, twisted off the cap, and placed the pen on the paper.

Maybe ten seconds passed when Will reached for the paper. He picked up the pen and was about to sign when he said, "What is this I'm signing?"

"It's just something we have to get signed if you're going to talk to us and help us out. It says you don't want to talk to a lawyer right now." Barclay lowered his head to try and look Will in the eyes. "You still want to help us, right? If you want to speak with a lawyer first, that's fine, but then we have to stop what we're doing; you'll have to find a lawyer and then wait for them to get down here. Probably talking several hours." Another silence, maybe twenty seconds long, then "Up to you, Will, but we'd sure like to go ahead and clear this up."

Will made a move to sign, paused, then signed the form.

The pen hadn't lost contact with the paper when Barclay snatched the paper back and plucked the pen from Will's hand. "Excellent, Will. Thank you." He put the piece of paper inside the manila folder. "Now, I asked you if what was showing on the monitor there looked familiar, and you acknowledged that it did. You'd be correct."

Barclay leaned back in his chair, swiveled just a bit, and said, "That is a mockup of your parent's living room as it was the day of the shooting. Well, at least the furniture, anyway. Each piece you see there—the chair, the coffee table, and the couch—are the actual pieces from the scene." He waited for a reaction. Getting none, he continued: "The woman in the chair—your chair—is a firearms expert with the Alabama Department of Forensic Sciences. She's holding a twelve-gauge Browning Citori." This got Will's attention. "Oh yes, we're using your gun in this demonstration."

"Demonstration?" said Will looking from the screen to Barclay then back to the screen.

"That's correct. We reenacted the shooting as you say it happened."

"You say 'the way I say it happened' as if I was lying about it."

"Just an expression. I wouldn't read too much into that." Barclay poised his finger over the keyboard and said, "Do we have it right so far? Where the furniture is situated, and how Ms. Richards is holding the gun?"

After a few seconds of staring at the screen, Will nodded stiffly.

"Good," said Barclay and hit the spacebar. The video began to play. "If you see anything we got wrong, speak up, ok?" He did not expect a response, and Will did not give one.

The video played silently, and eight seconds after playback began, the Citron's muzzle flashed, the gun kicked, the dummy's head exploded, and the cigarette ash was gone; the lack of sound made for an eerie effect. The spacebar was pressed once again, and the screen went still.

"So, how did we do?" said Barclay.

"Fine," Will said with a shrug.

"Oh, come on now," Barclay said as he stood, his momentum pushing his chair backward. "We had actual scientists work on this demonstration. Rulers, protractors, hell, they probably used string and a compass, too, and the best you can do is 'fine?'" He walked the length of the table toward the television. When he got there, he turned to Will and said in a much more serious voice, "I just need to know one thing—and I advise you to think very hard about how you answer this question." He leaned on the table and jabbed a finger at the television as he said, "Is that how it happened?"

The color had drained from Will's face. He stood up, bumping his knees on the underside of the table, and grabbed the edge to steady himself. He put his hands in his pockets as he turned to look out the bank of windows and down into the court square, his gaze coming to rest on the large green-patinated cast-iron fountain. No one else in the room moved. The faint ringing of a desk phone sounded in the distance.

Will took a deep breath and opened his mouth to speak before seeming to reconsider. Fitz opened his mouth to respond, and Barclay squeezed his shoulder. After a few seconds and without looking away from the window, Will said, "I'm pretty sure you know that's not how it happened." He turned and said, "How did you know?"

"I'll be honest; this has been bothering the hell out of me for nearly four years now. I've discussed this case with a hundred people or better. Shown the photos to some of the top law enforcement minds in the country, and it took a greenhorn lawyer to figure it out." Barclay was now looking down the table at Clayton, which prompted Fitz and Will to also look at the prosecutor. Will turned back to looking out the window, and Barclay continued, "It was the cigarette ash." He walked down the table to pick up a photograph and then returned to the television. "Your father's cigarette at the scene still had an entire cigarette's worth of ash attached to the filter, whereas in the demonstration you just watched, the ash is gone.

"That demonstration proved Clayton's hypothesis correct. He saw what everyone up to this point had missed: if the gun truly were fired from the distance you say, the ash would not have withstood the pressure wave from the gunshot."

The room was silent save for the cool air blowing through the ceiling vents. Seeing that Will wasn't going to speak, Barclay approached and stood beside him, adopting the same distant gaze, and said quietly, "Where was the gun when you pulled the trigger?" More silence ensued, but with a direct question hanging out there, Barclay waited him out.

After nearly a minute and without breaking off his gaze,

Will said, "I put both barrels right here." He pointed to the middle of the bridge of his nose. As Barclay was about to speak, Will continued, a smirk tugging at the corner of his lips: "Fucker saw it coming too." A mirthless laugh escaped him as he said, "He was asleep. Fell asleep with that cigarette in his hand as he often did when he'd been drinking." He shrugged. "I put those two barrels right on his nose and pulled the hammers back. The click of the hammers woke him up. He opened his eyes, and I pulled the trigger."

EPILOGUE

"WHERE ARE YOU TAKING me?" she said with a laugh.

"For the last time, it's a surprise. You'll see when we get there." Barclay guided a blindfolded Brittany down the stone front steps of their house. He had one arm around her back and a hand on her inside elbow, making sure she did not fall. She had no clue where she was going, but the crunch of the crushed rock driveway under her feet led her to believe she was going for a ride.

The SUV sat in the circular drive perpendicular to the entrance. He stopped at the passenger side, opened the door, and helped her into the car, then ran around the front and slid into the driver's seat. As he eased through the driveway, he put down all four windows and opened the sunroof.

It was a beautiful spring Friday afternoon. The air was on the cool side of warm, with not a cloud in the sky and the scent of gardenia blossoms riding on the breeze.

This was that perfect day. The first day coming off winter when you knew spring was here to stay. Duncan was killed almost nine months ago, and it had been seven months since Kingery had gone missing. The whirlwind that had been Barclay's life since then made this day even more special.

❖   ❖   ❖   ❖   ❖

SEVEN MONTHS AGO

The morning after the events at the Pickens' family farm with Barclay, Veronica, Malik, and Kingery, the last billboard Barclay's Uncle Jack would see built was completed. Barclay had been there with a few other friends and family, and, despite the early hour, they shared in a champagne-soaked celebration. While everyone was toasting the sale of Jack's business, Barclay was enjoying the relief akin to a ten-ton weight being lifted off his shoulders.

A day was given for the dust to settle when Barclay called an impromptu meeting of the investigative team in the conference room at Duncan's office, which had remained empty since his death. Molly Pheiffer had given Barclay a key to the office to assist her in getting everything in order. No one, not Barclay or Molly, was in any hurry to undertake the task of going through the things of a dead loved one, so the office was in the same condition as Duncan had left it. Barclay chose that spot to avoid raising questions about what they were all doing together. A meeting at the police station or the district attorney's office would be little more than a dog whistle to the unbridled rumor mill that is the local criminal justice system.

Detectives Wayne Drummond and Tina Crump and DA Investigator Winston Fitzsimmons sat around a round walnut table as Barclay recounted everything the investigation had uncovered. He included all the new information he had discovered in Charleston and the ensuing two weeks. He did not mention anything, however, about the late-night events at the Pickens farm.

He laid out, in detail, the plan surrounding Veronica Lane's disappearance. He told them about how it was carried out, the extent of Kingery's involvement, and, in a moment that sucked the air out of the room, he recounted that it was Kingery who had killed Duncan Pheiffer. When asked why Kingery had murdered Duncan, Barclay nudged the group down a path that allowed them, not him, to supply the motive.

Drummond surmised, "I bet Duncan told Kingery about the cell phone, and he killed him before it could be fully investigated."

Barclay merely sat back and gave the occasional bump, which, in their collective excitement, none of them even recognized.

He did not mention Kingery's moonlight confession; instead, he chose to attribute the information gleaned to Veronica Lane, who had agreed to be the conduit for the evidence. To Barclay, all that mattered was that the proper authorities were aware of the pertinent facts, enough to obtain an arrest warrant for Richard Kingery. After that, his work would be done. Barclay knew there would never be a trial.

They worked over the next three hours organizing forensic reports, cell phone tower records, maps, and other indicia of Kingery's knowledge of the innocence of Clements and then his guilt in the murder of Duncan Pheiffer. Finally, Drummond summoned the Towne County SWAT team for a rendezvous at 4:30 the following morning to snatch Kingery out of his slumber. All the SWAT team knew was that they were serving a murder warrant. The secrecy had them all on edge because serving arrest warrants, especially for homicides, was among the most dangerous tasks they undertook, so a good plan was mission-critical. Barclay had gotten District Attorney Maggie Gamble to call the head of the SWAT team and tell them she wished to maintain strict operational secrecy because they could not afford word of the target to leak. She did this out of her trust in Barclay because not even she knew the target was her own chief assistant. Barclay knew he was taking a risk not telling her, but he would make sure she was not caught unawares when the takedown happened.

One person he did tell was Molly. He and Brittany invited her for dinner, informing her they knew who killed her husband. The wounds were still raw, but it seemed she had no more tears left to cry, which was just as well. Barclay knew what the police would find when they raided the house—or rather what they weren't going to find—and for the first time, he worried about that. If only Molly could know the truth. Perhaps one day he could give her some assurances, but probably not.

He held on to some guilt for not telling SWAT who the target was, but he also knew there was no security risk in a rushed plan in this particular case. The raid went off without a hitch. Doors were breached, flashbangs detonated, then nothing. No one was home.

There was blood throughout the kitchen, however. Of course, a single pint of blood isn't a significant quantity, but in a kitchen, with its non-porous tile and granite surfaces, it appeared much more voluminous.

SWAT cleared the house, and the crime scene investigation team was called in. During their tour of the property, the ever-indomitable Detective Drummond observed: "This setup is just like the Lane case."

That afternoon Barclay called Luke Jackson and informed him of the eleventh-hour developments in the fast-moving case. He forwarded him everything he would need to vacate Charlie Calvin Clements' guilty verdict, and Mr. Clements was out and back home before the sun set. Luke had a myriad of questions, but he knew enough not to ask a single one.

Press conferences were held with just enough vague details to paint a clear picture of Kingery's guilt in killing one man and falsely convicting another while withholding enough information under the guise of an "ongoing investigation." Hence, no one from the press or the public looked too intently into the case.

A plea was made by the district attorney herself to assist law enforcement in locating a rogue prosecutor so they could see that justice was served. Following that, a national news program called Maggie for an interview. The producer promised to be fair and told her they merely wanted to help get the word out about their search for this fugitive murderer. The savvy DA replied in her most syrupy, southern accent: "Now you boys really want me to believe y'all are going to come down here to little old Towne just to help and not to make us look bad? Well, as we say in the South: 'No way, Jose.'"

In the first month, a veritable montage of Kingery sightings flooded the Towne Police secret witness hotline, but none proved to be of any significance. Over the following few months, attention on the case waned, and it was eventually relegated to a storage room shelf. It appeared to everyone involved that a long-time prosecutor, wise in the ways of both the criminal mind and police investigative techniques, had performed the perfect getaway.

The fallout for the district attorney's office was not insignificant. Lawyers came out of the woodwork wanting to re-examine not only cases Kingery had personally prosecuted but all cases prosecuted by the office since his employment. Maggie Gamble wasn't having any of it and welcomed the fight. Everyone ultimately agreed to a random sampling of fifty cases prosecuted by Kingery and fifty cases prosecuted by other attorneys who he supervised as chief assistant. After nearly six months, nothing even close to impropriety was found, effectively ending any claims of prosecutorial malfeasance.

Veronica Lane made an emotional, albeit brief, appearance. She went home for a few days before hitting the road to establish a new life for herself. Barclay met with the hospital's general counsel and advised her that pursuing any criminal charges against Veronica Lane would be unwise. He conceded they had evidence of her utilizing another nurse's ID card to swipe her way into the drug dispensary. However, due to the lack of security for dispensing the drugs, no one could know for sure—or at least beyond a reasonable doubt—that she had stolen any drugs. While using another nurse's ID was against hospital policy, it did not rise to the level of criminal conduct.

Barclay warned the hospital's attorney about two things: the first was exposing the archaic and inept system of dispensing drugs to nurses and the embarrassment that would cause the hospital, and second, prosecuting a woman who was manipulated by a chief assistant district attorney into faking her death and leaving her family behind all in an effort to protect himself. That was the narrative being peddled, and Barclay was perfectly fine perpetuating it. This is in addition to her actions resulting in Charlie Calvin Clements having his conviction overturned as being deemed heroic. She was a pawn in the plan of a master criminal mind. He made it abundantly clear to the hospital's attorney that choosing to prosecute Veronica Lane after all of this would not be a good look for the hospital.

By avoiding a criminal complaint and having the hospital accept her resignation, she could remain a nurse in good standing, allowing her to seek work wherever she opted to live.

Veronica and Barclay occasionally communicated, mainly by text, but the frequency of their contact trailed off as the months on the calendar fell away.

Veronica's cell phone, the burner that was the catalyst of the events of the past few months, was found by Barclay.

He, Brittany, and Molly were cleaning out Duncan's office on an unseasonably warm October day when he went to use the bathroom, and a thought struck him as he washed his hands. His mind went back to the last case he and Duncan prosecuted together: a possession of child pornography case in which the defendant was found in possession of over sixty-thousand images. The images were maintained on fourteen thumb drives the defendant had stored in a gallon-sized Ziploc bag secreted in his toilet tank.

Hands wet from the sink, he moved quickly and lifted the lid off the toilet tank. There, in a Ziploc bag submerged underwater, was a cell phone—*the* cell phone.

That evening, while Molly and Brittany continued work in Duncan's office, Barclay left to pick up pizza and beer for their dinner. He disposed of the phone sans battery and sim card in a sewer drain behind the restaurant; he tossed the battery in the restaurant's commercial dumpster, and he went by his office and shredded the sim card.

❈ ❈ ❈ ❈ ❈

PRESENT DAY

Barclay and Brittany were enjoying the beautiful spring day—windows down, sunroof open. Since leaving the house, he had driven between fifteen and twenty minutes when he made a u-turn in the road and came to a stop on the shoulder a few yards inside the marker denoting the Towne City Limits. He shifted SUV into park and ran around to let Brittany out of the car. She still had no idea what he wanted to show her.

Once out, he eased her clear of the hood, slipped the blindfold off, and watched her. It took a beat, but her face lit up, which in turn caused Barclay to do the same.

"Oh, honey," she said, "this is fantastic." They were looking at Towne's newest billboard and the advertisement it bore: ELECT BARCLAY GRIFFITH, TOWNE COUNTY DISTRICT ATTORNEY.

She hugged him tight and said, "That looks wonderful!" They stood there in silence for a long moment when she said, "I guess this is a little bittersweet for you."

"How do you mean?"

"This was something you and Duncan always discussed—you being the DA, him being your chief assistant—then he would correct you and say it would be the other way around." That drew a smile before she continued. "And now he's not here to experience with you. With us."

Barclay shrugged but didn't say anything. Then, after a minute, his voice took on a quiet, forlorn tone as he said, "I just want to do what I can to make you…and the baby proud." They both looked down at her belly, she rested her hand on it, and he placed a hand over hers, evidence of a pregnancy almost six months along.

Then he said, "It'll be fun having a little girl crawling around the DA's office when she visits her daddy." This lightened the mood as they both wiped their eyes.

"Yeah?" she said. "I don't know. I kinda think I want a little boy; I'll need someone to take care of me in my old age." They talked a little back and forth before deciding to head back home.

Barclay had just pulled onto the roadway and was accelerating when Brittany spoke. "I just had a thought," she said. "The first thing you need to do when you take office is to go after Richard Kingery. Finding him would be a hell of a way to start your term."

Barclay looked into his side mirror at the billboard receding in the distance and thought, *I wouldn't count on anyone finding Richard Kingery.*

❊ ❊ ❊ ❊ ❊

SEVEN AND A HALF MONTHS AGO
THE BLIND TIGER PUB
CHARLESTON, SOUTH CAROLINA

The conversation lagged, the weight of the subject matter taking its toll, and they fell into a companionable silence as they continued to drink beers and listen to the guitar player crank up his first set. Almost an hour passed with little conversation—none of it pertaining to the case—when the musician took a break. Barclay, Veronica Lane, and the appreciative crowd applauded, and the guitarist passed a tip bucket around as the pub-goers took this opportunity for fresh beers and a bathroom break.

Barclay returned to the table and, as he slid into his chair, said, "Held out as long as I could. Consider the seal broken."

More time passed as they enjoyed their beers, and the guitarist began his next set; they let the music wash over them. After a few songs had been played, Veronica interrupted the lull by closing the gap between her and Barclay, hair falling across her face, and saying, "You know I've got his blood." She flopped back into her chair, and let out a giggle punctuated with a hiccup.

Barclay paused, glass halfway to his mouth, certain he misheard her with the guitar player's tribute to 90s alternative music filling the packed pub. "You what?" he said, leaning in toward the middle of the table.

A languid, beer-laced smile spread across Veronica Lane's face as she drifted back in toward Barclay, their faces inches apart, the sweet smell of her alcohol-scented breath filling the narrow gap. "I said, 'I've got his blood.'" Reading his expression, she said, "Kingery's." She nodded, biting her lower lip. Then a laugh escaped her lips followed by a hiccup. She quickly covered her mouth.

He shook his head. *Was he hearing her correctly?* "How the hell did you manage that?"

She shrugged a lazy, drunken shrug. "I worked a blood drive for the blood bank at the courthouse one day. They needed extra phlebotomists, and the hospital thought it would be good PR to send some of their nurses to help." She drank the last of her beer and set the glass down a bit too hard on the table. "So when he donated, I grabbed his bag and took it with me."

"Wait, how do you just take a bag of blood? Aren't people, I don't know, watching the blood or something?" They had to almost yell to be heard over The Wallflowers' *One Headlight.*

She gave him an incredulous look. "Watch the blood? Why? Who the hell would steal blood?"

Barclay had a retort but kept it to himself. Instead, he said, "I thought that was supposed to be anonymous?"

She said, "Once it leaves the donation sight, it's all barcoded and unable to be identified as to the donor. But"—she pointed a finger dramatically in Barclay's face—"if you, oh, I don't know, say, mark it and pay close attention to where it gets put, then in the chaos of closing everything down at the end of a long day, you slip out the blood bag and put it in your tote then no one is the wiser." She laughed again.

"What did you do with it?"

Lazy drunken shrug. "Same thing that I did with mine. Put the glycerol in it and put it in the garage freezer. What's good for the goose and all that."

Barclay was processing all of this when she banged her empty pint glass on the table and said, "How *the fuck* did I allow that slimy sonofabitch to have something to hold over my head for the rest of my life."

Her unexpected burst of anger, combined with the sharp rap of her glass on the table, caused something to click into place in his mind.

She had Kingery's Blood which meant he *had Kingery's blood.*

Their waitress arrived as if summoned by the banging glass. She dropped off two more beers and plucked the two empties and the sandwich plate off the table. The alcohol from the beers was relaxing his brain, and that was a good thing. He did some of his best thinking in this state: not exactly drunk, not exactly sober. It served to declutter his mind like tidying up a paper-strewn desk leaving only the essential stuff to view.

A plan was forming in his mind. It was a little crazy—make that a lot crazy. The major negative with ideas that originated in this state, he had learned over time, is that they had to be properly vetted. Was it truly a good idea let loose, broken free of sober constraints, or was it, in fact, a drunken idea that had no place in a teetotal world?

Barclay heard the opening chords of a song from the guitar player at the front of the pub. The tune was familiar, but he couldn't immediately place it—the idea crowding in on his mind. He raised the fresh beer to take a drink but paused—a smile tugged at the corners of his mouth.

AUTHOR'S NOTE

I BEGAN THE JOURNEY that would become *The Hero Rule* in 2013. I had a nugget of an idea and an affinity for writing and, I believed, a measure of writing ability. I had no idea what I was truly stepping off into, so I did the only thing I knew to do: I started writing.

As I would soon learn, however, being able to craft a well-written sentence, a paragraph, or even a chapter is a far cry from effectively telling a cohesive story that can be sustained for 100,000 words, hold a reader's attention, and keep them invested.

My goal with *The Hero Rule*, above all, was to tell an authentic crime and mystery story where the mechanics of a criminal investigation are real and the dialogue rings true. I wanted to tell an honest story—no shortcuts, no embellishments.

Writing *The Hero Rule* was a lengthy process owed largely to making certain every aspect of the investigation and story was based on available and readily used science and investigative techniques, many of which I have dealt with personally in cases I have prosecuted. Making sure every connection is solid and every advancement in the story is credible and logical is no easy task. I want you, the reader, to know that I took no liberties with any aspect of the investigative process and developing the story. I only allowed the evidence to give what it was capable of giving and nothing more. I sweated every detail because

I want the reader to trust that what they are reading is real and accurate even if it is a novel. That, to me, makes for the most compelling story.

Towne, Alabama is a fictional location thus it is a product of my imagination, but it is not without inspiration. Portland and Charleston, however, *are* actual places and I did my best to show them in their best light.

The first draft of *The Hero Rule* took almost five years to complete, and throughout the writing process my respect grew for the art and, indeed, the craft of writing and those who do it so well. I came to the realization that telling even a good story did not necessarily mean a well-written story. In fact, though I liked the story I had created, it was a bloviated mess. I won't bore you with the minutia of draft after draft, rewrite after rewrite other than to say it took another year or so to have it to the point where I felt I could allow another person to read it. And even then it was anything but a story worthy of publication.

And now, ten years after I typed those first words, whether or not it is worthy of publication is a question best answered but the readers, but published it is.

Few things are scarier than putting yourself or your work out there for derision or approval in any manner let alone something in the realm of the creative such as the written word. For me, however, the fear of failure is far outweighed by the fear of regret. For in effort, there is risk, but idleness produces no rewards.

The Hero Rule has been presented to you in all of its glory and glorious flaws. I can only hope you had a fraction of the enjoyment in reading it that I had in writing it. For if so, you will have enjoyed it immensely.

Thank you,
Brandon

LET ME HEAR FROM YOU

Question: Did Barclay's actions
encompass the hero rule?

Email me at Brandon@brandonhughesbooks.com and let me know what you think or just drop me a line to say hello. Also, I will gladly join your book club or any social group either virtually or in person to discuss The Hero Rule or the writing process with you.

Also, please take a moment to visit BrandonHughesBooks.com and sign up for updates regarding my next novel. Who knows, perhaps you will help me choose the design for the cover. Maybe you can have a character named after you. Want a free book? That, too. But I have to know you're out there.

Please take a moment to leave a review on Amazon, Goodreads, or wherever you purchased this book.

I look forward to hearing from you.

ABOUT THE AUTHOR

BRANDON HUGHES brings two decades of experience in the criminal justice system to craft an authentic mystery novel and utilizes his real-world knowledge to take the reader inside the inner workings of a criminal investigation. Criminal cases he has handled have been featured on 48 Hours, Generation Hustle, and The Dr. Phil Show.

The long and short of it is, Brandon has stories to tell and a passion to tell them.

When he isn't writing, Brandon enjoys cooking, reading, and cheering for his Auburn Tigers. He and his wife Karen are empty nesters save for their chocolate lab Murphy. They live in Auburn, Alabama. The Hero Rule is his first novel.

Visit him online at:
BrandonHughesBooks.com

Printed in Great Britain
by Amazon

22591616R00202